THE PROMISE OF HAPPINESS

"I love you, Gennie," Roarke said in a hoarse whisper.

Genevieve caught her breath. She looked up at his face, a face that had haunted her since she'd first laid eyes on him seven years before.

She lifted her hand to his cheek and stroked it gently. "I love you, Roarke," she admitted softly, giving voice at last to the secret she'd carried in her heart.

His eyes seemed to burst into flames of joy as, ever so slowly, he brought his lips to hers. His kiss was so sweet, so compelling, that Genevieve nearly melted in his lingering embrace.

"Oh, God, Gennie, I need you. I need to wake up to you every morning, to give you children, to embrace each and every day with you for the rest of our lives. Marry me, Gennie," he said against her lips. "Please."

Harper
Monogram

SUSAN WIGGS

EMBRACE
THE DAY

HarperPaperbacks
A Division of HarperCollinsPublishers

HarperPaperbacks *A Division of* HarperCollins*Publishers*
10 East 53rd Street, New York, N.Y. 10022

This book was previously published by Paperjacks Ltd. in 1988
under the author name Susan Childress. It is herein reprinted
by arrangement with the author.

Cover illustration by R.A. Maguire

First HarperMonogram printing: January 1993

Printed in the United States of America

HarperPaperbacks, HarperMonogram, and colophon are
trademarks of HarperCollins*Publishers*

10 9 8 7 6 5 4 3 2 1

For my parents, Nick and Lou Klist, with love

Acknowledgments

My thanks to Jay, my heroically patient husband; Charlotte Childress Wiggs, Biblical scholar; Betsy Moize of *National Geographic* magazine; Walker Merryman of the Tobacco Institute; and Joyce Bell, Alice Borchardt, Arnette Lamb, and Barbara Smith, my literary best friends.

Special thanks to Gretchen Gay for her proofreading skills.

PART I

And cheerfully at sea,
Successe you still intice,
  To get the pearle and gold,
  And ours to hold,
Virginia,
Earthe's onely paradise.

MICHAEL DRAYTON, 1606

1

London, 1774

Tick, tock.

The clock had measured the moments of Roarke Adair's life from the instant he was born. The relentless regularity of its ticking had been present through all the small triumphs and large tragedies of his twenty-two years. The mulberry case, yellow with age, had been rubbed a thousand times by his mother's loving hands; the small whimsical halfpenny moon in the face had been traced by his chubby fingers years ago. Although a tiny sliver was missing from one of the corners, the clock had suffered minimal abuse from Roarke's father. Such had not been the case for Roarke and his mother.

Tick, tock.

The pawnbroker cocked his grizzled, patchy head and listened to the clock, poking at its time-worn casing with a pudgy finger. He raised narrowed eyes to Roarke Adair.

"Two pounds-ten," the broker said at last.

Roarke's breath drew in with a hiss, and his jaw tightened. The paltry sum would have been laughable if he hadn't needed it so badly. Still, it was about two pounds more than he had and fourteen shillings more than the last shop had offered him.

Tick, tock.

Still Roarke hesitated. It was no easy thing, parting with the only legacy his mother had left him. The last reminder of her small life. But Matilda Adair—ill these ten years, dead these ten days—would have understood her only child's dream. Even a dream so dearly bought.

Tick, tock.

"Three pounds even, sirrah, and a sight more than it's worth," the pawnbroker said, persisting. He set down a stack of coins with an air of finality.

Roarke gave the slightest of nods. Then he swept the silver from the counter. The clock went onto the shelf, and the claim ticket went into his pocket, forgotten. But Roarke would carry the familiar rhythm in his heart for the rest of his days.

Tick, tock.

He joined Henry Piggot, the colonial agent, in the street outside. Noting the absence of the clock, Henry raised an inquiring eyebrow. Roarke told him the amount.

"It's not enough, my friend," Piggot said bluntly. "'Twill barely cover the price of passage, and then there're the taxes to be paid on the farm you've inherited." He patted the folded land titles in his pocket.

"I know." Nearby, a beggar woman stretched out a gnarled hand and mumbled an entreaty. Almost without slowing his pace, Roarke put a single copper into the hand.

"By the Eternal, man!" Piggot swore. "Why the devil'd you do that?"

Roarke shrugged. "Maybe to remind myself. However little I have, 'tis a sight more than most folks."

"Won't be for long if you keep that up." Piggot gave a snort of disgust and then turned the subject. "Now, what about the fare? The *Blessing* sails in less than a week. You mentioned a lady cousin . . ."

"No," Roarke said quickly. "Not Angela. We hardly know each other. I couldn't ask her for the money."

"What's this?" Piggot demanded. "A show of pride, eh? 'Tis hardly the time for that, my friend."

Roarke said nothing, but he took the packet of deeds and titles from the agent, and they started toward the West End.

Henry Piggot knew immediately, from the grim set of Roarke Adair's jaw as he left the residence in Bedford Row, that the young man had been unsuccessful with his lady cousin. Roarke closed the door quietly. But he brought his fist down so hard on the stone ledge at the top of the steps that Piggot blinked. It was the action of a man frustrated too many times by life.

Piggot took out a small ivory pick and worked at his teeth, studying the young man with a mixture of interest and sympathy.

Roarke Adair looked out of place in the elegant West End setting, a great colorful oak standing amid severely pruned hedgerows. His best set of clothes consisted of a frock coat straining against broad shoulders and concealing a cotton shirt that had seen better days, breeches of a rather muddy color, and boots that, even after unmerciful brushing, still bore dark seams of wharf-side coal dust. A profusion of flame-red hair had been tied into a queue at his nape, and strands of it escaped a somewhat battered tricorn.

The packet of papers was clutched in Roarke's great rough, freckled hand. A hand that, more rightly, should have been closed around the handles of a plow. With an odd start, Piggot realized he was looking at a farmer. A man who belonged with the land even more than one who had been born to it.

Piggot put away his toothpick and sighed. It was a damned shame that Roarke's only living relative, Angela Brimsby, had apparently declined to help him. But for the money needed to pay the taxes and fare, Roarke could own his uncle's legacy, a good, solid farm in Dancer's Meadow, Virginia.

Roarke crossed the street and fell in step with Piggot. He

folded his mouth into a grim line and stared straight ahead with penetrating blue eyes.

"Did they even listen?" Piggot asked at length.

Roarke shrugged. "Angela tapped her teeth with her fingernail and looked worried that I'd soil her settee. Her husband, Edmund, kept his nose buried in a snuffbox." He gave Piggot a crooked half grin. "They were a bit unprepared for me. Angela's mother and mine were sisters, but her family found that easy to forget. We were always the poor relations from St. Giles." His grin disappeared. "She was quite happy to take the claim ticket for the clock. It was the only thing she ever envied my mother."

"Didn't you explain about the farm?" Piggot demanded. A Virginian for the past twenty years, he was a great proponent of the colony and for weeks had been trying to locate Roarke Adair. "By the Eternal, the Dancer's Meadow tract has been a working farm for a decade. Over a hundred bushels of corn an acre! A man can ship half of that down river, and the taxes don't even exceed five shillings."

Roarke looked annoyed. "Which is five shillings more than I've got."

"I know, I know. I'd lend you the sum myself, but I'm about strapped. Been doing other men's business in England for a few months now, and all I've left is a small bride price."

"A bride price?"

Piggot grinned and patted the coin purse concealed inside his waistcoat. "Bit of a shortage of women in some parts. Every so often a man'll send to England for a bride."

They walked along in silence for a time, passing staid brick façades fronted by neat boxed hedges, watching the occasional passage of a gleaming coach with painted doors and the procession of fashionable people out for a stroll in the fresh spring evening. Then Piggot asked, "What'll you do, Roarke?"

"I don't want to think about that right now."

Piggot nodded. "Come along, then. I know a place that'll get you drunk for a penny, dead drunk for tuppence, and then provide the straw for free."

* * *

Prudence Moon's small, fine hands twisted a handkerchief in her lap, and her eyes filled with tears.

"God forgive me, I knew it was wrong, but I gave myself to him."

At the sound of her friend's whisper, Genevieve Elliot tore her gaze from the bustling wharf-side scene to stare at Prudence in disbelief.

"Pru?" She placed her hand on Prudence's arm. "For God's sake, Pru, what are you talking about?"

Prudence swallowed, and tears spilled down her cheeks. "Mr. Brimsby," she said brokenly, "I—we're lovers."

"Bloody hell," Genevieve breathed, forgetting this once to avoid shocking her gentle friend with rough language. She tried to summon an image of Prudence Moon enfolded in the arms of the man who employed her as governess to his children. The image wouldn't form. Edmund Brimsby was one of those faceless, self-possessed individuals whose life would leave no mark behind, and Prudence so painfully proper and shy that even Genevieve, who was often accused of being fanciful, couldn't imagine the scenario.

"Brimsby?" she asked. Surely she'd heard wrong.

But Prudence nodded miserably. "It all began last Christmas. Edm—Mr. Brimsby came to the schoolroom and told me . . ." She crushed her fists into her moist blue eyes. "It doesn't matter what he told me. The fact is, we became lovers that night and have been for four months since. And the worst of it is, Genevieve, that I did nothing to stop myself. I lived for his nightly visits and died a little each time he stayed away, thinking he had done with me."

"Oh, Pru . . ." Genevieve took the girl's fragile hand in her work-roughened ones and stroked it gently. A wind blew across the Thames, stirring up a hellish and dismal fog of coal dust.

"I'm pregnant, Genevieve."

The sounds of the Thames wharf seemed to rise and swell in Genevieve's ears, but even the shouts and clamor of the dockworkers couldn't drown out the dreadful truth of what

Prudence had just revealed. Genevieve lifted her eyes to the gulls wheeling overhead with the absurd hope of finding the answer to her friend's dilemma somewhere above. But she saw only the ever-present dull layer of London smoke and heard the gulls' screams mingling with the cacophony of the wharf.

"Does Brimsby know?"

Prudence shook her head. "Nor shall he. I shall have to leave. I've heard there are places for women like—" She choked on a sob and buried her face in her hands. The sound of her crying tore at Genevieve's heart and filled her with a feeling of such helplessness, that she ached.

"Where will you go, Pru? You've no family, no friends but me, no money—"

"I'll manage."

Genevieve looked at her dubiously. She was small and frail, like a little blond porcelain doll. Prudence Moon was remarkably intelligent in things like geography and French, but she was not at all resourceful. Her life had always been ordered by someone else; first by the parson who'd reared her and now by the family she served. She'd never had to do for herself. She wouldn't survive a week on her own.

As they began walking back to Bedford Row, Genevieve tried again. "Brimsby is wealthy, Pru. He could give you a house somewhere, an allowance—"

Prudence shook her head. "Edmund is many things, but not generous or careless with his reputation. He'd deny the child was his."

"Sweet Christ, Prudence, and you fell in love with the bounder!"

"I love him still. I can't help it."

Genevieve felt a prickle of exasperation. "For God's sake, Pru—." She stopped herself, unwilling to add to the guilt that already consumed her dear friend. Pursing her lips, she hefted her basket of laundered goods to be delivered. At the top of the basket, couched in ladies' fine linens, was a calf-bound volume of *Gulliver's Travels*.

Prudence was more than a friend. She'd taught Genevieve to read and had awakened a voracious hunger in her for learning. Like a thief, Genevieve escaped the stench of her father's tavern to meet with Prudence, to learn things she'd never dreamed of knowing. She stole an education a girl of her station had no business having. But today there would be no reading, no animated discussion, no admonitions from Prudence to keep her East End speech in check.

In silence they walked the rest of the way, emerging from the noisy squalor of the docks onto a wide, tree-lined avenue. The West End was an oasis of stately quiet. The smoke was lighter here, letting in the sweet spring air tinged with the scent of cherry blossoms and budding flowers.

Genevieve and Prudence entered number thirty-six Bedford Row through a servants' entry in the back. Prudence looked abominably pale and shaken, and Genevieve meant to take her immediately to her room. They passed through the scullery and made their way to the back stairs.

Genevieve nearly collided with a young boy, Andrew, the Brimsbys' son. He gave her a dismissive glance and pushed past her.

"Miss Moon, you must come," he insisted, pulling Prudence through the passageway toward the schoolroom. "Emily has spilled ink all over the map I was drawing and—"

"Miss Moon! Is that you?" Angela Brimsby arrived on a swish of silk and lace. Touching a pampered hand to her brow, she frowned at Genevieve.

"Lord, haven't I had my share of scruffy visitors today!" she snapped. Without glancing at her son, she propelled him back toward the schoolroom. "You should have left the laundry in the kitchen instead of traipsing through— Never mind, just leave my things and get Meeks to pay you. I hope the linens aren't scorched this time—"

Mrs. Brimsby broke off and gave Genevieve a keen look. "As long as you're here, you might as well make yourself useful." She extracted a slip of paper from her bodice and handed it to Genevieve. "Take this to Pembroke's pawnshop and instruct him to deliver the clock to me first thing in the morning. He'll be paid when the piece is in my hands."

Genevieve gave Prudence a helpless look and started for

the kitchen with her basket. She stopped, though, when Angela's strident voice addressed Prudence in anger.

"Where have you been, Miss Moon?" she demanded. "The children are completely unsupervised. It's difficult enough now that Nurse has given notice—"

"'Tis my afternoon off, ma'am," Prudence said softly.

Angela's skirts rustled as she paced in agitation. "The afternoon is nearly over. Now, if you've concluded your visit with the *laundress,* I'd like you to go to the schoolroom and hear the children's lessons."

Little Emily appeared, grabbing at Prudence's sleeve and howling that Andrew had pulled her hair.

"Yes, ma'am," Prudence said wearily. There was a vaguely greenish cast to her complexion, and she swayed slightly, putting her hand against the wall.

"That's better," Angela said above Emily's howling.

As Prudence turned, her narrow shoulders sloping in misery, Genevieve was filled by a fierce, protective instinct. Her basket hit the floor with a thud. She stepped in front of Angela and tossed her dark head in defiance.

"Prudence isn't well. She's going to her room."

Angela's nostrils dilated. "What did you say? I won't have any cheekiness from—"

Prudence put a hand on her friend's arm. "Genevieve, please. I'll be fine."

"No, you won't, Pru. I won't have you working yourself to death."

Angela's face reddened beneath the layer of powder that concealed a trace-work of flaws. "See here, girl. You are forgetting your place. I suspect it's your influence that's causing Miss Moon to be so troublesome."

At that moment, Edmund Brimsby entered the passageway, wiping a film of snuff from his lip and frowning at the sound of raised voices. Genevieve's green eyes flicked over him contemptuously. She resented him, from his immaculately wigged head to the tops of his perfectly polished shoes. He was a comely man in a soft, almost effeminate way.

"What is this? I just stopped Andrew from fairly breaking Emily's arm." His voice was clipped and nasal, with tones schooled into him by England's finest academies. "Why aren't the children at their lessons?"

"I'm glad you're here, Edmund," Angela said. "Prudence is shirking her duties and is being encouraged, I fear, by this, this slut off the streets."

Genevieve felt her fists close into small knots of outrage. Prudence begged her with a glance to hold her temper. She managed, just barely.

Edmund Brimsby cleared his throat, obviously annoyed by this small disaster in his well-ordered household.

"Miss Moon, the children are in need of supervision. Please say goodbye to your friend and see to them."

His wife made a sound of disgust, clearly dissatisfied with her husband's mildness.

Hearing this, Edmund pressed on. "Miss Moon, I pay you a good wage, and for that, I expect some measure of cooperation."

Genevieve couldn't help herself. Prudence was defenseless against the man she claimed to love and his haughty, domineering wife. She wouldn't stand by and watch her friend being ordered about.

"You're a fine one to talk about cooperation," she shouted at Mr. Brimsby. "Prudence has done a bloody sight more than the work expected of her."

He stared at her coldly. "I suggest you leave straight away. And don't expect my wife's patronage again. You and your common ways are no longer welcome in my house."

"Common, am I?" she raged. "God blind me, then, Mr. Brimsby, how do gentlefolk behave? I wonder if you know just why Prudence is so ill."

Prudence gasped. "Genevieve, *no—*"

But Genevieve was too angry to stop. "'Tis because you've gotten her with child, you bleedin' sod, and if that's your idea of gentlemanly behavior, then I believe you could use a lesson or two from a 'commoner' like me!"

The silence that followed her tirade hung in the air, a tangible, throbbing tension. At last, pale and tight-lipped, Angela spoke.

"Those are filthy insinuations."

Genevieve thrust her chin up. "Mrs. Brimsby, I'm sure your husband will deny every word of it, but that won't alter the truth. Prudence is ruined, and the bugger should bloody well face up to his responsibilities."

Prudence began sobbing softly, hands covering her face.

"Get out," Angela Brimsby ordered. "Get out, or I'll have you thrown out onto the street." She opened her mouth to summon a footman.

Genevieve ignored her. Her arms went firmly around her shuddering friend.

"Will you be all right?"

Prudence nodded weakly.

"Pru, I know it wasn't my place to speak out for you, but I couldn't stand to see the way they treat you. There now, go up to your room and rest a bit. I'll be back soon."

She gave the Brimsbys a glower that promised certain trouble should something ill befall her friend.

She left the quiet avenues behind and wended her way back to the seedy East End, a maze of muddied, rank-smelling streets and alleys, shadowed by top-heavy buildings that nearly met in crooked arches over the roads. A few blocks east rose the grimy edifice of Hawksmoor's church, empty of worshipers. No one made the mistake of identifying the poor as Christians.

Creaking carts lumbered by, and hawkers called out, offering the last of the day's spoiling fish or limp vegetables. With a stab of premonition, Genevieve studied the women who came out to barter with the vendors. They wore ragged dresses and dirty aprons and had pale, thin faces creased by worry and want. Invariably, three or four hungry-eyed, bare-legged children clung to their skirts. The women were hardly older than Genevieve's own seventeen years.

She walked on, fighting a now-familiar feeling of restlessness. She didn't want to end up like these creatures, hopelessly trapped in the slums, destined to eke out her life and die before her time, as much from loss of spirit as from disease and want.

As she turned down Farthing Lane, an alley of singular tawdriness, she tried not to see the poverty around her. At the head of the lane were a few crumbling, rat-infested residences inhabited by an unending procession of the transient poor. A moneylender's office, halfway down the street, operated on the very fringes of the law. Across from it a brothel was thinly veiled as a boardinghouse. Worst of all, the butcher's shop at the end of the lane strewed offal out into the gutters for all to see and smell. Some said London had sanitary wagons to take care of the leavings, but Genevieve had never seen one anywhere near the vicinity.

Sighing heavily, she approached her father's tavern. The alehouse was marked by a peeling sign that bore a crude picture of a sheaf of barley. Elliot's was frequented by a regular scruffy crowd of workmen and idlers, sailors and traders from the wharves. Though unappealing, the place was packed to the walls every night because the ale was cheap and plentiful and no one objected to the illicit gaming that took place in the back room.

Genevieve walked around back to the cramped upper quarters she shared with her parents and two brothers. She deposited her empty basket and made ready to shoulder the even more unwelcome burden of the night's work in the tavern. Hours would pass before she could return to the loft where she made her bed.

"Well, miss," said her mother. "You took your time getting back."

"It's a long walk."

"Aye, well, you've missed supper and they're bangin' their tankards downstairs."

Genevieve sighed. The meat pasties she and Prudence had shared on the wharf would have to suffice.

"I'll go." She tied on an apron and neatened her cloud of dark-brown curls with a comb. She knew her appearance didn't matter to the revelers below, but Prudence's influence had given her a sense of propriety that made her want to present herself at her best. She kept her corner of the sleeping loft clean, her two sets of clothes well-mended. Each week she trudged to St. Martin's to bring in fresh straw for her pallet.

Short and slight though she was, Genevieve had to stoop beneath the beams of the stairwell that led down to the taproom. The noise and smells of the room greeted her before she actually emerged. Raucous laughter and bawdy remarks mingled with the clinking of the stoneware and pewter tankards. She stepped into the taproom and was immediately met by the pungent scents of tobacco and malt and strident requests for service.

"A pint 'ere, girl, and be quick about it."

"Bring that tray o' rolls, will ye? We're fair t' starvin'!"

"I'll have gin; the beer 'ere ain't fit for swine!"

Through years of practice, Genevieve had learned to heft a tray loaded with mugs, carefully snaking her way about the crowded room. For the better part of two hours she waited tables ceaselessly, until at last the drinking slowed. Then she went to the sideboard to wash tankards, arms submerged to the elbows in tepid water.

Her father, Watney Elliot, came to sift through the handful of coins she had in her apron pocket. He was a man of middle years, small and compact, but possessed of a crude sort of arrogance that gave the impression of a much larger man. His hair was brown and tightly curled, showing no sign of gray. His sharp, small eyes darted, missing nothing. He quickly summed up the take and pocketed it.

"Should be more," he grumbled. "You could do much better, girl."

Genevieve ignored him and continued with her washing. She'd endured her father's complaints for a lifetime that suddenly felt much longer than seventeen years.

"Look at you, girl, stern as a judge, when you know well and good these men would pay extra for a smile, or a glimpse of bosom or leg."

She whirled on him, green eyes snapping with outrage. "I don't doubt you'd bloody well have me sell my body if it would fill your pockets."

"There's worse ways of turning a coin, miss. You're a

cheeky one, always have been, when you should be thanking me for keeping your belly full and a roof overhead."

"I owe you nothing. Everything you've given me I've earned, and if your bleedin' customers expect any more than their ale from me, they're sure to be disappointed. If it's a dockside whore you want working here, you'll have to look elsewhere."

"Listen to you, talking like that high an' mighty governess friend of yours. You wouldn't put on airs if I—"

Genevieve pushed past him, unwilling to listen to more. "Excuse me," she said coldly. "I've work to do."

Through the rest of the evening she was plagued by what had transpired earlier in the day. A hundred times she wondered if she'd done the right thing in exposing Edmund Brimsby. Things would undoubtedly go badly for Prudence now, but at least Brimsby would be obliged to look after her. A small pension and a house on some quiet street perhaps. That was all Prudence needed. Genevieve would settle for nothing less for her friend.

Roarke Adair despised the city of his birth. London was a human anthill, and not a very clean one. He had a dim memory of his mother saying sadly that the soot of the wharves might never be washed off, even as she scrubbed away at his ankles in the tiny, battered tin tub. The noise and the smells and the smoke were inescapable, day and night.

The street Piggot took him to was among the worst Roarke had ever seen. He looked away from a vacant-eyed beggar crouched in a doorway and gritted his teeth. Now that Angela had denied him a chance to escape poverty, he could well join the beggar one day.

Stooping beneath a peeling sign, Roarke followed Henry Piggot into the tavern. The taproom was dimly lit by a single lantern on the mantel and a few candles impaled on rusty iron spikes. The crowd was a seedy assortment of idlers and day workers who swore fluently and laughed loudly. Roarke and Piggot found a table near the rear door.

Piggot raised his hand to call for service. "See there," he said, gesturing at the girl who approached. "Not the sort of wench you'd expect in a place like this."

Roarke raised his eyes and found himself staring at a remarkably pretty girl. She was young, maybe sixteen, with dark-brown hair rippling over her shoulders. The features of her small, heart-shaped face were fine, almost dainty. Her person was unexpectedly clean for a wench in a place like this. There was an odd poignance about the perfectly cut squares that patched her skirt, the hem of which was just a shade too short.

As she neared the table, Roarke amended his first impression. The girl wasn't merely pretty. She was a beauty.

"Two pints," Piggot said, pressing a coin into her hand. Her uninterested gaze swept over the two of them, and she went to fetch their ale.

"A cold fish," Piggot grunted. "Won't even talk to the regulars."

Roarke said nothing. He didn't blame the girl. The men in the tavern weren't fit company for warehouse rats. When she set a tankard in front of him, he gave her a smile. She hesitated just for a second, looking nonplussed at his gesture of genuine friendliness. He held her eyes with his.

"I'm Roarke Adair. What's your name, girl?"

"Genevieve. Genevieve Elliot." She spoke without expression.

"Genevieve . . ." Even his voice was smiling at her. "I think I'll call you Gennie. That seems to suit you better."

"It doesn't matter to me, sir," she replied tartly.

He ignored her tone. "What are you doing here, sweet Gennie? It's obvious you don't enjoy your work."

"What would you have me do, sir?" she said challengingly. "Go a-begging in the streets?"

"No, you seem much too clever for that. You speak well. Have you had any schooling?"

"Of course not. But" —she flung her head up proudly— "I can read and do figures."

"Well done, Gennie. But what good do such accomplishments do you?"

"Look, sir, I've not the time for idle chatter—"

"Sure she does, gentlemen," Watney Elliot interjected jovially. He gripped the girl's arm, halting her retreat to the sideboard. Watney hadn't failed to notice the size of Piggot's purse. He fixed a fierce glare on Genevieve. "You'll speak to the men," he ordered, and shoved her onto a stool.

Roarke almost changed his mind about talking to her when she turned the full force of her resentful gaze on him. He'd already drunk far too much at other taverns and was in no condition for entertaining a girl with conversation. But something about her compelled him to speak.

"Your father?" he asked, jerking his head at Watney.

She nodded.

"He treats you badly."

"I give him little enough in return."

Roarke clenched his fist. His own frustration earlier today somehow projected itself onto her. "Why don't you leave, then, Gennie?" he demanded.

"And where would you have me go?" she asked, equally fierce.

Roarke gave Piggot a canny look across the table. "The colonies. My friend from Virginia tells me 'tis paradise on earth."

The first spark of real interest animated the girl's face. Her eyes, fringed by dusky lashes, attained a sudden sharp sparkle that came from deep within her. To Roarke's dismay, however, that bright look was focused on Piggot.

"I wonder if you could tell me how much truth is in all I've heard of Virginia."

A bittersweet mood overcame Roarke as he leaned back and drew on his tankard. Virginia was Piggot's favorite subject, and he applied himself to it with gusto, expounding on the perfection of his adopted homeland: vast farms swelling with bounty, rivers and forests alive with game, cities that were shining jewels of prosperity.

As the girl grew more interested, Roarke became more morose. He'd wanted Virginia so badly. And he'd come so close to his dream. But not close enough.

Piggot finished his monologue and raised his mug high. "To Virginia," he proclaimed.

Genevieve noted the surprise of several nearby patrons. They'd all heard the news of Boston's defiance the year before and hadn't heard many toasts raised to the colonies since that tea-tossing episode.

But Genevieve Elliot smiled. The smile had nothing to do with Roarke, but its brilliance was so striking that it took hold of something deep within him. Then Piggot invited him to the gaming room behind the taproom, and he reluctantly followed.

When her father shouted stridently, Genevieve obeyed, covering her annoyance as she always did. She hurried into the cramped, dusty little game room. A circle of men huddled over their cards, seemingly oblivious to her presence. A mug had shattered and spilled on the floor, and she began to clear it away.

Genevieve found herself studying Henry Piggot. He was the first real colonial she'd ever met. An odd sort, not entirely trustworthy-looking yet possessed of a sort of worn elegance and an unusual turn of speech that set him apart from Englishmen. He was middle-aged and clad in clothing that had seen better days. His stubby, inelegant fingers protruded from ragged gloves, and in one hand he held an ivory toothpick, which he applied to his teeth from time to time.

Roarke Adair, whose sharp, intense stare disturbed her, lounged in the doorway. He was striking in appearance, but Genevieve didn't like him. She'd chafed under his probing questions and the way he looked at her, seemingly reading the restless longing that possessed her. At least he had sense enough not to join in the game. Watney Elliot cheated with great competence. Under Roarke's disconcerting gaze, Genevieve let the pieces of stoneware slip, and they fell to the floor with a startling crash.

One of the men looked up. "Gets prettier every day, does your daughter, Wat."

"She's not for the likes of you, Sim. Not with all the fancy ways she's been learning." Watney Elliot gave a gravelly, drunken laugh.

Genevieve grimaced and went back to clearing the mess. Mercifully, the idle talk turned from her, and the men began asking Piggot about Virginia. Between the betting and clinking of coins and tokens, she learned that he was some sort of agent for a tobacco planter named Cornelius Culpeper.

"I'm to set sail for Chesapeake a few days hence on the *Blessing*, out of Bristol. Doesn't leave me much time for my final bit of business."

Chester Molls, one of the regulars, raised a grizzled eyebrow. "I thought you were trading for household goods. Don't seem too hard, here in London."

Piggot nodded his balding head. "I've got all that. But I've yet to find Mr. Culpeper a wife. Women are few and far between in the western part of Virginia, and he's been a long time finding one."

"You don't say."

Again Piggot nodded. "Years past, they used to send them by the boatload, sixty, seventy at a time. All a man had to do was pay the passage—a hundred twenty pounds of tobacco—and he had him a wife. 'Tis less common now, and we've still four men to every female in some counties. Not very good odds for a lusty lot like the frontiersmen. Anyway, I've a decent sum for a woman, and I've found naught. Those who are suitable wouldn't go, and those who'd come along aren't worth the price of passage."

The men had a good chuckle at the strange predicament and went back to their game.

Genevieve gathered up the fragments and went outside to put them in the dustbin. When she returned, she noticed Roarke still in the doorway, observing some sort of argument among the players.

"You can't be betting what you don't have," Piggot was saying to Watney Elliot. The others had laid down their hands, and the wager was between the two of them.

"I'm good for it," Watney insisted, clutching his hand of cards to his chest.

"What have you got to put up?" Piggot asked. He'd suddenly become quite businesslike.

Watney's red-veined eyes flicked about the table as he

sought an answer. He was desperate to stay in the game; it was clear from the set of his jaw that he had a winning hand.

Genevieve pursed her lips. She'd heard the argument countless times before. What, she wondered, would he wager this time? There was precious little aside from the night's take, or perhaps her mother's prized new iron stove. Distracted and angry, she dropped the dustpan she was holding.

Watney Elliot exploded. "Worthless slut! I've thinking to do, and I can't concentrate with all that racket." He leaned back in his chair and shoved her hard. "Get out!"

Ears burning with outrage at being treated so, especially in this unsavory company, Genevieve moved toward the door. A strong arm descended in front of her face.

"Just a moment." Roarke Adair's voice rose above Watney's grumbled curses. He stood squarely in the doorway, blocking Genevieve's exit. "I've a solution to your problem, Mr. Elliot." He looked contemptuously at Watney.

Watney narrowed his eyes. "And what might that be?"

Roarke strolled into the room, his head brushing the timbered ceiling. "I believe Mr. Piggot is carrying the sum for a bride price from his employer."

Piggot shook his head. "I may be, but I'll not be lending—"

"That wasn't what I had in mind. But tell me." He jerked his head toward Genevieve. "How much is she worth?"

Genevieve gasped softly. Her initial dislike of Roarke Adair deepened by fathoms.

Piggot, however, seemed pleased as understanding dawned. If he won the hand, then Cornelius Culpeper's money would be his, and he'd have procured a bride at no cost. He studied Genevieve, who backed against the wall, aghast.

"She's a mite young."

Watney was grinning by now, acting as if the idea had been his own.

"Seventeen's plenty old, Henry. And she keeps a good house, does most of the chores for my wife. Any man here can vouch for her maidenhood; she's chased every one of 'em off at one time or other." Laughter rippled from the men, and Genevieve's blush of outrage crept to the tips of her ears.

Piggot hesitated for a long moment, his small eyes appraising. Then he nodded almost imperceptibly.

"She'll do. Show your hand."

Still grinning broadly, Watney laid out his cards with obvious relish. It was a hand of straight black clubs. Genevieve felt weak with relief. For once she was glad her father was so adept at cheating. She shot a look of pure venom at Roarke.

Piggot stroked his grizzled chin. "Very good, Watney. Very good indeed." He shrugged exaggeratedly and rolled his eyes up.

Then, almost playfully, Piggot showed a hand of high red, beating the clubs roundly.

"That ends the evening for me, gentlemen," he said jovially. "I'll be around in the morning to make all the arrangements. The girl's to be married by proxy here in London." He gave Watney a severe look. "And don't even think about not honoring your end of the bet. The girl's mine. I've got a small crew of sailors from the *Blessing* who'll back me up."

Watney Elliot spluttered and fumed, but he was beaten, and he knew it. Even his cronies were struck by the enormity of what he'd done. They called the game at an end and slowly trickled back into the taproom.

Genevieve had been in a state of numb shock, but she recovered when she looked up at Roarke Adair's rugged profile.

"What right had you?" she demanded. Her green eyes glinted with outrage. "By what right do you come meddling here?"

He seemed slightly bemused by her temper. "I merely made a suggestion, Gennie. 'Twas your father who gambled you away."

"What kind of man are you, to think in terms of buying and selling a woman like so much chattel?"

He faced her, growing serious. "I've been watching you,

Gennie. You strike me as uncommon in a number of ways. You don't belong in this seedy tavern, waiting tables and taking abuse from your father. You'd have rotted here, Gennie. Virginia will be good for you—"

"And who in bloody hell are you to decide I'd be better off wed to some colonial lout?"

He reeled a little as he straightened his hat and prepared to leave, looking utterly satisfied with himself. "You'll see, Gennie. You'll see." And then he was gone.

Watney sat alone at the table and drained a mug of ale. The idea that he'd just gambled away his daughter didn't distress him so much as the fact that he was about to lose her income and her help in the tavern. There was no remorse in his drunken eyes, no word of apology when he looked up at Genevieve.

"I've always known you for a bloody sot," she said matter-of-factly, painfully concealing her horror at what had transpired. "Now I see you've not so much as a shred of decency."

"There now, 'tis no way to be talking to your father, girl."

She whirled on him and unleashed her anger, eyes snapping with fury, voice brittle with bitterness. "Don't call yourself my father. What have you ever given me but a cuff on the ear and a foul curse when you thought my earnings too meager or my housekeeping too poor? You've never had so much as a soft word for me. I'm not at all surprised that you'd send me away for the price of a night's gaming. I'll go to Virginia, aye, and gladly, if it means never having to look at your besotted face again!"

She left Watney staring agape and disappeared up the back stairs, where her mother waited, cowering.

"Genevieve, you don't know what you're saying—"

The girl regarded her mother for a long moment, her bosom heaving with emotion. Her poor, grasping mother, who'd done nothing all her married life save submit to her louse of a husband, producing three children in quick succession. Her sin was that of ignorance; she knew of nothing better to strive for.

"'Twill be a burden for you once I'm gone, Mum," Genevieve said evenly, having regained control of herself. "But perhaps 'tis for the best. My absence may get the boys out to the yards, working again." She thought contemptuously of her brothers, who hadn't earned an honest day's wages in months.

"Must you go, Genevieve?" her mother asked blankly.

The girl pressed her lips together. Why couldn't her mother be stronger, why couldn't she insist that this nonsense be stopped and some other way found to compensate Piggot? But the woman accepted this turn of events with characteristic apathy: spiritless, downtrodden.

Genevieve sighed. "I'm going to bed." She left her mother and went behind the thin curtain in the loft to be alone with the thought that tomorrow she was to be married by proxy to a man she'd never met.

2

Angela Brimsby set her teacup down firmly and smiled across the table at her cousin. She'd never thought to see him again, having practically laughed him and his fool idea of claiming land in Virginia out of her house, but things were different now. Summoning him back had been one of her more brilliant ideas.

Smugly, she congratulated herself on having escaped the wild looks of his branch of the family. Roarke, with his mane of thick red hair and eyes that reminded her of a storm-tossed sea, looked as crude and elemental as the rugged land he longed to claim. She sat quietly, awaiting his reaction to her proposal.

Roarke leaned his long form back in a French armchair, draping himself negligently on the expensive piece. Angela's smile wavered, but doggedly she kept her expression pleasant.

"Sounds a bit cold-blooded, even for you, Angela," he remarked mildly.

" 'Tis a perfectly logical solution. You'll need a wife if you mean to be a proper farmer."

She selected a sticky sweetmeat from the tray before her.

"I truly doubt you'll do any better than Miss Moon. Admittedly, the girl lacks a certain degree of style, but she is educated and knows her place. As a wife, she'll be quite satisfactory."

"What does Edmund have to say about this?"

Angela's face closed. "Edmund has no opinion on the subject. He'll not oppose the plan."

"I can't help but wonder why you'd want to give the girl up, Angela. If she's as fine a person as you say—"

"Let's just say Miss Moon and I have had our differences. Now, what say you, Roarke? Will you refuse me, and return to the docks, or will you agree to my plan? I'll send you to Virginia in grand style, with a wife by your side, so you'll have a proper start. Where's the harm in that?"

Roarke narrowed his eyes at her. "I don't know," he said slowly. "But I'm sure it exists. What prompted this change of heart, Angela?"

"Really," she sniffed, "you're questioning an extremely generous offer, Roarke. Let us just say that I suddenly realized that as your only living relative, I owe you this chance."

Roarke sat silent for a long time, certain there was more to his aunt's scheme than she was saying. But something inside him strained with impatience and warned that a chance like this wouldn't present itself again.

"I'll speak to Miss Moon," he said at last. "If she is agreeable, then we'll make arrangements."

Roarke glared at the clock in the Brimsbys' drawing room. Its ticking measured twenty minutes with maddening regularity. Unpleasantly, he was reminded of his mother's clock. What an irony that he needn't have sold it in the first place. He'd never get the timepiece back, now that he'd given the claim slip to Angela, who had undoubtedly recovered it from Pembroke's shop at the first opportunity.

His thoughts fled as Prudence Moon appeared soundlessly. Pale faced and somberly dressed, she kept her eyes averted. The hand she extended was icy cold.

"Good day, Mr. Adair. Mrs. Brimsby has informed me of your offer."

"Then you'd best accustom yourself to calling me Roarke."

"As you wish." Prudence seated herself tensely on a straight-backed chair.

Roarke frowned. Her manner made him feel more like an executioner than a man come to claim a woman for his wife.

"Prudence," he said, trying not to frown anymore, "I know the circumstances of our courtship—if you could call it that—are unusual, but I believe you'll like Virginia. By all reports, it's a veritable paradise." He watched her hands twisting in her lap. "Prudence, what is it? Angela told me you were eager to go, having no family here and no source of income—"

"I'll go, Mr. . . . Roarke. I'll go with you to Virginia."

She looked so small, so fragile. But when she raised her china-blue eyes to Roarke, he was surprised to see a glitter of determination.

"I won't lie to you, Prudence. Life won't be easy in Virginia."

"It can't be any worse than here," she countered, her voice growing stronger with each word. "Let us be married, Roarke."

His face broke into a grin. Prudence knew then that she'd never regret her decision. The piece of her heart that had been ravaged by Edmund Brimsby would never mend, but she vowed not to think of that once she was wed to a man so fine as Roarke Adair.

"I'm told the crossing isn't bad in springtime," Roarke said to Prudence as a hired coach bore them into town, to a magistrate's office.

Prudence regarded him expressionlessly. Despite her willingness to marry him, an air of melancholy clung to her, evident in her eyes and in the hand that reached up unconsciously to smooth the already perfect lace at her collar.

Roarke scowled, then brightened, remembering something. "You'll find a companion on the *Blessing*. There will be another young woman aboard, by the name of Genevieve Elliot."

For the first time a spark of interest lighted Prudence's eyes. "Genevieve!" She smiled at Roarke's amazement when he learned of the unlikely but precious friendship that had grown between a West End governess and an East End washerwoman. Roarke suddenly felt a slight and welcome lessening of guilt over what had happened in the tavern the night before.

"Roarke, how did you manage this?" Prudence asked.

He looked down at his hands. "I'm not terribly proud of how it came about," he admitted. "I don't know what possessed me to do it—I was deep in my cups at the time—but I suggested her father wager her in a card game with a man called Henry Piggot, who's been sent here to find a wife for a Virginian planter."

This brought dismay to Prudence's soft eyes. "How could you? Poor Genevieve—Roarke, *why?*"

He shrugged. "I know nothing of your friend, except that she doesn't belong there in Farthing Lane, serving unwashed louts while they ogle her and make sport of her. The thought came to me suddenly that she'd be much better off in Virginia."

"You shouldn't have taken it upon yourself . . ."

He thought for a moment, recalling the girl's outrage, the hatred seething in her gemstone-hard eyes. "Regrets occurred to me too late, I'm afraid." He sighed. "If Genevieve is truly averse to going to Virginia, I'll see Piggot today and settle with him."

Prudence nodded. "It is best." She stared at him for a long time. "You've done a foolish thing, but you're a good man, I think, Roarke Adair."

He glanced at her sharply, taken aback. Slowly, a smile spread across his face. "We'd best go and be married now, Miss Moon," he said, helping her down from the coach.

*   *   *

Genevieve left the ink-and-paper-scented office in a pensive mood, walking a few steps behind a rather self-congratulatory Henry Piggot. She didn't feel any different, but following an unceremonious signing and stamping of papers, she was a married lady. Mrs. Cornelius Culpeper of Virginia Colony.

"We're off to Southampton tomorrow," Piggot said as they reached the head of Farthing Lane. "The *Blessing* sails the day after."

"I'll be ready."

He studied her with small keen eyes. "I dare say you will. 'Tis best you bring little with you. The *Blessing* is a cargo ship with scant room for passengers' effects." Taking in her worn, drab clothing, he pressed a few coins and bank notes into her hand. "Use this to get whatever you need for the voyage."

Genevieve covered her surprise as Piggot walked away. He couldn't know he'd just given her more money than she'd ever had in her life—close to five pounds. Carefully, she folded her hand around the notes and coins and placed them in her apron pocket.

Her hand brushed against a small piece of paper. Frowning, Genevieve took it out and stared at it. Spidery writing, woefully misspelled, described a certain hooded wall clock that had been left at a pawnship. Genevieve had a sudden image of Angela Brimsby thrusting the paper at her, commanding her to take it to Pembroke's. In the ensuing argument the slip had been forgotten.

Genevieve hurried to the shop and presented the claim to the pawnbroker. He set a clock before her, and she studied it closely, curious as to why Angela Brimsby would want it. The timepiece was decades old, oddly handsome. Charming even, with a halfpenny moon peeping through a hole in the dial. Below the face was etched a small inscription:

Behold this hand, observe ye motion's trip,
Man's precious hours, away like these do slip.

A sudden smile lit Genevieve's face. All at once she knew exactly what she'd bring to Virginia with her.

She left the shop with the clock concealed beneath the laundry in her basket. A small victory over Angela Brimsby, but she felt a certain grim satisfaction in it.

As she trudged toward the tavern, it struck Genevieve that this would be her last night of servitude in the taproom. That a life of another sort of servitude awaited her in Virginia didn't matter. Nothing could be as degrading as her existence here in Farthing Lane.

She had no idea what to expect beyond the cramped, sooty bounds of London, but a tremor of excitement eddied through her at the thought of the adventure that lay ahead. Smiling to herself, Genevieve envisioned vast green fields rolling out in all directions, a grand planter's house, perhaps a sun-warmed garden where she could while away the hours . . .

Lost in thought, Genevieve didn't notice she wasn't alone. Then a long evening shadow suddenly crossed her path, and she heard her name spoken.

"Miss Elliot."

She spun about, her heart quickening inexplicably. Roarke Adair was silhouetted against the smoke-hazed sun, his dark red hair gleaming beneath his tricorn. He was even more maddeningly handsome sober than he'd been drunk.

"You're early, Mr. Adair. The pub hour hasn't begun yet."

His rugged features remained serious. "I've done more than enough drinking. I came to see you."

"Why?" she demanded acidly. "To see that I held up my father's end of the bargain?"

"If I thought there was a chance of your forgiving me, I'd apologize. But never mind, I'll just find Piggot, pay your father's debt, and things will be as they were."

She glared at him. "Is that so?"

"Aye. Mind you, I still think you'd fare much better in Virginia, but the choice is yours to make. It shouldn't have been decided by a draw of cards."

"Your wisdom is a bit tardy, Mr. Adair," she remarked sarcastically.

"Miss Elliot—"

She laughed harshly. "There is no more 'Miss Elliot,' not anymore. I am Mrs. Cornelius Culpeper now."

He stared, his blue eyes searching her face. Almost to himself, he said, "I should have known Piggot would waste no time. But 'tis only a proxy marriage . . . You might get an annulment."

"Mr. Piggot is taking me to Southampton tomorrow."

Roarke frowned. "That doesn't leave much time."

Genevieve's resentment kindled hotter. Even with good intentions, Roarke Adair was proving himself as meddlesome as ever.

"You've done quite enough interfering in my life, thank you," she said. "If I didn't want to leave England, be assured I wouldn't. I don't approve of what you did, but perhaps Virginia will be a good thing for me. You were right in thinking I despise this London slum. So let me go."

He stared at her for a long moment. "Are you sure, Gennie?" he asked.

She almost winced at the gentleness she heard in his tone. She raised her small chin proudly.

"Quite sure, Mr. Adair. But don't start patting yourself on the back. I don't feel at all beholden to you for this."

"I'm not asking you to. Nor am I asking you to forgive me. But I do hope you'll tolerate me for Prudence's sake."

She stopped walking and stared at him. "Prudence?" she asked, her voice rising a little. "How do you know Prudence?"

"Not as well as a man should know his wife," Roarke said simply.

Genevieve's knees began to feel weak and watery. She leaned back against a nearby building for support as Roarke quickly explained what had happened. Angela Brimsby, that viper, was Roarke's cousin. She'd duped the sod into marrying Prudence.

"Gennie?" Roarke was frowning at her. "Are you all right?"

She straightened up quickly, hoping he hadn't guessed at the thoughts that shot through her mind. Drawing a deep breath, she said, "Prudence is my only friend. I'm pleased we'll both be in Virginia." Seeing his face soften, she scowled. "But if you ever do a thing to hurt her, Roarke Adair, I'll find out. I'll find out, and I won't be merciful."

To her surprise, he grinned broadly. "I dare say you won't, Gennie. But don't worry. I've given you little cause to trust me, I know, but I'll do right by Prudence."

"See that you do," she said stiffly, and fled down the street to the tavern.

3

Genevieve's parents and brothers were assembled in the empty taproom, where she waited the next morning for Henry Piggot.

Her mother held out a fraying shawl. "Take this. You'll be needing it to keep warm on the crossing."

Thanking her, Genevieve added the shawl to her small bundle of belongings, which consisted of a single set of clothes wrapped around the clock. Her father gave her a linen purse containing a knife and some eating utensils.

"You'd best be looking out for wild Indians," said her brother Tom. "I've heard stories down at the docks—"

"I've survived seventeen years in the meanest slum in London. I have no fear of savages."

The door swung open. Piggot arrived, and Genevieve said a subdued goodbye to her family. She felt the finality of it without regret. The family had always been like strangers living in close quarters, never really seeming to reach one another. The bond, Genevieve realized, had to be deeper than blood alone. It had to be forged by love . . . a thing that had never touched the Elliots.

For the first time in her life, Genevieve left the teeming

city of London. Sitting quietly beside Piggot in a hired coach, she marveled at vast expanses of rolling meadows, neat thatched farmhouses, and fresh-faced people going about their business at a relaxed pace. It was like another world here in the countryside, everything soft and green, so blessedly quiet, the sky a blue she'd never seen before.

When they reached Southampton, they found the tiny walled port shrouded by a gentle springtime fog that swirled above the river Test and beyond the West Quay, where the *Blessing* was anchored.

Genevieve looked out upon the world from a seat atop an empty wooden barrel, watching barks and small shallops being laden with weathered crates. Her favorite sight was that of departing ships, their sails puffed out proudly by the wind, disappearing over the horizon to ports unknown. Now that her destiny had been laid, she was anxious to be on her way.

Finally, Piggot escorted her unceremoniously to the West Quay. The *Blessing* lay ready, her full bow and sleek stern cutting a handsome profile against the sky. A small group of women had just boarded. They were an oddly matched lot, bound, as Piggot explained, to find husbands or work as bonded servants in Virginia.

Genevieve eyed the group curiously, pitying them. There was a mousy girl, painfully plain, who quailed before a brash, loud-talking young woman with painted lips and unnaturally yellow hair. Older ladies, widows perhaps, clutched nervously at the rail, their eyes revealing their worries about what awaited them. Genevieve was glad she wouldn't be subjected to the humiliation of bonded servitude.

She climbed the wooden gangplank and set foot on deck. Barefooted crew members in loose breeches and leather jerkins scurried about and climbed through the rigging, making ready to unfurl the sails.

"Wait here," Piggot said. "You'll be shown to your quarters with the other women."

She nodded and relaxed against the rail. The soft, salty

breeze lifted her dark curls, cooling her face and shoulders. She hugged her bundle close and smiled into the wind.

Suddenly, a movement caught her eye. She looked around in time to see Prudence and Roarke stepping onto the deck.

It *was* Prudence, but not the retiring young governess Genevieve knew. The girl looked glorious. Pale, as usual, but not in an unhealthy way. There was an unmistakable air of assurance about Prudence that Genevieve had never seen before. She hesitated, her eyes going to Roarke Adair, the handsome, vital presence at Prudence's elbow. He bore himself stiffly, yet calmly, surveying the activity with sharp blue eyes. He bent and murmured something to Prudence, who nodded and watched him as he strode toward the stern, where blocks of chalk were being brought aboard to be used as ballast, later to be ground into plaster in the colonies.

Once Roarke was gone, Genevieve made her way to Prudence, stepping over lengths of stout rope and wooden grates.

"Hello, Pru."

"Genevieve!" Prudence embraced her. "'Tis a miracle, is it not, that we're to be together in Virginia? And neighbors at that, Mr. Piggot says. Your Cornelius Culpeper has property near Dancer's Meadow, in Albemarle County."

Genevieve couldn't help the smile that tugged at the corners of her mouth. "If you could call my being gambled away in a card game miraculous."

Prudence's face fell. "Roarke told me. He's sorry, Genevieve."

"Never mind. I wasn't happy about the way this came about, but now that it's done, I'm ready for an adventure." She gave Prudence a sideways glance. "You aren't angry with me, are you, for blurting out everything to the Brimsbys?"

"No, Genevieve. Lord knows where I'd be if you hadn't spoken out."

Genevieve swallowed. "Still, I'm sorry. I've since realized that it's not a good thing to go meddling in other people's affairs."

Prudence smiled. Genevieve was glad to see her smiling

again. "Never mind. We're still the best of friends, are we not? Truly, I think fate brought us together on this ship. Roarke has promised we'll see each other often."

Genevieve frowned at the way his name trilled on Prudence's lips. "You really don't mind, do you?"

"No." Prudence fingered a small gold locket on a thin chain that had been concealed inside her gown. "I've not been able to simply wash my hands of Edmund, but in time, I think, I'll put him from my mind."

Hesitantly, Genevieve asked, "And what of Roarke Adair?"

"There now, I know you don't like him. But you mustn't judge him. He only suggested what he thought best for you." Prudence gave her a canny glance. "Much as you did for me, Genevieve, in speaking your mind to the Brimsbys."

Chastened, she nodded. "But he seems such a rough, wild sort."

"He's been ever so kind," Prudence insisted. Her hand strayed to her midsection. "He'll be a fine father."

Genevieve stared. "He knows, then? He understands?" Somehow she couldn't imagine Roarke Adair welcoming another man's child.

"Oh, no." Prudence said quickly. "I dare not tell him now. Later, after we've been married some weeks, I'll surprise him."

"Prudence! Bloody sakes, you mean you'll let him believe the babe is his?"

"Of course. It'll come early, but that often happens, I'm told."

Quiet laughter issued from behind them. Prudence's face drained of color as she and Genevieve spun about to find the source. The brash yellow-haired woman from the docks was lounging at the rail, picking absently at a bit of dirt under her fingernail and grinning broadly.

"Mornin'," she said in a husky voice. "I'm Nell Wingfield." She stared at Genevieve and Prudence until Prudence fell back against a grate, looking faint. Nell laughed again and wandered off, swaying her hips so audaciously that one of the sailors in the rigging nearly lost his footing.

"She heard," Prudence whispered faintly. "That woman heard us talking."

"There now, and what if she did?" Genevieve replied.

"You're right," admitted Prudence, relaxing visibly. "Roarke would never believe a tale told by the likes of _her_. Besides, in a few weeks he'll be too excited about the baby to listen to gossip."

Genevieve shook her head slowly in disbelief. She'd always thought Prudence above deception. "I've no great compassion for Roarke Adair," she said, "but still, I think the poor sod deserves to know—"

"Never," Prudence said flatly. "I don't want an innocent child to suffer for the mistakes of others. Actually, it was Mrs. Brimsby's idea. She forbade me to tell the truth and warned me what it could do to the child."

Suddenly, unexpectedly, Genevieve pitied Roarke Adair. What a convenient dupe he'd been, arriving at the perfect time to save the reputations of the Brimsbys and Prudence Moon.

"I must go," Prudence was saying. "Roarke has secured a cabin for us, and I'd like to get settled. Where will you be staying, Genevieve?"

She grimaced. "Below, with the other women. I suspect Mr. Piggot has plenty of Mr. Culpeper's money, easily the four pounds for private quarters, but he's not about to part with it for my sake."

"Poor Genevieve. Please, if you need something—anything—do call on us. Roarke is exceedingly generous."

Genevieve turned away. There was nothing hard about refusing the generosity of Roarke Adair. Spying some of the other women descending a narrow ladder, Genevieve decided to follow them, to see where she would be spending the next several weeks.

The women's quarters were small even by Genevieve's standards. Eight narrow bunks lined the sides of the lower deck. There was a tiny area for stowage beneath each one and not enough headroom to stand. Six of the women had claimed bunks, and Genevieve took a seventh. She looked bleakly at the damp, lumpy mattress. It smelled of mildew and was probably crawling with vermin.

Then Nell Wingfield came in, cursing volubly as her ragged red skirt caught on a splinter. Her garish presence seemed to fill the tiny space.

"Is this the only one not taken?" she demanded, indicating the single empty bunk. When no one responded, she looked about. "Well, it ain't to my liking. I prefer this one, beneath the lantern beam." She stood, arms akimbo, before the mousy girl who occupied the bunk. The girl resignedly began to gather up her things.

"Leave Amy be, Nell Wingfield," one of the older ladies said.

"Shut up, you," Nell snapped. She turned again to Amy. "And you—get your arse up."

Genevieve felt herself grow tense. The women would have to live in these close quarters for weeks, and it wouldn't do to have Nell placing herself at the top of the pecking order right at the start. She jumped up, undaunted by Nell Wingfield's brashness, outraged by her bullying.

"You've no right to that bunk," she stated angrily.

"And who have we here?" Nell purred, falsely congenial. "Ah, the conspirator from above decks . . . A pretty little piece, and feisty, too." She frowned suddenly and shoved Genevieve away. "One side, wench. I'll sleep where I please."

Cheeks flaming with anger, Genevieve grabbed Nell by the sleeve and, with a great push, flung her on the empty bunk.

"Sleep there, and don't be bothering Amy again."

Nell was upon her instantly, hissing and scratching like a great buxom cat. Emitting foul curses, she took Genevieve's breath away with a fist to the stomach.

Genevieve was no stranger to brawling. Half her childhood, it seemed, had been spent defending herself against bullies. Guided by the wisdom of the East End streets, she wrestled Nell to the planks, finally subduing her by straddling her and pinning her hands beneath her knees.

Nell cursed and thrashed, but Genevieve held fast, her

wiry, compact strength well able to best Nell's larger size. "For the last time, Nell, you're to leave all the others alone."

"You damned little chit," Nell ground out. But she ceased her struggling, and Genevieve knew she'd surrendered—for the moment. Genevieve walked calmly to her bunk, acknowledging Amy's tremulous smile of gratitude with a nod. For the second time in her life she'd made a friend. Behind her, Nell cursed again.

She'd also made an enemy.

Genevieve witnessed the *Blessing*'s departure from a tiny skylight above the bunks. The women had been instructed to stay below, out of the way of the busy crewmen. She heard the tattoo of running feet above decks, the squealing of chains and pulleys, as the tide swept in and wind swelled the sails.

Some of the women worried and prayed, clutching white-knuckled at the beams as the *Blessing* lurched away from shore. Genevieve felt strangely calm. It occurred to her that she was leaving behind everything she'd ever known. Something inside her quivered at the thought. She was being offered a new chance in life, a chance to become whatever person she chose to be, a person unhindered by the past, unlimited by the future.

Without quite realizing it, Genevieve found herself thinking, Thank you, Roarke Adair. Just as quickly she reeled in that thought, retracting her misplaced gratitude. He may have landed her where she was now, but he'd never hear a word of thanks from her.

After some time, Genevieve realized the *Blessing* was picking up speed, pushing smoothly out to sea. She left the women's quarters, garnering a glare from Nell, and went above decks.

The sight of the *Blessing*'s sails, puffed out like the breasts of giant birds, was breathtaking. Genevieve leaned against the rail, looking out at the misty, flat horizon. Behind were the gray-brown cliffs of England and dark waters with ominous jutting rocks. Ahead lay Start Point and

Land's End, and beyond that, the endless expanse of the open sea.

She tasted salt on her lips and felt moist air on her cheeks. The unpleasantness with Nell ebbed away, and a slight smile curved her lips.

Moments later it disappeared. Roarke Adair materialized suddenly at her side.

"It didn't take you long to make a formidable reputation for yourself, Mrs. Culpeper." His face was stern, but there was an unmistakable glint of humor in the uncompromising blue of his eyes.

She bit her lip. "How did you know?"

"Seems there're no secrets on shipboard. We all live too closely for privacy. News of your fight with the Wingfield woman spread like lightning."

"I didn't think. I'm off to a bad start, then."

"Certainly not. You're something of a heroine now. 'Tis clear Nell Wingfield meant to run things among the women, but you bested her."

"I had to. If I'd let her have her way today, she would have deviled us all through this voyage."

Roarke chuckled. "She won't trouble you again, Gennie. That's the way it is with bullies. They need to be shown their place, and you did that."

"I'm glad you're pleased," Genevieve said dryly.

He raised an eyebrow at her. "Touchy, aren't you?"

"I don't want to be known as a harridan. And I don't think this is amusing at all."

"I see." He grew serious, intense. "You know, Gennie, your eyes shine when you're angry. And your cheeks are flushed a remarkable color—like a ripe plum."

She felt her face grow hot and turned away. "You shouldn't talk like that, Mr. Adair."

"Gennie—"

She jumped away. "Stop calling me that!"

But he moved close, impaling her with his blue-eyed stare. "The voyage is long, and the days lonely. You're starved already for companionship, Gennie. I can see it in your eyes."

"Go away, Roarke Adair. I despise your attitude toward me. You admire my skills at brawling; you pay me pretty compliments and expect me to fall at your feet."

His eyes hardened. "This is an honest offer of friendship, Gennie."

"I suggest you try your charms on your wife, then. Because I happen to know that Prudence needs your friendship more than I." Genevieve fled, her mind in a turmoil of anger and something worse, something she might mistake for softness if she didn't despise Roarke Adair so.

The voyage went smoothly under the expert guidance of Captain Chauncey Button, who chose the shorter, more turbulent northern route over the balmy southern way, making for the waters about Greenland. The *Blessing* got a good offing well clear of the Bay of Biscay, thus avoiding the treacherous coast of Cape Finisterre.

The ship was cold, perpetually wet, and conditions below decks were barely tolerable. A candle lantern cast a dim yellow light over the women's quarters, where the air reeked of vomit, bilge, and unwashed women.

The older women huddled on their bunks, praying and talking of the past and trying to avoid thinking about what lay ahead.

But Virginia was all Genevieve could think about. She was delighted to find that Amy Floyd was as eager as she. Surprisingly well read, Amy often talked of her fascination with the American natives.

"It almost seems unfair, doesn't it," Amy said, "that most of the tribes have been forced to migrate from Virginia. 'Twas their land before any Englishman ever set foot on it."

"All the better," Nell Wingfield snorted. "Murderin' savages."

"They're hardly savages," Amy insisted. "Did you know their chiefs rule by the will of the people, selected for their wisdom and ability? 'Tis a sight better than we have in England; we're stuck with whomever the Hanovers happen to give birth to."

The ship lurched and threw Nell against a beam. "I'm getting good and bloody tired of this," she said peevishly.

Mrs. Dobbins bobbed her head. "I wish I could have had a private cabin, like that young Mrs. Adair."

Nell laughed unpleasantly. "In her condition she needs all the comfort she can get."

Genevieve stiffened. "Nell—"

"Aye, the woman's got more than seasickness plaguing her—"

"That's enough," Genevieve said loudly. "You'd do well to keep your gossip to yourself, Nell Wingfield."

"Gossip, is it?" Nell cocked an eyebrow.

"Some people," Amy suggested pointedly, "have nothing to say for themselves, so they invent things about others."

Genevieve sent Amy a grin and plucked idly at a frayed spot on her skirt.

"Bloody hell," she said, "I'll be lucky if this rag holds out for the rest of the voyage."

"We'll fix it," Amy said brightly, kneeling beside her bunk to look for her etui. The tiny lacquered box inlaid with gold filament was her most prized possession. Amy looked up from her searching, her brow creased by a frown. "My etui is missing," she said.

Only Genevieve saw Nell's hand creep furtively to a fold in her apron. Genevieve sighed wearily. It wasn't the first time Nell's light fingers had struck. But Genevieve wasn't in the mood for another scrap.

"God blind me, you've found it!" she declared suddenly, yanking Nell's hand from her pocket. "Good for you, Nell; you knew Amy'd be wanting it." She pried the little box from Nell's hand and tossed it to Amy, who stifled a giggle. Ignoring Nell's mumbled curses, they set to mending Genevieve's skirt, listening to high waves licking like giant tongues against the hull as Mrs. Dobbins read from her Bible in a quavering voice.

When the weather settled, Genevieve escaped to the upper decks, keeping a sharp eye out for Roarke Adair. She wasn't one to avoid confrontations, but this man was like none she'd ever encountered before. He seemed to see

through the air of brash insouciance she'd learned to culti-
vate long ago in the mean London slums. Roarke's blatant
friendliness reached out and grabbed some part of her that
she preferred to keep locked away.

She spent hours with Prudence, however, for during the
day Roarke took himself off to other parts of the ship.

Prudence wasn't weathering the voyage well. She was
constantly ill, and Genevieve became something of a nurse-
maid, emptying the bucket, bringing cool cloths for her
friend's brow, coaxing her to sip a bit of salty broth. But
even under daily care, Prudence's condition worsened. By
the fifth week of the voyage she'd grown thin and hollow-
cheeked and frighteningly gray about the eyes and lips. Day
by day her strength seemed to ebb away, and no amount of
coaxing from Genevieve could reverse the alarming trend.
Prudence had lost her initial good spirits and spoke frequently of Edmund, whispering her secrets to the North At-
lantic winds as she fingered the small engraved locket he'd
given her.

Genevieve bit her tongue when Prudence declared her
love for Edmund Brimsby. The man had done his worst to
her; how could she still think fondly of him? Unbidden, another thought crept up. How could Prudence resist Roarke's
cheery attentiveness, the tenderness with which he treated
her?

The ship had no surgeon, but one of the crewmen, called
Brother Tandy, was known to have some skill in doctoring.

With tar-stained hands, Tandy examined Prudence, lifting
limp, birdlike limbs and shaking his head. He murmured a
few questions and listened intently to her barely audible re-
plies. His eyes passed over the tiny rounded rise in Prudence's midsection.

When he looked up at Genevieve and Roarke, he was
grinning broadly.

"Good God, man," Roarke blustered. "Can't you see this
is no time to be joking? My wife is seriously ill."

But Brother Tandy continued to smile. "Not seriously ill,
sir. Seriously pregnant."

Genevieve held her breath, silently willing Brother Tandy

not to speculate on how long Prudence had been in this state. But even if he had, his assessment wouldn't have been heard. Roarke's whoop of delight would have drowned it out.

"A child!" he roared, his voice ringing through the decks. "Glory be, Prudence, we're to have a child!" There was a look of such naked joy on his face that Genevieve had to tear her eyes away from him.

Roarke danced a little jig, bumping his head on the ceiling beams before kneeling at his wife's side. He took her hand firmly in his.

"I never dreamed it could happen so soon, love," he said in a softer voice.

Prudence brightened a little at his tone. "Are you truly happy about this, Roarke?" she whispered.

He nodded. "There's nothing a man wants more than a child from his wife."

"I think I'd like to start writing in my journal again," Prudence announced one day. "Genevieve, do you think you could find it in that bag under the bunk?"

Genevieve was astounded at Prudence's rapid improvement, for she'd been so horribly weak. But Roarke's pleasure at the prospect of the baby seemed to give her strength. She searched for Prudence's little calf-bound volume, but it wasn't to be found.

"Are you sure you brought it, Pru?" she asked.

"Of course I did,—" Prudence's hand flew to her mouth. "Dear God, Genevieve, I left it in London! I remember now, I was hurrying so in my packing—"

"Don't worry; you'll have another one in Virginia."

"But you don't understand, Genevieve. That journal contains my innermost thoughts; it was my only outlet for the longest time. If anyone should read it—"

Genevieve patted her hand. "Does it really matter, Pru? You'll never see any of those people again. I'm glad you left the journal; you don't want to drag old secrets into your new life with you."

"You're right, Genevieve," Prudence admitted. "Ah, I'm lucky, aren't I, to have Roarke. He's been more gentle than ever since learning about the baby."

"I'd best be going," Genevieve said suddenly. It never failed to bother her that Prudence had become complacent about Roarke, that she took all he offered her without a bit of guilt.

With Prudence on the mend, Genevieve spent more time alone over the final two weeks of the voyage. She tried not to rise to Nell Wingfield's taunts or to fight with the women over cooking their meals on the smoky little fire-box in the galley. She found herself thinking more than ever about her new home in Virginia. She even began to wonder, as she never had before, about the husband who awaited her.

Virginia's shores rose like a gray-green lump on the hazy horizon.

"It won't be long now," Roarke said, coming to stand behind Genevieve at the rail.

She looked around sharply. As he stood staring at her, she became suddenly aware of her unkempt state. It had been weeks since she'd looked in a mirror, but she knew she was at her worst. She refused to feel ashamed. She lifted her chin proudly and looked into the wind as Roarke Adair spoke.

"You must be anxious to meet Culpeper," he ventured.

"Perhaps."

"It's not so bad, marrying a stranger. It worked out well for Prudence and me. Still, you mustn't expect too much, Gennie. I've been talking to Piggot, and he admits Culpeper is somewhat older than you and a bit loose with his money."

Genevieve sniffed. "I hardly expected a prince."

He smiled, the lines of his rugged face suddenly soft. "What an odd little bird you are, Gennie. Somehow I get the impression you don't think much of yourself."

"Why should I? My life was spent in a house where I was treated no better than a dog. My future was gambled away for the price of a round of cards. That's hardly the way a person of any worth is treated. I have no overblown sense of my own value, Mr. Adair." She spoke matter-of-factly, without a hint of self-pity.

Roarke smiled again. "You're hiding, Gennie."

"What the hell—"

"That's just what I mean. You're hiding behind the rough talk and bravado of a razor-tongued guttersnipe. But inside, I know there's a sensitive girl with a loving heart, as surely as I know that beneath the grime and ragged clothes is a woman of uncommon beauty. I saw it the first time I laid eyes on you."

4

The port of Yorktown hummed with activity
the *Blessing* was brought to dock. Grand houses fronted th
wide mouth of the river. Frame and brick buildings mingle
along a few paved streets. Stores and warehouses were bu
with the river at one door, the street at another. Genevie
watched avidly, her attention arrested by the green palisad
of the forest beyond the town, the wild, tall cedars and pin
and the bushes that exploded with blossoms of a deep pin
color.

The people clustered around the wharves looked differe
in subtle ways from those she'd left behind. The men wo
plain shirts and breeches, and the few women she saw we
garbed in homespun. There was a sturdiness about the
people, a certain assurance in the way they bore themselve
an aura of hope, that set them apart from Londoners. Gen
vieve stared curiously at the Negroes, whose coffee-colore
skin and tightly curling hair were unfamiliar to her. Su
denly, she looked forward to joining this assortment of pe
ple, to being a friend and neighbor to some of them.

She disembarked with the rest of the women, unsure

what to do. She approached Mr. Piggot, who was speaking agitatedly to Mr. Ratcliffe, the ship's merchant.

". . . couldn't have foreseen this," Piggot was saying.

"That doesn't matter. It's up to you to come up with the money."

Genevieve cleared her throat. "What's the problem, Mr. Piggot?"

His eyes flicked nervously toward the ship's merchant. "Never mind, girl. I'll take care of—"

"My passage hasn't been paid, has it?"

"No, miss," Ratcliffe said.

She whirled on Piggot. "You had more than enough money. What have you done with it?" A sickening dullness settled on her when she recognized the look on his face. The defensive thrust of his jaw, the narrowed eyes. She'd seen it many times in her father. The bloody sod.

Coldly, she said, "You gambled it away on the ship, didn't you?" His lack of response confirmed it. "I suspect Mr. Culpeper will not take this kindly. Mr. Ratcliffe, as soon as my husband arrives, he'll take care of my debt."

Now both men looked uncomfortable. For the first time, Genevieve saw genuine regret in Henry Piggot.

"Culpeper's dead," he mumbled.

"*What?*"

"I'm told he succumbed to swamp fever a fortnight ago."

Genevieve shook her head in wonder. "Bloody hell. I'm a widow before I was ever a wife." She couldn't mourn for a man she'd never known. All she felt was a sense of amazement at the absurdity of her situation.

"I'm sure he left an estate," she said to Mr. Ratcliffe. "Since we were married at the time of his death, he must have left me—"

"There's more to tell," Piggot said, growing more ill at ease by the moment. He took out his ivory toothpick and fingered it distractedly. "Cornelius Culpeper was a good man, a kindly man. But he was irresponsible. He left a mountain of debts. Everything he had has been seized except for a small farm in the West. I myself am one of Culpeper's creditors. I shall have to sell the Albemarle farm in order to recoup my loss."

Genevieve sat down on a crate. Her shoulders drooped. "Some bloody fix I'm in now."

Captain Chauncey Button approached them, his deeply creased face thoughtful. "I'm sorry, Mrs. Culpeper," he said to Genevieve.

She gave him a thin smile. He was probably more sorry than she; it was to him that the fare was owed. Chauncey Button didn't have long to worry. A few moments later he was smiling and watching Roarke Adair count the fare into his hand.

Genevieve gripped his arm, wavering between relief and outrage. "I won't be beholden to you, Roarke Adair," she vowed.

He nodded. "Exactly. Let's just call this a payment for my past mistakes."

She frowned at him. "How did you suddenly come into so much money? That first night we met, you hadn't two coppers to rub together."

Roarke said nothing. But, briefly, his eyes flicked to Prudence, who was standing beside their bags. In that instant, Genevieve understood. She was furious with herself for ever feeling sorry for Roarke Adair.

"It was the Brimsbys, wasn't it?" she demanded softly. "They settled money on you to marry Prudence."

He looked so angry that she stepped back. Anger was something she hadn't seen in him before. Genevieve stared at him, determined not to flinch if he hit her.

"You're not to speak of this again," Roarke said, cautioning her in a low voice. "Not ever. I mean to do right by Prudence, to be a good husband to her. Where's the fault in that?"

Without waiting for her answer, Roarke turned on his heel and stalked over to Prudence.

Somewhat at a loss, Genevieve followed a small crowd of people to a dusty warehouse that smelled sharply of dried tobacco. Almost immediately, Roarke appeared at her side. There was no trace of anger in his eyes now.

"I still want to be friends," he told her.

Genevieve looked away. The women from the *Blessing* were gathering in the warehouse, surrounded by curious on-lookers.

"Like cattle up for the slaughter," observed a man nearby. He was lean and long-jawed and wore a fringed hunting shirt and buckskin pants. He tipped a hat of gray animal fur at Roarke. "How do? My name's Luther Quaid. I hear you're looking for a guide to Albemarle County . . ."

The men fell to talking while Genevieve and Prudence watched the proceedings in the warehouse.

The affair was demeaning. Although Nell Wingfield preened and threw back her skirts to afford a view of her strong legs, behaving much as she'd done on the docks in England, the rest of the women hung back and looked nervously at the men who pressed in around them.

Bids were shouted at the ship's merchant from a blur of faces, old and young, grizzled and cleanshaven, grinning and frowning.

Henry Piggot joined Genevieve and Prudence. "You'd best offer yourself," he suggested. "You'll be needing a master . . . or a husband."

Genevieve narrowed her eyes at Piggot. *"No . . ."*

"You're alone now, and penniless. You have nothing."

Genevieve flung her head up and directed a fierce look at him. "Alone, aye, and penniless, too. But I've the strength of my hands and back. I'll get work."

Piggot shook his head. "The only work you'll get is the kind done flat on your back."

Her mind raced. She'd noticed a single tavern in the port called Swan's. But would they want a Londoner fresh off the boat, with the stench of the slums still clinging to her? Then a thought pushed its way into her mind. Slowly, a smile crept across her face.

"Didn't you say that Cornelius Culpeper left a tract of land in the West?" she asked.

Piggot nodded. "In Albemarle County."

"Is it not mine now that he's dead?"

This time Piggot frowned. "Aye, but not for long. I intend to have the land sold."

She clutched at his arm. "Let me farm it, Mr. Piggot. I'll pay you what you're owed."

He snorted and began idly working at his nails with his ivory toothpick. "You? Alone? What does a London tavern wench know of farming?"

"Nothing," Genevieve said fiercely. "But I'll learn, I'll—"

"Give the girl a chance," Roarke said suddenly, his eyes taking in Genevieve's look of utter determination. "'Twas you who got her here, after all."

Genevieve sniffed. Roarke had conveniently forgotten his part in suggesting the wager. But she held her temper; Piggot seemed to be wavering.

"A year," she said quickly. "Give me a year, Mr. Piggot. If I fail, the farm is yours. If I'm successful, you'll be paid."

Piggot smiled. He was never one to resist a wager, especially one he couldn't lose. He went to the ship's merchant, scratched a quill over a bit of paper, and presented it to Genevieve.

"There's our pact, Mrs. Culpeper," he said. "Put your name to it and the farm's yours."

Genevieve's heart swelled with enthusiasm. She read the document, then signed her name with a flourish and gave the paper to Piggot, who left in a jovial mood, to gossip over the bizarre wager with his cronies. Genevieve looked up to see Roarke grinning at her.

"What are you looking at, you sod?" she demanded.

Laughter rumbled from him. "I believe I'm looking at a farmer, Gennie Culpeper."

Luther Quaid's flat-bottomed boat brimmed with eager new settlers. The buckskin-clad trader declared they were all as green as the Virginia laurel that grew in profusion along the banks of the James River, but he liked them.

Standing at the tiller, he studied his passengers. Seth Parker, the only one not fresh from England, was solicitous of his new bride, Amy. They'd be fine, building a life on

Seth's modest plot near Dancer's Meadow. They had youth and hardiness and the beginnings of what would become an abiding love.

The Adairs were a different story. Roarke was as strong and hale a man as Luther had ever seen, with his bright hair and keen eyes and hands that looked as though they could span a white oak. He'd do well by his uncle, who ten years earlier had carved out a good tract in Dancer's Meadow. Roarke was a likely heir to that legacy.

Pity his wife wouldn't live to enjoy it, Luther thought with a sudden, unwelcome premonition. Prudence had a look about her that he'd seen before: a pallor, a languor that spoke of some weakness of blood—and of character. That, coupled with her utter lack of interest in this whole adventure, would finish her. Virginia's bounty was a wild one; to harvest it, one needed a good supply of mettle.

At least Genevieve Culpeper wasn't lacking in that. But looking at her, her eyes bright with interest, her movements quick and animated, Luther concluded that she had a good chance. He had every intention of helping her. There was nothing he liked better than to see someone—woman or man, white or red—take a piece of land and shape it and make things grow. Odd, that bit about making things grow. Somehow the person working the land grew right along with it.

Genevieve noticed Luther Quaid looking at her and gave him a bright smile. He was unlike anyone she'd ever met: long-jawed and hawk-nosed, clad in strange garments he'd claimed to have hunted from the land, with shoes he called moccasins laced up to his knees.

She crossed to the tiller and sat down beside him, trailing her hand in the silky waters of the James. Along the banks the wind hissed through the cedars and catbirds flitted among the reeds.

"All these trees make me feel awfully small," she commented. A mosquito hummed in front of her face, and she slapped at it.

Luther handed her a small vial. "Pennyroyal," he said. "Keeps away the insects."

Gratefully, Genevieve rubbed it on her skin. "You know the river well, Mr. Quaid."

He nodded. "I was born in Albemarle County, right under the Blue Ridge. My pa was an Indian trader. Last thing he traded for before he died was a wife for me."

Genevieve's eyes widened. "Your wife's an Indian?"

"Chippewa. I took her to my hearth when she was a mite younger than you. But she claims I'm married to this here river."

Privately, Genevieve agreed. Luther Quaid had an uncanny way of reading the river. He seemed to know every nuance of it, the way it reached over rocks, swirling, sucking, doing things that only Luther could anticipate. He was the proud captain of two boats, one that made the gentle run from the Falls of the James to the coast and another above the falls that braved the up-river rapids. They'd made the transfer a few days earlier. The new countryside was wild and colorful, and Genevieve decided she was more eager than ever to make her home here.

The companionable silence on the boat was broken only by birdcalls and the constant thrum of mosquitoes and occasionally by Amy Parker's shy laughter, which Seth delighted in coaxing from her.

Prudence stayed in the small cabin, hiding from the untouched splendor of the woods rising up all around them. She preferred being alone with her thoughts and her broken dreams, sharing little with Genevieve, sharing even less with Roarke.

When he emerged from the cabin, looking somewhat bewildered and not a little frustrated, Genevieve caught herself smiling at him. When a biting fly buzzed near him, she held out the vial of pennyroyal.

"Good hunting here," Luther commented. "Let's see if we can scare us a turkey for our supper."

Genevieve watched as they brought the boat to a bank of deep-red clay. Roarke looked more rugged than ever in the Virginia wilderness, sleeves rolled up over strong, corded arms and his face growing ruddy in the sun. Although he was a newcomer to the colony, he already looked as though he belonged here.

She settled down with one of Luther's books as the two went off to hunt. In less than twenty minutes she heard several cracks from the rifles. Shortly after, Roarke burst from the woods, his face glowing with pride as he held his quarry aloft. Even Prudence emerged from the cabin to see what the celebration was about.

"Look there, love," Roarke boomed, giving the limp bird a shake. "First turkey I ever bagged." He swooped down and planted a kiss on Prudence's brow. His only reward was a wan smile. As Luther took the bird off to clean it, Prudence shivered with revulsion and went back to the cabin without another glance at her husband. Roarke's face suddenly lost its boyish glow.

Genevieve felt resentment rise sharply within her. Why couldn't Prudence share in Roarke's pride? Bringing home food to his wife was clearly important to him, but Prudence acted as if it were nothing. Genevieve was inches from telling Prudence as much, but she stopped herself. She was hardly an authority on being a wife. Determinedly, she took up Luther's well-worn agrarian manual again.

"What's that you're reading?" Roarke ventured, lowering himself to her side.

She said nothing but held up the book so he could see the title.

He grinned. "You'll have to tell me, Gennie. I've no head for reading."

Genevieve looked at him in surprise. "You can't read?"

He shrugged. "Barely. Never had a teacher. I was working the docks practically from the day I could walk."

She continued to stare, searching his face. Although he was smiling and spoke offhandedly, she thought she perceived a note of wistfulness in his tone. Roarke Adair, for all his boundless self-assurance, was a man who knew his limits. Suddenly, Genevieve realized he had dreams of his own, too. She wondered why that had never occurred to her before.

" 'Tis a book on farming," she said slowly. "If I'm to be a planter, I'd best be learning what I'm about."

Two days later the craft slid up a wide estuary of the Rivanna, called Dancer's Creek. Luther poled to a weather-beaten dock. Genevieve, who had been sunning herself and talking to Amy, sat up, eyes sharp and seeking. Brambles grew down the bank, spreading over a barely discernible track. While Luther secured the boat, Roarke attempted to help Genevieve to the poorly constructed dock. She pulled her arm away quickly and scrambled up to the creaking planks.

"What it it, Gennie?" he asked, mildly annoyed.

She took a step back. The wood felt brittle and insubstantial under her feet.

"I don't like having things done for me, that's all."

Shaking his head, he handed up her bundle of things. "Bit of a heavy parcel there," he commented.

She snatched the bundle, which contained her clock, from him. "I can manage, Roarke Adair." He climbed to her side and stood looking up the bank at the farmhouse. "I hope so, Gennie," he murmured, frowning at the neglected structure, which was surrounded by an equally dilapidated barn and several outbuildings. In front of the house rose a tall hickory tree, ragged and gray of bark, at home in the setting. "You're sure to be tested if you mean to live here."

The house had been built in haste. Its walls leaned slightly, and the logs had weathered to a dull gray. The structure was buttressed at one end by a large stone chimney. But Genevieve didn't see the flaws. She stared at the two cleared hills rising behind the house, just waiting to be planted.

Luther looked at her dubiously. "Ain't much," he stated.

Genevieve shrugged. "I never wanted much." She gave another look at the hills and then she and Roarke entered the house. She wrinkled her nose at the musty smells of old smoke and disuse. There was a single crudely hewn stool and an old crate standing on end for a table. The bedstead had a mattress covered with a hide and blanket, nearly rotted through to the floor. A few rusting utensils hung on hooks over the hearth. The fireplace had deep jambs and a long crane for cooking. A money scale provided unexpected ornamentation over the mantel. Genevieve put a finger on the scale and laughed.

"I'll have to find some other use for this," she joked, moving the brass scale aside. She set her bundle on the puncheon floor and slowly unwrapped it, extracting the clock. "This will do better over my hearth than the money scale," she commented, setting the clock in place. She wound the timepiece and smiled at the sound it made.

The ticking accentuated a sudden, heavy silence. Thinking Roarke had gone, Genevieve turned.

He hadn't gone. He was regarding the clock with an expression she was hard put to read. His eyes widened in shock, then narrowed in outrage, while the corners of his mouth pulled down with a sadness she didn't understand.

"Where did you get that?" he asked quietly, his eyes locked on the clock.

Genevieve tipped her chin up. "It was to be delivered to Angela Brimsby, but I claimed it from the pawnshop instead." She grinned sheepishly. "A bit of pettiness, I admit, but at the time I wasn't feeling too kindly toward Mrs. Brimsby."

A sigh slipped from Roarke. "I see."

"Why do you ask?"

"That clock is—was—"

She squinted at him. "No doubt you think it too grand for the likes of me."

He shook his head. "No, Gennie, 'tis not that at all."

He seemed about to say more, then hesitated. "You'll give the clock a finer home than Angela Brimsby ever would have." Reluctantly, he dragged his eyes from the mantel and turned away.

Genevieve watched him, bemused. Then she went and lifted a corner of the blanket on the bed, coughing as a little storm of dust met her face.

"You can't live here," Roarke said from the doorway.

She shot him a determined look. "Can't I, Roarke Adair?"

"'Tis little more than a hovel, girl."

"The roof seems sound enough." She stamped her foot. "And look, a good wooden floor."

He shook his head, motioning for Luther to join them. "Come with us, Genevieve. Luther says we're only three miles upriver from here. You can live with us until you get this place in better shape."

"No."

His jaw tightened in impatience. "Damn it, Gennie, why not?"

She turned about, filling the room with her presence. "Because this house is mine, Roarke. It's where I belong now."

Roarke visited almost every day, always in late afternoon, soaked with sweat from his work. He was never empty-handed. Ignoring her protests, he brought her honey and vegetables from his farm; brown eggs or a bit of butter or cheese.

"You're kind to do this," Genevieve told him sincerely, "but I don't need your generosity; I have to learn to do for myself."

"I expect you will one day, Gennie," he said assuredly.

"I can't keep waiting for one day, Roarke."

He gave her a long, measuring look. "I don't guess you can, Gennie. Very well, let's go fishing."

"Fishing!"

He grinned. "'Tis well to grow crops, but that takes time. If you really want to be able to fill your belly, you'd best learn to fish."

It wasn't quite what Genevieve had meant, but she followed him down to the river bank for her first lesson.

"Damn, but you're an impatient woman," Roarke muttered. He frowned at the empty hook Genevieve had just hauled from the river, sure she'd caught a fish.

"You can't simply jump at the first sign of a bite," Roarke continued. "Give the devil a chance to snare himself."

Genevieve pursed her lips and baited the hook again. She didn't like appearing incompetent before Roarke. It had been three weeks since her arrival at the farm, and she wished she had something to show for it.

She cast her line into the river and gave Roarke a smug look. It was a perfect cast. The current pulled the line until it was taut, and Genevieve stood staring at it, willing a fish to take her bait.

The river was bountiful. In moments, Genevieve felt a distinct tug on her line. Immediately, she started to haul it backward.

Her motion was stopped by Roarke. Stepping directly behind her, he brought his arms around her and grasped the rod, closing his hands firmly over her own.

"No, you don't," he said into her ear. "You're not going to let this one make off with the bait." Together they watched the line being pulled to and fro. Then Roarke gave it a quick tug. Fins flashed, and the sun glinted off a yellow underbelly.

"A good-sized bass, Gennie," he said with a laugh. "Easy now . . . pull away, girl."

His arms felt hard and strong about her. He smelled faintly of leather and sweat and wood smoke. Chasing a strange quiver of feeling away, Genevieve helped him land the fish. They regarded the plump, flopping bass in the grass beside the river.

Roarke gave her shoulders a little squeeze before releasing her. "You see, Gennie, it's easy. Tomorrow I'll show you how to set a seine for them."

She looked away to hide the flush that stained her cheeks. "Will you stay to supper?" she asked. "I'm not much good at catching fish, but I know a thing or two about cooking them."

Roarke thanked her but said, "I'd best be getting back home to Prudence."

"How is she?" Genevieve asked quickly. She felt slightly

guilty being here with her friend's husband, with her insides all aflutter in some strange, forbidden way.

"Doing well," Roarke said as he began cleaning the fish expertly with a thin-blade knife. "She's been asking after you, Gennie. Why don't you come for a visit? The house is plenty big for guests. You could stay the night."

Genevieve shook her head quickly. "I can't, Roarke. I've too much work to do around here." Automatically, her eyes went to the small kitchen garden behind the run-down house. It bore nothing edible yet, but Genevieve had carefully cultivated the ruined plot, hoping to coax some of the turnips and onions and potatoes from their wild state.

"You've been working too hard, girl," Roarke said. "Every time I come by, you're toiling over something or other."

"I don't mind the work. I like it, in fact. For the first time in my life, I'm doing something for me, Roarke, and I like the way that feels."

He nodded in understanding. But then he asked, "What good is it, though, if you've no one to share it with?"

"You'd best get back to Prudence," Genevieve said quickly, taking the gutted fish from him.

Genevieve shaded her eyes at the westering sun, then looked down at the neat, newly weeded rows of the garden. The rich, red-brown soil was nourishing a nice summer crop of vegetables. It was a fine thing, Genevieve decided, bringing things from the earth. She glanced up at the twin hills behind the house. The land there was rich, too. Luther had said it had borne two seasons of tobacco. But there was too much land for one woman to work. Not for the first time, Genevieve wished there were some way to use the land again.

She sighed, and nearby a cat gave an answering mew and stretched, blinking long, lazy eyes at her. Roarke had brought the cat a week ago, saying it might be good company. It wasn't. The little beast only seemed interested in sunning itself and occasionally murdering a bird or field mouse.

"Day's almost over, cat," Genevieve said. "I thought sure I'd be finished with the weeding by now, but it looks like I've another day's work here." The cat purred and dug its claws into the dirt.

"Fat lot you care," Genevieve said, but she was smiling. She bent and pulled up a final weed. On the way back to the house, she stopped to fill her apron with some raspberries that grew wild along the fringes of the dooryard. Then she went inside, the cat padding silently behind her, and stirred the embers in the grate.

She and the cat shared a meal, shrouded by purple twilight, the sounds from the woods swelling with the coming night. Genevieve tried not to think about the fish she was eating. She told herself firmly that she should be thankful for the river's abundance. But, Lord, she was tired of the taste of fish. She pushed her plate over to the cat, allowing him to devour her portion.

Then she added some sticks to the fire and waved her apron at it until if flared up. It wasn't nearly cold enough for a roaring blaze, but Genevieve's lamp oil had run out, and she wasn't ready to retire for the night. Taking up one of her books, she thumbed through it until she found her place.

In appreciation of her interest in reading, Luther Quaid had been by with more books on farming. Sometimes he even brought her a plump, freshly skinned rabbit or offered a sample of venison, dried and jerked by his Indian wife. Genevieve looked forward to Luther's infrequent visits. He wasn't a talkative sort, but he brought news from town and was always ready with some practical advice to help her along.

Genevieve turned her eyes to her own fields, illuminated now by a full moon. Always her attention went back to those two grand, gently rounded hills. There was a boundless richness about the brown fields, rippling like corduroy over the acres. Genevieve stared at the land for a long time. It was hers, and what she did with it was up to her.

Slowly, like the moon breaking from a bank of clouds, a smile spread across her face.

5

"*I haven't any* money," Genevieve said.

Digby Firth brought the tips of his fingers together and regarded her sternly from beneath brows that resembled graying bottle brushes. "How much do you know about growing tobacco, Mrs. Culpeper?"

She looked down at her pink dimity dress, sent to her by Prudence, who was fast outgrowing her clothes, and bit her lip. Not for the first time, her conviction wavered. It was a fool thing, coming to Yorktown with Luther Quaid. A woman alone, she had no business trying to revive her farm. But she squared her shoulders and faced the tobacco factor with determination.

"I know very little, sir, except what it smells like being smoked in a tavern. But I've been studying about cultivation. The soil on my place is excellent. It's borne only two seasons of tobacco."

"'Tis a hard crop to bring from the earth. There is a never-ending cycle of cultivation. If one small task is improperly performed, it could mean ruin. Every step, Mrs. Culpeper, requires skill, judgment, and a good bit of luck."

"I understand that, Mr. Firth. I've studied Mr. Charing's treatise inside and out."

He tamped a small wad of tobacco into a pipe, held a flame to it, and frowned severely through the strands of blue-gray smoke that encircled his head.

"Why, Mrs. Culpeper?" he asked. "Why would you want to start up a tobacco farm? 'Tis an uncertain, sometimes cruel existence—"

She regarded him steadily, gathering conviction. "I want to make things grow, Mr. Firth."

The bushy eyebrows raised, but the look he gave her was not unpleasant.

"Just how do you propose to go about this, Mrs. Culpeper?"

"With your loan, I'll buy seed, equipment, and a horse and hire workers to help me prepare the seedbeds in January. I'll need help again in April, when it's time to transfer the plants to the main fields, then at harvest time."

"Mrs. Culpeper, you do realize that your first crop won't even be shipped until next spring? You'll have no income at all until then."

"I've been without money for five months, since I arrived in Virginia."

"Tell me, Mrs. Culpeper . . ."

"Yes?"

"Just what makes you think you'll succeed?"

"I'll succeed, Mr. Firth. Because I won't allow myself to fail."

He stared at her in her fading frock, hands folded in her lap. There were traces of dirt under her fingernails. Her face was browned by the sun, and freckles dusted her nose and cheeks. When she lifted her eyes to him, Digby Firth decided to give her the money.

He smiled to himself. People would raise their eyebrows and wonder if, in his dotage, the hardheaded Mr. Firth was getting soft, showing compassion for a young widow alone in the world. But that wasn't true. He hadn't become wealthy by doling out charity. He'd done it by making himself the smartest, most intuitive tobacco factor in Yorktown.

And as he looked at the young woman across the desk, Digby Firth knew that the glint of tenacity in her eyes wasn't just a show of bravado. Genevieve Culpeper would succeed. Her farm was small, negligible by Virginia standards, but even a modest crop could be sold for a tidy profit in the markets he knew so well.

He dipped his quill and scratched out a hasty note. Pushing it across to Genevieve, he said, "Take this to Norris Wilmingham. He's two doors down from Flowerdewe and Norton. He'll give you everything you need."

Not until Genevieve was out in the road did she allow herself to believe Digby Firth was actually going to help her. But looking down at his note, she realized he'd been more than generous. Her whoop of joy startled several passers-by, who turned in surprise to watch the pretty dark-haired woman skipping down the street.

As she was passing a warehouse, a man sprawled out into the street in front of her, so close she almost tripped over him. A derisive laugh issued from the warehouse.

"We'll have no niggers doing a white man's work," someone said. "Get back to the fields where your kind belongs."

At first, Genevieve thought the man was a drunken brawler being ejected from the warehouse. But looking into his coffee-brown face with its clear, bright mahogany eyes, she realized he was quite sober.

"Excuse me, ma'am," he said, getting to his feet.

Genevieve picked up his battered tricorn and handed it to him. "Are you all right?"

The man nodded, replacing his hat.

"What was that all about, sir?"

He shrugged. "I was just trying to hire myself on for an honest day's work."

"Why didn't they hire you?"

He looked incredulous. "Didn't you hear the man? I'm not fit to do a white man's work." Shaking his head, he muttered, "Waited forty-five years for my freedom. I guess the price for that is watching my family starve. Better I stayed a slave."

Genevieve moved her eyes over the man. He was gaunt and wiry, his cheeks hollow and creased by deep lines.

"You mustn't talk like that, sir," she said quickly.

"I guess not," he said, brushing off his clothes.

She put out her hand. "I'm Genevieve Culpeper, of Dancer's Meadow in Albemarle County."

Slightly taken aback, he shook her hand. "Joshua Greenleaf. Lately of Greenleaf Plantation, in King and Queen County. My master freed me in his will. At the time, I thought he was doing me a favor, but . . ."

"What do you know of growing tobacco, Mr. Greenleaf?"

"All that the better part of my life has taught me, ma'am."

"How badly do you want to work?"

"I got a wife and six young'uns, ma'am."

An audacious grin brightened Genevieve's face. As they walked together toward Wilmingham's, they struck an agreement. Genevieve told Joshua right off that she had little money to pay him, but that he'd share in any profits they made. His wife and four sons and two daughters would have a roof over their heads, if they didn't mind the work of converting the barn on her place into a home.

Genevieve listened carefully as Joshua Greenleaf presented his family to her. Mimsy, his wife, was a stout, cheerful-looking woman with a smile as wide as Chesapeake Bay. Calvin, a boy of eighteeen, was as tall and lean as his father, with the same glint of intelligence in his eyes. He was the only member of the family who wasn't smiling; he regarded Genevieve with hostile skepticism. The other three boys, Curtis, Phillip, and Eustis, were scruffy and playful looking, but they paid their respects in a mannerly way. The girls, Caroline and Rose, gawked at Genevieve, openly curious. She knew they'd inundate their father with questions as soon as her back was turned.

Quickly, Joshua sketched out Genevieve's plan. Calvin turned away with a snort.

"Slaves again," he said darkly. "and this time she gets us without bidding at the auction house."

"That's not what I offered," Genevieve said firmly. "I'm talking about a partnership, Calvin. Your father and I will be equals."

"So we all starve together."

"No, we all get rich together," Genevieve insisted.

"That's just what I mean to happen," Joshua added.

At that, Mimsy Greenleaf burst into tears. Genevieve swallowed hard to relieve the tension in her throat. She, too, felt like weeping with relief. After all the months of being alone, wondering whether she'd ever do anything other than scratch out a meager existence on her lonely farm, her life was suddenly full of plans and people and hope.

Dancer's Meadow was a tiny hamlet embraced by the Rivanna and Dancer's Creek, dwarfed by the line of the Blue Ridge to the west. Its single street, unpaved and dotted by tree stumps, was lined with a few buildings that managed to look neat despite the dust.

The town boasted one tavern. Its name, the King's Arms, was the only grand thing about it. Walls of rough-hewn timber and plaster surrounded the dirt-floored taproom, which was furnished with stump-legged tables clustered around a large central hearth.

A few patrons had gathered at the front door to look across the road at the trading post. Roarke joined them when he heard Genevieve's name mentioned.

"Lookee there," said Elkanah Harper, gesturing with his mug of cider. "The Widow Culpeper's got herself a gang o' slaves." She was standing on the dock, supervising the unloading of Luther Quaid's boat.

"Lot o' seed there," said Simon Gray, the barkeep.

Elk Harper's boy, Wiley, came running into the tavern, puffing with exertion. "They ain't slaves," he announced. "I heard Mrs. Culpeper say they was business partners. They're gonna raise tobacco."

Roarke couldn't suppress a grin at the open-mouthed astonishment on the men's faces. They'd always regarded Gennie with curiosity and not a little resentment; she'd made it clear from the start that she was quite happy without a husband.

He wasn't at all surprised to hear of the plan. It was exactly like her, plunging headlong into a plan so audacious that it just might work.

"Tobacco, eh?" Elkanah slurred. He liked to call himself a philosopher so as to excuse his disdain for an honest day's work, but everyone else knew him as the town drunk, one who had a tune for every occasion. "What's a green Londoner know about tobacco?"

The other men laughed in concurrence. "She'll be wiped out by summer," Simon claimed. "Maybe then she won't be so disdainful of us menfolk."

Roarke knew then that Simon had been one of Genevieve's victims.

"Like to lay odds on that, Simon?"

The barkeep laughed. "Hell, yes, if you're fool enough to bet in her favor, Roarke." Simon scratched his head. "I'll give you three to one she doesn't even see a crop through to the first harvest."

Roarke raised his mug. "Done," he said, and took a long drink to Gennie's health.

Seth Parker had hewn a stump into a low seat for Amy. She called it her weeding stool, and the profusion of herbs and flowers that grew around it attested to her care. Seth brought out two stools from the house so that Amy and her friends could sit in the herb garden in the soft autumn sun.

Genevieve sipped her tea, savoring its rich herbal flavor. "This is lovely," she said to Amy. "What is it?"

"Raspberry, comfrey root, sassafras. Seth won't allow a single leaf of English tea in our house."

"Roarke is the same way," Prudence admitted. "He's very much in sympathy with Boston and won't stand for paying the tax." She set her cup aside with a little *moue* of distaste. Leaning forward conspiratorially, she added, "But I managed to lay in a supply of good English tea. Rather dear, but Roarke knows nothing of it."

Genevieve and Amy exchanged a look. Amy excused herself to check on the bread she was baking. Genevieve forced the matter of the tea from her mind and turned her eyes to the brooding line of the Blue Ridge to the west.

"It's beautiful here, isn't it, Pru?" she said.

Prudence shrugged. "In a wild sort of way, I suppose, it is." Catching the look on Genevieve's face, she added, "I know you're disappointed in me, Genevieve. But I just can't be happy here."

"Good God, Pru, why not? You've a lovely house, a husband who treats you like a queen—"

"I know," Prudence said with uncharacteristic fierceness. "But I'm not like you, Genevieve. When you left London, you left nothing." She lowered her eyes. "I left the only thing that truly matters to me."

"Edmund Brimsby," Genevieve said dully.

"I loved him. I love him still."

Genevieve stifled a curse. "How can you love the man who ruined you?"

"You talk as if I have a choice. But it's not like that, Genevieve. I can't help what I feel."

"What about Roarke?" The question leaped to her lips before she could stop it.

"I'm grateful for all he's done for me. He'll be a good father to the baby. Genevieve, I wish I could be a better wife to him, but I can't. Roarke's a strong, bighearted man. He deserves better than me." Prudence gave her friend a sudden look of surprise. "He needs someone more like you, Genevieve."

Genevieve felt a jolt of understanding, a blinding clarity. She knew then that she wanted Roarke. Wanted him in a way that made her cheeks flame, in a way that she must, at all costs, deny.

"Gennie, you're behaving like a child," Roarke said, frowning at her.

"You're not my bloody nanny, Roarke Adair!"

Prudence gave her hand a gentle squeeze. "Roarke wants

you to come to meeting with us because he cares about you, Genevieve. We both do."

"I've no time for churchgoing."

"Nonsense," Roarke said. "All of the Greenleafs have gone to the slave church at Scott's Landing. You'd do well to look to their example in observing the Sabbath."

She opened her mouth to protest again, but Roarke was lifting her out of his cart and tugging her into the church before she could speak. Mercifully, they sat in the back, away from the curious stares of the townspeople. Genevieve kept her eyes downcast, her hands folded firmly in her lap.

Furtively, she stole glances at Prudence and Roarke. He'd settled comfortably beside his wife, making a cushion for her by placing his arm behind her waist. Prudence smiled distractedly at him and began fussing with a bit of lace on her bodice. Genevieve became fascinated by Roarke's hand at the small of Prudence's back. Great strong fingers were making tender circles there in a mindless rhythm of gentle affection. Prudence gave no indication that she'd even noticed his solicitousness.

Resentment prickled within Genevieve. *She* would never be so indifferent to that touch, she—

Suddenly, a fragment of the Scripture that was being read penetrated her thoughts. She imagined a note of accusation in the Reverend Carstairs's voice.

" '. . . Flee also youthful lusts; but follow righteousness, faith, charity, peace, and them that call on the Lord out of a pure heart . . .' "

Genevieve fled from the church. But as fast as she ran, she couldn't escape the guilt she felt at what she'd been thinking.

"Bloody hell," Genevieve breathed, regarding the loaf she'd just brought from the oven.

"Ma," Rose Greenleaf whispered, "Miz Culpeper's swearing again."

Genevieve smiled a little sheepishly. "I'm sorry. It's just

that I can't seem to bake bread. Look at this! Flat as a hoecake."

Mimsy Greenleaf hid a grin behind her hand. Her husband's partner—Genevieve wouldn't stand for being called the mistress—tried hard in the kitchen but simply had no talent for cooking and baking.

"That's all right," Mimsy said, shooting Rose a look to quell the girl's giggling. "We'll break it up into the stew tonight." She bent over the hearth and gave the pot a stir.

Genevieve inhaled the fragrance of the bubbling small-game stew. Phillip, the Greenleafs' youngest boy, was a cunning hunter and was always bringing in a rabbit or squirrel, sometimes even a buck, which Mimsy transformed into a sumptuous meal.

"Luck was smiling on me the day we met," Genevieve declared. "I don't know what I would have done without you." She turned her eyes to the window, where in the distance she could see Joshua and the boys carving furrows in the late-autumn fields with the new plow. Ordinarily, Genevieve was out there toiling alongside them, but she'd fallen into a hole and twisted her ankle. Mimsy wouldn't hear of her working until the sprain had healed.

So Genevieve stayed with Mimsy and Rose and Caroline in the kitchen. The Greenleafs had made a cozy home in the barn, but Joshua had yet to finish the chimney. At Genevieve's insistence the girls slept in her house, where it was warmer.

A shout brought her limping to the door. Curtis, Eustis, and Phillip ran tumbling down from the fields, calling out in delight.

"Mr. Adair! Mr. Adair, what did you bring us?"

Roarke swung down from the seat of his cart, his big arms spread wide to receive enthusiastic hugs from the boys. As always, he pretended ignorance as the youngsters repeated their question but soon relented and took out three pieces of maple-sugar candy.

Smiling, Genevieve stepped out onto the porch.

"You'll spoil the boys, Roarke Adair."

"Those fine fellows?" He laughed and doled out candy to

Rose and Caroline, who giggled and ran back into the house. "Never, Gennie. Besides, I'd best get used to young ones. I'll be a papa soon."

"How is Prudence?" she asked quickly. Unlike Roarke, she knew Pru's time was coming sooner than anyone else expected.

"As a matter of fact," Roarke said, "I'm here to collect you. According to Mrs. Weems, the midwife, we'd best hurry."

The cart creaked beneath them as they drove toward the Adair farm. The acres that rolled by the river road were brown and sere, the trees stark and stately against the sky. A grouse rattled in the brush at the roadside, startled by their passing. Overhead, geese wheeled and cried out, spreading silver-gray wings that matched the color of the sky.

Genevieve glanced over at Roarke. The months of outdoor work had deepened the color of his skin, and the sun had burnished red-gold highlights in his hair. Roarke looked totally at ease in his surroundings—strong, confident, full of vigor.

He caught her staring at him and grinned. "I'm a Virginian now, girl. An American."

"An Englishman," Genevieve contradicted.

Roarke's eyebrows descended a little. "Maybe not for long. Plenty of folks aren't too happy with the way England's been treating her own."

Genevieve nodded, conceding his point. Every so often, Luther Quaid arrived with a copy of the Virginia *Gazette* from Williamsburg, which regularly contained long lists of Parliament's abominations in the colonies. There had been talk of breaking away from the mother country, turning the colonies into a confederation of their own.

"Such things don't concern us," she told Roarke. "It's all we can do to coax a livelihood from the land."

"You'll be concerned enough when you get a taste of the tariffs they put on your tobacco," he said darkly. Then he looked thoughtful. "I've decided to put in extra corn next season. For the people of Boston."

"You'd best forget politics, Roarke Adair," she said firmly. "You've a farm to run and a child on the way."

The moment she said it, she was sorry she'd brought it up. Roarke's eyes grew slightly harder, as if some unpleasant thought had stirred in his mind.

"Our wedding night was but seven months ago," he remarked, watching Genevieve closely for a reaction.

She flushed and looked away.

"Prudence is a good deal more than seven months along."

"I know nothing of such things," she insisted, now blushing furiously.

"Did Prudence ever tell you whose child this is?"

Genevieve couldn't bring herself to meet his hard gaze. "You'd best speak to Prudence about it, Roarke."

"Prudence and I speak of nothing," he said. Genevieve stiffened at the note of bitterness she heard in his voice.

"Roarke—"

"Don't make me pretend, Gennie, not with you. Prudence and I attend church together, we go calling, we set our table for the parson . . . But it isn't right. I don't even know who my wife is, Gennie. And she doesn't care who I am."

Privately, Genevieve was astounded that a woman married to Roarke Adair could keep her mind off her husband at all. He was such a powerful presence, his booming voice and deep, rich laugh impossible to ignore. But she was quick to rally to her friend's defense.

"Roarke, she hasn't had an easy time of it. She's never really had anyone in her life. How can you expect her to know what to do with a brute like yourself?"

He laughed at her assessment of him, and his mood grew lighter. "Perhaps you're right, Gennie. Perhaps I've a few things to learn myself."

*   *   *

"Sweet—merciful—God!" Prudence's scream pierced the stillness of the November night, bringing Genevieve to her feet. She'd been dozing after spending most of the day mopping Prudence's brow and soothing her as her labor progressed.

But now, in the darkest hour of the night, there was no consoling the woman who suffered on the bed. Prudence's hand clamped convulsively around Genevieve's, the veins on it standing out with tension.

"Please, Pru, try to relax," Genevieve said helplessly.

Mrs. Weems, the midwife, was more matter-of-fact. "Every labor has its dark moment," she said, studying her patient with an experienced eye. "It passes quickly."

But there was nothing quick about the birthing. A day and a half before, Prudence had taken to her bed with vague twinges in her back. Sharp pains had started soon after, but the baby seemed to be making no effort to join the world.

Genevieve sat at the bedside and put her arms around Prudence, who moved her head from side to side in a delirium of pain.

"Please, God, I want to die," she said through gritted teeth.

"Pru, don't—"

"Leave me alone!" Prudence said with sudden fierceness.

Mrs. Weems shook her head at Genevieve's frantic look. "She don't know what she's sayin', Genevieve. Don't pay no mind to her rantings."

By the time the pink light of dawn tinged the sky, Prudence no longer spoke. She merely shivered and gulped quick, uneven breaths of air and shook her head as if to deny what was happening to her.

Even Mrs. Weems could no longer mask her concern. She lifted Prudence's wrist and felt her pulse.

"She's weakening."

Prudence's eyes flew open, and she let out an unearthly howl. Then she began to grunt through clenched teeth, eyes wide and unseeing.

Mrs. Weems rushed to her and let out a whoop of gladness as she spied the top of the baby's head. "It's coming!"

she called, clasping her hands to her chest. "God be thanked, it's coming."

A baby boy slid into the midwife's hands.

Genevieve froze, staring. And then tears began pouring down her cheeks. Never had she seen anything so utterly beautiful, so fine, so sweet. The baby was a healthy red color, and as Mrs. Weems daubed at his nose and mouth with a bit of linen, he coughed and let out a small, thin cry.

"Fetch her husband," Mrs. Weems said, laying the baby beside Prudence as she began tying off the cord.

Genevieve was out the door in an instant. "Roarke!" Her cry was a shout of gladness. "Roarke, where the devil—"

He appeared in the hall, haggard and unshaven, lines of worry showing around his eyes.

"It's the baby, Roarke," Genevieve called. Before she knew what she was doing, she leaped to him and felt the pressure of his arms wrapping about her. The embrace lasted only a moment, but it was enough for a familiar feeling of unease to begin creeping into Genevieve's heart. But today it was easy to push aside.

"It's a boy, Roarke," she said. "You've a fine son. Come see."

Taking his hand, she led him to the bedroom. He stopped in the doorway, letting his eyes adjust to the dimness within. Then, hesitantly, he approached the bed.

"Prudence?"

At the sound of Roarke's voice she opened her eyes and smiled weakly. She moved the quilt aside to reveal a small ruddy face.

"Isn't he beautiful?" she whispered. "Such a fine little lad . . ." Her voice trailed off, and she closed her eyes again.

Roarke was fascinated by the baby, and more fearful than he'd ever been in his life. How could anything be so small? So perfect?

Genevieve pushed him forward, holding a candle so he could see. Roarke knelt beside the bed and touched the blanket that swaddled the child. Then, growing bolder, he ran his finger along the wizened little cheek.

The child turned his head toward the finger and opened his tiny mouth. Roarke felt a sting of emotion in his eyes. It didn't matter that the child hadn't sprung from his loins. The boy was his now, in every sense of the word.

While Roarke marveled over the child, Mrs. Weems busied herself with Prudence. She removed the bed linens and toweling. Watching her, Genevieve felt a shiver of fear. So much blood . . . There wasn't an inch of linen that wasn't soaked.

She followed the midwife out into the hall. "What's wrong?" she asked. Her voice was low, as if she were loath to give voice to something dark and unimaginable.

"She's very weak," Mrs. Weems explained. Her face was somber. "She's spilled enough blood for a dozen birthings, and it shows no sign of stopping."

"What—what does that mean?" Genevieve demanded, terror pounding through her veins.

Mrs. Weems brushed a tear from her cheek. "She's bleeding to death, Genevieve. She won't last another night."

"No!" Genevieve stifled a sob with her fist, nearly breaking the skin of her knuckles with her teeth. "You're wrong, Mrs. Weems—"

"I wish I were, lovey. I wish I were. But I've attended too many birthings to be mistaken about this. 'Tis a risky thing, bearing children."

Genevieve almost wished the baby would begin crying again, if only to break the silence that crowded into the darkened room throughout the day. But the child was as patient as an angel, bearing the clumsy, inexperienced way she cradled him in her arms with great calm, sucking occasionally from a small twisted cloth that had been dipped in water.

Roarke merely sat and stared at Prudence's inert form, looking bleak and helpless as he watched his wife slip away. From time to time, Mrs. Weems came and exchanged the blood-soaked rags for fresh ones.

The blood never seemed to stop. Genevieve shivered and

tried not to give way to panic. The horror, the helplessness of watching the dearest friend of her heart die, was almost too much to bear. So she clung to the baby and watched his mother and didn't bother to wipe away the tears that, like Prudence's lifeblood, flowed copiously.

"I never should have brought her here," Roarke said, his voice thick with self-loathing. "I never should have listened to Angela Brimsby. Prudence wasn't strong; I saw that from the first. But my own selfishness kept me from heeding that warning."

"It's not your fault, Roarke," Genevieve whispered. Bitterness twisted in her gut at the thought of the Brimsbys. Such fine, upstanding Londoners. So rich and secure in their neat little life. Prudence meant nothing to them. Edmund had planted the child that was killing her, while he himself was untouched by scandal and tragedy. Genevieve had never before realized she was capable of the cold hatred she now felt.

Afternoon slid into evening. Mrs. Weems had engaged a wetnurse, a French Indian woman named Mimi Lightfoot who had lost her husband and baby to fever. Mimi slipped into the room and built up the fire in the grate. Then she placed a candle on the bedside table and withdrew, her face pinched with regret. Neither Roarke nor Genevieve spoke to her.

Finally, as the first stars of twilight began to wink in the sky, Prudence stirred. Roarke leaned forward, hope springing to his eyes.

"The baby . . ." Prudence breathed.

Genevieve came to the bedside and held out the child, who was just waking from a long nap. He opened his tiny mouth and yawned delicately. She laid the bundle beside Prudence and brought her friend's arm about the baby.

Prudence squinted and blinked, as if she were having trouble seeing. Then her eyes seemed to focus, and her lips curved into a smile of unbearable sadness.

"He is worth it," she said, mouthing the words, too weak to give voice to them.

"He's a fine boy, Prudence," Roarke assured her.

She looked at him as if seeing him for the first time. Her smile softened and became even sadder. "And you're a fine man, Roarke Adair. I was lucky to share even a small part of my life with you." A wistful look crossed her face. "'Tis a shame, my husband, that I waited until now to tell you that."

Roarke gripped her hand. Then Prudence reached her other hand out to Genevieve, who stood at the other side of the bed.

"My dearest friend," she murmured, her voice even fainter than it had been before. "What joy I had in you."

"Oh, Pru . . ." Genevieve choked, feeling herself begin to tremble from head to toe.

"You mustn't cry for me, Genevieve. Please. You must live for me. Virginia was not my destiny, but it's yours. You're thriving, Genevieve. I like to think I've given you something by teaching you to read."

"Pru, you've taught me so much more than that."

"Then use it, Genevieve. Use it, and make me proud of you."

Genevieve brought her friend's small, cold hand to her lips and pressed a kiss on it.

"I will, Pru. I swear I will."

Prudence's eyes fluttered shut, and Genevieve sobbed aloud, certain she was gone. But the eyes opened again, to look upon the child.

"Hance," Prudence said, using the name she'd chosen. "Keep him well. He is innocent of my crimes."

Roarke met his wife's gaze. "Of course, Prudence."

"You are so good, both of you," Prudence murmured, coughing softly on the words. "Would that I had a fraction of your goodness . . ." Slowly, she turned her gaze to the window, where stars sprayed across a blue-velvet sky.

And then it was over. Prudence simply gave herself up to death. There was no movement, no dramatic sound or final plea for mercy. It was as if Prudence had been frozen in time, staring out the window with unseeing eyes, unconsciously facing eastward, toward the man she'd never stopped loving.

"No!" Genevieve sank to her knees beside the bed. Roarke shook his head, moved his hand gently over Prudence's face to close her sightless eyes, and took the baby into his arms.

Then he came around the bed and lifted Genevieve to her feet.

"She's gone, Gennie," he stated. "She's gone, and we've work to do."

Genevieve clung to Roarke's strength and slowly gained control of herself. Brushing the tears from her face, she gazed down at the baby.

"Indeed we have, Roarke Adair. This young man will need a good bit of love."

They walked to the door together, to find Mimi Lightfoot and begin the melancholy business of mourning. Roarke hesitated and looked back at the slight form on the bed.

"I never even knew her," he whispered hoarsely.

Genevieve swallowed hard. "I did, Roarke. Oh, God, but I did."

6

Genevieve stood at the top of the main field, leaning on her mattock. The twin slopes below her shimmered as the springtime sun began to draw the dew from the grass. Mimsy was in the kitchen garden fussing over her peas and potatoes. The bright yellow calico kerchief she wore on her head stood out amid the muted browns and tender greens of the garden. Near the barn, which had become a home with a newly mortared chimney, Rose was pegging laundry to a line stretched between two sassafras trees.

Closer to Genevieve, Joshua and the boys worked at transplanting tobacco seedlings, as they had done starting at dawn every morning for a full month now. Joshua caught her looking at him and grinned, motioning her to join them. Lifting her skirts above her mud-caked boots, she started down the slope.

"Finest seedlings I ever saw," Joshua remarked. "The leaves are the size of bank notes."

Genevieve smiled at him. Like Joshua, she hoped to see the crop transformed into cash. The land was bountiful, but there were some things they couldn't take from it, like hogsheads and hand presses and farm equipment, which they needed more and more with each passing day. She bent and dropped a seedling onto one of the tobacco hills that had been prepared.

Looking down at the plant, she said, "I've done that so many times, I swear I could do it in my sleep."

"You're a born planter, Genevieve. We'll be done by the first of June the way things are going. And the Lord's seen fit to bless us with plenty of rain."

Genevieve grimaced at the mention of rain. Despite what Joshua said, she had a hard time regarding it as a blessing. It had drizzled steadily for the past few weeks, soaking her and the Greenleafs to the bone before each day was done. But Joshua insisted it was perfect planting weather, so she endured it.

"I can't believe we'll be finished in two weeks," she said, working on another seedling.

Joshua nodded. "Never drove myself or my boys so hard at Greenleaf. I guess knowing part of this is to be mine makes all the difference."

"You'll have earned more than your share, Joshua," Genevieve said.

They worked in companionable silence for a time, until Curtis burst into song. Genevieve smiled. The boy was irrepressible, as tireless as his father. He had a beautiful voice, as sweet and pure as a bird's song. Mimsy called him her singing angel. Quietly, so as not to mingle her own less tuneful voice with Curtis's, she began to hum along.

She wished, for Joshua's sake, that the eldest boy, Calvin, had some of Curtis's humor. Calvin was a handsome, brooding youth with a quick mind and an even quicker temper. Genevieve sensed a restlessness in Calvin that reminded her a little of herself, the way she'd been back in London. Cal seemed to be straining at the bit of his life, reaching for something just out of his grasp.

Genevieve had hoped last winter that he would find fulfillment on the farm, but it was not to be. Calvin worked as hard as any of the Greenleafs, but he worked without conviction. Of all the family he was probably the most intelligent, the most high-minded. And the most frustrated.

Still humming, Genevieve began to work beside Calvin. As always, he pretended not to stare at her; as always, she pretended not to notice. Usually, Genevieve didn't try to breach the young man's wall of silence, but today she wanted to share her high spirits. The farm was bursting with new growth, and the weather promised a sun shower rather than rain. Genevieve paused to shade her eyes, turning to look at the mountains. Today the ridge was a line of repose, blue distances and flat layers of wispy white clouds.

"Back in London," she remarked, "you could never see the sky for all the smoke. If someone had told me then about these colors, I wouldn't have believed them."

Calvin merely shrugged and savaged a weed with his mattock. "Guess I been looking at Virginia too long to be impressed by it."

"What are you impressed by, Cal?"

He gave her a sharp look, somewhat taken aback by her question. And he said nothing.

"You've a fine family, Cal. If we're successful at this business, you'll have a good life."

"Maybe so, Miz Culpeper."

"Then why are you so unhappy?"

Again that sharp look. Calvin had very dark, penetrating eyes. "I guess," he said slowly, "I don't want the life of a planter."

"What do you want, Cal?"

He folded his lips into a thin line and went back to his planting. But this was the longest conversation Genevieve had ever coaxed from Calvin, and she pressed on. "Cal, I don't like to see you like this. Please, if there's anything I can do—"

Finally, she noticed a glimmer of interest in his eyes. "There might be, Miz Culpeper."

"Oh?"

"You could teach me to read." He spoke challengingly, as if expecting her to refuse.

She nearly dropped the seedling she was holding. "Teach

you to—God blind me, Cal, why didn't you say so? I've few enough talents, but I can bloody well read. And I'll try my best to show you how it's done."

Calvin didn't smile, but there was an unmistakable softening of his features, and one corner of his mouth turned up slightly. Then he went back to his planting.

Rose Greenleaf had named the horse Victor, insisting that such a fine beast needed a noble title. Genevieve knew the farm plug had seen better days, but the animal was tractable and strong. Victor had a plodding gait that suited Genevieve just fine. She was inexperienced at the reins and never failed to be nervous when driving the cart.

She went into town intending to find the Reverend Carstairs, hoping he'd forgiven the fact that she'd run from his church in October and never been back. Today, it seemed, half the town was gathered at the trading post.

It was to this post that farmers brought their wares to be sold downriver and came to trade for the supplies they needed. And, most important, it was where the settlers received news from other parts of the world.

Genevieve got out of the cart and hitched Victor to a rail. She smoothed her fading calico dress and hoped the hem would conceal her dusty boots. Roarke had insisted on giving all of Prudence's dresses to her, and she'd always felt a little guilty at how quickly they succumbed to the dirt of the fields.

As if the very thought of Roarke had summoned him, Genevieve heard his voice calling her name. She swung around, feeling an inner tremor at the sight of him. It always happened like that. Genevieve had decided long ago that she would probably spend the rest of her life trying to hide her feelings for Roarke Adair.

She smiled and brushed a wisp of hair from her cheek.

"Gennie," he said, "you look wonderful, like you've been touched by the wind and sun. Virginia is the best thing that could have happened to you."

Still smiling, she teased, "You're still trying to justify persuading my father to gamble me away, Roarke Adair."

He scowled. "I'll never live that down, will I?"

"Never mind. I'm looking for Mr. Carstairs. Have you seen him?"

The scowl disappeared. "Don't tell me you've finally decided to join the flock?"

She shook her head. "I've survived this long without going to church. But I want to borrow some books from Mr. Carstairs. I'm going to teach Calvin Greenleaf to read."

His blue eyes grew warm with appreciation. "Well, that's fine, Gennie. That's just fine. You'll be doing the lad a great favor."

"I hope so. His parents aren't too sure. They insist that reading will put all sorts of crazy notions into Cal's head and ruin him as a farmer."

"Maybe so," Roarke mused. "Maybe it'll turn him into something more." He looked thoughtful for a moment. "You're a good woman, Gennie, to do this for the lad."

She flushed and looked away. " 'Tis a small enough favor. I only hope I can do it."

"You will, Gennie," Roarke assured her. "Mr. Carstairs is down at the docks. Luther Quaid just came in."

Together they approached a little knot of people clustered around the rickety wharf. Genevieve nodded to Amy and Seth Parker, asking after Amy's health and being informed that the baby would be born in just a few weeks.

As Luther unloaded his usual supplies, he traded gossip with the locals. Then, with a dramatic flourish, he produced a well-worn copy of the Virginia *Gazette*. He held it high with a strange, somber look on his face.

Genevieve pressed forward to see. She squinted; all the reading she'd been doing on farming was weakening her eyes. But the words on the page leaped out at her.

". . . the Troops of his Brittanick Majesty commenced hostilities upon the people of Massachusetts province . . . we are involved in all the Horrors of a civil War. . . . The sword is now drawn. God knows when it will be sheathed."

Mr. Carstairs read the passage aloud. The group around

him fell silent as they listened to an account of battles and bloodshed that had occurred in remote New England a full month before. British soldiers, marching to the towns of Lexington and Concord, had been engaged by a small militia.

"Civil war . . ." Genevieve glanced over at Roarke; her breath caught at the look on his face. For some time there had been talk of unrest in the colonies, bitter complaints about Lord Townshend's unfair revenue schemes and the highhandedness of the British ministry. But no one in Dancer's Meadow had realized the situation was so volatile.

"There's more," Luther Quaid said above the babble of voices. "Patrick Henry mustered an army and marched on Williamsburg. No blood was shed, but Governor Dunmore was forced to pay for the powder he confiscated."

"Roarke . . . ?" Genevieve laid her hand on his arm. As everyone began to talk at once, she asked, "What does this mean?"

The intense look left his face, although he remained thoughtful. "That the trouble's reached our own Virginia, Gennie. No telling how far it'll go."

"How far can it go? What can a few angry colonists—with no army and no money—hope to accomplish against the British army?"

"We've got something," Roarke said thoughtfully.

Her eyes widened at the word *we*. "And what is that, Roarke?"

"We have America, Gennie. 'Tis no small resource."

They walked away from the dock to sit together beneath a spreading oak tree. Genevieve leaned her back against its trunk and looked at Roarke. She didn't want to think about war.

"How is the baby?" she asked. She hadn't seen the child in over a month, being so busy with the spring planting.

"Thriving," Roarke said, a warm look coming into his eyes. "Mimi Lightfoot swears the little nipper gains weight every day."

Genevieve studied Roarke as he spoke. At first she'd been

terrified he'd reject a child sired by another man. But she'd underestimated the generosity of Roarke's heart.

"You're a good papa, Roarke," she said warmly.

"I'm working at it." He drew his knee up to his chest and stared up at the budding leaves of the tree. "I feel a bit inept when it comes to this business of being a father. There's nothing about my own father worth remembering, so I'm on my own."

"You'll do it well," Genevieve insisted. "Just like you do everything else. Hance is a lucky little boy."

He smiled. "There's no reason the child shouldn't be treated as my own."

Genevieve couldn't help the hand that went out to Roarke and laid itself on his arm. "Take care," she said, getting to her feet. "I'd best be seeing Reverend Carstairs."

Watching her walk away, Roarke frowned. Genevieve never failed to leave him bemused. One moment she was scolding him for trying to give her advice or spoiling the Greenleaf children, and the next her lovely eyes were suffused with warmth at some small thing he did or said.

Every so often he thought he sensed a deep longing in Gennie that made him want to reach out to her. But her independent ways warned him off. She wore her self-reliance like armor, protecting herself against those who would be close to her, disdaining sentiment. Roarke drew idly in the dust with his finger. He simply didn't understand the woman. Sometimes he didn't even understand himself.

The clock above the mantel in Genevieve's house ticked faithfully, but real time was measured on the farm by the progress of the crop. As Joshua had predicted, the transplanting was completed by June, and this was followed by a long season of ripening and growth. But the days that slid by were far from idle. Each field required regular attention. There were the daily chores of hoeing and battling weeds, in addition to topping the plants and removing the secondary shoots put out by the roots.

Genevieve was tireless during this time, as were the

Greenleafs. In the scalding heat of high summer and in the soft rains that came down from the Blue Ridge, they worked the fields. In the evening they shared a meal, their food growing more bountiful with each passing week. Mimsy's kitchen garden fairly burst with beans and squash and turnips, and Phillip's propensity for hunting put meat on the table. It was a full, busy time for Genevieve, a time of hope, a time when she allowed herself to dream.

Her evenings were never lonely now that she had her project with Calvin. Although Genevieve swore she knew little of teaching, he was an apt and eager pupil. She soon had him reading Ben Franklin's worldly witticisms and studying the rules of language in Dilworth's speller, which Mr. Carstairs had lent her. Even during the day, when they paused for dinner beneath a shady tree, Genevieve would often take up a stick and set Calvin to drawing his letters in the dust. When Mimsy saw that her son was beginning to read, she brought forth a tattered Bible that had once belonged to her mistress at Greenleaf. Now, instead of looking askance at Calvin's new skill, she delighted in hearing him read the Scriptures.

But Calvin had little interest in the Bible. Luther Quaid had brought him a battered copy of Judge Sewall's "Selling of Joseph," an antislavery tract. Genevieve was surprised by the power of Calvin's reaction to it. She was even more amazed when he began to pen his own ideas on slavery. Ideas that, she knew, would bring all the slave owners of Albemarle County down about his ears if they ever knew about them. But never once did she try to discourage him.

One evening in late August, as Genevieve was listening to Calvin read from Jonathan Edwards's treatise on freedom of will, she found she had trouble concentrating on her pupil. Calvin had a deep, musical voice, and he was reading now with growing confidence, but there was a restlessness within Genevieve that detracted from her enjoyment at hearing him.

For months she'd suffered from vague pangs of loneliness, although she told herself it was absurd. She had the farm, and the Greenleafs. Still . . .

Calvin stopped at an unfamiliar word and looked up. He waited a moment for Genevieve to prompt him, as she usually did, but she said nothing, only sat there with a wistful expression on her face.

"Miz Culpeper . . . ?"

Genevieve started. "What it is, Cal? Oh, do you need a word?"

"I believe I've finished for the night."

"Oh. Very well. Say goodnight to the family for me." He nodded and placed the book on a shelf, then walked toward the door.

Thinking Calvin had gone, Genevieve leaned her elbows on the windowsill and looked outside. Luther Quaid had brought a piece of glass for the window, but Genevieve hadn't yet prevailed on Joshua to set it into the frame. The glass would be welcome come winter, when the wind blew relentlessly down from the mountains, but now in high summer, Genevieve savored the gentle breeze that wafted in.

She found her gaze drawn down to the Greenleaf house. Joshua had cut a large window into one wall, and she could see the members of the family moving about. It was a scene of cozy intimacy; Genevieve felt slightly guilty watching as little Rose tripped by, and then Joshua appeared, sweeping Mimsy into a firm embrace. Fighting down an unbidden twinge of longing, Genevieve turned away.

Embarrassed, she found herself facing Calvin. "I thought you'd gone," she said, feeling her face redden.

Inexplicably, Calvin himself seemed ill at ease. This was unusual, as the young man ordinarily exuded confidence in everything he did.

"I was just thinking how quiet and lonely it must get up here at night, Miz Cul—Genevieve."

She smiled. "That it does, Cal. I don't mind the quiet, really I don't." But he had seen her staring longingly out the window and knew she was lying. Genevieve forced herself to look at him and tried to laugh.

"In truth, I sometimes dread the night. Especially when the wolves howl. It makes me feel so cut off from everything, so utterly alone."

"You ought to marry again, Genevieve. Marry proper this time, and start a family. You're never alone once you got family."

"But you're my family, Cal. You and your parents and brothers and sisters. I couldn't ask for better than I already have."

"Ain't the same thing," he insisted, stepping closer to her. "A person's got to have something more than that."

The next moment, Genevieve found herself pulled against Calvin's tall, wiry frame and felt his mouth push down on hers. At first she was so shocked that she couldn't react. But then she brought her hands up and pressed them firmly against his chest, pushing herself away.

"Cal!"

There was a rebellious look in his eyes as he reached for her again. "I ain't a boy, Miz Cul-Genevieve. I'm the same age as you. There's plenty I know about women. Plenty I know about you, that you probably don't even know yourself."

Genevieve backed away. She wasn't afraid, but deeply disappointed. With his embrace, Calvin had changed the terms of the friendship that had been growing between them all summer. She held up her hand to him.

"You don't want this, Cal, not really. What was it you were reading from your mother's Bible . . . 'Stolen waters are sweet, and the bread eaten in secret is pleasant . . .'"

It was the wrong thing to say. Calvin's eyes hardened to gleaming ebony. "Looks like you suddenly got religion," he sneered. "Mighty convenient timing." He turned away sharply. "I thought you were different from most folks; thought you could look at me and see a man, not a nigger. But you can't, not any more than the slave owners in Dancer's Meadow."

Genevieve winced at the bitterness in his voice. "Cal, it's not that. It's just that—"

He strode to the door. "Goodnight, Miz Culpeper. Thank you for teaching me to read. I reckon I can get on by myself from now on."

He disappeared into the gathering twilight. It was the last time Calvin ever set foot in Genevieve's house.

Genevieve knew immediately upon reaching town that something was wrong. The fact that she'd barely slept the night before, worrying about the confrontation with Calvin, added to the tenseness of her nerves. She was on her way to the trading post to send her monthly letters to Mr. Firth and Henry Piggot, which informed them of the farm's progress and begged Piggot to be patient. She drew up her horse at the end of the road and shaded her eyes with her hand.

A dozen men milled about, clad in dirty hunting shirts and buckskins, conspicuously armed with rifles, knives, and tomahawks. Squinting, Genevieve caught sight of Roarke and another tall man with a head of flaming red hair. She remembered George Rogers Clark from a visit he'd made the previous summer. The presence of the Indian fighter and frontiersman caused a prickle of apprehension to slither up her spine.

Bouncing her heels against Victor's flanks, Genevieve joined the group massed in front of the trading post. Victor shied a little at the sight and smell of the unfamiliar horses. Genevieve herself recoiled at the smell of bear grease and the sight of scalps of spiky black hair hanging from some of the saddles. She dismounted and went to Roarke's side.

She greeted Captain Clark, who nodded gravely, and then asked Roarke what had happened.

"There's been an Indian attack," he reported in a subdued tone. "The Parker farm was hit."

Genevieve stumbled back. Her knowledge of the ways of Indians was scant, but she'd heard terrifying tales about redskins who, infrequently, rode down to attack white settlers.

"Sweet Christ," she breathed, raising her hand to her throat. "Are they—?" She broke off, unable to give voice to her fears.

"Seth and the baby were killed," Roarke said quietly. "Amy is missing. Kidnapped, probably."

Swallowing hard, Genevieve asked, "Why, Roarke? How could this happen?"

Hearing her question, Captain Clark stepped forward. "Retaliation, ma'am. Chief Logan was a friend of the whites until his family was slaughtered by Greathouse's gang. After that, Logan declared open season on the white man."

He pushed back his wide-brimmed hat and shook his head. "It's unusual, an attack this deep into a settled area. From the look of the Parker farm, this was a band of strays, three or four at most."

Genevieve tried not to show that she was trembling. "But why the Parkers, captain? Amy was fascinated by Indians; she would have offered them her hospitality."

The rugged frontiersman's face clouded. "Seth Parker's brother was in on the Greathouse massacre."

"What will become of Amy?"

"If she's cooperative, she may be adopted. The Indians have a ritual that purges a person of all white blood and makes them a member of the tribe."

"And if she fights them?"

"Indians have exquisite ways of torture."

Quaking inside, Genevieve found herself hoping that Amy wasn't a captive after all, that she'd met a quick, merciful death. Knowing how much her friend loved her husband and baby, she guessed that Amy wouldn't want to go on without them.

Captain Clark spoke to Roarke. "Some of the men are going back up to the farm. If we can determine the direction the redskins took, we might be able to overtake them."

Roarke walked to his horse. "I'll go along, too."

Without hesitation, Genevieve mounted and rode up alongside him.

"You'd best get back to town," Roarke said curtly.

"I'm coming with you."

"Gennie—"

"Amy was my friend." She tipped her chin at a stubborn angle.

"Just stay close," Roarke said, relenting.

Genevieve gave a little cry of alarm when they reached

the Parker place. A thin wisp of smoke rose from the blackened timbers of the barn. A few chickens scratched aimlessly in the dust in front of what was left of the house. Its sturdy logs hadn't succumbed entirely to the flames. Most of it was intact, but the door hung at an awkward angle.

Roarke and the others went inside. Genevieve's eyes blurred with tears, and she stood outside for a moment, trying to compose herself, trying not to look at the butchered carcasses of the family dogs. Then, taking a great gulp of air, she stepped into the doorway.

Roarke turned, his face pale and taut. He put out a hand to keep Genevieve from coming inside.

"Gennie, no—"

But she brushed past him, determined to face what had happened to Amy.

Furniture had been overturned, and cooking utensils were strewn randomly about. Bedding and clothing lay in twisted heaps on the floor. Genevieve's eyes fastened on a small wooden cradle pushed up against the hearth. The blankets were soaked with blood. A tuft of hair—sweet God, Amy had been so proud of little Ruth's golden hair—clung to the side of the cradle. And on its wooden edge, a tiny hand print of blood could be seen.

There was something so poignant and horrifying in that hand print that Genevieve nearly fainted. She sagged against Roarke, murmuring curses against the savages who had taken the life of a tiny baby.

Roarke put his arms around her and led her back outside. "Stay here," he said quietly. "I'll be back in a few minutes." Before he went into the house again, he turned. "Are you all right, Gennie?"

She managed to nod. As soon as he was gone, she sank to her knees and watched her own tears splashing down onto the trampled remnants of Amy's herb garden.

By the time Roarke returned, she'd stopped crying. Pale and trembling, she rode beside him back to town. When they were almost there, he reached into his shirt pocket and drew out a small lacquered box.

"I found this," he said. "I'm surprised the Indians over-looked it. Did it belong to Amy?"

Genevieve nodded and took it. Something tugged at her heart as she placed it in her pocket. It had been the only thing of value Amy had brought to Virginia.

"I'll keep it for her," she said, fiercely hoping for her gentle friend's return.

When they reached town, Clark and his men were forming up to leave for the frontier. They planned to comb the area for the Indians, though without much hope of finding them. Redskins, Captain Clark explained, were swift travelers and knew the land even in the dark of night. Chances were they were well up into the Blue Ridge by now.

To Genevieve's surprise, she recognized Calvin Greenleaf among the frontiersmen. He was clad in clean breeches and a loose shirt and had a small pack of gear in his arms. One of Clark's men was helping him saddle a horse.

"Cal!" she cried, jumping down and running to him. "What are you doing?"

He gave her a cold stare. "Looks like I'm joining the captain's company."

"Don't be silly, Cal; you don't know anything about fighting Indians."

"Don't guess I do," he said. "But I reckon I'll learn pretty quick."

Genevieve swung around to face George Clark. "You can't do this!" she cried. "He's only a boy."

The captain looked at Cal for a long moment. "He's man enough to know his own mind. He's willing to leave his home with no promise of pay, glory, or food. I can't ask for more than that."

She turned her gaze back to Calvin. Suddenly, she under-stood the glitter of determination in his eyes. Even before last night, Calvin had been restless, seeking something her small farm couldn't offer him.

"I hope you find what you're looking for out there, Cal,"

she said quietly, turning her gaze to the hazy blue line of mountains in the west.

"Reckon I might, Miz Culpeper," he remarked, turning away.

"It's best you let him go," Roarke said behind her. "There's no putting blinders on a man like him." Laying his arm across her shoulders, he walked her back to her horse.

Genevieve turned and gave Cal a last look. Before he followed the contingent out of town, he raised his arm in salute and sent her one of his rare smiles. Genevieve knew then that what Calvin was doing was right.

7

"Steady now . . ." *Roarke* said gently, watching Genevieve as she sighted down the octagonal barrel of the Pennsylvania flintlock rifle he'd brought her. "Don't tense up, but be ready for the kick when she fires."

Genevieve's arms ached beneath the weight of the long gun, and its curly-maple forepiece was slick with sweat from her hands. Steadying herself, she closed her eyes and turned her head slightly in anticipation of the thunderous report.

"No, no." Roarke chuckled, taking the rifle from her. "You can't very well close your eyes if you mean to shoot at something."

Genevieve shook her head. "Roarke, I'm hopeless. I still don't know why you insist on putting a gun in my hands."

"I've told you before, Gennie, I want you to learn to defend yourself. Here. Try again."

Taking the rifle in hand again, she followed his instructions more closely. Peering down the length of the barrel at a distant tree, she squeezed the brass trigger. Flint struck the frizzen and made a hot spark, igniting the powder in the firing pan, which in turn exploded the powder in the barrel.

Genevieve was instantly flung to the ground, ears ringing

and nose burning with the acrid scent of powder. Then Roarke was at her side, frowning with concern.

"Gennie—"

She coughed and sat up, wiping black powder from her face. "I'm all right. But I hope you're finally satisfied that I'll never learn to shoot."

"Not at all, girl. It just takes practice. Phillip Greenleaf is no bigger than you, and he's one of the best hunters in the county. Come, I'll show you how to load."

Genevieve watched as he screwed a small swab of tow into the end of the barrel, tamping it in with three swift strokes of the ramrod. This was followed by a carefully measured amount of powder and then the bullet itself, wrapped in a bit of greased patching.

As Roarke drew out a minute amount of priming powder, Genevieve realized that her concentration had strayed from the gun to the man loading it. The play of muscle in his arms as he seated each step with the ramrod, the glint of sunshine in his hair as he bent to his task, made Genevieve long to touch him. She pressed her arms firmly to her sides.

Half-admiring, half-annoyed, she continued to watch him. He was remarkable—so sure of himself, so competent in all he did. He farmed the land as if he'd been born to it and handled a gun like the most seasoned frontiersman.

"Is there nothing you can't do, Roarke Adair?" she mused, more to herself than to him.

He looked at her in surprise. "What manner of question is that?"

She flushed a little. "I was just thinking how well you do everything. I've seen you shoe a horse, fix a plow, even hammer out a tool at the smithy. You're a wonderful father to Hance, and everyone in Dancer's Meadow is envious of your corn crop."

"You're making too much of me, Gennie. Besides, you're the one they all admire."

She snorted. "I'm the one they all laugh at behind their hands."

Roarke shook his head. "I never told you this, but last

fall some of the men in the King's Arms laid bets you wouldn't last a single season."

She drew herself up indignantly. "Oh? And just how did you bet, Roarke?"

The sound of his deep laughter rippled over her. "I won a shilling from every one of the sods."

Joshua had never asked Genevieve about the night preceding Calvin's departure for the frontier.

"Always figured the boy'd take a different path," was all he'd said.

Mimsy had taken her eldest son's departure hard, but she, too, had understood. Curtis and the others were proud to have a brother who was an Indian fighter.

Genevieve knew Joshua wasn't brooding over Calvin now. He was grinning broadly, his face dappled by the late-September sun streaming down through the leaves of the hickory tree in front of the house. Genevieve eyed him curiously. She'd never seen him look this way before. He seemed about to burst with anticipation.

"What is it, Joshua?"

"Follow me," he said, leading her up to the high fields, the first they'd planted in the spring. Genevieve walked happily in his wake, wondering what new bit of tobacco lore he was about to reveal to her.

Joshua stopped at the top of the field and hunkered down beside a tobacco plant. "Look at it," he said, taking hold of one of the broad leaves. It was slightly grayish and spotty. For a moment, Genevieve thought he might say the plants were diseased, but the merry gleam in his eyes told her otherwise.

"It's ripe," he said simply. "Lord be thanked; I was afraid this cold spell would do us in. But I think we've weathered it. We can start the cutting."

Genevieve had known the harvest was near, but she couldn't help the rush of gladness she felt. She jumped into the air with a whoop and threw her arms around Joshua. He swung her about, laughing.

"We did it, partner," he chuckled, setting her down.

Genevieve had never felt such supreme satisfaction. As Joshua went to call the boys and fetch the scythes, she hugged herself and raised her face to the autumn sun. Its warmth fell like a golden curtain over her, full of promise, full of hope.

The curing barns were more than half-full of drying tobacco. Bundles hung, bound by the stems, brushing Genevieve's shoulders as she worked. Joshua and the boys were in the fields, cutting through the acres. Curtis's voice rose in song after song, bringing a holiday air to the farm.

But Joshua's face when he entered the barn was grave. Curtis was with him, no longer singing.

"There'll be a hard freeze tonight," he said quietly.

Genevieve set down the bundle she was holding and wiped her hands on her apron.

"Can the crop withstand it?" she asked.

Joshua shook his head. "It's been too cold for too long. Everything that's not harvested by morning will be lost."

She felt a leaden chill in the pit of her belly. "But we've only got half of it cut."

He nodded glumly. "Crop was small enough to begin with. We don't even stand to recoup what we've spent."

Genevieve squeezed her eyes shut. Even so, a tear crept out from beneath an eyelid. She tried not to feel defeated, but so much was riding on her first season.

"I guess," she said slowly, opening her eyes, "I've been fooling myself into thinking we'd make good. I'm sorry, Joshua. I didn't mean to dupe you into working for me."

"Don't take on like that, partner," he said. "Let's go get in what little we can. Come on, Curtis."

But the boy was nowhere to be seen. Unnoticed by Genevieve and Joshua, he'd managed to slip off somewhere. Grumbling a promise to take a willow switch to the lad, Joshua led the way up to the fields.

They worked all through the day at breakneck speed, flinging the tobacco onto a sled made of wooden planks and depositing the leaves in the sheds without stopping to strip and bundle them. Mimsy and the girls pitched in, using kitchen knives. But they were too few, and the plants too many. There was no way they'd be able to finish before nightfall.

Already the wind was skirling down from the heights of the Blue Ridge, which had become an uneasy cauldron of scudding clouds and uncertain winds that bore the bite of a killing frost.

Genevieve battled a feeling of hopeless despair, applying her scythe savagely to the stalks. As the sky softened and darkened to purple, the tears came again. She'd played for high stakes, and lost. Piggot would sell the farm out from under her. Never had failure tasted so bitter.

She was so intent on savaging the plants and despising her own foolishness that she didn't hear Curtis Greenleaf's shout.

Only when the bobbing of torches caught her eye did she give her attention to the boy. Curtis was fairly dancing up the road to the farm, singing and shouting the whole way. And, incredibly, he was followed by a string of people.

They came on foot, in wagons, a few on horseback. Genevieve recognized Roarke instantly, sitting proudly on his roan stallion.

"God blind me . . ." she breathed. There were dozens of torches flickering up the path, as if lighting the way for a small army. The men shouldered scythes and rakes, and the women toted gingham-topped baskets of food and kegs of cider and lemonade. Picking up her skirts, Genevieve ran down the hill.

"Roarke?" she asked, feeling suddenly self-conscious as she recognized what seemed to be half of the population of Dancer's Meadow. "What—"

"They've come to harvest our tobacco!" Curtis shouted. "Said they'd work all night if they had to!"

Genevieve sent Roarke a questioning look. His white teeth gleamed in the torchlight as he grinned. "You should've asked, Gennie. It's the only way you're going to get help from your neighbors."

"But I can't pay a crew, Roarke. I simply—"

His fingers bit into her shoulders. "Gennie, when are you going to get it into that thick head of yours that there's such a thing as neighborliness? These people want nothing, except to see that they do lose those bets they made against you."

"Oh, there might be a thing or two," the Reverend Carstairs said with a grin.

Genevieve braced herself. She expected him to summon her to meeting once again, to give thanks to his God for her good fortune.

Carstairs read her reaction correctly. His laughter rang out. "Not that, Genevieve Culpeper. I've no doubt you'll be a proper churchgoing woman someday, but not until you're ready. No, I just want you to promise to join us at the harvest dance once this is all over." He laughed again at her sigh of relief.

It was a novel thought, that the people of Dancer's Meadow would want to include her in their celebration. Along with a rush of happiness, she felt a lump rise in her throat.

"I'll oblige you there, Reverend," she said brightly. "It will be my pleasure."

Already the men were swarming over the fields, cutting furiously with their backs to the biting wind. The women were gossiping and slicing pies and setting out portions of chicken. Genevieve threw herself into the work, unmindful of the pain of raw and blistered hands. With so much help, the work would be finished in hours. Her hands went to her cheeks and came away soaked with tears of joy.

As the last of the tobacco was hauled to the sheds, she approached the Reverend Carstairs. "Thank you," she told him, her voice breaking. She looked at the weary, smiling faces of her neighbors. "Thank you all."

Reverend Carstairs shook his head, reaching into his coat and extracting a Bible. "We'd best be thanking him who is truly responsible for this," he said, moving beneath a torch.

" 'Sing unto the Lord with thanksgiving,' " he read. " 'Sing praise upon the harp unto our God; who covereth the heaven with clouds, who prepareth rain for the earth, who maketh grass to grow upon the mountains . . .' "

Genevieve felt Roarke's arm slide about her shoulders, and for once she didn't shy away from him.

The next day, weary to the bone and weak with relief and gratitude, Genevieve settled down and penned a letter to Digby Firth in a firm hand. The crop was in and safely drying. In just a few months a thousand hogsheads of Virginia's finest strain of tobacco would be shipped down river to Yorktown.

"I can't very well go to a party like this." Genevieve looked dubiously at her worn frock.

Mimsy opened her mouth to disagree, but there was no arguing about the dress. Like all the much-mended frocks Genevieve had gotten from Prudence, it was drab and hung limply about the girl's slight figure. Mimsy folded her mouth into a determined line.

"Wait here." She ran lightly from the kitchen and down the path to her house. While Genevieve waited, she shook her head. Even though the Reverend Carstairs had commanded her appearance, she was apprehensive about joining the close-knit community of Dancer's Meadow, a community that regarded her as an oddity and frowned on her insistence on equal partnership with a Negro.

But Mimsy was determined for her to go. The kitchen became a beehive of activity as Curtis rushed in several times, emptying buckets of water into a small round tub. Mimsy added a pot of boiling water from the fireplace and a handful of dried rosemary from a spice tin. She ordered Genevieve into the tub and applied harsh homemade soap, scrubbing her head mercilessly and drying the girl's hair with vigor. Then, while Genevieve stood shivering before the fire in her shift, Mimsy shook out the dress she'd brought with her.

She smiled fondly, holding it up for Genevieve to see. "I wore it the day Joshua and I pledged ourselves at Green-leaf."

It was lovely, of soft blue cotton sprigged with lilacs. The sleeves were puffed at the shoulders and then tapered to tailored cuffs. There was even a bit of lace clinging demurely to the collar.

"Oh, Mimsy," Genevieve said, "I couldn't."

"Nonsense," the older woman said impatiently. "This dress hasn't seen dancing in a sow's age. I'd be proud to have you wear it." She took up her sewing basket, threaded a needle, and stabbed quickly at the fabric. "The length is fine," she said, speaking around the pins protruding from her mouth. "But I'm a mite stouter than you. I'll just take in this seam here, and here. . . ."

Her hands moved like lighting over the cloth, jabbing two quick, tapering seams on either side. All the while Genevieve argued and protested, but Mimsy would have none of it. She finished altering the garment and slipped it over Genevieve's head, doing up a long row of tiny buttons in the back and securing a lilac sash snugly about the waist.

She brushed out Genevieve's sable curls, not relenting until the locks shone brightly and caught the light. Mimsy added a pair of combs and a sprig of dried laceweed to the curls and stepped back to survey her work.

Her brown eyes gleamed with merriment. "You look like a princess," she said, beaming.

"Go on, Mimsy, it's only a dress," Genevieve laughed. But then Rose burst in and stopped to stare.

"Miz Culpeper . . ." she breathed. "You're beautiful." Genevieve laughed at the note of disbelief in Rose's voice, realizing that the girl had never seen her in anything but a worn frock, muddy boots, and disheveled hair.

"She's going to a party in town." Mimsy bustled Genevieve out the door, throwing a shawl around her shoulders and giving her a blanket for the wagon. Even the brilliant sun of late afternoon hadn't driven away the autumn chill.

Genevieve settled into the wagon and shivered. Not with the cold, but with nervousness. She had no idea what to expect when she reached Dancer's Meadow, having thus far avoided the various church socials and merry corn-huskings. It occurred to her that this was the first time she'd be seeing

Roarke socially, without the pretext of work to be done. Twisting her hands about the reins, Genevieve drew a deep breath and gave them a determined flick.

The fiddler's playing was nearly drowned out by the stomping and hooting of the townspeople. A mass of smiling faces was burnished by the slanting light of a westering sun. Roarke whirled his partner about in a sweeping motion, full of good humor. The harvest had been a good one for all. The fertile region wrapped by the sweep of the Blue Ridge and its many rivers and creeks had been generous.

The last notes of a merry reel scraped to a halt, and the dancers milled over to long boards supported by sawhorses. The boards groaned under the weight of great kegs of cider and ale and all manner of foods prepared by the women. Roarke went and drew a mug of ale. Over the babble of voices he heard the creaking of a wagon and looked up the road. Drawing his breath, he set his mug down and went to meet Genevieve.

Nothing, not even his frequent midnight dreams, could have prepared him for the sight of her. She dropped her worn shawl, untied her bonnet, and lifted her hand in greeting. Sweet God, but she was lovely. Her loosely styled hair gave her small face a soft, winsome look, and the pretty frock she wore draped the intriguing lines of her figure to perfection.

Roarke's blue eyes warmed at the sight of her. Before she could jump down from the wagon, he was there, grasping her firmly about the waist and swinging her down to his side. A smile played about his lips as he stared at her.

"Hello, Roarke." Even her voice was lovely tonight, bearing little resemblance to the hard-bitten speech she'd once used in the London slums.

"Lord, but you look fetching tonight, girl," Roarke said. His grin widened as he watched a delicate blush stain her cheeks. Behind them the fiddler took up playing again.

"Come dance with me, Gennie," Roarke urged softly, taking her arm.

"Roarke"—her blush deepened—"I haven't any idea how to dance."

He laughed deeply and gestured at the crowd, which was forming two lines, ladies facing the gentlemen. "And do you think these backwoods louts know any better?"

The next thing Genevieve knew, she was added to the line of women. Roarke stood across from her, extending his hands. Music and laughter and clapping created an irresistible rhythm, which she joined in effortlessly. Never had she felt so giddy with happiness. No one asked anything of her, except to enjoy the company, which she did immensely.

Roarke made sure she was greeted by all. As the hours slipped by and a great bonfire was ignited, she began to feel a kinship with the people of Dancer's Meadow. She spoke to Cyrus Hinton about planting and discovered that Kimberly Estes hailed from London. She felt sorry for Fannie Harper, whose tired face bore a bruise from a recent scuffle with her hard-drinking husband, Elkanah.

As always, talk meandered to the problems with England. People discussed the news from the northern colonies, where civil war had broken out in earnest. Rebels who called themselves patriots had battled the redcoats at a site called Bunker Hill, and a Connecticut man named Benedict Arnold had seized Fort Ticonderoga, in upper New York. It all seemed remote and unlikely to touch the lives of the farmers who danced in the dusty main street of Dancer's Meadow.

But some of the men didn't see it that way. Although New England seemed as distant as the mother country, Nathan Scammel declared that the colonists in the north were his brothers and announced that he meant to find a regiment somewhere and join the fighting. This raised a few cries of alarm from the women, but Nathan was young and unattached, a wandering type who always seemed to be looking for adventure. Most of the other men were reluctant to leave their farms and families.

During this discussion, Genevieve watched Roarke closely. He listened with a thoughtful frown.

"You're not thinking of joining the rebellion?" Genevieve asked, holding her breath.

He threw back his head and laughed. "Gennie, my girl, I don't even know the way to New England. The fighting would be done by the time I got there." The appreciative murmurs of laughter that ensued convinced her that most of the men were of like mind.

They danced some more and feasted on the huge meal the women had brought. After supper the smaller children curled up on folded quilts near the bonfire, but the adults barely slackened their pace.

Only when the big round moon had set did the party begin to dwindle. One by one, the revelers drifted home-ward, bundling children into wagons or carrying them in their arms. Mr. Carstairs stood up, reeling slightly.

"Must be going," he mumbled, earning a prod from his portly wife. He drew a watch from his pocket and squinted at it. "Lord in heaven, 'tis the Sabbath already!" He scooped up his little daughter, Jane, and wove down the street to his house, scolded all the way by Mrs. Carstairs.

Roarke chuckled at the sight and stretched his long legs out toward the fire. "Good man, that Carstairs. Has me going to meeting every week now."

"I'd say you've become a full-fledged citizen of Dancer's Meadow," Genevieve said.

He lifted an eyebrow at her. "And what of you, Miss Gennie?"

"I feel more a part of this place than I did my own family in London," she admitted. "But I'm still an outsider here, Roarke. I'm too different from everyone else. I'd never be able to sit still for a quilting bee or sermon."

"You ought to give it a try, girl. You might find some-thing you like."

"I've found it, Roarke. I like growing tobacco, and I'm good at it."

" 'Tis a solitary life you lead, tucked up on your little plantation."

"I've the Greenleafs. I never lack for company." She looked down at her hands, feeling his eyes on her.

"Do you mean that, Gennie?" he asked gently.

"Of course. I have everything I need at the farm."

"You're young for a widow, girl. Haven't you thought about marrying again?"

She felt her throat tighten. Something told her she shouldn't be having this conversation with Roarke Adair. He had an uncanny way of bringing her feelings to the fore, laying open raw emotion within her and making her feel weak and vulnerable.

"I like things just the way they are," she said carefully. "I don't need a man running my life for me."

Roarke placed a finger under her chin and tilted her face up to his. "Why can't you look at me when you say that, Gennie?" he asked.

She narrowed her eyes in defiance. "Because you'd just argue with me, and I don't feel like arguing."

"You mean you don't feel like *losing* an argument."

"Or anything else, either, Roarke."

Luther Quaid helped Genevieve from the boat with an exaggerated flourish, holding her hand as if guiding an important lady from her yacht. She laughed and stepped lightly onto the wharf at the mouth of the York River.

"I'll be ready to leave tomorrow morning," she promised him. "Mr. Firth never lingers over business." As she walked past the customshouse toward the tobacco factor's offices, there was a decided spring in her step. Her eyes moved appreciatively over the city, which at one time had been the busiest tobacco port on the Chesapeake. The magnificent houses up on the cliffs above the town were from that earlier era, built by shippers and merchants in a style that rivaled the finest European abodes. Genevieve's gaze lingered on the handsome two-story red brick house of Thomas Nelson that dominated the town, aptly situated to overlook the shoreline that fanned out in front of it.

Yet there was nothing about the splendor of the bustling town that called to Genevieve. The years in London had left a bitter taste in her mouth. She much preferred the remoteness of Albemarle County, where sometimes the stillness was so complete she could hear the barn cats bedding down in the straw.

But Genevieve didn't mind her infrequent visits to the city. Especially not today. Today she was to collect the money for her first shipment of tobacco.

She burst into Mr. Firth's office, her cheeks blooming from the bite of the January air.

"Did you see our tobacco, Mr. Firth?" she asked, not even pausing to greet him. "Every pound of it passed inspection at the Falls. What do you think?"

He tried not to let a smile mar the usual severity of his countenance. But she saw the mirth tugging at the lips beneath his thick mustache.

"I think, Mrs. Culpeper," he said easily, "that 1776 is going to be a very good year for you." Feigning nonchalance, he unlocked a coffer near his desk and extracted a heavy cloth bag, setting it in front of her.

Genevieve was almost afraid to touch it. "Hard currency?" she breathed.

"Aye, and a good sum of it, too. I made a sweet deal with a Frenchman in the Indies. I'll be sailing there myself next week. No bank notes for you, Mrs. Culpeper. These days they're not worth the paper they're printed on."

" 'These days,' Mr. Firth?"

"We're at war, my dear, although it may not seem so in Dancer's Meadow. The British burned Norfolk the first day of this year."

Her hands flew to her face. Norfolk! That meant the fighting had moved to Virginia!

"I didn't mean to shock you, Mrs. Culpeper," Digby Firth said quickly. "But you'd best get used to the idea that all thirteen colonies could well be consumed by civil war soon."

Somehow the notion that there had been fighting on Virginia soil made it all seem real to Genevieve. She'd read the papers all winter, noting that there were several firebrands in the Virginia assembly calling for independence, but she'd dismissed it as politics.

"What's to happen?" she wondered.

The big Scotsman shrugged. "Who can say? Both sides thought the whole thing would be over in a matter of months, but now it looks like the end is a long way off. The patriots, as they called themselves, are a stubborn lot. They won't give an inch, and neither will Parliament."

"How will the war affect me?"

"Shipping will be interrupted by blockades and such. But you're secure in that you've a good cash crop. The demand for tobacco won't go away. The French are clamoring for it."

"I won't let it interfere with my business, Mr. Firth," Genevieve said with conviction, picking up the purse of gold and silver. "I've worked too hard to let a mere war ruin me."

At that, Digby Firth laughed. "Mrs. Culpeper, I think I believe you."

Gales of laughter issued from Genevieve's house on a waft of spring-scented air. Luther Quaid had just delivered a large package of goods Genevieve had ordered when she was in Yorktown two months earlier, using the small bit of money that hadn't been turned back into the farm. Reaching into the crate, she drew out a length of mulberry calico and handed it to Mimsy.

"This reminded me of you," she explained, giving her friend a hug. "You're so good with the needle that I just knew you'd make a fine dress for yourself."

Rose received a doll with a beautiful bisque face and a blue velvet dress. She clutched it reverently to her breast and fingered its black ringlets.

"I'll call it my Gennie doll," she whispered. Genevieve smiled and tried to ignore the sudden image she had of Roarke Adair. She'd thought his nickname for her a private affair, but apparently others had noticed.

There was a set of lead soldiers for Eustis and a small mouth harp for Curtis, which he tried immediately, tapping out an exuberant jig as he played. Caroline received a fine string of beads, and Phillip exclaimed over a shiny new hunting knife. Finally, Genevieve drew out the last item from the crate. She handed a paper-wrapped parcel to Joshua, who gave her a questioning look.

"Genevieve, you shouldn't have—"

"Just open it. It's for both of us—partner."

Ripping into the paper, he extracted a heavy iron brand.

"Our tobacco mark," Genevieve explained. "With both our initials." The *C* was intertwined with the *G* and surrounded by a wreath of leaves in a handsome design. Mimsy brought a jug of cider out, and the celebrating became so loud that no one heard a hammering at the door. Finally, it burst open.

Curtis's harp dropped to the floor, and the room fell silent.

Foreboding twisted within Genevieve as she approached the visitor.

"Hello, Mr. Piggot," she said cautiously.

But there was nothing friendly about the way he was looking at her. Removing his tricorn to reveal his balding head, he strode into the room.

"It's taken a while, Mrs. Culpeper," he said darkly, "but I understand you're now in a position to settle your late husband's debts."

8

Genevieve shifted uncomfortably on the settee in the sitting room of Roarke's house. She hadn't set foot in his home since the night of Prudence's death, and she didn't want to be here now. But with Henry Piggot breathing down her neck and Mr. Firth gone to the Indies on business, she didn't know what else to do.

The room, kept painfully tidy by Mimi Lightfoot, bespoke Roarke's presence even when he wasn't there. His polished rifle hung above the mantel, and a few toys he'd carved for Hance were in a basket near the hearth. An extra pair of boots, clean but well-worn, stood near the door. Above them hung his coat, to which his scent still clung.

Genevieve avoided touching any of Roarke's things, as if her touch would bring her closer to him than she cared to be. She sat twisting her work-roughened hands in her lap. The sound of a footstep behind her made her jump.

"I take it there's more to this call than just a social visit," Roarke prompted, striding into the room with Hance balanced on his hip. As he spoke, the baby tugged at the leather whang that tied Roarke's hair into a queue at the back of his neck.

While she groped for words, Genevieve watched the pair of them. Hance was a child of uncommon beauty, as fair and sweet-faced as Prudence, yet with a decided streak of mischief in his bright blue eyes. He called Roarke Papa, and Roarke seemed as proud as if he'd actually fathered the boy. With genuine affection, Roarke embraced the child of a woman who had never loved him.

"Gennie . . . ?" Roarke asked, stirring her out of her musing.

"Please, Roarke, this is hard for me." She bit her lip. "I'm afraid I'm about to take advantage of your friendship."

"Then why don't you just say what you came to say and be done with it?" Roarke only pretended impatience. Actually, he wished Genevieve would call on him more often.

"I need money," she said hurriedly, as if to rid herself of the words. "The fall harvest is coming up, and we need hogsheads and a lot of new equipment."

He wasn't able to mask his surprise. "But I thought you'd made a small fortune off your first crop, Gennie. It was all the talk last spring—"

"We had to turn all our money back into the business."

"*All* of it, Gennie?"

She swallowed hard. If she was going to humble herself before Roarke, he might as well know everything.

"Henry Piggot has taken every bit of my profits as partial payment for Cornelius Culpeper's debts. I still owe him several hundred pounds."

"Piggot was here?"

"Yes. Last spring."

"Good God, Gennie, why didn't you tell me?"

"There was no point, Roarke. You'd only have lost your temper, and I would have had to pay him anyway. I signed an agreement with him when we first arrived in Yorktown, remember?"

"What about Joshua?"

She sighed. "Strapped. He's put everything he has back into the farm. Even if he had the money, I wouldn't ask him to take on my liability." Genevieve was growing irritated with Roarke's questioning. "Look, Roarke, if you don't want to help me, just say so, and I'll try to hold out until Mr. Firth returns from the Indies. The man trusts me to make good my word."

"I trust you, Gennie," Roarke said in a placating tone. "And I mean to help you. Now, how much do you need?"

Suddenly, the sitting room seemed to grow very hot and oppressive to Genevieve. As if sensing her mood, Roarke took her hand and led her outside, to a shady spot under a sycamore tree in the yard.

The hour that ensued was one of the most painful Genevieve had ever endured. It was one thing borrowing from Dibgy Firth in a business agreement, but it was quite something else asking Roarke for money. The transaction was so personal, so oddly intimate. She felt like she was baring her very soul to him there in the sun-dappled yard.

As he counted out a sum of money, he watched her with one eye. "You know," he said with studied casualness, "there is another way to straighten things out."

"Oh? And what is that?"

"You could marry me."

She nearly choked with surprise. Then, recovering, she drew her brows into an angry line. "Don't be ridiculous, Roarke. You can't afford to take on my debts."

"I'd be willing to try, Gennie."

She forced herself to ignore the note of tenderness in his voice. "If I ever decide to marry, Roarke Adair, it won't be because I need money. I intend to approach it from a position of strength. You'll never find me the weaker partner."

He stared at her for so long that Genevieve felt herself growing restive. What was he thinking? Why would he make her such a preposterous offer?

Roarke read the questions in her eyes. He could have told her that he wanted to marry her because she fascinated him, with her spitfire temper and the steely determination with which she faced life. He could have told her that he'd been captivated by her beauty since the first time he'd laid eyes on her in her father's tavern.

He could have told her that he was falling in love with her.

But Roarke said nothing. Genevieve was too wrapped up in her own troubles to listen to him now. Besides, he could practically hear her snort of derision at the words he longed to say. No one had ever loved her, Roarke knew, and she'd never learned to love anyone except Prudence. It was a damned shame. Gennie had so much to offer, yet Roarke had no idea how to unlock the door to her heart.

He gave her the money and barely listened to her promise to repay him. The amount comprised the better part of all the cash he had, but he didn't care if he never saw it again. All that mattered was that Genevieve needed it. And if money was all she'd accept from him, then he'd have to content himself with that.

He was about to see her out when a boy rode in from town. It was Mannie Hinton, his neighbor's son. The fifteen-year-old was known around town for his riding tricks, although at the moment he seemed only interested in speed.

"Mr. Adair!" he called. "Mr. Adair, look!" Mannie swung down from his horse and shoved a battered copy of the Virginia *Gazette* into Roarke's hands.

"I'm not enough of a scholar to muddle through this," Roarke grumbled, handing the paper to Genevieve.

She scanned the paper curiously, squinting and feeling the now familiar throb of exertion behind her weakening eyes. At first the words made little sense to her, but then she looked up at Roarke in amazement.

"'Tis about a document adopted last July by the Congress in Philadelphia," she said, rubbing her eyes. "It seems the colonies have stated their grievances against King George and declared independence from Britain."

Roarke gave a low whistle. "A new nation," he said quietly, digesting the news. "I guess that makes us citizens of, of—" He paused, groping for the word.

"The American Republic," Genevieve replied, catching the phrase that had been used in the paper. "We're a bloody republic now."

She leaned against the trunk of the sycamore and read the rest of the news to Roarke. The patriots had run aground three British frigates off Charles Town and now held that city. In distant New York a mob of rebels had pulled down a statue of King George and sent if off to foundries to be made into ammunition for the Continental Army.

It all seemed so strange. Somewhere not so very far away people were fighting and dying for a cause that Genevieve and Roarke barely understood.

Little by little the war found its way to Dancer's Meadow. The King's Arms changed its name to Liberty Tavern, and some of the British sympathizers in the area moved away. A liberty pole was raised, and people learned to make do without British goods. The women's quilting circle at the church abandoned their homey art and worked instead on making bandages for the army. Every now and then one of the town's young men would go off to enlist, fresh-faced and eager to defend his rights. A few came back months later, faces lined, world-weary, unwilling to talk of the reality of war: endless, seemingly pointless marches, smoky battles, dreadful shortages. Some never returned.

Genevieve remained preoccupied with the work of the farm, scraping together every bit of money she could to stave off her creditor, Henry Piggot, who made his presence felt by purchasing the old Parker farm.

She owed money to Roarke, too. He seemed to have forgotten the debt, but it hung over her every waking moment. She was beholden to him and wouldn't rest until she saw the debt paid.

On Christmas Day she made her way to his house through a biting wind, a small cache of coins concealed at her waist: the first installment of her payments to Roarke. She also had a small bag of shells she'd collected in Yorktown for little Hance to play with.

Roarke greeted her before a warm, crackling fire in the keeping room. Before Genevieve knew what was happening, he'd taken her wrap and peeled off her gloves and was chafing her icy hands between his broad, warm ones. Discomfited, she snatched her hands away and reached for her purse.

Roarke didn't even allow her to open it. "You're not going to deprive yourself just to pay me back," he ordered, turning away. "Good God, woman, 'tis Christmas, and all you have on your mind is business."

"I won't have this debt weighing on me," she insisted, reaching for the money again.

He turned back, eyes full of fury. "Damn it, Gennie, listen to yourself. 'Tis not the way of friends to speak so. You've an account book where your heart should be."

Stunned by his anger, she dropped her gaze from his storm-tossed eyes. Feeling the color rise to her cheeks, she conceded to herself that he was right. Lately, her life consisted of nothing but numbers: how many hogsheads to be rolled to the river and shipped, how many pounds of seed she could afford, the amounts owed to Mr. Firth, Piggot, and Roarke . . . Yet she refused to apologize for trying to keep her farm afloat.

She dropped to her knees beside Hance, who was playing on the floor nearby, and handed him the bag of shells. He crowed with delight, and Genevieve was rewarded with a wet kiss. Then Hance waddled off to show his new possessions to Mimi Lightfoot.

When Genevieve looked back at Roarke, he was smiling, all anger gone from him. She felt weak with relief.

"I was a mite hard on you, girl. I guess because I don't like you being so hard on yourself."

She nodded, feeling suddenly awkward. Then Roarke dropped a parcel into her hands. She tried to look disapproving, yet the sparkle in her eyes was one of pure pleasure.

"You shouldn't be giving me presents," she scolded.

"Always trying to tell me what to do, aren't you, Gennie?" he laughed. "Well, I won't have it. Go on, open your present."

She sent him a dubious look but pulled obediently at the bit of string around the small parcel. She extracted a flat box with rounded ends and eyed it curiously. A jewel box? She nearly thrust it back into Roarke's hands. Never would she accept—

"It's not diamonds and pearls," he chuckled, as if he'd read her mind. "I know better than that."

Relieved, Genevieve lifted the lid. A delicate-looking pair of spectacles peeped out at her.

"Roarke . . ." she breathed, lifting them out as if they were the most magnificent thing she'd ever seen. How had he known she'd been longing for a pair of spectacles? For months she'd strained her eyes over ledgers and printed matter, always earning a piercing headache for her efforts. But she hadn't a penny to spare for such a luxury.

"Thank you," she whispered, so touched by his thoughtfulness that her voice shook. "How did you know?"

"I'm a thickhead, as you've often pointed out," he said gently. "But I do notice some things. About you, I notice everything."

She raised her eyes sharply. The note of tenderness in his voice hadn't escaped her. Color flooded her cheeks.

"Try them," he prompted, a bit gruffly. "The grinder who came peddling them through town claims to work miracles on weak eyes."

Reverently, she unfolded the little hinges and tucked the wires behind her ears. She blinked once, slowly, and then again. She looked up at Roarke, who stood just a heartbeat away. Never had she seen his dear, rugged features in such sharp focus. Had the tiny fans of humor always been there, beside his eyes? Were the freckles that dusted his face always so faint she hadn't noticed them before? Emotion robbed her of breath as she gazed into his eyes.

Roarke had remarkable eyes, she realized, like shards of sky smiling down at her with tiny laugh lines in his tanned flesh. Genevieve supposed she'd seen this before, of course, but the feeling pounding through her veins now was completely new. She refused to consider whether it was the improvement from the spectacles or something more that triggered her reaction.

Roarke laid his hand lightly on her cheek. It was a tentative touch, as though he were afraid she might bolt like a frightened doe. Genevieve trembled, but she didn't pull away.

"Merry Christmas, Gennie," Roarke murmured. He bent and brushed her lips with his.

With a soft gasp, she turned away, her face flaming. Roarke watched her with an ache of longing that was familiar to him by now. The very first time he'd laid eyes on Genevieve, he'd known she was special. But it had taken him a long time to admit to himself how very much he wanted her.

She wasn't as indifferent as she wanted her to believe. Roarke smiled, remembering the way she'd just been staring at him with those new spectacles perched so charmingly on her nose.

Prudence was two years dead, and it was time he found another wife. And no one but Genevieve would do. Debt or no debt, he'd have her.

"Gennie," he said softly, coming up behind her. He grasped her arms. "Gennie, I think it's time we talked about—"

She fled from him then, crossing the keeping room quickly to stand by the fire. Dreading what she suspected he was about to say, Genevieve turned the subject. She snatched up a packet of papers, which Luther Quaid had brought from a recent trip to Philadelphia. It was the only thing at hand she could think of to shield herself from facing her feelings.

"What's this?" she asked hurriedly, glancing at the newspaper. The Pennsylvania *Journal*. She looked at the publication date: December 19, 1776. "'Tis not often we get anything so recent." Genevieve knew she was babbling, but she couldn't stop herself.

Roarke gritted his teeth in frustration. "Gennie, listen to me—"

"No!" The sharpness of her tone startled even her. Softening a little, she said, "Don't, Roarke. Don't spoil a lovely Christmas by starting an argument."

"I didn't intend to argue, Gennie."

"But I would have," she assured him.

Stifling an impulse to sweep her into his arms, Roarke stepped back, gritting his teeth. She wasn't ready.

"Very well," he said. "Why don't you try out your new spectacles?"

She sent him a grateful look and turned her eyes to the paper she was holding. The words were so sharp and clear that they seemed to leap from the page. Sitting down, she began to read aloud from an essay by the patriot firebrand Thomas Paine.

Genevieve's voice wavered over his powerful denunciation of the deserters and the Continental soldiers who intended to flee homeward the moment their commissions were up. " 'The summer soldier and sunshine patriot will, in this crisis, shrink from the service of his country,' " Paine scathingly wrote. " 'But he that stands now deserves the love and thanks of man and woman. . . .' "

She stopped reading for a moment. The writing was powerful, compelling. It made her think too much, moved her to feel things she didn't want to feel. Glancing up, she saw a similar effect etched on Roarke's features. He seemed to have forgotten the matter he'd brought up moments ago, his attention held fast by Paine's words.

"Go on," he ordered gruffly.

His intensity scared her. So far no one she'd been close to had been touched by the civil war. But the way Roarke was looking—

"Keep reading," he said.

She forced her eyes back to the page and went on, wishing she'd never picked up the paper. Paine called all men of heart to arms, to defend the land that had given them so much.

Genevieve finished reading and set the paper aside. Slowly, she looked up at Roarke. Then, dropping her eyes to the big, calloused hand at his side, she saw evidence of the hard conviction she'd been dreading for months: the quiet clenching of a fist.

"You're a fool, Roarke Adair." Genevieve paced in front of the small contingent of men assembled at the head of the main street of Dancer's Meadow. In the blinding brightness of the January sun, they were slapping one another on the back and talking of the high adventure that awaited them at the frontier.

Genevieve didn't share their exuberance. That manly heartiness would soon disappear once they tasted the hardship of the trail, the bite of an Indian's tomahawk. Since the arrival of Sergeant Alfred Lasher a week earlier, a shadow had dropped over her life. Lasher had been riding the counties of the back country, seeking men to defend the Western wilderness areas against Indians who had lately been armed by and allied to the British.

"You're wrong, Gennie," Roarke said, securing a pack to his roan stallion. "I *was* a fool when I ignored the calls to arms. I was willing to work the land but not to fight for it. I'm late to admit my obligation, but I'm willing now."

"Willing to die, Roarke?"

"Aye."

"What about Hance?"

Roarke glanced over at the handsome towheaded lad gamboling on the town green with Mimi, enjoying the sunshine.

"My son will grow up free. A Virginian—an American. Not a British subject."

"And your farm?"

"Gennie, the land's so rich the corn practically grows wild. Cyrus Hinton and his boys will take care of things while I'm gone."

"Just where are you going?" she asked fiercely.

He shaded his eyes and turned westward, toward the blue wall of the mountains, which concealed a heartless, forbidding wilderness. "We're to rendezvous with Captain Clark in Kentucky. I guess I'm going to war." He sounded a little incredulous at the idea. Shrugging, he angled a rifle-barreled gun across his saddle. When he swung back around, the look on his face nearly crumbled the wall of indifference she'd erected around herself.

"Is it really Hance and the farm you're worried about, Gennie?" he asked softly.

She bit her lip. Deep down she had an urge to fling herself

into his arms and ask, What about me, Roarke? There are no tidy arrangements that can be made for me. Not when I've grown to depend on you so, to need you. Like the soil needs the rain and the warmth of the springtime sun . . .

But she caught herself. It was preposterous even to consider that a plea from her would deter Roarke from—

"Gennie?" He was waiting for an answer.

She blushed, realizing she'd been staring. "Of course I'm only worried about Hance and the farm. What else could there possibly be?" As soon as the words, sounding so flippant, so indifferent, were out of her mouth, she regretted them. A look of pain crossed his face. Yet Genevieve couldn't bring herself to retract what she'd said.

Roarke was asking for an admission on her part that he meant something to her. But she couldn't say that now, not when he was going so far away with these rough-looking frontiersmen, most of them shockingly scarred by Indian fighting . . .

"Why Captain Clark?" she asked suddenly, desperate to turn the subject. "Can't you join a local regiment?"

"I don't much care for authority, for mindless obedience," he explained. "If I'm to follow a man into battle, it has to be someone I respect. Someone who embodies all the traits he expects to find in his men. George Rogers Clark appears, by all reports, to be that sort of man."

"I see." Then, remembering something, she handed him a bag of coins. "Mr. Firth sold my crop. This is the rest of the money I owe you."

Roarke grinned. "I won't have much use for that where I'm going. Keep it for when I get back."

"What if you don't come back?"

He grinned even more broadly. "Then keep it in trust for Hance."

Genevieve felt a flicker of anger. "How can you be so casual about this?" she hissed, striking his chest lightly with her fist for emphasis.

He captured her hand with his and held it against his heart, his mood changing abruptly from joviality to intense seriousness. His eyes drilled into hers as he spoke.

"Feel it beating?" he demanded hotly. "Faster than a treed squirrel, Gennie. If it sounds like I'm joking, it's because if I don't, I might just burst with panic." Seeing her lips tremble, he let a low groan escaped him. "Oh, God, I don't want to leave you, Gennie," he said.

Then, in full view of the entire assemblage in the center of town, he kissed her, long and hard, putting the full force of his frustrated longing into the embrace.

It never occurred to Genevieve to stop him, to be embarrassed at being handled so in front of the crowd. She drank the memory of his smile from his lips, and when he lifted his face from hers, her cheeks were drenched with tears.

"Goodbye, Gennie," Roarke said, his eyes devouring her.

Unable to speak, she nodded and backed away. Their hands lingered together for a moment, then dropped. Finally, Genevieve found her voice.

"Roarke," she said brokenly, trying to smile, "I hope you win your war."

9

Ahead of Roarke, Jim Ray was slashing frantically at his leggings with a hunting knife so they wouldn't hamper his escape. Behind him, Jim's brother Bill's screams tore through the misty forest, praying to a God that didn't listen, begging for mercy that was not granted by the Shawnee war party.

Above the vicious yipping of the Indians, Roarke heard a dreadful, ragged breathing and realized it was his own. The harshness of it startled him.

It was the sound of fear, as raw and pure and elemental as the Kentucky woods.

The Indians had been chasing Roarke and his companions for almost a league, having discovered the Virginians collecting sap for maple sugar in a glade outside the fort at Harrodsburg, Kentucky.

"Roarke Adair, ye tenderfoot," Jim Ray had yelled. "Get that pistol primed!"

Roarke had almost laughed, thinking Jim was making a joke. But then he'd looked up to count at least a dozen faces, fiercely painted red and black. He and the others had lit out toward the fort.

The fort . . . Roarke saw its palisades beyond the clearing ahead of him, and his legs pumped ever harder, defying muscles that screamed with fatigue. But the fort might as well have been a thousand leagues away. For it was being peppered from every quarter with musket shot from Blackfish's braves.

Roarke had lost sight of Jim Ray. He risked a glance behind and saw that the tall yellow feather chasing him was gaining ground. The brave, accompanied by a slim youth, gave a murderous scream and raised his tomahawk high. Roarke plunged on, topping a slight rise. A fallen tree, its girth nearly half of Roarke's height, lay ahead.

He dove behind it, shielding himself with underbrush. The yellow feather and the youth passed him. Roarke's hands shook as he primed his pistol, but it was ready by the time the braves returned to search for him.

Despite the drizzling cold, Roarke felt beads of sweat break out on his brow. A moccasin-clad foot landed not three feet in front of his face. He was so close to dying he could taste it. Not for the first time, he wondered what the hell he was doing out here in this wilderness, killing when he had to and being hunted like an animal every time he set foot outside the fort. At times like this it was easy to forget the lofty goals of freedom and independence. Easier still to long for the comfort of his own hearth and home, for Hance's merry laughter, for a glimpse of Gennie's face . . .

The Shawnee brave let loose with a howl of triumph when he spotted Roarke. But he hadn't seen the pistol. The howl became a macabre gurgle as the pistol exploded and gore blossomed from his chest. Roarke felt a momentary surge of power as he rose from his hiding place, taking a dark, forbidden pleasure in having bested the enemy.

But the feeling was driven away as he heard a sound of horrible grief.

"Notha," the Indian boy screamed. "Notha, Notha . . ."

Roarke recognized the word: "my father." A shiver rippled through him. He could only wonder what it was like for the boy to see his father die this way.

The youth stopped abruptly and looked over at Roarke, who had just finished reloading his pistol. Although only a child of perhaps twelve, his eyes smoldered with a hatred so fierce that Roarke grew cold. It seemed a sin against nature for a child to look that way.

"Roarke Adair," the boy shouted to the wind, mimicking the name he'd heard Jim Ray use earlier in the maple glade. Then he darted off into the forest, saying the name over and over again like a strange chant, as if to burn it upon his memory. Roarke didn't understand the rest of the babbling, yet he'd never heard a vow of revenge spoken more clearly. He knew he should dispatch the youth with his pistol. But nothing could have compelled him to do it, to take that young life as he'd taken the father's.

There was a wintry lull before spring burst upon Kentucky. The men within the compound at Harrodsburg protested the cold as they were sent out to cut pickets to repair the stockade, which joined the outer walls of numerous cabins. Others were busy prying Indian musket balls from the palisades. Lead was precious to the small company of men in the fort.

Roarke's friend Will Coomes grumbled at the chore. Flipping a bullet out with the tip of his knife, he said, "More fodder for you, Beelzebub. Maybe this'll be the one you put into Blackfish's stinkin' hide."

Roarke grinned. A seasoned woodsman, Coomes had the quirky habit of talking to his rifle.

"I don't mind the work, Will," Roarke said. "Life in this fort is dull as death."

Coomes raised a skeptical eyebrow. "The hell you say, Roarke."

"Well, 'tis dull so long as no one's trying to break into the fort and scalp you."

Coomes nodded at that. Conditions at Harrodsburg were abominable. The filth of mud and animal dung and human waste created an unholy stench. The men—rough frontier sorts who lived by a code of violence—were weary and irritable and given to picking fights.

It was a shame, Roarke reflected, that the Kentucky wilderness was such a treacherous place. It should be a land where things grew and thrived, not where men killed and died. There was something profound about the pristine forests, with their rich, earthy smells and the babble of springs pouring forth from every crevice of rock, that made the violence seem an ungodly affront against nature.

Roarke thought of home, and Hance. And Gennie. Always Gennie. It was absurd that he should feel she was such a part of him, when she'd never given him so much as an inkling of encouragement.

"Ye look like you're longin' for home," Coomes suggested.

Roarke nodded. "Aye. But it's getting hard to remember I ever had a home. My own son wouldn't know me from Adam."

"Doubtless your wife's keepin' your memory alive."

"My wife died birthing him."

Coomes made a clucking sound of sympathy. "At least you've only the boy to miss. Me, I've got the prettiest gal in Pennsylvania waitin' for me."

Roarke had a sudden vision of Genevieve and remembered the taste of her lips when he'd kissed her goodbye. "I know all about missing a pretty woman," he said gravely.

They worked in companionable melancholy as mist gathered on the brims of their hats and dripped in front of their faces. Roarke moved down the wall a little, seeking more musket balls. He spied a rain-soaked bit of paper and picked it up.

"What's that?" Coomes asked.

Roarke's brow darkened. "A Shawnee's calling card. The English have them leaving us broadsheets from Detroit. Seems they think they can persuade us to give up with a lot of flowery promises."

Coomes snorted, and Roarke crumpled the broadsheet, casting it aside. But there was one thing he couldn't argue with. The situation in Kentucky was desperate.

Harrodsburg and Boonesboro were the last remaining American strongholds. And they weren't so damned strong after all. Harrodsburg huddled tenaciously beside the river, its cabins brimming with women and children and the sick and wounded. A few fires in the compound had been spattered out by a persistent stinging rain that soaked the canvas of the men's tents and caused the horses to hang their heads against the dreary chill. Roarke dug his knife into the wall and tried not to think about the past week.

It was inhumanly cold. Cold enough to debilitate a man. But not a Shawnee. Roarke clenched his fist until his fingers bit into his palm. He'd been fighting Indians for weeks, and he still wasn't used to the savagery.

The Shawnee, armed with new British-issued weapons, disdained the appalling weather. They'd withdrawn, yes, but everyone in the fort knew they'd be back.

The actual battle was never the worst of it, Roarke reflected. It was always the aftermath, the pain of the wounds and the horror of loss, that was the hardest to endure. The satisfaction of having survived was always a momentary thing. The cold, empty feeling of having drawn blood and killed stayed with a man, haunting his sleep.

Roarke shivered. The Indians didn't merely kill; they butchered. They crushed skulls and peeled away hair and flesh; they severed limbs and gutted bodies. With each new clash, Roarke learned a new horror.

Americans fought as if they were up against a herd of charging buffalo. Powder was dumped, unmeasured, into the muzzle. A mouthful of balls was spat down the barrel, the touchhole pricked, the weapon primed heavily and then fired away. No time was spared for patching; the scattering bullets usually found Indian flesh, for the Shawnee fought in a close-packed ring.

Some of the Kentucky frontiersmen heeded the lessons of the Indian wars too well. They believed that the way to defend the frontier was to kill Indians until they'd killed them all. They were merciless with the enemy, with the enemy's women and children.

Roarke glanced over at Bard Tinsley, who was idly whittling toothpicks a few yards away. One of the man's ears had been chewed away by a redskin, but the scars on his character were deeper even than that on his flesh. The man had a seemingly insatiable appetite for blood and women. He wore the scalps he'd lifted with pride, adorning himself shamelessly with the hair of dozens of victims.

Roarke grimaced and looked away from Tinsley. On days like this he was hard put to remember what the hell he was doing out here, sleeping in the rain and eating raw game and killing Indians . . .

"Lookee there," Coomes said suddenly, pointing at the clearing. "'Tis Lawton Powell." The scout had been sent out from the command post to discern Chief Blackfish's next move.

"Who's that other rider?" Coomes wondered. "Jesus, a darky! We don't see many of 'em out here."

The man with Powell was wiry, clad in buckskins and a wide-brimmed Kentucky hat. When he tipped the hat back to reveal his face, Roarke ran down to the clearing.

"Calvin Greenleaf!" he shouted, clapping the young man on the back when he dismounted.

Calvin still retained an intense, brooding look, but he seemed pleased to see Roarke.

"Hello, Mr. Adair."

"That's *Sergeant* Adair, boy," Lawton Powell said quickly. "Show some respect."

Roarke gave Powell, who disliked Negroes almost as much as he hated Indians, a withering glance. "We don't wear uniforms out here, and we don't stand on rank."

He walked toward the stockade with Calvin, showing him the bag of shot he'd pried from the walls. Coomes still worked there, singing to Beelzebub.

"How are they?" Calvin asked suddenly, his voice betraying his hunger for news of the family.

"Your family was well when I left. All healthy. Proud of what they're doing. Missing you."

Calvin nodded. Then, with a studied casualness that made Roarke wonder, he asked, "Miz Culpeper?"

Roarke was stabbed again by the memory of Genevieve.

God, but he missed her. "Same as always," he told Calvin. "Proud, feisty, determined as hell. Now, what about you?"

"I like it out here," he said, although he grinned with irony and wiped a drop of frigid rain from the tip of his nose. "I've been clear to the Mississippi."

Roarke gave a low whistle. "So it's true, then. Major Clark's going straight for General Hamilton's throat."

It was an awesome thought, turning the whole of the western wilderness into a giant theater of war. But Roarke didn't have time to ponder the matter with Calvin.

He realized suddenly that Coomes had stopped singing. He pocketed his bag of shot. Somewhere in the woods a wild turkey gobbled.

Roarke stiffened and felt an icy prickle at the base of his spine. He'd been in the wilderness long enough to distinguish the call of the turkey from an Indian's imitation. The sound he'd just heard was definitely human.

As he picked up his rifle and primed it, Roarke's blood pumped hard in anticipation. His every sense felt sharp and clean, and his muscles rippled with strength. But it wasn't a pleasurable sensation. It was merely his instinct for survival.

The sound of yipping issued from the forest. Coomes was already aiming his rifle. "Here's your chance, Beelzebub," he told the weapon gamely. The yipping grew louder, and Calvin shot Roarke a questioning look.

"Blackfish," Roarke said darkly. "He's back."

Roarke dropped to one knee with a curse. His gun belched flame and acrid smoke. In the distance a brave let out an unearthly squeal of agony and did a curious macabre death dance, clawing at the eruption of blood and flesh that spread across his middle. Roarke gritted his teeth and swore again. He despised killing. He hated it even more than he hated the Shawnee.

"Let's go," he said to Calvin and Will. The three of them scaled the palisades and dropped into the stockade to brace themselves for another of Blackfish's unholy assaults.

The first American victim was a man named Hank, who'd brought his family down from Logan's Fort. Two braves dragged him into the clearing in front of the fort,

screaming wildly as they sliced the living flesh from his body
and lifted his scalp, waving the bloody mass in fierce defiance.

"Murdering devils," Roarke muttered, reloading. Behind
him a cry went up from Hank's widow, and livestock scurried frantically through the mud. Roarke hunkered down at
the ramparts, trying as the others were to lure Blackfish
from the protective woods. The war chief wheeled his dark
horse to and fro, never stopping, never letting his eyes leave
the fort. He'd be a hard one to bring down, too cunning to
endanger himself. And his braves were too loyal to allow it.

Above the thunder of battle, Roarke heard his name being called in a dreadful, high-pitched voice he remembered
from the previous day. He looked down to see the yellow
feather's youth pointing at him and dancing in agitation.

Roarke glanced over at Will, who was stationed nearby.
Coomes's face had gone pale.

"Mighty bloodthirsty for a young'un," Coomes said.

"What's he yelling about?" Roarke asked.

"Calls himself Muga—Black Bear. And he's vowing on
you the most unholy kind of death I ever did hear tell of. He
won't be a boy for long, Roarke, especially since the redcoats are arming the Indians to the teeth."

"Man's got no business buying me such things," Mimsy
Greenleaf grumbled. But her eyes shone as she fitted a spin-
dle onto the new spinning wheel Joshua had come home
with. That, together with the broadloom he'd given her to
celebrate the Christmas of 1777, were the first hints of
Joshua's growing prosperity. Although Mimsy scolded his
extravagance, she adored his gifts.

Genevieve watched in fascination as Mimsy's foot
worked the treadle and the mass of combed wool in her
hands became, inch by inch, a long strand of thread.

"First thing I'm going to make," Mimsy declared, "is a
decent shawl for you, Genevieve."

"Mimsy, you don't have to do that."

"No, but I will. That old rag you've been wearing has

seen better days. We're not paupers anymore, Genevieve. No reason to live like 'em."

"I'm touched, Mimsy. I would've bought myself a shawl in York the last time I was there, but—" She broke off, not wanting to worry Mimsy.

She'd already said enough to arouse Mimsy's ire. "It's that man Piggot again, isn't it? The one who bought the Parker farm. He's still after you for Culpeper's debts."

Genevieve nodded glumly.

"When's he going to quit hounding you? Can't anything be done?"

"I've tried, Mimsy. Even Digby Firth has looked into the matter. But Cornelius Culpeper died owing Mr. Piggot a great deal of money. Even the change in government doesn't eradicate that."

"Well, it ain't right. You been working like a plow horse for nigh on four years, and every time you make a little money, you got to give it to that man."

"But every time I do, it brings me closer to independence."

Mimsy shook her head and agitated the treadle more vigorously, plucking from her bundle of wool with an expert hand. "You're too independent, Genevieve. Independent and hardheaded."

"Is that so bad, Mimsy?"

"I don't know. I shouldn't judge, but—"

"But what, Mimsy?"

The older woman set aside her spinning and cupped Genevieve's chin in her warm hand. "Look at you, girl. You're twenty-one years old, at a time in your life when you should be having a little fun. I haven't seen you so much as smile at a man since Roarke Adair left over a year ago."

Genevieve flushed. "I like my life, Mimsy," she insisted. "I like farming, and being with you and your family."

"What about a family of your own?"

"I've got enough to keep me busy, Mimsy. Especially now. General Washington sent out a plea for tobacco from Valley Forge last winter, and I mean to give what I can. He's sent Dr. Franklin to France to negotiate loans using Virginia tobacco as collateral. My hands are full; I don't need a man. I think I've proven that."

But Mimsy only shook her head again, unconvinced. She felt a little guilty being so happy and fulfilled with her family, while every night Genevieve closed the door to her little house and sat by the fire beneath the clock, spectacles perched on her nose, alone with her borrowed books and silent dreams and private yearnings.

10

The trading post in Dancer's Meadow swarmed with people. These days Luther Quaid's arrival was always a thing of note; the citizens were hungry for news of the war, which was entering its fourth year. But this time the clamoring wasn't for news. The stir was created by a passenger. Genevieve moved closer to see, pressing in among the women.

"Brazen as brass, she is," Mrs. Carstairs was whispering. She drew little Janie into the protective folds of her skirts.

"Who in heaven is she, anyway?" asked Sally Hinton.

Genevieve stood on tiptoe and spied a nimbus of bright yellow hair peeping from a grand-looking hat. The brim of the hat lifted, and Genevieve found herself, frozen in amazement, staring at Nell Wingfield's wide, brash smile.

"God blind me," she breathed. She'd never thought to see the woman again, but here she was, looking as if she owned the world. Stepping closer, Genevieve realized Nell wasn't quite as grand as she'd initially appeared. Her clothes were as flamboyant as her manners, yet they were shabby, too, made of cheap cloth and fraying in spots.

The years had hardly left a mark on Nell. Perhaps her

mouth was a little harder, her body a bit less firm. But she was the same Nell who had brazened her way to Virginia aboard the *Blessing* five years earlier.

Nell's gaze swept over the curious villagers and rested on Genevieve.

"Little Genevieve Culpeper," Nell mocked, her gaze moving pointedly over Genevieve's faded linsey-woolsey frock. "You look positively rustic." Nell's speech had changed. The sharp dockside edges of her words had softened to a somewhat counterfeit gentility. But her eyes were the same, Genevieve noted. There was a dangerous glitter in them that told her clearly that they were still enemies.

When Mrs. Carstairs realized Genevieve was acquainted with Nell, she stepped forward, avidly curious. "Who is she?"

There was a great irony in introducing Nell to the minister's wife. Genevieve forced a smile. "Nell Wingfield and I made the crossing together on the *Blessing.*"

"I am here as the guest of Mr. Henry Piggot," Nell explained grandly. Genevieve's smile fled, and silence fell over the crowd.

That name was known to most of Dancer's Meadow, and no one thought any better of Piggot than Genevieve did. He'd become a champion of Tory interests in Virginia, scouting out likely farms to raid, betraying caches of food and gunpowder to the British army. Piggot seemed to have an uncanny sense for subterfuge and betrayal. A sense that was well rewarded.

Nell smiled smugly. "I can see my benefactor's reputation precedes him."

"We're patriots here, Nell," Genevieve said.

"I'm not here to fight a battle," Nell sniffed. "Mr. Piggot has sent me to take possession of the Parker farm, which he bought some time ago."

The ensuing silence was tense. Like all the townspeople, Genevieve was filled with distaste that the Parkers' misfortune should benefit Nell.

But Nell didn't notice. She gestured grandly at a mound of trunks and bags. "My servants won't be able to manage all my things. Would anyone care to help?" She patted the fat reticule at her waist. "Good, hard currency; not those worthless Continental dollars you see these days." She pursed her lips. "Now, can someone show me my new home?"

No one moved. Finally, the tension grew so thick that Genevieve stepped forward, risking the town's displeasure but unwilling to cut Nell dead her first day here. "I'll show you, Nell," she said quietly. She glanced over her shoulder at Joshua Greenleaf. "Perhaps when you and the boys are through at the wharves you could help."

"A mite civil to your slaves," Nell suggested as they walked away.

Genevieve bristled. "They're not anyone's slaves, Nell. Joshua is my friend and business partner, and he's a free man."

Nell pursed her lips in disapproval as she motioned to her own servants: a mulatto boy of about twelve and three maids who looked similar enough to be sisters. They walked to the western end of the street and turned onto an over-grown path that led up to the abandoned farm. The cabin, vacant for nearly four years, looked forlorn and weather-beaten. Vines grew up the charred walls, and the chimney had crumbled at the top.

There was a poignant melancholy about Amy's flower garden. She'd been so proud of it. Now the plot was choked with weeds; the bedraggled tops of a few marigolds gone to seed were the only remaining evidence of Amy's care. The weeding stool Seth had made was slowly rotting.

"Looks like a bloody wasteland," Nell grumbled.

"It used to be a home," Genevieve said softly, remember-ing the sight of Amy seated in the dooryard, crooning to her baby while tending her flowers and herbs. Briefly, she told Nell what had happened to the Parkers.

"I always knew she'd come to a bad end," Nell stated. "Never did have much of a spine." She placed her hands on her hips. "I'll do better than our little Amy, to be sure. Henry's doing business in Williamsburg now, but he'll be sending crews to help with the spring planting. He means to grow corn for whiskey." Nell's eyes gleamed with pride. "I've four more niggers in addition to these."

"Congratulations," Genevieve said wryly. The sarcasm in her voice completely eluded Nell.

"You should think about owning slaves yourself," Nell suggested.

Genevieve felt her eyebrows gather into a frown. "I would no more own another person than I'd try to possess the moon or the stars."

Nell shook her head. "You never did put much store in convention, Genevieve." She poked around the yard, peeked briefly into the cabin, and then turned back to Genevieve.

"It'll be a while before this place is fit for me to set foot in," Nell declared, "so you might as well tell me about yourself, Genevieve. Last time I saw you, Henry was trying to find a husband for you in York.

"There were no takers, as I recall," she added cattily.

"I haven't suffered for that," Genevieve said hotly. "I'm growing tobacco on my own."

Nell shrugged, clearly unimpressed. "And what of dear Prudence?"

Genevieve swallowed. Even now the memory of her troubled friend brought the ache of tears to her eyes.

"Prudence died in childbirth over four years ago."

Nell took a moment to digest this. "Such a pity," she murmured, but her voice was so bright that Genevieve suspected her sincerity. "Surely Roarke Adair has remarried? He was such a great, strapping young man."

"Roarke lives alone with his son. There's a woman named Mimi Lightfoot who takes care of the boy for him."

"*His* son?" Nell said. "Surely, he's not that much of a dupe."

Genevieve recalled with chilling clarity that Nell had guessed Prudence's secret on the *Blessing*. Drawing herself up, she faced Nell squarely.

"You wouldn't dare have the bad taste to insinuate that Hance is anything but Roarke's own," she said hotly, doubling her fists. "Not ever, Nell."

Nell regarded the small, hard fists and seemed to be remembering their scuffle on the *Blessing*. She turned the subject quickly, loath to tangle with Genevieve.

"Well, I'm alone until Henry returns, and Roarke is no doubt in need of company. I must pay him a call."

"He's off fighting in Kentucky, Nell. For the patriots."

"Then he'll be back before long," Nell said confidently. "The rebels have been driven completely from every stronghold on the coast. General Cornwallis has the entire South firmly in hand."

Genevieve threw back her head. "Not for long, Nell. We've the French with us now."

Nell smiled maliciously at Genevieve's vehemence. "My, but you've become quite the little patriot, haven't you? Doesn't it matter at all that you were born an Englishwoman?"

"I was born in the meanest slum in London. Our 'mother country' never gave me anything but an empty belly and every disease that poverty could spawn. How can you expect me to be loyal to England?"

Roarke tried to think of anything but the cold. He found that he couldn't. Lord God, but it was inhumanly cold. There was no getting away from it. For nineteen days the company had slogged through icy marshes and frigid streams, sometimes so deep in winter floods that rifles and powder had to be held for hours above the head by arms trembling with weakness.

Even the signal, bloodless victories at Kaskaskia and Cahokia had failed to sustain Colonel Clark's men through these two hundred Godforsaken miles to the Wabash.

Fort Sackville, at Vincennes, was their destination. Colonel Clark was determined to wrest the stronghold from General Hamilton, Britain's legendary scalp buyer.

Rafts had been built to ferry the patriots across the Wabash. Roarke was on the first raft, along with Calvin Greenleaf and Bard Tinsley, to find a good landing site on the other side of the churning yellow river. They battled the current until their limbs shook and then came ashore amid brush and barren trees and sodden river grass.

"Ah, deliverance!" Tinsley exclaimed, unstopping a flask of grog.

The drink never reached his lips. The river had delivered them into the hands of a Shawnee war party.

Only Calvin made it back to the raft. He threw himself aboard, clutching at a branch and calling desperately for Roarke and Bard to join him.

But the Indians had placed themselves in the way, leering from their red-and-black painted faces.

"Go on with you, Cal," Roarke shouted. "Go!" He had the momentary satisfaction of watching Calvin drift to safety on the swift current. Then a nearby movement caught his eye.

"Roarke Adair."

Roarke stared. There was only one Indian who knew his name, who spoke it like the vilest of curses. Black Bear. The lad had grown taller and fiercer in the two years since the clash at Harrodsburg. But the hatred in his eyes was as fresh as if the killing had happened yesterday. And the other Indians with Black Bear—a half dozen of them—clearly shared the brave's blood lust. They beat their chests and rattled their bear-claw necklaces and shrieked with savage triumph.

Bard Tinsley, great, grizzled Indian fighter that he was, sank sobbing to the ground.

There was some talk among the braves, and Roarke felt their eyes on him, assessing him. The muscles of his legs tensed, and then he hurled himself at the tallest brave, knocking him aside to plunge into the woods.

But the days of the starving march had weakened him, slowed him. Four of the braves threw themselves on him in a pile of greased limbs and brandished tomahawks. Roarke tried to fight, but even the effort of drawing air into his lungs was too great. In minutes the Indians had stripped him of his knapsack and knife and bound his wrists behind his back. He and Bard Tinsley were half dragged, half marched, up an overgrown trace, prodded by spears and jabbing fingers, taunted by braves who burned with hatred.

* * *

The sound of ragged sobs awakened Roarke. For a moment his mind, cobwebbed by pain and hunger and cold, worked sluggishly as he looked at his surroundings. Then the sting of a hissing rain brought him fully conscious, and he remembered.

He remembered the four-day march to the Shawnee camp, the vicious glee of his captors. He remembered that he was going to die, and not kindly.

"Stop that infernal weeping, Bard," he snapped. "Do you think it'll help anything?"

"B-by the Almighty, but I'm scared, Roarke," Tinsley said. "They mean to butcher us like a pair of bucks. These redskins ain't got a shred of human decency in 'em."

Roarke turned away. Tinsley was a fine one to talk of decency. Back in Harrodsburg the man had bragged incessantly about his part in the Greathouse massacre. He'd chuckled over raping a pregnant squaw and then carving the unborn child from her belly with his knife.

Firelight flickered from the center of the small camp. A few of the Indians idled near the bound prisoners, jeering in their gutteral, aspirate tongue. While Tinsley hid his face, Roarke stared at them. There were families here, he realized. Families that had undoubtedly lost members to the white man.

A woman wandered nearby. At first all Roarke could discern was a smudged face and a ragged-looking dress. Then the woman stepped back, and her face was illuminated by orange firelight. Roarke felt a faint prickle of recognition taunting his sluggish mind.

"By God almighty," he breathed, stretching out his bound hands. "Amy Parker! Amy, it's me, Roarke Adair!"

She made a small sound and shrank away, looking over her shoulder. Then she edged forward slowly, cautiously. She was about to speak when a brave barked an order and jerked her by the arm. As she was dragged away, Roarke heard a faint thud on the earth beside him.

His hands snaked out and captured the small knife Amy

had dropped. He thrust it quickly between his knees to conceal it while he worked away at the leather that bound him.

Black Bear appeared with another brave who resembled him so closely that Roarke was certain the two were brothers. They laughed and chattered as they stood over the prisoners, no doubt planning a gruesome revenge for their father. Black Bear displayed a belt of scalps, dangling them in front of Roarke's face.

They reeked of dried blood. There were scalps of brown and white, and a blond one, the hair so fine it could only have been taken from a baby.

"Devils," Roarke said through gritted teeth. Then an even worse thought crossed his mind. General Henry Hamilton, the Hair Buyer, would pay for the scalps. Roarke regretted that he'd never get to Vincennes to let Hamilton know exactly what he thought of him.

There was movement among the Indians. The women and children were ordered away, and a group of eight braves, including Black Bear and his brother, clustered around the prisoners. Tinsley was taken first, probably because he was beginning to annoy the Indians with his ceaseless crying. The braves dragged him away.

Roarke was able to close his eyes to the sight of Bard's torture, but he couldn't dull his senses of hearing or smell. Tinsley's screams streaked through the air and rose heavenward to the stars of twilight. Roarke shivered to his very bones at the sound. When the smell of Tinsley's burning flesh wafted to his nostrils, Roarke felt a dreadful sickness well up in him. He worked with renewed strength at the leather thongs.

Bard Tinsley died slowly, screaming his life away as his flesh was fed, bit by bit, to the roaring campfire.

When the screams subsided, a new sound could be discerned. At first, Roarke thought it was another war party, but then he recognized the shouts and curses of his comrades.

"Shemanese!" the Indians shrieked, and scurried for their weapons. The Virginians descended like a pack of unruly wolves, snarling and slashing with knives and spitting at the Indians with pistol and rifle fire.

Roarke left off his careful sawing and, with a huge surge of strength, broke the leather thongs. He freed his ankles and leaped to his feet.

And found himself staring into Black Bear's enraged face.

The brave howled and lunged. But Calvin Greenleaf was quicker. He leaped upon Black Bear, gouging out one of the brave's eyes as he wrestled him to the ground. Grimly, Calvin crushed his knee into the brave's chest, deftly binding him with a length of rope.

Roarke's surge of strength left him as he regarded Black Bear. The youth had never had a chance to be a youth because of him. Despite the horror of his gouged eye, which was pouring blood, Black Bear bore himself magnificently as Calvin jerked him to his feet. The brave's good eye still gleamed hatred and defiance at Roarke. And, oddly, triumph.

Too late, Roarke realized why Black Bear had that look. Something more vicious than a wildcat landed on his back.

Black Bear's brother. Roarke roared with pain as a tomahawk was buried to the haft in his shoulder. Before he could recover from that horror, he felt the blood-slick steel of a knife blade at his neck. He crouched low, toppling the brave to the ground. His hand closed around Amy's knife. It slipped with amazing ease between the brave's ribs, slicing human flesh like butter.

Black Bear gave a shriek of rage when he saw his brother die. The vengeful hatred in the youth's eyes had doubled.

Indians were running everywhere, racing for cover in the dark woods. Roarke spied Amy Parker slipping away, hand in hand with a tall brave. He placed himself in front of them. The brave showed no fear, but he kept glancing toward the woods.

"Let's go," Roarke said to Amy. "Quickly, now."

Incredibly, she appeared to be torn.

"My God, Amy," Roarke said, "we can take you to safety!"

The brave tugged at her hand and muttered something.

Amy shook her head. "I'm not going, Roarke."

"But you'll be home, Amy, think of it—"

"Home? There is no home without Seth and little Ruth. I am a Shawnee now, Roarke." She glanced at the brave. "Coonahaw is my husband. And his babe stirs in my belly."

"But these people are savages, Amy! Murderers—"

She looked pointedly at the bloody knife clutched in his hand. "And you, Roarke Adair?" she asked.

Then she fled into the forest with the tall brave.

The Virginians captured seven Indians without losing a single man. There was a holiday air about the group as they made their way to the fort.

"Vincennes is ours," Will Coomes said excitedly, fairly dancing along the trail. "By Job, we pulled a mighty trick on the old Hair Buyer, we did! Got most of the town on our side like we did at Kaskaskia and convinced Hamilton that we were a thousand strong. Every one of us did the work of ten men!"

Roarke was in too much pain to celebrate with the others. He could feel the blood seeping from beneath the hastily bound bandages on his shoulder and neck. He reeled slightly, battling lightheadedness. He had to be carried into the fort.

When the men saw the Indian captives, they whooped with glee. They begged Colonel Clark to execute the braves.

Clark was no Indian killer; he never had been. But he was enraged by the scalps that adorned the captives' belts. And he knew there was a way, at last, to show Hamilton's Indian allies that the Hair Buyer was something less than their beneficent White Father. He ordered the execution to take place near the church.

There was a clamor among the men; each wanted to lay open an Indian skull in full sight of the Hair Buyer.

Through a haze of pain, Roarke gripped a railing near the main gate and watched. Black Bear was last in line. Although doubtless in pain from his damaged eye and fully aware that he was about to be killed, the youth looked as fierce as ever.

"Redskins believe it's a sacred thing," Coomes explained, "to die by an enemy's hand."

Roarke looked away. He'd done enough killing and seen enough dying for a lifetime.

The Indians filed past the church. Roarke found himself admiring Black Bear. The youth bore himself so proudly. And he was so quick when he broke from the group and lit out for the gate road.

A cry went up, but Black Bear sprinted like lightning. Only Roarke, who had been walking away from the spectacle, was near enough to stop the brave.

He didn't know whether it was lethargy or compassion that made him step aside. Black Bear looked incredulous for a split second, and then the familiar veil of hatred dropped over his face. He spoke Roarke's name like an oath, and ran for the river.

"Jesus, Roarke," Coomes said, aiming his rifle. "You let the devil get away."

Roarke moved the barrel of Will's rifle aside. "Don't," he ordered gruffly. "Let him go. I've robbed the boy of a father and a brother; I can at least let him have his life."

Coomes shook his head. "It don't pay to get all soft-hearted over a redskin, Roarke. You did him no favor, showing him mercy like that. The Shawnee take it as an insult. And now you've got an ungodly enemy out there who won't rest until he busts up your life like you did his."

"I doubt I'll be seeing him again."

"Injuns have long memories, Roarke. Black Bear'll carry his grudge against you to the grave, I swear it."

Roarke tried to sit up when Colonel Clark entered the cabin. Pain knifed through him at the movement.

"Lay back down, Roarke," the colonel said. "That shoulder's going to be mighty tender for a while."

"Six months is more than a while," Roarke told him darkly. Those months were missing from his life, missing in a fog of delirium. Following the surrender of Vincennes, his wounds had festered and a fever had settled in, holding him in its grip for weeks on end. The camp physician, with his leeches and regular bleeding, had weakened Roarke nearly to the point of death.

George Clark removed his hat and pulled a stool up beside the bed. "I'm sending you to Harrodsburg to recover fully," he said, keeping his keen gaze level. "And then I'm sending you home, Roarke," he added.

"I'm not all that bad off," Roarke protested.

"I can see that. You're a strong man, Roarke. A good fighter; you use your head and not your heart in battle. But our work out here's about done. The British have lost the frontier to us."

Roarke ran his tongue over his fever-dried lips. "What about Detroit?"

Clark shook his head. "We haven't the means to take it, not for a long time. I've had to divide my forces between Vincennes, Cahokia, and Kaskaskia. And there's a fort to be built at the Falls of the Ohio."

"Sounds like you'll need men," Roarke said, moving restlessly on his cot. He tried to sit up again, and was rewarded by a blinding flash of pain.

Again, Clark moved his head slowly from side to side. "You've fought your battles, Roarke, and fought them well. I couldn't ask for a better soldier than you. But it's time for you to go home." Clark held up his hand to forestall a protest. "You're no murderer, Roarke. You're too good a man to be killing redskins year after year."

"But I've done it," Roarke said darkly. "For nearly three years, I've done it."

Clarke nodded. "Aye. 'Tis a funny thing, this business of killing. With each life you take, you lose a little of yourself. That's why Bard Tinsley was the way he was in the end. Nothing but a hollow shell of fear and hatred."

Roarke agreed silently. Tinsley had lived like an animal. He'd died like an animal, too, at the hands of his prey.

"You've given more than any one man should have to give," the colonel continued. "I'd say you earned a trip home. Just like you earned a grant of land in Kentucky, should you ever care to claim it."

Roarke swallowed. "Are you sure—"

Clark grinned and held out a flask of grog. "Go home, Roarke Adair," he said. "Go home, and farm the land like you were meant to do."

11

The hooded wall clock struck four, and Genevieve sighed, aware that she had hours of work ahead of her. She pushed her spectacles back up on her nose and applied her quill determinedly to the ledger book she was working in. Lord, she thought, let 1781 be a good year for me. Let there be enough money this year . . . enough for the farm, and enough to get Henry Piggot off my back once and for all.

She worked and reworked the column of figures. But any way she added it, the result was the same. Her profit margin was too slim to free her of debt.

She slammed the book shut with a thud. A long silence ensued, punctuated at regular intervals by the clock's ticking. Normally, the sounds of the Greenleaf family filled the air, but this was Sunday. Every Sunday the family made a pilgrimage to Scott's Landing, where they attended services at a slave church.

Genevieve hated Sundays. She'd been invited more than once to go to meeting in town, but always she demurred. Despite the openness of the people of Dancer's Meadow, she still felt like an outsider. And so she kept to her house, busy-

ing herself with endless tasks, trying not to acknowledge the
pervasive, bleak loneliness that enveloped her every time she
paused to think.

"There're worse things in life than being lonely," she
grumbled to the cat, who was sunbathing beneath the window.

But at the moment she couldn't think of anything worse.
The clock's ticking seemed weighty today, pressing on her,
nearly driving her to distraction. When an odd clanking
sound drifted in through the window, Genevieve welcomed
the interruption.

But caution had been schooled into her by the six years of
the war, especially after British raiders had made their presence felt in Albemarle County. Automatically, her hand
strayed to the Pennsylvania rifle hanging by the door, to see
that the weapon was primed and loaded.

She walked out on the porch. The clanking grew louder,
and then a mounted figure appeared below, on the river
road. Genevieve had an impulse to step back inside and bolt
the door. These days the area was rife with deserters—British, Hessian, and Continental—who would kill for less than
a good meal.

The man raised a hand, and the brim of his hat lifted.
Genevieve clutched at the door frame, not daring to believe
her eyes. She'd seen that face so many times in her secret
dreams that she thought she was dreaming now.

But the man rode closer, and the clanking of his weapons
and utensils grew louder, and she knew he was real.

"*Roarke!*" That yell, bursting with joy, didn't even sound
like her own voice.

She tumbled from the porch at breakneck speed, running
out into the sunlight, calling his name again and again like a
song.

But Genevieve stopped at the end of the yard, suddenly
unable to go on. The years on the frontier had changed
Roarke. His fringed hunting shirt and leggings garbed a figure that was much leaner than she remembered, and he and
his mount were so laden with gear that every movement
created noise. He sported a full, coarse beard that was a

deeper red than the unevenly cropped flame-colored hair that peeped from beneath a wide-brimmed Kentucky hat.

He was a stranger, grizzled and unkempt, as raw as the frontier itself. Genevieve realized she was a little afraid of him.

But the smile he gave her as he dropped from his horse was so sweet, so heartachingly familiar, that Genevieve felt something inside her melt. She took a hesitant step, and then an old hidden longing propelled her into his outspread arms. He swung her about and buried his face in her hair, inhaling deeply. Genevieve laughed and cried and gloried in the strength of his arms and listened in awe as he murmured her name in a voice rough with emotion.

Finally, he set her down and cupped her face in his hands, a smile dancing in his blue eyes.

"I've not the words to say how much I've missed you these four years, Gennie."

"Have you, Roarke Adair?"

"More than I can say."

Her heart filled with a feeling so warm that she caught her breath. She looked away so he wouldn't see the emotion welling in her eyes.

"Have you been to your farm yet?"

He shook his head. "I rode in from the north. I'm on my way there now."

She walked him back to his horse and watched him mount, feeling awkward. There was so much she wanted to say to Roarke, yet so little came to mind. "Hance has grown into a fine boy," she commented at last.

"I've lost so much time with the lad. He won't even know me."

"You'll make it up to him, Roarke."

"I just hope I can."

Secretly, Genevieve hoped so, too. Hance needed a father badly. He was indeed a fine boy, as she'd said, arrestingly handsome, with Prudence's pale-blond hair and china-blue eyes, and he was thriving on the bounty of Virginia's land. But something about the youngster disturbed Genevieve. Hance had a streak of wildness in him that went beyond boyish mischief. He was willful and demanding, occasionally even cruel. But Genevieve wouldn't tell Roarke this. It was up to him to assess the boy's character.

Roarke paused before turning his horse.

"Gennie?"

That name, spoken in his deep voice, never failed to stir her. She looked up at him inquiringly.

"I'll be back. Will you see me tomorrow?"

She smiled at him. "You never have to ask that, Roarke. Of course I'll see you. In fact, I insist on it." Her eyes moved over the long scar that issued from his collar and wound up toward his jaw line. "I want you to tell me what sort of man the frontier has made you. And I want to know whether or not you think you've won your war."

"Are you really my pa?"

Roarke set aside his shaving blade and brushed away the last strands of his beard, rubbing his hand over the newly exposed flesh. God, but it felt good to be clean again, to be home. He grinned and swung the little boy up into his lap. "That I am, son. You don't remember me, do you?"

Hance shook his bright head solemnly.

"I was off in Kentucky, fighting Indians."

The lad brightened. "Did you kill a lot of them?"

"Only when I had to, son."

"What were they like, Papa? Were they like Mimi, and Mr. Quaid's wife?"

Roarke smiled to hear Hance call him Papa, forcing away the savage images that the thought of Indians recalled to him. "They were different. They dressed in animal skins and beads and feathers. In summer they wore almost nothing at all. But they're people, Hance, just like us. The children play with dolls and cry when they fall down and scrape their elbow. They grieve when something bad happens."

A memory stabbed at him: Black Bear, screaming his name like a battle cry.

"Why were you fighting them?" Hance inquired, looking curiously at Roarke's pensive expression.

"Because they sided with the redcoats."

"Did you win the fight?"

Roarke frowned, remembering Colonel Clark's confidence at their last parting. "I think so, son."

Hance began fingering the straps of Roarke's saddlebag. "Did you bring me something?"

Roarke smiled. "There wasn't much to be had in the wilderness." He reached into the bag and took out a geode bowl. "The Indians eat from this," he explained. He handed the crystal-lined bowl to Hance and watched the boy's eyes grow wide with appreciation.

Then Roarke drew out some other gifts—a bear-claw necklace, quill work, a handful of polished agates. "These are for the Greenleafs."

Hance dropped the bowl and grabbed at the bear-claw necklace. "Mine!" he said loudly. "I want them all."

Roarke knew that this sort of possessiveness was normal in children Hance's age. He also knew better than to give in to it. "Sorry, lad," he said mildly. "One for each of you. Tomorrow we'll go over to the Greenleafs, and you can help me give out the presents."

But Hance leaped from his lap, clutching the saddlebag. "No!" he shouted, stamping his foot. "Mine!"

Roarke stood up. "Hance, please."

The boy was furious now. "The Greenleafs aren't your sons—I am! And I can do anything I want with the presents."

He hurled the necklace into the fireplace with all the fury of his boyish indignation. The string broke and the claws scattered over the hearthstones.

"It was mine," Hance mumbled.

Roarke clenched his jaw, though he was careful to betray neither anger nor surprise at Hance's outburst. He bent and retrieved the necklace.

"Since you broke Phillip's necklace," he explained calmly, "I'll have to give him your bowl."

"No!" Hance screamed. He whirled on Roarke, his face dark red with fury. "I hate you! Why did you have to come back anyway!" Hance leaped for the geode bowl.

But Roarke held him off. "I'm giving this to Phillip, Hance. And if I find you trying to take it from him, I'll do to you what I probably should have done a few minutes ago. I'll take you across my knee. Now, why don't you pick up those bear-claws, and we'll see if we can get them back on the string?"

"No." Hance turned away sulkily. As he left the room, Roarke heard the boy mutter, "Mine," under his breath. This time, Roarke ignored it. He'd give Hance time to get used to his being back. But not much time. Roarke had already figured out that the boy would require more than a little training.

The hogsheads rolled down the river road at a lumbering pace, stirring up red-brown dust as the Greenleaf boys guided them to the wharf. Genevieve basked in a glow of pride; it was their best crop yet. A few of the townspeople milled about, admiring the yield, shaking their heads with the wonder of it.

"They still can't get over you," Roarke said, grinning down at Genevieve. "A few years ago no one would have believed that a woman and an ex-slave could raise so much as a turnip between them."

As they were laughing together, Nell Wingfield sidled by, sporting a new hat of outrageous proportions.

"'Tis a tidy bit of tobacco there, Genevieve," she said. "Henry will be most pleased."

Genevieve's face clouded. Henry Piggot would indeed be happy to learn of her farm's bounty. He'd been absent for the duration of the war, but she didn't doubt that Nell kept him informed of things in Dancer's Meadow. The constant dread of his arrival weighed on her mind.

Hance, riding high on his father's shoulders, plucked a paste grape from Nell's hat.

"Lookee there, Papa," he chortled. "It's not real! I wondered why the birds stayed away from her."

"Give that back, you little urchin!" Nell huffed, grabbing for the bit of fruit.

"No," Hance said merrily, slipping to the ground with youthful agility. "You've got enough fruit on your ugly old hat."

"Hance . . ." Roarke strode off in pursuit, concealing a grin of amusement.

Nell glowered after him. "Impertinent child," she sniffed. "He could use a good whipping. I'm surprised a man like Roarke would tolerate such manners." She narrowed her eyes at Hance. Roarke had reached him and was extracting the paste grape from his hand. "But then," Nell continued, "we can't hold Roarke responsible for the boy's nature, can we?"

Genevieve shot her a warning glance. "Don't speak of it, Nell. Don't ever speak of it. If you do, I swear, I'll make you sorry."

Hance landed a kick on Roarke's shin and ran down to the river, howling like an Indian.

"Blood will tell, Genevieve," Nell said cattily. She gave a moist, red smile to Roarke, who handed her the paste fruit. Just as she was leaving, Nell seemed to remember something. She handed a folded piece of paper to Genevieve.

"Read that to me, will you?" she said. "The writing is too poor for me to decipher. I dislike straining my eyes."

Genevieve hid a smile as she donned her spectacles. Nell could barely read her own name. Glancing down at the paper, she said, "It's from someone called Desmond Sloat."

"An associate of Henry's. A British procurement officer."

But Genevieve didn't hear. She stumbled back against Roarke, gasping with disbelief.

"Henry Piggot is dead," she breathed, staring at the letter. "He was killed on a farm near Fairfield."

Genevieve's mind reeled as images of Piggot swam through her thoughts. Piggot, her creditor, her tormentor, was gone. She drew a deep, shaky breath.

And then relief set in. Relief so dreadful and so profound that Genevieve was ashamed of herself.

*   *   *

Genevieve's gaze moved dubiously up the trunk of the enormous hickory tree in her yard. Roarke had climbed to the first great crook and was moving out onto a spreading limb.

She shaded her eyes and squinted against the shafts of sunlight that filtered through the hickory, dappling her face.

"Roarke, do hold on with both hands. You'll fall."

He stopped working for a moment and grinned down at her, shaking his head. His smile was more dazzling than the sunlight above.

"Well, now, I can't very well tie these ropes if I'm clinging for dear life, can I?"

"Just be careful," she said primly. But, watching him, she knew she needn't have worried. Roarke secured the ropes using both hands, straddling the branch with his ankles hooked together, the sinews of his thighs straining against the taut fabric of his breeches, holding him in place effortlessly. He finished knotting the ropes and looked at Genevieve.

A hot blush crept to her cheeks when she realized she'd been staring in frank admiration at his thighs. The blush grew hotter when Roarke's wide grin told her he'd seen. He grasped the rope and let himself down, dropping to the grass in front of her. But he said nothing, only stooped and picked up a plank of lumber that he'd cut and sanded. He passed the ends of the rope through two holes in the plank and tied them. The he stepped back to admire his handiwork.

"You didn't have to do this," Genevieve said.

"Nonsense, girl. Every child needs a swing. Hance loves the one I made for him."

"But there aren't any children here. Joshua's youngest is twelve now."

"Well, then," Roarke said, lifting Genevieve up and setting her on the swing, "it appears we old folks will have to enjoy it."

"Really, Roarke," Genevieve protested. She gasped when he gave her a push that sent her sailing toward the sky.

She'd never been on a swing before; she'd never even thought about it. But as the soft early-autumn wind rushed through her hair, it never occurred to her to object to the frivolity of playing like a child when there was work to be done.

Roarke was enchanted by the picture she made, sable curls flying out behind her, eyes sparkling like gemstones as she began to laugh. It was rare that Genevieve let down her guard and gave herself up to pure pleasure, so damned rare . . .

Suddenly, Roarke knew that he wanted to make her laugh every day, not just on these occasional visits. And, just as suddenly, he knew with shining certainty that she was ready at last to hear what he'd ached to tell her for years.

When Genevieve arched forward, he caught her at the waist and lifted her out of the swing. Roarke's face must have betrayed the emotion that pulsated through him, because she stopped laughing to stare at him, cocking her head to one side.

He grasped her by the shoulders and drew her so close that she could feel the urgent pounding of his heart.

"I love you, Gennie Culpeper," he said in a hoarse, throbbing whisper.

She caught her breath. The honesty of his admission stunned her at first. And then a warm, pervasive feeling seeped through her to the very core of her being. She looked up at his face, a face that had haunted her since she'd first laid eyes on him seven years before, in the smoky, dim atmosphere of her father's tavern.

She lifted her hand to his cheek and stroked it gently. Unlike all the other times they'd been together, there was now an absence of tension. At last she felt completely free to touch the face she'd thought of with forbidden adoration for so long.

"I love you, Roarke," she admitted softly, giving voice at last to the secret she'd carried hidden in her heart for years.

His eyes seemed to burst into flames of joy as, ever so slowly, he brought his lips to hers. His kiss was so sweet, so compelling, that Genevieve nearly melted in his lingering embrace.

"Oh, God, Gennie, I love you. I need to wake up to you

every morning, to give you children, to embrace each and every day with you for the rest of our lives.

"Marry me, Gennie," he said against her lips. "Please . . ."

In the past she'd had a hundred reasons for not wanting a husband. But now not a single one came to mind. She knew only that she loved him and wanted him and would never be complete without him.

"Yes, Roarke," she heard herself saying. "Yes, *please.*" She wound her arms around his neck and gave herself up to the rush of giddy joy that enveloped her. All the promise of the happiness to come was in Roarke's kiss. Genevieve knew, with heart-stopping certainty, that she was happy for the first time in her life.

Mimsy Greenleaf appointed herself the bride's seamstress, lending her expert hand to an extravagant assortment of new dimities and calicos and linsey-woolsey fabrics with enthusiasm. She gave special care to the length of green-sprigged cotton Genevieve had chosen for her wedding gown. Mimsy's unerring eye for design and detail created a dress prettier than any Genevieve had ever seen.

She wore it one late-September morning, standing on a half-round stool while Mimsy took up the hem. The gown felt perfect. Its snug bodice hugged her torso, rising to a wide, lace-edged neckline. The full sleeves were gathered just below the elbows. Rose, who had inherited her mother's talent, had woven purple and green ribbons into the front of the bodice and into the sash at the waist. As she had for days, Genevieve felt herself on the verge of song. She hugged herself and tried to stand still.

"Just a few more inches," Mimsy said, speaking around a mouthful of pins. "I declare this hem must be four yards around."

"I'll probably trip over the skirts," Genevieve said.

"When have you ever tripped over anything?" Mimsy snorted. "You seem to do everything just right, Genevieve. I don't know how we'll get on without you when you leave here."

Genevieve laughed. "Give Joshua a little credit, Mimsy. I couldn't leave the farm in more capable hands."

"Are you sure you want to give it up?"

Her eyes turned to the window, to the twin hills that rose behind the house, gray-green with ripe tobacco. She'd poured sweat and tears over every acre of that land; she'd loved it, hated it, praised it, cursed it, and finally made things grow.

But where she was going there would be a lot more growing to do, and she'd be doing it with Roarke. She felt no tug at the idea of signing the entire farm over to Joshua. She and Roarke wouldn't need it. Everything they needed was at Roarke's farm.

She was ready to leave. Ready, because what awaited her commanded her heart like a plot of land never could.

She gave Mimsy a fond pat. "I'm very sure," she said firmly. Then her face burst into a smile. "Roarke's here!" He was coming up the road on his big roan horse, holding Hance in front of him on the saddle.

"Hold on, girl," Mimsy scolded when Genevieve leaped from the stool to greet him.

"But I want him to see the dress."

"No, you don't. It's not fitting. He'll get an eyeful soon enough."

Genevieve agreed that tomorrow was soon enough. Mimsy helped her out of the dress and slipped on one of her usual day gowns. Without stopping to put on shoes, she ran from the house to greet Roarke.

She paused to lift Hance from the saddle and placed a kiss on the boy's shining head, which was warm from the bright autumn sun. He scampered up to the fields, where Joshua and his sons had begun cutting the tobacco.

Roarke dropped to her side and caught her in an embrace that took her breath away. At first, Genevieve had protested his frankly affectionate demonstrations, which he indulged in regardless of who was watching. But now she savored the sweet warmth of his kisses and the strength of his arms folding about her. She wanted the closeness as much as he did.

"Tomorrow, love," Roarke mumbled against her hair. "God, it's an eternity until then."

Genevieve agreed. Always she felt this inner fire at his nearness. Something within her strained for completion and she could hardly wait for the moment when she could give her whole self to him.

"I can't stay long," Roarke said regretfully. "I never knew there was so much to be done for a wedding. Mr. Carstairs has agreed to officiate."

"I'm glad," Genevieve said. "It's kind of him, considering I haven't set foot in his church in six years."

"He's happy to do it, Gennie. Cy Hinton and I finished setting up the garden at my house. We'll be wed right under the sycamore tree, where I first proposed to you."

Genevieve blushed. "I'm surprised you remember that, Roarke. As I recall, I wasn't very civil to you about it."

Laughter crinkled in his eyes. "I didn't mind, Gennie. I knew you were in love with me even then, but you were just too damned stubborn to admit it."

She struck him lightly on the chest. "You flatter yourself, Mr. Adair."

"Do I, Gennie?" His eyes held hers compellingly.

At last she shook her head slowly from side to side. All the denial, all the reasoning with herself, had been in vain. She knew it now; she felt safe admitting it.

"I've always loved you, Roarke Adair," she said, her throat aching with emotion. "Always."

"Then don't be so sad about it, little love," he told her gently, taking a tear from her cheek with his thumb. "The only sad thing is that we took so long to do anything about it."

Genevieve nodded. A stiff breeze blew down from the Blue Ridge, tasting of winter's chill. She stepped into the circle of his arms.

"Hold me, Roarke," she said, seized by some inexplicable sense of urgency. "Hold me and tell me that this is really happening, that it's not just a dream."

"It's no dream, Gennie. I have to get Hance and go back now, but after tomorrow we'll never be apart."

She buried her face against him and breathed in his fragrance. He smelled of sunshine and clean earth. "Swear it, Roarke," she said. "Swear we'll always be together."

He placed a finger under her chin and tilted her head up to face him. "I swear, little love," he whispered, and claimed her mouth in a kiss that told it far more eloquently than words.

As Genevieve watched him ride away, she was full of a happiness so brilliant that even the single cloud that scudded over to obscure the sun couldn't dim it. The intensity of her joy frightened her a little. Good Lord, she thought incredulously, why would fate smile on me like this? *Me.* I've done nothing in my life but bring a few pounds of tobacco from the earth, and yet I've managed to win the love of the finest man in God's creation.

She refused to look at the shadows cast by the clouded sun. To put any meaning in that event would be to question her joy.

The clock ticked somberly in the late afternoon. Mimsy had gone to put the finishing touches on Genevieve's dress. Joshua and the boys were out of sight, over the rise in the more distant fields. Rose was helping Mimsy, and Caroline, who possessed Calvin's urge to read and learn, was practicing her skill reading the Scriptures to her mother and sister. She hoped one day to attend a Quaker school in Philadelphia that Luther Quaid had told her about.

Genevieve was alone in her house, listening to the clock and thinking about Roarke. She'd sleep here for the last time tonight. No wave of mawkish sentimentality washed over her at that. The house had never been anything but the sole legacy of Cornelius Culpeper, the husband she'd never met, who'd unwittingly dealt her many cruel years of hardship by leaving her his debts.

A movement on the road caught her eye. The afternoon sun glinted on the painted side of a coach, causing her to wonder. There were few coaches in Dancer's Meadow; even horses were getting scarce because of the war. The coach rolled up and crunched to a halt on the gravel drive. A black footman jumped down from the box and went around to open the door.

Henry Piggot emerged.

Genevieve's hand flew to her mouth, and she made a small sound of helpless denial. You're dead, she said mutely. You were killed while looting farms at Fairfield. But even as those thoughts tore through her mind she realized that a mistake had been made. A mistake that would cost her her happiness.

Abandoning futile denials, she opened the door to him. His bulk had increased over the years. He was massive now, filling the doorway.

Genevieve stared at him and forced herself to speak. "Hello, Mr. Piggot."

He smiled humorlessly around the ivory toothpick that protruded from his mouth. "Back from the dead, it appears. I'm afraid I found it expedient to contrive my own demise. You see, the patriots were about to seize me for spying . . . But it's all blown over now. The rebels are doomed, and I've work to do." He fingered the packet of papers in his hand. "Debts to call in."

Genevieve fumbled as she put on her spectacles to peruse the fading papers he showed her. Her fingers were like ice as she clenched and unclenched her fists at her side.

"I don't have that sort of money in hard currency," she told him shakily.

He shrugged. "Very well, I'll take this farm, then, and all your darkies."

She slammed her fist down on the table, upsetting a clay bowl of Mimsy's peppers. "You'll never have this farm, Mr. Piggot, and those 'darkies' are not mine to give." Silently she blessed the fate that had kept him from coming earlier. If he'd come just a day before, the farm would have been half in her possession. But she and Joshua had made the official transfer yesterday. She no longer owned the tobacco concern, and so Piggot wouldn't be able to take it from her.

She explained that to him with relish.

He looked unconcerned. "I'm sure you'll be able to find some form of payment. I understand you're to be married shortly. In a town as small as Dancer's Meadow, tongues can't keep from wagging about an impending wedding. Your husband will simply have to—"

"No!" Genevieve felt herself growing panicked. The debt amounted to a small fortune. Roarke didn't have that kind of money; he'd lose his farm. And even if he could afford it, it wasn't fair to force him to assume another man's debts. He deserved a wife, not a liability.

"Does anyone else know you've come?" she asked Piggot.

He shook his head. "Not even the fair Nell. I've had to keep my presence a secret here in patriot territory."

Genevieve emitted a shaky sigh. "Roarke is to know nothing of this."

"Then what do you propose to do, Mrs. Culpeper?"

Genevieve turned away and went to the window, unmindful that the papers Piggot had brought were cast to the floor by her movement. What, indeed, was she going to do? The gilded mantle of contentment that had shrouded her since she'd agree to marry Roarke suddenly fell away, leaving her naked and exposed to a cold feeling of hopelessness. What a fool she'd been to believe fortune had finally smiled on her. There had always been obstacles; there always would be.

As she gazed eastward, the afternoon sun glimmered on the placid river. Genevieve had a sudden wild surge of hope. Maybe, just maybe, there was a way to get the money. Digby Firth had been generous to her in the past, and she hadn't disappointed him. It would mean, of course, that she couldn't marry Roarke tomorrow, that she couldn't even risk telling him about her problem. She clenched her fist at her side.

He would understand. He had to understand.

12

She went alone with Piggot in the coach he claimed to have hired, although she suspected he'd commandeered it in the name of the British army, using the small arsenal of weapons concealed within. The urge to explain her journey to Roarke was tempting, but she knew better than to ask for his understanding. Because he'd do more than understand. He'd insist on taking on her debts.

She wouldn't let him do that. She didn't want them to start their life together with the shadow of debt hanging over them.

Genevieve had little to say to Piggot during the long trip to Yorktown, but she listened eagerly to his reports on the war. A staunch Tory, his account was colored by loyalty to the British, but his tale alarmed her nonetheless.

"General Cornwallis has things nicely in hand," Piggot said. "He marched deep into Virginia last summer; 'tis a wonder the farms around Dancer's Meadow were left alone. He burned tons of tobacco and grain, slaughtered horses and cattle . . . I heard he sent Governor Jefferson and the Virginia assembly fleeing into the woods to escape his cavalry."

"He sounds like a butcher," Genevieve said peevishly.

Piggot shook his head. "Cornwallis wants an end to this as much as anyone. He's trying to smash Virginia's will to resist."

"He won't succeed," Genevieve said determinedly.

"We'll see about that, Mrs.—"

"Mr. Piggot!" One of the black footmen gestured in alarm at the road. A small, bedraggled contingent of people approached.

Genevieve gaped at their condition. The men looked as if they hadn't eaten in days. One of them waved a hunting knife in a pitiable show of bravado.

"Mercy," a man groaned. "Please . . ."

"Keep going," Piggot directed his men.

But Genevieve jerked the coach door open. "These people are starving, Mr. Piggot. We're less than a day away from Yorktown. We can spare the food we've brought."

Piggot knew there was no arguing with the woman. He settled back with an exasperated sigh as Genevieve handed sacks of cornmeal and beans to one of the men. Then she gave him some salted meat wrapped in oilcloth.

The children attacked the food with heart-rending vigor. The man thanked her profusely.

"What are you doing out here?" Genevieve asked. "Have you no home?"

"Not anymore, ma'am. We used to live down in Little York, but General Cornwallis, he sent us all away. Said there wasn't enough food for his soldiers. Turned us out without so much as a by-your-leave. You ain't heading that way, are you, ma'am?"

"I am, sir."

His eyes widened. "Don't do it, ma'am. There's gonna be fightin'."

Genevieve looked back at Piggot, who shrugged. "Lafayette's probably going to try a last stand. Nothing to worry about."

*   *   *

Curtis Greenleaf had grown into a strapping, bandy-legged lad of seventeen, with arms sinewed by years of working tobacco. He was handsome and clean featured and had an air of strength and fearlessness about him that his mother proudly attributed to his devotion to family and Scripture. Still, as he dropped from Victor's back on the drive in front of Roarke Adair's house, he felt a shiver of apprehension. He didn't relish having to tell the red-haired giant that his bride-to-be was missing.

He found Roarke with Mr. Carstairs and some of the farm hands in the arbor at the back of the house, moving a number of benches to face a small flower-decked gazebo beneath a spreading sycamore tree.

Roarke looked up when Curtis cleared his throat. "You're a few hours early, lad," he said with a grin. "And I thought *I* was the impatient one."

"Mr. Adair, could I talk to you?" Curtis jerked his head toward the house.

Roarke slung his arm around Curtis's shoulders as they walked away from the others. Noting Curtis's unsmiling countenance, Roarke said, "You're still planning on singing at my wedding, aren't you?"

Curtis swallowed. There was no point in delaying any longer. "Mr. Adair, you know I'd be honored to sing for you and Miz Culpeper. But she's gone, sir. This morning we went up to the house and she wasn't there. Her bed hadn't been slept in."

Roarke stiffened in anger when he heard Genevieve's name on Nell Wingfield's lips. Genevieve had been the source of gossip all day, with people speculating over her hasty departure, relishing the small scandal like a sweetmeat.

"You mustn't be so morose about Genevieve," Nell was saying with her canny red smile. "There always was a bit of the odd bird about her. I'm not at all surprised she got a case of the cold feet the minute a decent man like you offered for her."

"You're hardly one to be talking of decency," Roarke

growled. He stalked away from Nell, mounted his horse and galloped to Genevieve's house. He wanted to be near her things, to touch and smell them, to see if any of her essence was left for him to savor.

He wanted to know why she had left him.

The clock had stopped. Roarke wound it for the first time in more than seven years, yet the act was as familiar as if he'd performed it daily. He moved his hands over the dial, which appeared to have been faithfully polished.

A soft curse escaped him. If only Genevieve had been so careful with his heart . . . He turned away from the clock, shaking his head.

The autumn sun slanted in through the windows, laying its yellow glow on the simple, rough furniture there, illuminating the small things of Genevieve's life . . . a life Roarke had wanted desperately to share. He'd thought he'd had her at last, after all the years of battling her will, chipping away at her defenses, finally forcing her to admit her love for him.

He'd been wrong to push her. But how could she have left without even a word of explanation, without taking so much as a single belonging? That was the odd part, the part he didn't understand. Even Amy Parker's prized needle case still rested on the mantel. Genevieve had sworn never to part with that.

Something didn't fit, Roarke knew suddenly. There was more to this than he'd guessed. Perhaps Genevieve had left against her will. Not kidnapped; there were no signs of a struggle, and besides, the Greenleafs would have heard. But something had compelled her . . .

The only thing out of place was a small slip of paper covered with spidery writing. It lay in a corner near the door, forgotten, overlooked. Swiftly, Roarke bent and picked it up.

Frowning and moving his lips, Roarke tried to make sense of the document. It was a bill of indebtedness, signed

by Genevieve and Henry Piggot. He squinted at the date—
19 May 1774.

Roarke's mind worked at breakneck speed. Bits and
pieces of nearly forgotten memories suddenly came together:
Genevieve, dazed at the wonder of unexpected widowhood,
putting her name to the paper; Piggot's odd manner in the
warehouse back in Yorktown; the surprising ease with
which he'd relinquished the farm to Genevieve; his veiled
promise to settle things one day . . .

Roarke turned the paper over. Another message was
scrawled there, unrelated to the debt, as if the paper had
been used in haste. The message had to do with a sum of
money paid to Henry Piggot for services rendered to His
Majesty's Army. This, too, was dated: 12 August 1781.

But Piggot was dead; Roarke had been there when Nell
had gotten the letter from Desmond Sloat.

Roarke's jaw tightened as he realized that the report had
been mistaken—or deliberately false. Piggot was alive, and
determined to have his due from Genevieve.

"Oh, God, Gennie," he murmured. "You should have
come to me . . ." But that wouldn't have been like her.
Proud little fool that she was, she would try to cope on her
own. There was only one person she would have been willing to approach with her problem: Mr. Firth of Yorktown.

It galled Roarke that she hadn't asked him for help. Furious, he bolted homeward to throw together the few things
he'd need for his journey.

Tension thrummed through the silent streets of Yorktown.
Moving like a wraith in the deep-velvet autumn night,
Roarke crept past the merchant house of Flowerdewe and
Norton to the offices of Digby Firth. Redcoats were every-
where, patrolling the streets and manning the heavily armed
redoubts. Roarke knew he'd be questioned if he were seen.

A lamp burned low at the back of the house. Roarke tried
the door; it swung open into an empty storeroom. He made
his way to the light, which glimmered from the library.

Digby Firth looked up when a large shadow darkened his

door. His eyes widened, but he said nothing. He motioned for Roarke to close the door.

"Have a care, man," the Scotsman whispered. "I'm quartering three officers upstairs."

"Seems like the whole town is playing host to the redcoats," Roarke said darkly.

"Aye, I've been trying to stay on neutral ground throughout this whole thing, but the British army's about worn its welcome thin."

"Has Genevieve been to see you?" Roarke asked, losing all patience with the discussion.

Digby shook his head. "I'm not expecting her. Why?"

Quickly, Roarke explained. Digby's bottle-brush eyebrows descended as he stroked his whiskers. "Poor little lass," he mused. "She's worked harder than a dozen men and has accomplished more than a score of them. She doesn't deserve this."

"I know, Mr. Firth."

"I'd help you if I could. You know that, Roarke." His full eyebrows worked thoughtfully. "But I'm penniless. I've allowed myself to trade in Continental dollars. What little cash I have is worthless. But where could the lass be?"

The journey to Yorktown was riddled by unexpected delays; Piggot's coach became mired, and they were stopped constantly by British patrols and bands of homeless refugees. It was another week before they arrived.

Genevieve suspected immediately that the British had more to deal with than General Lafayette. Redoubts had been dug across the network of creeks at the port and in the center of town where the main road ran. The ramparts of each redoubt bristled with lines of palisades angled outward. Embrasures were adorned by cannons. A half mile from where Genevieve and Piggot descended the road, Yorktown's rooftops could be seen. They were surrounded by a jagged semicircle of inner fortifications. The Union Jack flapped overhead.

Suddenly, the British guns spoke. Cannons and muskets barked from the redoubts.

Genevieve burst into Digby Firth's library, eyes wide with fear at the sound of booming guns. Dirty and unkempt from days of travel, she looked like a lost child. But to Roarke she had never been more beautiful. He scowled at Henry Piggot, who stood behind her, and then swept her into his arms.

"Damned proud woman," he chided gently, filling his senses with the taste and feel and smell of her.

She broke down in the face of his tenderness. "Roarke," she wept, "I can't marry you now. Everything you have would go to Mr. Piggot if—"

Digby Firth stepped forward, touched by Genevieve's despair and the adoration that shimmered in Roarke's eyes. "I know a way," he said, "to absolve you from liability. Now, 'tis not much to my liking, mind you, but it'll allow you two to be together."

"Good God, Mr. Wakefield," Roarke said to the hastily summoned magistrate. "This is preposterous. Are you sure there's no other way?"

Phineas Wakefield shook his head. "We must adhere to tradition in this. The smock marriage is a little-known bit of common law, and it must be perfectly clear that you've complied. The theory is that a woman who comes to a marriage without even the clothes on her back brings no debts to her husband. It's the only way to exempt you."

Roarke expelled his breath with a hiss. "'Tis a damned strange notion. I don't—"

The door to the library opened slowly, and Genevieve stepped into the room. Roarke, Digby, Phineas, and a disgruntled Piggot turned as one to stare at her. As tradition dictated, she was barefoot and bareheaded, clad only in a thin lawn smock with a torn hem and fraying ribbons.

Instinctively, Roarke moved to throw his coat around her. But she pushed him away, lifting her chin proudly.

Muttering complaints about the primitive custom, Digby lowered the wick of the lamp.

Roarke felt a painful inner lurch at the sight of Genevieve, standing beside him so determinedly. Despite the thin rag she wore, she looked magnificent. Her bare arms were bronzed by the sun, and taut muscles shaped them beautifully. Her hair, unbound as common law commanded, tumbled down over her shoulders in a rich cascade of dark sable. She displayed no missish modesty; she didn't quail or try to cover herself.

The others weren't watching her closely enough to guess, as Roarke did, at the depth of her humiliation. He felt her shiver slightly and saw her bare flesh shrink in mortification. Never had he thought her love for him would have to bear this awful test. Humbled by her bravery, her quiet dignity, Roarke wanted to lay himself at her feet and beg her forgiveness. He wanted to die for her.

As if she'd sensed something of what passed through his mind, Genevieve slipped her hand in his.

"'Tis a small price to pay, Roarke Adair," she assured him in a whisper, "for a lifetime with you."

Her words nearly brought him to his knees. "I love you, Gennie," he whispered.

Phineas Wakefield was decent enough to make short work of the ceremony. He said but a few words, set the documents before them to be signed, and pronounced them wed.

After Genevieve had hurried into her clothes, Digby Firth saw them to the door.

"Be happy, you two," he said, beaming from behind his whiskers. "No one deserves it more than you." He looked pleased with himself and turned to see what Henry Piggot was making of his cleverness.

"A right canny turn, wouldn't you say, Mr. Piggot?" he asked, not bothering to mask a little smirk.

Piggot's eyes narrowed, and the breath wheezed from him in short, angry gasps. He directed his anger at Genevieve.

"You've just caused me to lose everything," he said in a

low, deadly voice. "It was my doing that you were able to build a life here at all."

"Yes, you let me build a life, and then tried to take it from me," Genevieve said. "You should have known you wouldn't succeed."

"Oh, no?" Piggot asked maliciously. "I wonder what I'd be able to recoup for turning in a known rebel." He laughed at Roarke's amazed expression. "Didn't think I'd use that against you, did you?" he asked.

Before anyone could react, Piggot plunged his bulk from the library, calling for the officers who slept upstairs.

Urging Roarke and Genevieve to hurry, Digby led the way down a back alley to the livery, where they hitched Roarke's horse to a serviceable farm cart. In minutes the couple were headed northward, keeping to the shadows to avoid the watchful British guard.

"Where are we going, Roarke?" Genevieve asked in a small frightened voice. The muck of Black Swamp sucked at the roan's hooves.

"To Williamsburg for now," he said darkly. "It's patriot ground."

She nodded. He looked at her, her small face grimy and tired looking, her hands twisting in her lap. Curving his arm about her, he kissed her temple.

"Ah, Gennie love," he murmured, "'tis not the way I had our wedding planned. I didn't even think to bring the ring I'd bought you. You've been cheated of your chance to be a bride—for the second time, I fear."

Hearing the regret in his voice, she immediately straightened and stopped feeling sorry for herself.

"'Tis not being a bride that I want so badly," she declared, "but being your wife. And I've a whole lifetime to do that."

"Aye, but no woman should have to spend her wedding night fleeing in a farm cart."

"I want to spend it with you, Roarke. And I am. I ask no more than that." She grinned up at him. "You'll find me demanding enough later on, I'm sure."

*   *   *

The journey consumed the remainder of the night. Roarke had to move cautiously, aware that the horse and cart were valuable commodities for an army that needed to transport big guns and supplies. Neither of them slept. Morning found them wearily celebrating their marriage with a quiet meal of corn pudding in Raleigh Tavern. A scruffy-looking man approached them, staring with disbelief.

"Roarke Adair! By Job, I gave you up for dead at Vincennes!"

Roarke grinned and shook his head. He'd never spoken of the circumstances of his discharge to Genevieve; until this moment he'd nearly forgotten the months of fever and hopelessness. He stood and pumped his old friend's hand.

"Genevieve, this is Will Coomes. Will, my wife." Roarke swelled with pride as he claimed her for his own. "What brings you to Williamsburg?" he asked.

"We're marching to Yorktown!" Will said excitedly. "By Job, I wouldn't miss it for all the world, Roarke. It's to be the biggest siege of the war. Washington means to drive the redcoats from Virginia's shores."

Roarke gripped the edge of the table. "Washington? Last I heard he'd set his sights on New York."

"That's just what he wanted everyone to believe. He had Clinton guessing right down to the end. But he's here! And de Grasse is in the bay with twenty-nine ships and some three thousand troops from the West Indies."

"I'll be damned," Roarke said slowly.

Will drained his mug of cider and stood up. He lifted his hat to Genevieve. "We march in an hour." He directed a meaningful look at Roarke. "It's Captain Langston's regiment, Roarke. He needs all the good men he can get."

Genevieve watched her husband closely as they finished their meal. Only because she knew him so well did she see, in the depths of his eyes, the conflict warring within him.

"It could be the final battle," she ventured, thinking of the patchwork of southbound companies they'd seen assembling in Williamsburg.

"Aye. Let's hope so."

"You want to be a part of it, don't you, Roarke?"

He looked up sharply, and a denial leaped to his lips. "I have everything I want in you, Gennie. You and Hance, and the farm . . . I'm no soldier. I found that out when I was on the frontier."

"Just because you don't like soldiering doesn't mean you don't love freedom, Roarke." Genevieve had to force the words from her mouth. "Don't you understand? Everything you went through in Indian country will finally make sense if you see it to the end."

He looked at her, dumbfounded. "But Gennie, it'll mean leaving you—"

"I can wait," she said with more resolution than she felt. "Virginia can't."

He swallowed hard. She was so brave, so selfless, sitting across the table from him with the tears bright in her eyes and her jaw clenched hard against trembling.

He reached across the table, eyes brimming with emotion. "Sweet Gennie," he said. "I don't deserve you."

She clasped his hands and smiled. "Go with them, Roarke," she said with sudden, fierce conviction. "Go, and win your war."

"What the hell is that?" Roarke said, moving aside a low-hanging branch to peer through the woods. They were on the road to the front, and the company had veered off into the trees at the sound of a scuffle up ahead.

Lieutenant Colonel John Mercer, whose Virginia militia was marching with Langston's legion, put a spyglass to his eye and squinted.

"By God!" he exclaimed with a laugh. " 'Tis the French cavalry! Must be the Duc de Lauzun—he's got Washington's only horse soldiers. Looks like he could use a hand, lads."

The French, resplendent in their gorgeous uniforms, had charged a British contingent, which was guarding a heavily laden wagon train and a herd of cattle. Mercer and Langston formed up their lines and marched down into the fray.

It was Roarke's initiation into European-style warfare. Rather than shooting from the cover of underbrush at darting targets, the American columns marched boldly and let fly a blast of fire directly into the British charge. Sulfuric smoke and screams filled the air. The Frenchmen babbled in their own tongue, and the Americans raised a battle cry of jubilation as they slashed and hacked their way into the heart of the British guard.

Roarke didn't want to kill again. But when a redcoat rose up before him, sword raised, Roarke sent a musket ball into the man's middle. He hated the feeling of dark victory that rose within him and ached for the peace of his farm and Gennie's arms.

Moments later, at a shout from Colonel Banastre Tarleton, the redcoats dispersed, leaving their wagon train and livestock behind. The allies sailed their hats into the air as the first flush of victory took over.

And when, three days later, it was announced that the allies would open their trenches to the infantry that night, rebel fervor reached a fever pitch. Roarke joined in the drinking and singing as lustily as the next man. But as he bedded down for the night and looked up through the trees at the winking spray of stars overhead, his only thought was for Genevieve.

He whispered her name to the October wind and closed his eyes to form her image in his mind. He was still a little in awe of the fact that she was his wife. All the years of desiring her and being denied by her were finally at an end. She was safely on her way back to Dancer's Meadow. At last they'd make their home together.

Guns rumbled in the distance. The British, who had withdrawn from their captured redoubts to the inner fortifications, were probably firing on the sappers and miners in the trenches.

Roarke opened his eyes again and lifted a silent plea to the stars. There was a time when he'd felt so hopeless on the frontier that he hadn't cared whether he lived or died. But he cared now. Because Gennie was waiting for him. Let me keep myself alive, he begged to the stars, so I can hold her in my arms again.

The cart creaked beneath the weight of the Quaker family who had agreed to accompany Genevieve as far as Scott's Landing. They were kindly, and their children seemed to respect her pensive mood, leaving her to her thoughts.

There was joy in being married to Roarke, and she clung to that. Still, when she thought about the thousands of men making their way to Yorktown, she was seized by a terrible dread. It was possible, she admitted, that Roarke might do as Cornelius Culpeper had done. He might make her a widow before she'd had a chance to be a wife.

The appearance of a small company in the road ahead tore her from her thoughts. They pulled the cart to the roadside and hid amid a cover of underbrush.

But the British raiding party spotted them almost immediately. In minutes the cart and horse were surrounded.

The Quaker man settled back, sighing with resignation and drawing his family to his breast.

But Genevieve was furious. She leaped to her feet, planting herself in front of the British commander.

"You bloody thief!" she railed. "Would you steal from a woman?"

The redcoats laughed at her. " 'Tis the most expedient way," the commander joked.

Battling a pounding fear, Genevieve drew herself up. "Would you kill a woman for this cart?"

"Nay," said a voice from behind. "That won't be necessary."

Genevieve gasped. Henry Piggot insinuated himself between her and the officer and thrust her roughly aside.

"I was hoping for the chance to settle things with you, Mrs. Adair," he said, grinning. "The law has exempted you from debt, but in my mind you still owe me dearly."

"I have nothing," she told him through clenched teeth.

But Piggot shook his head. "You've a rather valuable

commodity right here, Mrs. Adair," he said, nodding at the cart and Roarke's horse.

"You infernal bloody sod!" Genevieve said. The redcoats sniggered in delight at her temper.

Piggot reached for her. She closed her eyes to his avid face; the blood pounding in her ears nearly drowned out the catcalls of the redcoats.

Her eyes flew open at the sound of staccato yells from the woods above the road. Like a pack of wild dogs, a group of men descended on the raiding party. In minutes the rebels had the redcoats howling back down the road.

All except Henry Piggot. Ignoring the fighting around him, he shoved Genevieve up against the cart, incautious in his fury. She heard herself scream.

"Let her go," someone commanded. The voice was full of quiet rage. Genevieve turned with a gasp of recognition.

"Calvin Greenleaf," she said, her knees nearly buckling with relief.

With reflexes made quick by years of Indian fighting, Calvin's arm snaked out and captured the back of Piggot's collar. The Englishman was dragged away, flailing and cursing.

Too late, Genevieve saw his knife. She cried out, but the blade had already found a home in Calvin's middle. She expected the young man to faint with the pain.

He didn't. If anything, his rage increased as he wrapped his arms about Piggot's neck. There was a dreadful snapping sound, and Piggot's body went slack.

Only then did Calvin allow himself to crumble. He slithered to the ground, using Piggot's bulk to cushion his fall.

Trebell's Landing was the scene of a jostling, noisy crowd pressing its way in around the supplies that were being unloaded. The chaos was overseen by the despairing French commissary Claude Blanchard.

Genevieve looked about in a daze. Calvin's company, under the command of Major General Henry Knox, had asked for the wagon, and she'd given it gladly, along with the roan. The wagon was needed for Calvin and then to drag the allies' heavy guns over the sandy track from Trebell's Landing to the theater of war.

Genevieve sat inside a cramped tent, moving her hands absently over Calvin's sweating brow. The fever was a bad sign, the doctor had said. Infection had set in.

He was still lucid, though, and Genevieve clung to that. When he opened his eyes she forced herself to smile encouragingly.

"Can I get you something, Cal? Some water or—"

He shook his head and frowned at her. "You shouldn't be here," he grumbled. "Your husband thinks you're on your way to Dancer's Meadow."

"And so I would have been," she replied evenly. "But I had the good fortune to run into an old friend."

He grimaced and looked away.

Genevieve knew it galled Calvin that he'd been wounded by Piggot, not even in a proper battle.

"I've been talking to your lieutenant," she said. "According to him you've acted the hero more than once." She could see Calvin's eyes glazing over. The surgeon had warned her not to let him slip away. "Tell me about the Kentucky campaigns, Cal."

"A hundred yellow feathers," he said faintly, his mind wandering. "Braves, all of them, painted up like nightmares. It had been raining for days. Our powder was useless, the men half-starved. I didn't have any choice. Took all of their stores and ordnance . . ."

His lips curved into a smile, and suddenly he no longer looked like the world-weary soldier who had been brought to Trebell's Landing three days ago. Now Genevieve saw him as the youth she'd known: intense, burning with the will to achieve something for himself.

Yet he looked so weak just now. He was hurting. Genevieve went to the opening of the tent and looked out. The big guns of the Americans were being loaded onto wagons or dragged away by enlisted men, but there was still no sign of the hospital equipment the French had promised.

Genevieve ground her teeth in frustration. "Mr. Blanchard," she called to the harried French commissary.

He glared at her and tapped his foot impatiently. "Yes, madame, what is it?"

"The wounded men can't wait any longer, sir. Every bandage we have is soiled, and we need something to alleviate the pain."

"Sacredieu!" Blanchard exclaimed, stamping his foot. "De Grasse has ordered me to set up bake houses, and everything I need to function properly is still out on the Chesapeake!"

Genevieve could see that she'd get no help from Blanchard. He was an annoyingly fussy little man, enamored of order and precision. He was no more at home in Virginia than a lap dog on a coon hunt.

She glanced back at Calvin, who had begun to moan softly. Nearby, the surgeon was bandaging a wounded soldier and cursing the lack of medicines and equipment.

"What is it you need, sir?" she asked softly.

The doctor scowled at the unconscious man, whose face had been burned by mortar fire. Then he looked at Genevieve and rolled his eyes heavenward.

"A miracle, ma'am. That's what we need."

She gestured out at the bay. "Would some of the supplies from that ship help?"

"They'd do more good here than on the water."

It was all the impetus she needed. She ran down to the landing and lifted her skirts to wade out to a small dinghy moored at one of the docks. Behind her, she heard Blanchard's shouts of outrage. But by the time she turned to look at him, she was rowing smoothly out to the French ship.

The allied guns greeted the dawn of October 17 by belching death upon the British, who had been driven into a huddle within their crumbling fort. It had been storming through the night, preventing Cornwallis from ferrying his breakout detachments across the bay to Gloucester.

Roarke sat with his company behind the muddy trenches. He'd fought in several skirmishes over the past two weeks, killing more British than he cared to think about. The American soldiers were a tough, battle-trained lot who knew the land they were fighting for and used it to advantage.

Roarke had sustained a head wound from an explosion. The bandage kept slipping down over his shooting eye. But he was beginning to suspect that there wouldn't be much more shooting.

No more trenches needed to be dug. Now there was nothing to do but watch the artillerymen work the guns. By nine o'clock the return fire had ceased completely.

Finally, the sodden monotony was broken. A scarlet-coated man appeared on the crumbling parapet of the British horn works. The man beat with frantic desperation on a drum, although the sound was drowned out by the allied fire.

The Americans held their collective breath. By now every man was soldier enough to know what the drumming meant.

Soon after, an officer appeared, halfheartedly waving a white handkerchief. The pair began a slow trek toward the American lines.

The guns ceased to thunder. Roarke had never known a silence so profound. Only the melancholy tattoo of the drum could be heard now.

"La chamarade," a Frenchman nearby whispered. "The parley begins now."

The quiet that descended over York that night was not a peaceful one, although the rain and shooting had finally stopped. Roarke lay sleepless, wondering if a last, brash British mortar shell or cannonball would drop into their midst, killing him just when the end was in sight. He lifted his eyes to the remarkable decoration of stars in the cool, clear sky and put the notion from his head.

At dawn the harsh music of the Scots from the Seventy-sixth Regiment whined a salute to the allies. A jubilant reply came from the Royal Deux-Points regimental band. Roarke and his comrades scrambled to the parapet to see both sides crowded with men. He tried to summon rage at the enemy but found nothing within himself that resembled hatred.

The gouged, littered battlefield was all that was left of the ugly face of war.

Roarke looked away and shivered in the early morning chill. Perhaps, he told himself, the glory would come later, when the formal surrender took place. But for now there was only the silence to savor, and the thought that he'd finally be going home.

Some of the Americans were already leaving. Roarke was tempted to follow them. Then he remembered what Genevieve had said about seeing it through. He brushed the mud from his tattered coat and polished his boots.

The Americans and French formed a double line along the Hampton Road in readiness to receive the defeated British. In the afternoon the British marched from Yorktown to the strains of "The World Turn'd Upside Down."

Roarke noted that every Englishman kept his eyes trained on the French lines, not even sparing a glance for the Americans. It was as if they wanted to lessen their disgrace by surrendering to the French rather than the Continental Army.

No wonder, Roarke thought. The world's most powerful war machine had been defeated by a band of tattered, defiant rebels. But the Americans weren't about to be ignored. Their band burst into a blare of "Yankee Doodle," forcing the British, who had scorned and despised them for so long, to look them in the face.

When the sullen order to ground arms was given, the British began hurling their weapons into a pile in hopes of damaging them. General Lincoln, Washington's second in command, barked a curt warning. The defiance was cut short, and the arms were laid to rest with less violence.

Roarke stood and stared at the silver and brown pile of muskets and listened to the sobs and curses of the mortified British, until at last the ranks dispersed.

Washington's forces went to occupy Yorktown, and the patchwork of smaller companies dispersed. Drinking and celebrating began in earnest that evening.

But Roarke was ready to leave. He was no less jubilant than the men who clapped one another on the back and reveled in the heady sense of victory, but his jubilation was a quiet, fierce one. He was gathering up his few belongings in preparation for the journey back to Dancer's Meadow when Will Coomes found him.

"Leaving already?" Coomes asked, cocking his head so that his hat fell askew. "They've just unbunged a good supply of Jamaica water."

Roarke shook his head. "My part in this is done. I'm going home to give my wife a proper wedding and raise my son as an American." God, but it sounded good to say it. Roarke couldn't ask anything more.

But as he trudged up the road, he was enveloped by a great wave of loneliness. It was a long trip to Dancer's Meadow, and he didn't relish going it alone.

All up and down the Hampton Road people were celebrating. A good many of them were homeless, their houses having been destroyed in the siege, but they knew they'd rebuild, and this time it would be for a new nation. Roarke trudged past embracing couples and gamboling children and listened to the music and laughter and voices raised in song.

And then he heard his name being called. Faintly at first, then with gathering strength.

"Roarke! Roarke Adair!"

He stopped and froze. An arm waved frantically from the midst of the milling crowd on the road, and then Roarke saw a gleaming sable head and the adorable face he'd longed for in his dreams for weeks.

"Gennie!"

She twisted her way out of the crowd and ran toward him. He met her halfway on the road, filling his arms with her and swinging her about in the golden evening light. He didn't dare question her presence for fear of waking from the dream.

As if to convince him that she was real, Genevieve pressed her mouth to his.

"Roarke," she murmured. "Oh, Roarke . . ." Touching

the stained bandage that circled his head, she frowned. "You're hurt!"

"It's nothing, love. Nothing at all." He kissed her again, his mouth lingering over hers longingly.

"You've won your war," she said when they parted.

"It appears I have, Gennie love," he replied, giving her shoulders a squeeze.

Her eyes passed over the noisy throng in the road one last time.

"Then let's go home, Roarke. Let's go home."

13

"*Bless you,*" *Mimsy* Greenleaf whispered. "Bless both of you." She bent over Calvin's supine form and touched his face. Her eyes were brimming with tears when she looked up at Roarke and Genevieve.

"You've brought my boy home to me."

Joshua and the others came running as Calvin was taken to the house. The young man moaned and thrashed a little, but he was lucid enough to smile for his mother, Genevieve saw with relief. Quickly, she told the Greenleafs of Cal's bravery and how he'd sustained the injury. Mimsy and Joshua thanked her for staying with their boy, even as the Battle of Yorktown raged throughout the Chesapeake.

Roarke had a brief conversation with Joshua and Curtis and followed Genevieve to her house.

"I've an errand in town," he told her with a smile that was both charming and uncharacteristically mysterious. "Joshua will bring you around later."

Genevieve was a bit mystified that he couldn't wait for her to bathe and change, but she accepted his kiss without questioning him.

"I'll see you later, Mrs. Adair," he said.

She laughed with delight at her new title and declared that later was too long to wait.

For the last few days men had trickled back to Dancer's Meadow, bursting with the news of Washington's signal victory at Yorktown. The little settlement was littered by the celebration that had gone on, and the people who greeted Roarke as he went about his business were charmed by his plans for Genevieve. Hance was delighted to see his father, although he balked when Roarke announced that it was time for Hance to go with Mimi and wait in the church.

Roarke was leaning against a hitch rail in front of the trading post when Joshua and Curtis arrived in the cart with Genevieve.

His breath caught at the sight of her. She was wearing a pretty, beribboned gown of green. Her hair had been washed and brushed until it glowed like a dark halo around her small heart-shaped face. The afternoon sun streamed down on her bright head and cut golden facets of light into her eyes. She gave him a smile that drove away the chill of the November day.

Roarke held out both his hands, and she took them.

"Odd," she remarked. "The town seems deserted. I thought people would be celebrating the victory."

Roarke shrugged and pulled her across the street. "Come with me, Gennie," he said.

She smoothed back a stray lock of hair. "Where are we going?"

"To church, love."

"Roarke, no," she protested. "I just wouldn't be comfortable—"

"Gennie, please. I know folks were hard on you at one time, but give them another chance." He brushed his knuckles over her cheek. "Please."

She couldn't refuse him. "I suppose it will be all right," she said shrugging. "There can't be anyone around for me to offend on a Saturday afternoon."

"Of course not," Roarke said with a chuckle, then grinned at the sharp look she gave him.

When they reached the church steps, Genevieve began to grow inexplicably nervous. Dancer's Meadow was too quiet. Even Elk Harper, the ever-present singing drunk, was absent from his usual loitering post in front of Liberty Tavern.

But Roarke didn't allow her to hesitate. He opened the door and pushed her inside.

Genevieve gasped at all the smiling faces that turned to greet her. Everyone was there—nearly the whole town. Holding the door, Luther Quaid grinned and gave them a mock salute. Roarke left Genevieve at the doorway and made his way up the aisle to the altar, where Mr. Carstairs beamed from behind his prayer book.

Genevieve tensed for flight, mortified by the rapt attention that centered on her, even though not a single disapproving stare could be seen. But Joshua Greenleaf appeared suddenly at her side and took a firm hold on her elbow.

"Whoa there," he said in a low voice. "You're not thinking of leaving your groom at the altar, are you, young lady?"

"My groom . . . ? But—"

"Roarke didn't much care for what happened back in York. He thought you'd like to start your life together with a proper wedding. Now, ordinarily it's the girl's papa who gives her away. But I'd be obliged, partner, if you'd let me do the honors."

By the time Joshua finished his speech, tears were streaming down Genevieve's face. She was stirred to her very soul at this unexpected plan of Roarke's and the whole town's smiling complicity. Blinking through a sheen of tears, she put her arm through Joshua's and started toward Roarke. Curtis's rich young voice lifted in an Isaac Watts hymn, reaching a sweet crescendo as Genevieve arrived at the altar.

"Dearly beloved friends," Mr. Carstairs said in his ringing voice. "We are gathered here to witness and bless the union of our neighbors, Genevieve and Roarke." The preacher paused and looked at Joshua. "Who gives this woman in marriage?"

Joshua drew himself up proudly. He looked very serious and stern, although Genevieve caught a sparkle of humor in his eye as he said, "Her partner does." He placed her hand in Roarke's. For a moment his hand lingered over theirs, and he dropped his voice to a whisper. "God keep you both, my friends," he said, and stepped back to stand beside his son.

Genevieve looked up at Roarke with a smile so radiant that he blinked. Mr. Carstairs read: " 'Finally, brethren, whatsoever things are true, whatsoever things are honest, whatsoever things are just, whatsoever things are pure, whatsoever things are of good report; if there be any virtue, and if there be any praise, think on these things.' "

The words washed over Genevieve like a song of unbearable sweetness. When the time came to repeat her vows, she did so with all the conviction of her love for the man who stood beside her, the man who had turned her wearying, ordinary life into a gilded dream.

When Mr. Carstairs asked for the ring, Roarke proudly produced the one he'd lacked at the smock marriage, a band of braided yellow gold that gleamed like a piece of the sun on her finger. Then Roarke bent and gave his bride a kiss so full of gladness and passion that a collective sigh went up from the congregation.

Everyone pressed around the happy couple. Still astonished by the outpouring of good will, Genevieve was hugged and kissed and given all manner of advice. Contentment pervaded her whole being like a warm glow from a friendly hearth. At last, after all the years of feeling like an outsider, she was accepted. When portly Mrs. Carstairs professed the hope of seeing the Adairs—all of them—at Sunday meeting, Genevieve promised she would be there.

Somehow Roarke had managed to dissuade the townsmen from performing the drunken ritual of charivari, in which the newlyweds were tormented with bawdy tricks right up until they bedded down together. Roarke wanted nothing to mar their first night together as man and wife. As independent and hardheaded as Genevieve was, she evoked a strong protective instinct within him that made him want to shield her from any hint of humiliation.

They returned home late, replete with gifts and good wishes and the feast that had been amassed in haste by the church women. Hance, overwrought and somewhat confused by the day's festivities, had been put to bed by Mimi, and the big welcoming supper prepared by Roarke's neighbors had been cleared away.

Genevieve and Roarke sat in the keeping room facing a hickory fire that glimmered with fragrant warmth. Above the mantel hung Genevieve's clock. She stood looking at it for a moment and traced its yellow mulberry case with a finger.

"Odd," she mused aloud; "it seems to belong here, much more than it ever did in my house."

"Maybe because this is a home, Gennie," Roarke suggested. "Our home."

"Yes," she sighed, leaning against him. "Oh, yes . . . Roarke, did you know that this is the first thing I bought with my bride money from Mr. Culpeper?"

He shook his head, smiling indulgently.

"I was so unaccustomed to having money that I spent it without thinking. I suppose I could have used a new pair of shoes, something practical like that. But I was furious at Angela Brimsby that day . . . At first, buying it was a petty act of spite against that woman, but when I saw the clock it became more than that . . . 'Behold this hand, observe ye motion's trip,' " she read from the dial.

" 'Man's precious hours, away like these do slip,' " Roarke finished for her.

She turned and looked at him in surprise. "I didn't know you'd ever paid any attention to my clock, Roarke."

He laid his hand along her cheek. "Those were the first words my mother ever read to me." He smiled at her confusion. "She read them from that very clock, Gennie."

Her eyes widened. "Your mother . . . God blind me, Roarke Adair, you never told me!"

He told her then, holding her, looking at the clock, reviving memories of years past. But there was no pain now in speaking of his mother's suffering and his father's abuse because of the healing he felt as he held Gennie in his arms.

She moved her head from side to side, fighting tears, remembering Roarke's reaction when he'd first seen the clock. She should have realized then that the timepiece was as much a part of Roarke as his friendly smile and his big freckled hands.

"Why the devil did you let me keep it?" she asked softly.

He brushed the tears from her face. "Because I knew you'd keep it well, my love. I trusted you." Together they turned and went to the settee, to sit and watch the legacy and listen to its quiet ticking.

There was a quilt spread over their laps, which Genevieve stroked absently, moving her hands over entwined circles made from bright scraps of fabric. The quilt was a gift from the ladies of the church, and Genevieve was a little in awe of it. Every tiny stitch had been sewn for her and Roarke, by women she never would have guessed cared for her. On the mantel the clock chimed midnight.

Roarke set down his half-finished cup of peach brandy and turned sideways to face her.

"Happy, Mrs. Adair?"

She snuggled closer to him. "Mmm . . . More than I can say. More than I dare to be. If I died this instant, I wouldn't have a single regret."

He smiled softly. "Oh, but I would, Gennie."

"What's that?"

"It would be the supreme cruelty for you to leave this world before I've had the chance to make you mine."

She pressed herself against the warm breadth of his chest. "But I am yours, Roarke. Finally." But when she felt his hand glide gently around her waist, she realized she'd mistaken his meaning. He wasn't talking about the mere fact that she'd married him. Feeling a blush creep to her cheeks, she swallowed hard.

"Gennie," he said, instantly pulling away from her, "I didn't mean to embarrass you—"

She answered him with a kiss, sipping the sweet brandy

from his lips. "If I'm embarrassed, Roarke," she said softly, "'tis because I want to please you, and I've no idea what I'm about."

He felt his heart swell with gratitude as he took her face between his hands. "You need never worry about pleasing me, Gennie. And as for the other, you're wrong. You know exactly what you're about. You know how to touch me to my very soul, and a man can't ask for more than that."

"But—"

He silenced her with a kiss that sent her senses reeling. With their lips still locked, he scooped her up, quilt and all, and carried her to the bedroom. She gazed up at him in wonder, feeling no fear, only awe at the idea that he loved her, that he wanted her. Slowly, his fingers plucked at the ribbon that circled her waist.

"Roarke . . ." Her voice trembled with longing.

He put his finger to her lips. "Just let me love you, Gennie," he said. "Just let me love you."

14

Each time an unearthly, agonized groan issued from the bedroom, Roarke felt a shaft of pain as if it were he doing the suffering. He winced and ground his teeth and looked at the clock. Seven hours had passed since Genevieve's fluids had moistened the bed they shared. Six hours since she'd begun laboring in earnest. How much longer would it go on?

Roarke was terrified. Losing Prudence to this business of giving life had been painful enough. And for Prudence he'd only felt a sense of responsibility, an affection born of duty. Roarke knew it would finish him if he lost Genevieve, for he loved her with a consuming adoration, as though she were as necessary to his survival as the very heart that beat within his chest.

For ten months she had filled his days with joy. Her laughter as she played with Hance in the garden, the endearing briskness with which she handled, like a seasoned trader, the business matters of the farm, the startling sweet ardor she showed as she lay with him night after night . . . Roarke raked a hand through his disheveled mane. Sweet

Christ, he loved that woman. Every moan was like a hot dagger penetrating his chest.

Suddenly, Mimsy Greenleaf appeared at the bottom of the stairs. The sight of her, dressed in crisp cottons and a clean apron, reassured Roarke a little. She looked impeccably competent, not at all worried about her patient.

"It ain't right," she declared roundly. "Ain't right at all. I tried to tell her so, but she won't listen. She insists on having you with her, Roarke." Mimsy stalked across the room and took his arm. "Men got no business at a birthing, but your stubborn woman in there thinks different. Come along, now, but don't blame me if you don't like what you see."

Roarke hurried across the dim bedroom and knelt beside Genevieve. How could he not like what he saw? It was almost unbearable to witness her pain, but she had never looked braver or more lovely, even with her hair matted on her brow, her face contorted with agony.

"It hurts," she said faintly, the words squeezing from her between pains.

He peeled a lock of hair from her forehead and kissed her moist brow. "I know, love; I'd give anything to keep you from feeling it."

She tensed and gripped his hand. Roarke looked over his shoulder at Mimi Lightfoot and Mimsy, who were watching with quiet concern.

"Fetch the doctor from town," he ordered curtly. "Something's wrong—"

"No!" Genevieve had recovered from the pain enough to protest stridently.

Mimsy patted Roarke on the shoulder. "Nothing's wrong," she assured him. "Nothing at all. It's just the way of things."

He nodded and held Genevieve through another pain. From a distant part of the house he heard a small frightened cry.

"Hance!" he said. Morning had come, and the boy had awakened to an empty house. "Mimi, go see to him."

Mimi left the room to take the boy out of earshot, so he wouldn't be alarmed by Genevieve's cries.

"Roarke," Genevieve whispered, dazed by the last pain. "Roarke, promise me something . . ."

"Anything, love."

"If I—If anything happens to me, I don't ever want Hance to feel . . ." She grimaced. "He's ours, as much as if we'd given him life. I want him and the new baby to be as brother—" She arched on the bed, and her limbs began to shake.

"Christ, Gennie, don't take on so. Nothing's going to happen to you."

"Promise me, Roarke," she ground out.

"Of course, love," he replied. And he meant it. He loved Hance; the boy's willfulness and mischievous streak only made him more endearing. Genevieve had worked hard over the months to be a mother to Hance. She spoiled him shamelessly, giving in to his every whim and fulfilling his demands for attention, which were considerable. Hance called her Mama in a way that filled Genevieve with pride each time he said it.

But when, a few hours later, Genevieve gave birth to the son of his loins, Roarke nearly wept with happiness. Genevieve was unutterably weary, glowing with exultation. She watched with a full heart as Roarke himself bathed the child and then laid him in her arms.

"Roarke," she said, brushing her cheek across the baby's gossamer wisps of hair. "Roarke, we did it."

He sat on the edge of the bed and embraced them both, filling his arms with the most precious things he'd ever held.

Genevieve kissed him softly and gazed down at their son. "Hello, baby," she whispered. "Hello, Luke Adair."

Mimsy finished clearing away the linens and went to the door, motioning for Mimi and Hance. The little boy took a hesitant step toward the bed.

"Come on, son," Roarke said with a grin. "We named your brother Luke, just like you wanted."

Hance looked dubiously at the swaddled bundle in Genevieve's arms. "He's just a little mite of a thing."

Genevieve laughed. "Mimsy says he's big for a newborn. Eight pounds at least."

"Can I play with him?"

"I dare say he's a bit young for playing. But one day he'll need a big, strong brother like you to teach him to climb trees and swim and skip stones in the river."

"I don't think I want to teach him," Hance said, setting his jaw in the stubborn way Genevieve knew so well.

"Now, son," Roarke chided gently. "'Tis grand having a brother. You'll see—"

"I don't want a brother," Hance shouted, and his sharp exclamation startled the baby into crying. "I liked things just the way they were." He stomped from the room and slammed the door.

Genevieve jiggled Luke to quiet him and gave Roarke a helpless look. But Roarke only smiled. Not even Hance's outburst could mar his happiness.

"Hance has been the only child around here for nearly eight years," Roarke explained. "He'll come around, Gennie. He'll soon love our little Luke as much as we do."

15

"Mama!" Luke came running up the lane from the fields, his bare feet kicking up little puffs of reddish dust. The sun glinted down on his freckled, sunburned face.

"Mama," Luke repeated, "Hance wasn't at school again today. He lit out for Scott's Landing with the Harper boys. Parson Stiles said he'd come to a bad end, Mama." Luke stole a raspberry from the bowl on the porch table and popped it in his mouth. Then he poked out his lower lip in a pout. "Hance said if I tattled, he'd thrash me good, but I don't care. Seems I'm always smoothing the field for him. I just can't think of any more ailments to tell the parson, Mama." He flopped down on the bottom step and rubbed the soles of his feet in the dust.

Genevieve stroked her son's rumpled hair and hid a smile. At the age of six, Luke was the image of his father, with big rough features and hair the color of rain-wet clay. He had Roarke's solid build and stood a full head taller than most boys his age.

Luke resembled Roarke in temperament as well—dutiful, kind, with a strong sense of justice. The boy was no scholar, a fact the parson often pointed out, but ever since he'd been old enough to work in the fields, he'd done so without complaint. Luke was quick to understand that Hance didn't share his enthusiasm for farming.

"There now," she said gently, plucking a bit of dried grass from his hair, "You know how Hance is. He's nearly fourteen. He's gotten too old and too smart for the parson."

"Peter Hinton is fifteen, and he's always at school," piped a small voice. Five-year-old Rebecca Adair appeared on the porch with Israel, a dark-haired boy of four, and baby Matilda in tow. Genevieve smiled at her children, thankful that they were such a handsome, healthy lot, blessedly well behaved. But Hance . . .

"Hance isn't like other boys," Genevieve reminded them. It was true. Hance was different, so wise in unchildlike ways that it sometimes scared her. When he fled from school, it wasn't to idle the day away fishing or swimming. Often he would be found in the crook of a hickory tree poring over St. John's *Letters* or the essays of Tom Paine. Genevieve didn't mind that, but even more frequently Hance ran off to keep company with Wiley and Micajah Harper, sons of the hard-drinking ne'er-do-well Elk, of whom she heartily disapproved.

"It's not fair," Luke said obstinately. He traced a circle with his bare toe in the dust. "Papa never badgers him to help on the farm like he does me."

"Hance is busy learning other things." She shuddered to think what those things were.

Luke shrugged. "All a man has to know is how to plant a field and send his crops down the river."

Genevieve lowered her eyes. Luke was too young to understand that Hance had already begun looking beyond the tree-fringed boundaries of the farm. He wasn't made for growing corn and mending fences and clearing land. Roarke had taken him on several trips to Richmond, and Hance had returned full of enthusiasm for the rollicking life of the new capital. He seemed as intrigued by the blustering, self-important politicians of Shockoe Hill as he was by the flamboyant gamblers who plied their slick trade in Eagle Tavern.

Genevieve knew better than to suppose Hance's wild

streak could ever be beaten or cajoled out of him. She felt she owed it to Prudence to let him make his own choices.

"We must accept Hance as he is, Luke," she said firmly, "as the Lord made him. Come now, get that glum look off your face. Didn't your father want some help building the new springhouse?"

"It would've been done by now if Hance hadn't lit out with the Harpers."

"Never mind, Luke. You'd best get cleaned up. Remember about tonight."

Luke's dark moods never lasted long. They were like a spring rain: a burst of anger, and then the storm was over. His face blossomed into a smile. There was a spray of freckles across his nose that made him positively adorable.

"Papa's birthday!" he cried, running down the yard. The other children followed him, whooping with glee at the prospect of a party.

Genevieve smiled after them, shaking her head. Not even the wind changed as quickly as her children's moods.

Roarke Adair sat at the head of the table in a room that now brimmed with the faces of seven Adairs. He felt a fullness of heart that made him tremble inwardly; it was almost a sin for a man to have so much.

The remnants of a feast littered the table: a succulent haunch of pork, large earthenware bowls of vegetables, a crock of butter. Only a heel of bread remained from two loaves. The one item left intact was the big cake, heavy with nuts and iced by Mimi Lightfoot's skilled hand.

Roarke looked around at his family. Luke's eyes fairly devoured the cake. Rebecca managed to look prim and serious despite her curly cloud of ginger-colored hair and the freckles that dotted her nose. Israel had inherited his mother's delicate dark beauty and, it seemed, her intelligence and passion for books. Genevieve was fond of pointing out that he already knew his letters and could pick out some of the words of the Lord's Prayer on his sister's hornbook.

Genevieve herself sat at the opposite end of the table, looking as fresh and girlish as she had when they'd married seven years before. She held baby Matilda in her lap, jiggling the child to amuse her and brushing her lips across Mattie's hair, which was an unlikely but beautiful pale-blond color.

Hance lacked the younger ones' round-eyed wonder at the cake but was prepared to be pleasant tonight, a bit contrite over his truancy earlier in the day.

"You do me proud," Roarke said. "All of you. As of this day, I've been on this earth for thirty-six years, and I'm thankful for each and every day I've had." He caught Genevieve's eye and was rewarded with the brightness of her smile. "'Tis said a man should make a fond wish on his birthday," Roarke continued. "But not a one comes to mind. I've been blessed so many times over, with you children and the bounty of this farm, that I've nothing left to wish for."

Rebecca tugged at her mother's sleeve. "Can I give him my present now, Mama?" she asked impatiently.

At Genevieve's nod she climbed down from her chair, ginger curls bobbing as she approached her father. She climbed up into his lap and placed a limp parcel in his hands. Then she stepped back to watch him open it.

"Well, look at that," Roarke exclaimed. The sampler had obviously taken hours of the little girl's labor. To the delight of Mimsy Greenleaf, Rebecca showed a bit of talent with the needle.

"It's a Bible verse," Rebecca explained proudly. " 'I have refrained my feet from every evil way, that I might keep thy word.' "

Roarke gave Rebecca a hug. "Well, now, 'tis a lovely piece of work. We'll hang it in the keeping room, next to the mantel clock."

A second parcel was pushed shyly into Roarke's hands. He smiled down at Israel, then spilled a collection of brightly colored stones out onto the table.

"Gathered 'em all by myself," Israel said importantly. "I went all the way to the river bank at the end of the road."

"Thank you, Israel," Roarke said. He selected a light

pink stone, one worn smooth and polished by rushing water as if in a tumbler. "I believe I'll carry this one here in my pocket, for luck."

Luke's gift was a wolf he'd whittled from a bit of driftwood, surprisingly well made and properly ferocious looking. Brimming with pride, Roarke set it on the table.

Even Hance, who rarely displayed more than a wry tolerance for anyone in the family except the baby, had a gift. Reaching into his pocket, he produced a beautiful pipe carved from iron-maple burl with an ivory stem and silver band.

Roarke turned it over in his hands. "I've never seen the likes of this before," he said. "Where'd it come from, Hance?"

The boy thrust his chin up proudly. "I won it off a tobacco factor in Richmond."

Roarke set the pipe down. "Hance—"

"Won it fair and even in a game of loo, I did!"

"Your mother and I don't hold with gambling, Hance."

"You don't hold with anything I do," Hance fired back. His loud voice startled the baby, who began to wail. Hance snatched her up and stalked from the room.

Genevieve looked after him with a mixture of dismay and affection. Hance simply didn't understand that it wasn't the grandness of the gift that mattered but the spirit in which it was given.

The sound of Matilda's babyish cooing drifted in through the window, and Genevieve smiled. It was uncanny, Hance's attachment to the child. He'd never shown such affection for his other siblings, but right from the start he'd formed an unexpected bond with the infant. Perhaps it was her fair hair and blue eyes, which bore a slight resemblance to Hance's own coloring. Whatever it was, Hance was Matilda's most ardent admirer and her fiercest protector. And oddly, he seemed to need her as much as she needed him.

The mood in the dining room had quieted in the wake of Hance's angry departure. The children ate their cake and kissed their parents, and then Mimi came to put them all to bed. When Genevieve rose to help, Mimi waved her away.

"You just sit back with this old man of yours," she said cheerfully. "Or better yet, take your cider into the keeping room and leave the rest of us to find our ways to bed."

Genevieve sat before the hearth, listening to the ticking of the mantel clock and the sounds of her family settling in for the night upstairs. The back door slammed as Hance returned, his temper somewhat cooler, she hoped. Then Luke howled his older brother's name. The boys had scarcely ever gotten to bed without some sort of tussle. A sharp bark from Mimi silenced them. Israel began to sing tunelessly, as he was wont to do, but that stopped abruptly as it always did; the lad had a gift for falling asleep. Then Matilda fussed until Genevieve heard the rhythmic wooden creak of her cradle being rocked, probably by Hance. Finally, the soft murmur of Rebecca at her prayers could be heard, and then all was quiet.

Genevieve watched Roarke as he stirred the fire and added fuel. Blue flames wrapped themselves around the log, causing it to hiss softly in the settled stillness. Her heart filled with love as she watched him.

She'd never gotten over her astonishment at the depth of their love. Every moment they spent together was a small miracle, precious and fragile, to be guarded and kept close to the heart for safekeeping. Those moments, together with the larger miracles of their children and the success of their farm, brought a perfection to their lives she'd never dared dream of.

"Roarke."

He turned and smiled at the gentle warmth he heard in her voice. She patted the place beside her.

He wrapped her in his arms, inhaling the fragrance of her hair. "Gennie love," he murmured, nuzzling her neck. "Thank you."

She shook her head, tossing her curls. "Don't thank me yet, Roarke. I've not given you anything."

Rich laughter rippled from him. "Only everything a man could ever want."

He reached for her again, but she pushed him aside. Still

smiling, she handed him a small parcel. She pointed to the words she'd written. "For my husband."

He opened it slowly, with relish. With a gasp of pleasure, he held up a silver drinking cup. The metal caught the light as he held it in front of his eyes.

"Gennie, Lord, but it's fine. What's an old lout like me to do with such a fine piece?"

"What does any gentleman do with a proper drinking cup?" She tipped a bit of cider into it and held it to his lips. "You make a toast to your wife."

He raised it obligingly and nodded at her. "To card games," he said in his deep voice.

She lifted an eyebrow at him. "Card games, Roarke? But we don't hold with—"

"Shh," he said. "It'll be our secret. 'Twas a card game that brought you here, to Virginia. And eventually to me." He took a sip with a satisfied smile.

She shook her head. "You're impossible," she said, striking him playfully on the chest.

He brushed his lips over her temple. "Ah, Gennie, have I told you today that I love you?" He scowled a little. "I haven't. Nor did I yesterday, or the day before. I've been remiss, love."

"No, you haven't, Roarke." She nuzzled the warm flesh at the side of his neck. "I've learned that I needn't hear the words day in and day out. I know you love me. I see it in all the little things you do for me, the small smiles meant only for me, the way you hold my hand in church, your incessant boasting about the way I manage the farm . . ."

They came together in a fiercely tender embrace, celebrating their love in a way that transcended words and time.

In a distant part of the house, Matilda cried again. Then the back door slammed, causing Roarke to stiffen. It wasn't the first time Hance had disappeared into the night with Matilda, to whisper secret dreams to the baby under the stars.

Genevieve's brow furrowed. "I feel helpless when it comes to Hance. He seems so unhappy."

"That he does, love."

"It used to be so simple when the things that troubled him were a scraped knee or a stubborn pony. I knew how to fix those things. But now . . ."

Roarke nodded. "I feel the same way. But what can we do, Gennie? We can only give him love and guidance. We can't live his life for him."

"Roarke, do you think he knows?" Genevieve asked suddenly, lowering her voice.

He shook his head. "Of course not," he said curtly. "Mimi would never breathe a word, and Nell Wingfield . . . She's not one to trust, but she's stayed out of our lives."

"But I don't even feel like I know him anymore. Why won't he talk to us, Roarke?"

He shrugged. "He's a thirteen-year-old. Not a man, yet no longer a boy, either. Perhaps the best thing to do is allow him space, and time . . ." He fitted his arm around her and hugged her close. "Let's not worry about it, Gennie, just for tonight."

She kissed him. "Yes," she murmured, inhaling deeply, filling her senses with him. "Tonight, let there just be the two of us . . ." Roarke never let her worry for long.

Hance trudged back up the stairs, his parents' words echoing in his ears. He put Matilda back in her cradle, and she settled softly against her favorite shawl.

Resentment prickled within him. Why did they go on about him, wringing their hands and wondering about their own inadequacies? It was obvious all fault lay with him.

And what were the whispers about? What was it they were hiding from him, that even the razor-tongued Nell Wingfield didn't dare divulge? The secret was something they feared; Hance had heard it in their voices. He supposed it had something to do with his nature, that wild streak in him that even he could not control.

As he slipped into his nightshirt and crept beneath the sheets, taking care not to awaken Luke and Israel, who shared the other bed, Hance swore under his breath. His parents weren't inadequate; quite the opposite. If anything they were almost too indulgent, too forgiving of his many flaws. Genevieve, whom he'd always unabashedly called Mother, went out of her way to give him the same acceptance she gave her own children.

She shouldn't do that, Hance thought. She shouldn't have taken the load of corn to the gristmill last week when that was his duty. She shouldn't spend her money on books for him when she hadn't had a new frock in years. She should expect—demand—more from him.

And he should be willing to give more. Each night he went to sleep resolving to contribute more to the farm, the family. But when day dawned bright and golden, the woods so fragrant and blessedly empty, his good intentions fell away and Hance found himself stealing off to enmesh himself in anything but farming or school with the backwoods parson who could barely spell his own name.

Hance sighed heavily. God knows, he tried. He tried to be a good brother to Luke, but the big, handsome lad seemed to need nothing from his brother. He had no head for book learning, but was possessed of a God-given way of working the land. Never had Luke shown any interest in Hance's enthusiasm for political discussions and the odds of gaming.

Israel, quiet and pensive beyond his years, seemed to have no notion that Hance existed; the little boy's hero was Luke. As for Rebecca, the girl was so wrapped up in her confounded prayers and psalm singing that the only thing she spared for Hance was an occasional fiery condemnation that would do the Reverend Carstairs proud. She was fond of telling Hance that his idleness would lead him into the hands of Satan, occasionally succeeding in making him feel like a sheep-killing dog.

A small mewing cry issued from the room across the hall. Matilda was cutting a mouthful of teeth and had been having trouble sleeping lately. But Hance didn't mind soothing her, no matter how many times she roused him. Matilda was the one member of the family who didn't judge him. Granted, she was an infant, but from the day of her birth they had shared an almost mystical bond, which was Hance's one secret joy.

He padded across the hall to his parents' room, rounding the still-empty bed, and lifted the baby into his arms. Sighing, Hance rubbed his chin over the fine wisps of fair hair and inhaled Matilda's warm, milky fragrance. She quieted as soon as she recognized her brother and settled comfortably into the crook of his arm.

"There you are, little one," Hance whispered. "Did something give you a fright?"

She blinked and worked a tiny thumb into her mouth, giving Hance a look that made his heart swell. Grabbing a shawl from the cradle, he made his way down the back stairs again and out into the warm, dark yard.

It was a soft night of late summer, alive with the chirrups of crickets and tree frogs and the scents of ripening crops and mountain laurel. The new moon, with the old moon cradled in her arms, rose in a star-sprayed sky, hanging above the Blue Ridge and illuminating its rippling peaks. Across the towering barrier was an awesome forest, a patchwork of oak openings and prairie drained by a huge system of rivers and streams.

"See that, Mattie?" Hance said. "That's the Blue Ridge. There's a whole part of Virginia out there that we've never even seen, called Kentucky. Mr. Daniel Boone spied it all out, once upon a time."

Matilda waved a chubby fist toward the mountains.

"Me, too," Hance said, interpreting her gesture. "I'd like to go beyond the mountains, to the other side of the world. Reckon I will one day, and I'll take you with me, little sister."

The baby squirmed and burrowed her face into his shoulder with a small sound of contentment.

"Lord, but I love you, Mattie," Hance told her gruffly. She was the only one he could say those words to. Stroking the moist softness of her cheek, he smiled. And she answered him, wordlessly, with a round-eyed stare and a gurgle of unmistakable contentment.

16

Above the mantel the clock ticked ominously, ceaselessly, breaking the stillness in the house with its age-old rhythm. Summer blazed again over the land at the foot of the Blue Ridge, but Genevieve and Roarke sat gripped by the bitter chill of terror.

Outside, another rhythm could be heard: the sound of Luke's ax descending again and again on a log. It was his way of coping with the tragedy in the house, a way to empty his mind of everything but the screaming protest of his aching muscles.

Below the window, Hance and Rebecca argued volubly, raising their voices over Israel's confused sobbing.

"She'll be an angel soon," Rebecca insisted.

"Oh?" Hance asked cuttingly. "And what the hell is Mattie now, the devil's spawn at the ripe old age of three? Christ, Becky, what good are all your hymns and prayers if this is what your God does?"

"Hance," she gasped, "listen to yourself. You're talking blas-blasphony!"

He snorted derisively at her mispronunciation. But when she began to cry, he softened a little. "Go on and pray,

Becky, if it comforts you. But don't expect me to join you. Mattie already is an angel and always has been. No amount of psalm singing will convince me that this is just."

Inside the house, Genevieve agreed. She couldn't tear her eyes from Matilda, who lay flushed and wheezing in her arms, as she had for two days now.

"Let me take her, love," Roarke offered, his voice ragged with fatigue. "You'd best try to eat something, take a nap—"

"No. No, I've little enough time with her as it is." Genevieve shuddered at the sound of her own words. Shuddered because she'd spoken the awful, dark, gut-twisting truth. Matilda had lung fever, and it was eating up her barely lived life with dreadful speed.

"Oh, God, Roarke," Genevieve said. "Oh, God, I can't stand this . . ." The words came quietly, suffused with the full horror of all she felt.

"I know, love," he said. Unshed tears roughened his voice. "I know. Sweet Christ, I feel helpless." They'd had the doctor from town, and Mimi with her Indian remedies, and Mimsy Greenleaf, who years ago had lost one of her own to the same raging disease. But none of them could help.

Roarke lowered himself to the bed where Genevieve sat with the child and encircled them both with his arms. Sensing his presence through her delirium, Matilda clutched at his sleeve with a fever-flushed hand. Her eyes, tiny slits of blue in her swollen face, regarded him with confusion. Matilda was unable to comprehend the pain she was in.

"Oh, please, God spare her," Genevieve murmured. But she knew her prayer would be ignored. Matilda was too weak and small to battle the fires of this illness. She grew more feeble with each passing moment.

Genevieve tore her eyes away from the child and gave Roarke a tortured look. "What can we do?"

"Nothing," he told her. He wished he could comfort his wife in this time of aching sadness, but his own sense of grief and hopelessness equaled hers. " 'Tis the greatest ill we could ever be dealt, Gennie."

Her tears splashed down on Matilda's shawl. "How will we go on after this?" she asked brokenly.

"I don't know, love. I don't know. We have the others . . ." His voice trailed off. There was no comfort in that. The preciousness of all the other children could never fill the void Matilda would leave in their lives.

There was a sound of muffled protest outside the door—Mimi's voice. And then the door was pushed open.

"Hance, no!" Genevieve said, instinctively drawing the child against her. "The fever—"

"Fever be damned," Hance growled. "I'm sick of waiting out there, not knowing—"

Genevieve opened her mouth to protest again, but Roarke stopped her. "Let him, Gennie," he said quietly, and motioned Hance to the bed.

The boy shot his father a grateful look and approached slowly, fearfully. It wasn't the disease he was afraid of but of what he was about to see. Genevieve pulled back the blankets to reveal Matilda's pitifully flushed face.

He drew his breath in sharply. Even his darkest imaginings hadn't prepared him for this. Matilda looked unutterably fragile, her flesh burning beneath his touch, her breathing the faintest of wheezes, like dead leaves rustling in the wind.

Genevieve winced at the look on Hance's face: the disbelief as he stared at the baby, the naked terror that haunted and darkened his sky-blue eyes.

"She's very sick, Hance," she said quietly.

"She's dying." The words were torn from him.

Roarke put a hand on Hance's shoulder. "There's nothing we can do, son. Nothing but wait, and hold on to each other."

"Let me have her."

Woodenly, Genevieve handed him the child. With heartaching tenderness, Hance gathered her to his chest and turned away, toward the window.

The dormer gave out to the west. Hance's gaze moved restlessly over the acres of the farm. The gnarled white oak where he'd pushed Matilda in her swing, laughing as she

squealed, "Higher! Higher!" The patch of green where
they'd lain on their bellies, their chins tickled by soft grass as
they watched a cricket. In the distance the Blue Ridge
brooded in its soft haze, changeless, ever present.

"See it, Mattie?" Hance whispered. "See the Blue Ridge?
I said I'd take you there some day—to see the other side of
the world."

For a brief moment the glazed look left her eyes, and she
turned her face toward the light. Her dry lips curved into a
ghost of her sunny smile, as if forgiving Hance for not fulfilling his promise. Stricken to his core, Hance brought her
back to Genevieve.

The child's mouth formed the words "Mama" and
"Papa." Then she turned her face into Genevieve's chest and
died with the softest of sighs.

Genevieve felt the life shudder out of her child. She, too,
stopped breathing, her throat constricting painfully. But she
wasn't granted the mercy of death. Inevitably, she dragged
in a reluctant breath. She had to go on. She had to spend a
lifetime missing her baby.

Roarke took Matilda and covered the rapidly cooling
face with kisses, his entire body convulsed with ragged sobs.

"No." Hance whispered the word, desperately, stepping
back. Then he ran to the window and gripped the sill and
repeated his denial, screaming it this time.

Days of warmth and brilliant light ended the summer of
1790. The crops grew straight and tall, yielding bounty. But
within the family all was darkness. Genevieve went through
the motions of living, drawing her children to her with desperate ferocity. But there was a gaping hole within her heart
that couldn't be filled, not by Luke's steadfastness, nor Rebecca's constant prayers, nor Israel's quiet affection, nor
even the grief-tinged sweetness of Roarke's abiding love.

The farm prospered, and the children grew. Eventually,
Genevieve learned to smile again, but it was a smile haunted
by sadness, for life was no longer a dream fulfilled. The

nightmare of Matilda's death colored everything in shades of bleakness.

Hance was inconsolable. The one thing he'd loved above all others had been snatched from him. Unlike his parents, who grieved in quiet desperation, Hance raged. His temper flared at the slightest provocation. His absences became more frequent, longer. Often he escaped to Richmond, seeking out the lowliest of taverns, drinking and wenching himself into a state of torpor.

"I'm worried about him, Roarke," Genevieve said as they lay together in the dark one night. "I'm worried about the company he keeps and the things he does when he's away."

"I've tried to talk to him about it, love," Roarke said. He sighed and flung his arm over his brow. "But I can't stop him. If I'm too hard on him, we'll lose him completely."

"He's so angry, Roarke."

"Aye. At all the world and at himself, too, I think."

"People in town talk. They swear he'll come to a bad end."

"Do you believe that, Gennie?"

"I don't know. There's so much good in him, Roarke, so much he could share. But he keeps it all to himself."

He stroked her hair, weaving his fingers into soft curls. "He knows we're here, should he need us. 'Tis all we can do, love."

Genevieve hoped that a baby would come of that night, and all the years of nights that followed. She still loved Roarke desperately, even more deeply now with the tragedy they'd shared. A baby would give her new hope, new faith. But the fulfillment Genevieve longed for eluded her. It seemed she was as barren as the region of her heart Matilda had occupied.

17

"*Hance has a* gi-irl! Hance has a gi-irl!" Luke skipped around the periphery of the big new meeting hall, within earshot but out of fist range of his seventeen-year-old brother. Dancers swung each other about to a fiddler's scratchy tunes, creating patterns of gay cotton dresses and bright hunting shirts. Dusty boots beat a steady tattoo on the puncheon floor, the rhythm echoed by clapping.

Genevieve looked over Roarke's shoulder at Luke, who was darting about and grinning audaciously. The boy took every opportunity to tease Hance unmercifully, but it wasn't malicious teasing. And Luke was always careful to choose a time when Hance was too preoccupied with other things to retaliate.

"I think Luke's right," she said to Roarke as they moved among the circle of dancers. "Hance is smitten with Jane Carstairs."

Roarke chuckled. "And she with him, I'll wager."

"Why not?" Genevieve questioned. "He's handsome as the devil, with all that golden hair and his sparkling blue eyes. When he's not in a temper about something, he can be quite charming."

"Aye. But why the parson's daughter, of all the girls in town?"

Genevieve frowned. "Roarke, what are you saying?"

"That I don't trust the lad's manners," he admitted. "I don't believe much of my teaching took hold."

He squeezed her hand as they watched Hance and Jane slip out the door into the quiet summer evening.

"Hance has a gi-irl!"

Hance cringed a little as Luke's taunts came floating out after them. "Damn the little whippersnapper," he grumbled. "Rattles on like a bell clapper up a goose's ass. I'll give him what for when we get home."

"Hance," Jane gasped, "you shouldn't swear."

He laughed and laid his arm across her shoulder. Fascination always outweighed her outrage. "I've heard that before."

"You should pay it some mind then."

"Now, Janie, don't you start in on me. I get it bad enough from Rebecca. I swear my sister'd put even your father to shame with all her sermons and psalm singing."

"I haven't seen you at meeting lately, Hance," she reminded him.

He waved his hand. "And you're not likely to, Janie."

"Papa told me to stay away from you. Said you consorted with the Harpers. Said you were wild and unsettled."

Hance laughed. "So I am, honey. But—" he caught her against him, smiling at her soft gasp of surprise and pleasure —"that's what you like about me, isn't it?" He leaned down toward her pretty face, lips seeking hers.

She protested, but Jane always did. Just like she always gave in eventually. After a few moments her obligatory struggling ceased, and she softened in his arms. Hance covered her mouth with his while his hands slid over her ripe, young body. Urgency thundered through his veins, and he strained against her.

"Janie," he murmured against her lips. "Oh, honey . . ."

Hance knew far more of women than most boys his age. But his experience was with tavern girls. Jane was different, because she was so very proper—the preacher's daughter, as clean and fresh as new print on a Bible page.

Hance wanted to be the first one to write on that page. He'd been months working Jane up to this point . . .

He fitted his hand between their bodies, inhaling expectantly when his fingers splayed out over the rise of her breast. He'd never been so bold with Jane, but tonight, surrounded by the music of crickets and the smells of honeysuckle and budding sassafras, the moment seemed right. Just right . . . His hand slid down into the bodice of her dress. The warm, satiny feel of her flesh ignited the firestorm within him to new heights. Surely, she would yield to him now. Surely—

He was amazed that such a petite girl could possess such strength. Jane placed her hands against his chest and gave a mighty heave, causing him to stumble back.

"How dare you, Hance Adair?" she cried, hands flying to her flushed cheeks in mortification.

Confused and frustrated desire caused a buzzing in his head. He regarded the girl curiously. "Come on now, Janie, I was only—"

"I know exactly what you were trying to do," she stormed, wrapping her arms across her chest as if to shield herself from him.

"Where's the wrong in it? We're courting, aren't we?"

"We *were.*" Jane folded her lips into a prim line. "But not anymore, Hance. You're nothing but a rutting mule. Papa said you weren't good enough for me, and he's right."

"Janie—"

"Stay away from me, Hance. Go back to your fancy girls in Richmond. You deserve them."

With that, she flounced away in a flurry of calico and petticoats. Hance watched, amazed, as she paused at the door of the meeting hall, linked her arm with Peter Hinton's and strolled off with him.

Hance stiffened at the sound of laughter nearby. Sharp amusement, with a derisive quality, drifted through the scented air. Nell Wingfield appeared from the shadows near the meeting hall.

"Poor Hance," she cooed huskily. "I'm afraid you've got a lot to learn where girls are concerned."

"Excuse me, Miss Wingfield." He tried to push past her, but she placed herself in his way, holding a small silver whiskey bottle to his lips. Unthinkingly, he drank and was surprised at the smooth quality of the whiskey.

"Remember that taste," Nell said, smiling at his expression. "You'll never want raw corn whiskey or hard cider again."

Hance took another sip. This time he returned her smile. She really was a pretty woman. Years past girlhood, of course, but with a firm, generous body and lips that looked as if they could devour a man whole.

When she led him away from the meeting hall, off into the dark and up the road to her house, Hance knew he'd taste more than Nell's whiskey before the night was out. He'd already forgotten Janie Carstairs.

"Luther!" Genevieve hurried to the dock where he was climbing from his barge. "Did you see Hance when you were in Richmond? Lord, he's been away so long, nearly a year."

Luther Quaid took her arm and drew her aside. As they headed toward the trading post, he handed her a packet. "Corn prices are up again. You're going to be a wealthy woman someday."

Genevieve put the money away with a shrug. "We already have everything we need. Israel's turning into something of a scholar, though. We'll be sending him up to Williamsburg for a proper education when he gets older." She looked down at her hands, no longer roughened by labor. Lately, the most treacherous tool they wielded was her quill.

"Sometimes I think we have too much. There are days when Roarke simply sits idle, watching the farm prosper. It's almost as if the place doesn't need us anymore." She frowned at Luther. "You're avoiding my question about Hance."

He nodded and rubbed his hand thoughtfully on the sleeve of his doeskin shirt. "I seen him, Genevieve. He's living in a rooming house in Marshall Street, a fairly decent place. Has a decent job, too. He works for Horace Rathford."

"The assemblyman?"

Luther nodded. "I understand Hance takes care of his correspondence, runs errands and such."

"So why didn't you want to tell me, Luther?"

"He lives in a flamboyant manner, I guess you could say. Rathford's a mite fond of the lad; tends to fawn over him. I'm afraid Hance has a taste for the gaming tables, and women." Luther gave Genevieve a sideways glance. "Jamaica water, too, and . . ."

Genevieve pressed her lips together. What more could there be?

Luther shuffled his feet, looking ill at ease. "Look, Genevieve, maybe I shouldn't—"

"Luther, *please*."

"Fourteen slaves escaped from the Whitney plantation last week. Both Hance and Calvin Greenleaf were questioned about it. And not very kindly, I'm afraid."

Genevieve shook her head, not at all surprised. She'd never regret that she'd taught Hance to hate slavery, but she wished he could find a less dangerous way to hate it. And she wished, for the Greenleafs' sake, that Calvin would use a bit more discretion in his fight against the institution. Planters around Richmond were quick to distrust a black freedman, quicker still to hang one they didn't like.

Genevieve was seized by an inexplicable sense of foreboding when she said goodbye to Roarke the next day. They both knew his trip to Richmond would prove futile, for Hance was no farmer. It was absurd, she told herself, to have this sudden attack of nerves on a day when the January sky was as blue as a jay's wing and winter's chill had given way to brief warmth.

Added to that was her sense that she was falling ill. She'd been so tired these last few weeks, barely able to rise in the morning. Food nauseated her and—

"Sweet, merciful God," she breathed, clutching at Roarke.

"What is it, Gennie?"

She looked at him in confusion, almost afraid to speak. And then her foreboding was forgotten as joy blossomed in her heart. How stupid she'd been, not recognizing the signs that had once been so familiar to her.

She collapsed, laughing, against Roarke's chest. "I'm pregnant," she told him, suddenly suffused by a feeling that had been absent for years. A warm, protective feeling of contentment, a prelude to the nesting instinct that would come later.

Roarke recovered from his surprise and swept her up into his arms, swinging her about as rich laughter rippled from him.

"That's fine, Gennie love," he told her, setting her down gently. "That's just fine. 'Tis time we had a baby about the house again."

Her breath caught at the roughness she heard in his voice. The void Matilda's death had left in their lives was still there, contemplated during quiet moments, shading all the events of their lives like a small, gloomy cloud. Even a new baby wouldn't change that. But it was something to hope for, a new object for their love.

Roarke gave Genevieve a lingering kiss. "Hance will welcome the news. I'll hurry back," he promised. "Take care of yourself."

The news should have explained her foreboding, but it didn't. Within moments after Roarke left, she was seized again by a chilly feeling that she couldn't bring herself to think about.

*   *   *

"I swear, you're ornery as Balaam's ass, Becky—put that darned book away and help me," Luke said irritably, lifting a newly riven oak rail onto the ones below it. The bottom rails had gone gray and rotten over the years; it was time for a new zigzag fence of fresh, pale oak.

Rebecca frowned. " 'Tis the Good Book, Luke, and you've said a profanity about it."

"Well, it's no help in mending fences. Pick up that other end, will you?"

She sighed and slipped the small volume into her apron pocket. Her red calf-bound Bible, together with a small wooden bear that spun on a rod, had been gifts from Roarke for her tenth birthday. Prized gifts, beloved ones, from the father she worshiped almost as fervently as she worshiped her Lord.

"I don't see why we have to do this anyway," she complained. "Papa's fence was perfectly good—"

"This is better," Luke said with certainty, fitting the rail snugly in place. "I want to finish by the time Pa gets home from Richmond, to surprise him."

They worked in silence for a while. At age eleven, Luke was a big, strapping lad with a good mind for building things and an eye for useful innovation. Rebecca, a year his junior, was a sturdy little girl with a headful of tumbling, ginger-colored curls that defied the bonnet she tried to tuck them into. She was hard-working, although she showed a marked preference for reading her Bible and singing hymns over everyday work about the farm. As she worked, she began to sing, pausing between verses of a Watts hymn to stick her tongue out at Luke, who pretended to be in real distress over her singing. He began splitting more rails with the maul, trying to drown her out with its rhythmic thud.

"Well, well," said a harsh voice behind them, "what a godly little pair the two of you make."

Luke set down the maul and snatched off his hat. "Hello, Miss Wingfield," he said, unsmiling. He knew little of the woman from the other side of town, only that she'd been a Tory during the war and that the men she hired to work her farm, including the notorious Harper brothers, weren't of the very best character.

Unlike his parents, Luke knew why Hance had left Dancer's Meadow the spring before. Almost immediately after setting the town on its ear by forsaking Janie Carstairs when all the world expected them to marry, Hance had taken up with Miss Wingfield. He was discreet about it, going on foot so his horse wouldn't be recognized outside her house, but Luke shared a room with Hance. Night after night he'd awakened to the smell of whiskey and sharp, floral perfume. And the sound of Hance murmuring his lover's name as he slept off the drink and the passion.

And then Hance had left. Luke guessed that at last, Hance hadn't been able to abide a liaison with a woman old enough to be his mother.

Luke didn't like Nell Wingfield. Didn't like her strangely accented voice or the cloud of too-yellow frizz that framed her painted face or the unexplained animosity between her and his mother or the way she used to look at Hance.

"What can I do for you, ma'am?" he asked warily. Miss Wingfield didn't make social calls. She only appeared, with her false red smile and her husky voice, when she wanted something.

"I'd hoped your father could help me. One of my Negroes ran off two months ago, and three of my hands are laid up with the ague. I've a load of corn that needs to be brought down to the docks."

"Papa's away," Rebecca said, pressing her lips together in disapproval. Miss Wingfield's corn became whiskey—the highest quality, some said, but whiskey nonetheless. Nervously, Rebecca took out the little bear her father had carved her and began toying with it.

Nell sighed. "I don't know what I'll do, then." She eyed Luke keenly, as if just seeing him for the first time. Her gaze took in his green eyes, bright as sun-shot leaves, and the burnished red color of his hair.

"You favor your father," she said, her frank stare lingering on his freckled face. She gave Rebecca a slight nod. "You've your father's coloring but your mother's face."

Rebecca dipped slightly. "Thank you, ma'am." She knew full well Miss Wingfield hadn't meant it as a compliment. The woman hated Mama.

"Come along, then," Nell said briskly, turning away. "There's work to be done."

"Sorry, ma'am," Luke said mildly. "But we've work to do here."

Miss Wingfield drew herself up, eyes narrowed in anger. She looked about, down at the reed-fringed river bank and then at the rise of meadow land that obscured the house. "You've your parents' bad manners as well," she snapped, reaching out and gripping Rebecca by the arm.

"Let go of her," Luke said, his voice trembling with a quiet warning. "Let my sister go."

The reeds parted slightly as an angular, copper-hued face stared out at the three people above. Thin lips curled into a grin as the brave looked back at his companion.

"Thirteen summers, Meseka," he whispered. "Thirteen summers it's taken me. At last I've found him."

The other brave shook his head; the feathers that adorned his braids brushed against the reeds. "That is not your soldier, Black Bear."

"I know that. But we have found his woman and children. Hair like the flames of the council fire—I've seen it only one other time." The brave narrowed his good eye at his quarry and growled low in his throat. "It is even better than I'd hoped. I swore revenge on Roarke Adair for killing my father and brother. They were your people, too, Meseka."

He watched the small group above the river bank. The woman was berating the youngsters, who faced her with belligerence. "The white man prizes his family above his own life. Our payment shall come from Roarke Adair's family." He nodded at the woman, who was speaking irritably to the children. "She will be difficult. So will the boy. We'll kill him and take the woman and girl."

"Let us be quick about this, Black Bear," Meseka

warned. "Our kind no longer strays so deep into the white man's territory."

"It is well, then. We shall have no trouble surprising them."

In stealthy silence they prepared themselves, extracting several lengths of rawhide from their canoe and looping it into their breechclouts. Then, gripping finely honed tomahawks and knives of vicious steel, they leaped from the reeds, screaming with vengeful fury.

18

Roarke trudged up to the house, his mind far more weary than his legs, which had been hugging horse-flesh for too many days. He wondered how he would tell Genevieve about Hance. There was no kind way to put it, no way to disguise what Hance had become.

God, he didn't even know the boy anymore. The dandified townsman was a stranger to him, all brash talk and freewheeling ways, living a life Roarke didn't even want to understand.

He'd found Hance at Eagle Tavern, wearing a suit of clothes that would, years ago, have done Dandy Dunmore proud. Lace at his throat and wrists, a silk handkerchief protruding from the pocket of his embroidered frock coat. Roarke couldn't blame the ladies of the tavern for flirting with Hance, but the sight of Horace Rathford, so fawning in the attention he gave the young man, had given Roarke an unpleasant jolt. The middle-aged assemblyman commanded more respect and affection from Hance than Roarke ever had.

Roarke pulled the front door open to an odd absence of noise. The mantel clock's ticking sounded like thunder in the silence. Ordinarily, the children would hurl themselves at him, begging to know what he'd brought them and fighting to be the first to tell jumbled stories of a just-born calf, a newly lost tooth, a particularly brave injury.

Roarke went into the keeping room. It was dusk, and they would be sitting together after supper, Rebecca and Israel taking turns reading from the big Asbury family Bible.

Rebecca was nowhere in sight. Israel was reading in a faltering voice. " 'Deliver me, O Lord, from the evil man, preserve me from the violent man; which imagine mischiefs in their heart . . .' "

"There's my family," Roarke boomed good-naturedly. "Come, who has a hug for Papa?" Israel set down the book and flung himself into Roarke's arms. But he said nothing. He was more serious than usual; somber, even.

Roarke looked over the boy's tousled head at Genevieve, suddenly seized by a dark feeling of dread.

"Gennie, where's Rebecca? What—"

She took Israel by the shoulders and propelled him from the room. "Go help Mimi in the kitchen," she said. Israel obeyed with uncharacteristic muteness. Then Genevieve turned to Luke, who toyed absently with the dancing bear Roarke had given Rebecca, looking slightly dazed. His head was wrapped with a white bandage.

"Go with your brother, Luke," Genevieve said.

He tilted his chin to a mutinous angle, clutching the toy to his chest. "I'm staying. Papa'll hear it from me, since I'm the one responsible."

"Good God, lad," Roarke said. "Don't keep me waiting."

The boy's face was a mask of dreadful calm as he struggled to keep his voice even. "Two weeks ago, Becky and I were mending the fence down by the river. Miss Wingfield came by wanting something or other . . ." Luke took a long, shuddering breath and absently fingered Rebecca's toy.

"Two redskins jumped out of the bushes. I tried to stop them, honest, Pa! But they clubbed me good. Tried to scalp me, too, but Becky set to screaming so loud I guess they got scared." Luke's hand crept to a fading bluish bruise that peeped out from beneath the bandage. "They knocked me out cold, Pa. And—" finally his voice broke, and a huge tear crept down his pale, freckled cheek "—they took Becky and Miss Wingfield, Pa. Took them clean away while I was lying there."

Panic rocketed through Roarke. He looked helplessly from Genevieve to Luke. A dreadful pounding began in his ears. It was too much to comprehend. His Rebecca—his shy, pious little girl who'd never harmed a soul in her life—was gone, kidnapped by redskins. It was inconceivable. But he heard the truth in Genevieve's quiet, desperate crying and Luke's ragged, tortured sobs.

Roarke strained against the impulse to go charging up the river after her. He would do so, of course, but not before he had time to prepare himself.

"What's been done so far?" he asked tightly.

"I wanted to go after them, Pa," Luke said. "But Mama wouldn't let me."

"Luther Quaid went," Genevieve explained.

"And?"

"He returned two days ago, to report that they'd killed Elkanah Harper's wife, Fannie. She'd been gathering sage in the hills . . . Elk and his boys are searching now, too. Luther managed to follow the Indians up into the Blue Ridge, but they discovered him. They nearly killed him, Roarke. He was shot in the shoulder. Lord knows how he managed to find his way back."

The thunder in Roarke's ears pounded even more furiously. "The Indians—tell me about them."

Luke shivered and shifted his gaze to the hearth, where a small pile of coals glowed dully in the grate. "Shawnee," he said, wiping his nose with his sleeve. "Mr. Quaid said so. Faces painted red and black. One of them had an eye put out. It was all sort of grown over and scarred like."

A hard lump settled in Roarke's gut. Black Bear. He'd known it when Luke had first mentioned redskins. At last, just when Roarke's memories of the frontier campaigns were growing hazy and dimmed by time, the old enmity had resurfaced.

He ground a fist into his hand. How had Black Bear found him? He must have been searching for years, haunting every little hamlet and outpost in Virginia with a Shawnee's single-minded determination. His warrior's guile and cunning had served him well; he'd gone straight for the heart.

In the privacy of their room that night, Roarke was about to tell Genevieve about Hance. He changed his mind when she turned to him, eyes brimming with tears.

"I've no daughters left," she whispered, trembling in the crook of his arm. "No one to pick flowers with . . ."

"Gennie . . ."

She laid her hand alongside his cheek, shaking her head with heartaching sadness. "In a way, it's worse than Matilda. At least with Mattie we *knew*, Roarke, as awful as it was."

"Becky lives," he told her firmly, steadying her shuddering shoulders with a gentle squeeze. "She lives, and I'll find her, Gennie. I know Kentucky; I know Black Bear. I won't rest until his blood drenches my hands and I can feel my arms around Rebecca and smell her hair and hear her sweet voice again."

Genevieve shivered at the vow. She'd never known Roarke to be vengeful, to desire another's death.

Roarke agreed to wait until morning before he set out for the frontier. He held Genevieve against him, running his hand over the soft mound of her belly, where the baby was already in evidence.

"Gennie, will you be all right?"

He felt her nod against his shoulder. "I'll manage. Joshua will help with the farm." She propped herself up on one elbow and traced the side of his face with a finger. "But there won't be a minute, Roarke Adair, that I won't be missing you and my Becky." She clasped him fiercely to her and gave him a kiss of tenderness and need.

Their loving was sadly sweet, tinged with desperation. Neither would admit to the chilling possibility that they might never touch again.

*　　*　　*

Kentucky had changed. In the years since the birth of the new nation, its population had burgeoned to well over seventy thousand, if the figures Roarke had heard could be credited. Families from every part of the union were flooding to the fertile valleys and rippling grasslands that graced Kentucky, which had achieved statehood in 1792.

Roarke rode into Lexington, his supplies nearly gone, his horse hanging its head in exhaustion. But even through his fatigue and worry, he was able to appreciate how the town had grown. Once it had been a tottering collection of blockhouses in the middle of a canebrake; now it boasted cleared streets and solid buildings and a population of settled townsfolk. He sought lodging at a tavern called the Sheaf of Wheat, on Broadway, settling back to sip whiskey and plan his next move. Other men milled about the taproom, laughing raucously, joking among themselves.

"Well, lookee there, Beelzebub," drawled a voice. "'Tis our old friend Roarke Adair."

Roarke came to his feet and clasped Will Coomes's calloused hand.

"And I mean *old*," Coomes continued, his sharp eyes roving over his friend. "By Job, Roarke, you look like the years've been pressing upon your shoulders."

"Sit down, Will," Roarke said. "What the devil are you doing here, anyway? I thought you'd be settled down with your girl from Pennsylvania."

Coomes shook his head. "All through the war, I thought Livvie was in my blood. But 'twasn't her at all; it was this dad-blamed fine wilderness. Commands me like no mistress ever could. I couldn't stay away." He sipped his whiskey and studied Roarke, eyeing the fans of fatigue about his eyes and the look of utter bleakness that tugged down the corners of his mouth.

"What of you, my friend?" Coomes asked quietly.

Roarke's fist clenched around his clay cup. "I'm back because of Black Bear. He took my little girl."

Will said nothing but caught his breath with a hiss of fury.

Roarke's knuckles whitened, and the cup shattered in his hand, the liquid bleeding across the wooden table. "God almighty," he swore, "I showed that devil mercy back at Vincennes. I let him live, so he could do this to me."

"You knew better than to expect gratitude," Coomes reminded him. "You robbed him of an honorable death. A death he probably craved." Then he stood up.

"Give me an hour, Roarke," he said.

Roarke frowned. "An hour?"

Coomes gave him a crooked grin. "That's how long it'll take for me and Beelzebub to gear up for this hunt."

"You don't have to do this, Will."

Coomes grinned and hefted his rifle. "Hear that, Beelzebub? The man's tryin' to do us out of a fine adventure." He looked back at Roarke. "One hour. And then we head north, into Indian country."

Kentucky was still a place of majestic forests and rushing blue rivers shadowed by high, cave-dotted shelves. But now there was evidence of settlement; every so often they passed a centerless small community huddled against the threatening wilderness, locked around a narrow valley of hills and hollows. Even in the deepest woods they spied a big chestnut oak that had been skinned for its tanbark and left to die.

Traveling as they had in their campaigning days, Roarke and Will crossed the flatlands and climbed northward, to the wind-swept region of the Blue Licks, where salt bubbled up from the springs. They crossed the Ohio, wending their way along an old trace to the upper reaches of the Scioto.

They knew better than to attempt secrecy. This was the heart of Shawnee territory. Indian scouts were on intimate terms with every crook of the river, every patch of ground that was amenable to making a campfire.

The village was a cluster of wooden shelters. Children and dogs played in the dust beneath budding locust trees.

Women worked at their cooking and weaving chores, while the men sat in clustered groups, talking among themselves.

"What do you think?" Coomes whispered to Roarke. They had dismounted and were leading their horses up an overgrown deer trace, shielded by a midsummer canopy of murky green woods.

"I've been searching for six months," Roarke said darkly. "I aim to go in there and get my girl back."

"Just like that, eh?"

Roarke shrugged. "I've brought enough whiskey to gag a buffalo, and plenty of trinkets, too."

They approached the village openly in the full noontide sun of a balmy July day. The Indians were waiting for them; they'd probably been spotted days ago. People in Indian and Western dress gathered about the council house, looking more curious than hostile. There was a time when a lone white man had been an immediate target. But now the enemy was different. The unending tide of land-hungry settlers threatened the Indians, not the wandering frontier hunters.

Roarke held up his hand and spoke, retrieving the few words of Shawnee he'd picked up during the war years.

"Black Bear," he said. "Is he here?"

An aging chief wearing a headdress of fur stepped forward. A network of time-worn lines crept across his ancient face.

"Who are you?" His words whistled from the many gaps in his teeth.

"I am Roarke Adair. I seek the brave called Black Bear."

"Roarke Adair," the chief repeated, loudly so that all could hear. Then he spoke in English. "You killed Black Bear's father and brother. You dishonored him."

"His quarrel is with me. Not with my daughter and the woman he took."

The chief contemplated this for a moment. "You make bold to come here."

"I mean to settle things with Black Bear. Where is he?"

The chief gestured to the west. "Our people disperse like seeds to the wind. There is no room to share the bounty of the land, not when the white man stakes out claims as if trying to own a piece of the sky."

Roarke gave him some tobacco and a warm Dutch blanket along with several pieces of silver. The chief walked with him to the edge of the village. They stood on a grassy knoll, looking down at an endless expanse of green hills and dark forests. It was as wild a land as Roarke had ever seen, alive with birdsong and the soughing of the wind.

"She is out there," he said.

The chief nodded. "You will have to kill Black Bear to get her."

Roarke adjusted the brim of his hat. "I know. I should have finished our quarrel when we last met."

The chief turned and looked at the knot of braves behind him, who were arguing and gesturing.

Sadness pulled the lines of the old chief's face downward. "There are others who would quarrel with you, Roarke Adair. You and your friend both."

Roarke frowned at the braves, who had begun calling orders to the villagers. People lined the path to the council house, arming themselves with thorn-spiked sticks and whips of willow and wild grapevine.

Will Coomes swallowed hard and addressed the chief. "See here now, we're just passin' through. We've brought gifts—"

The old man shook his head. "You have intruded upon our lives. For that you must run the gauntlet."

"And if we refuse . . . ?" Roarke questioned.

Before the chief could answer, Roarke and Will were seized from behind, divested of all but their breeches, and brought to the head of the path. There was no question of a struggle.

"This is one thing I hoped I'd never be called on to do," Will said faintly. "Jesus, they're like a pack of baited dogs."

Roarke nodded. Lust for vengeance showed in the faces lining the path, in the fists clenched around the weapons.

"I don't wonder that they're eager to lay into us," Roarke said. "How many of them have lost a loved one to the white man?"

"Doesn't matter that it wasn't our doing," Coomes added glumly. "We'll pay the price. What'll it be, Roarke, me first, or you?"

"I'll go," Roarke said, straightening his shoulders. Privately, he hoped the Indians would spend their fury on his hide, sparing Will some of the pain. A look of determination hardened his face, and the Indians fell silent, watching him, tensing in anticipation.

The cry of a catbird rose up, and the wind hissed through the trees beside the river. Roarke flung his head back and stepped to the head of the double row of Indians. They stayed quiet, watching him, studying the play of sunlight across the breadth of his bare chest, the shafts of light that burnished his hair to a fiery crown of red and gold.

Roarke fastened his eyes on the council house, trying to empty his mind of the torture to come. He conjured up images of Rebecca: her sweet, earnest face, her voice lifted in pious song. Gathering the image about him like steel armor, Roarke plunged down the path.

Cries filled the air. Leather and green wood bit into the flesh of his back, his shoulders, his neck, stinging, laying open livid weals. Stones grazed his head and face, almost stunning him. Roarke stumbled but wove his way relentlessly to the council house. To fall would be to capitulate, to admit weakness.

And that Roarke would never do.

He reached the council house without having tasted the dust of the path in his mouth. Dripping with sweat and gore, he turned to face his tormentors.

Their disappointment at not having broken him was a fleeting thing. The Shawnee were great admirers of physical strength and stamina; that he'd weathered their torture meant he was worthy. They yelled approval to him.

As Roarke had hoped, the fury had lessened somewhat when Coomes ran the gauntlet. He endured it bravely, only staggering when he reached the council house.

Their wounds were cleaned with mineral-rich spring water, salved by bethroot poultices, and bound with cloth.

They were given a meal of venison and hominy mush sweetened with maple sugar, served in geode bowls.

Only when sparks rose from the council fires to the darkening sky above were the new adoptees allowed to rest.

Hours later a slight shuffling roused Roarke. He propped himself up on one elbow, blinking at the yellow brilliance of a late-morning sun.

A child of perhaps five stood in front of him, gnawing shyly on one finger and gazing at him with huge eyes.

Roarke blinked again. Those eyes . . . He'd never seen the like on an Indian before. They were a startling color of blue, so light and clear that they reminded him of a piece of the summer sky. He sat up and studied the child more closely.

Beneath a good covering of grime and bear grease, she was beautiful, a tiny, delicate woodsprite who had no business living the rough and tumble life of the Shawnee. A little turned-up nose, lovely pink lips pressed into a somber line, dainty hands and feet.

Roarke chanced a smile. It must have looked as bad as it hurt, his lips split and swollen by the previous day's rain of stones and whips.

But the child didn't flinch. She merely continued to stare until someone called out.

"Mariah! Where've you gotten to, girl?"

Roarke was startled to hear the King's English. Then a memory, dimmed by nearly fifteen years and a thousand miles, rushed back to him, and he staggered to his feet.

"Amy Parker," he said. "By God, Amy, it's you."

But he was looking at a stranger. A woman who was neither Indian nor white, but a strange mixture of the two; a combination that wasn't attractive. The years had streaked her hair gray and added sagging flesh to her doeskin-clad figure. A bulge in her midsection hinted that yet another birth would further mar her shape. The little girl sought refuge in Amy's ash-smudged skirts.

"I was wondering about those blue eyes," Roarke ventured.

"This is my daughter, Mariah."

"My father calls me Gimewane—Whispering Rain," the girl said quickly.

"Go and play, Gimewane." Amy chased her off with a pat. The child ran straight into the midst of a group of cavorting youngsters who were playing a game with a hoop fashioned from a wild grapevine. Almost immediately, Mariah was knocked on her backside by a tall boy.

"She seems a bit small for that," Roarke said.

But Amy only smiled. "Mariah will hold her own; she always does. The children tease her because of her white blood. Sometimes I think that's what drives her to run faster, jump higher, and yell more loudly than the rest of them."

Roarke wondered at the idea that white blood was considered a source of shame. "What about you, Amy?"

"I am the wife of Coonahaw. They treat me as a sister."

"Did you know I was here yesterday?"

"Of course. We all knew, Roarke."

Pain bit into his shoulder as he spun to face her. "By the Eternal, Amy, and you didn't try to stop it?"

She gave him a wistful smile. "No, Roarke. It is the way of my people."

"Your people?" he asked harshly.

She took his hands, that sad smile still tugging at her mouth. "You don't understand, Roarke. There is nothing about your world that calls to me. This is my home now. And these are my people."

"You're right. I don't understand. But there's something calling to me, Amy." He turned his eyes westward. "My daughter Rebecca."

Hance swept his arm in an arc across the green baize surface of the gaming table, scooping a pile of copper and silver toward him.

"That ends it for me," he said with a rakish grin, pouring the coins into his pocket. "Finest game of old sledge I ever played, gentlemen." He looked around the table at his companions and adjusted his stock. "I'll be going now."

"So soon?" pouted Maybelle, the barmaid. She leaned both hands on the table, artfully granting Hance a generous view of her considerable charms.

Hance flipped her a coin and stood up. "Sorry, love, but the assembly meets in the morning. Mr. Rathford will be needing my services."

"In the assembly," Artis Judd sneered, "or elsewhere?" Judd was peevish because Hance had just won his last two bits. Adair was a cheat; everyone had known it since the brash youth had moved to Richmond four years earlier. But he was too damned smooth to be caught.

Hance's head snapped up. "What the hell is that supposed to mean, Artis?" he demanded.

"Nary a thing, my friend," Judd said with a smile of unabashed insincerity. "Still . . ." He studied his fingernails intently. "Folks have been saying the old coot's gotten mighty tight with his pretty boy." Nervous laughter rippled among the listeners gathered around the table. It was the first time anyone had ever dared to give voice to something that had only been whispered about.

Tension coiled within Hance like an iron spring. He suspected there was more to the taunts than Artis's dislike for Horace Rathford, a man who held tenaciously to an unpopular antislavery stance in the assembly.

Hance thought about what Judd would not say in front of his cronies. Judd's wife, Carmen, was far too refined for a lout like Artis, something she had often told Hance at their trysting place, an abandoned mill a few miles above the Falls of the James.

But the attack on Horace Rathford's character filled Hance with fury. It was true the assemblyman had certain mannerisms that uncouth brawlers like Judd enjoyed making sport of. Truer still that Horace was too much of a gentleman to defend himself against gossip. Hance's eyes glittered dangerously at Artis, who rose to his feet.

"Take it back," Hance said. There was a disconcerting mildness to the request.

Judd's grin faltered a little. "There now, nothing's been

said, pretty boy. Or maybe it's the grain of truth that's got your dander up . . ."

Hance lunged at him, hooking his left arm toward Judd's jaw with lightning speed. Knuckle met flesh with a jarring crunch.

"You damned infernal little bastard," Judd snarled, working his jaw with a grimace. He planted his feet and clenched his fists in readiness to counter the attack.

The barkeep gave a nod, and the two men were restrained by others nearby.

Cursing, Hance twisted in the grip of a local planter and his burly black manservant, who started dragging him toward the door.

"I'll go," he told them in a low whisper of fury. They dropped their hands.

Having regained his composure, Hance began putting on his chicken-skin gloves. He hesitated and looked back at Judd. Peeling off one of the gloves, he flung it at Judd's feet.

"Tomorrow at sunrise," he growled. "At Schwab's Green, on the Chesterfield side of the James."

Judd stooped and picked up the glove, his merry eyes sweeping the taproom. "Gentlemen," he said with a chuckle, "I do believe this young pup has just called me out." He turned the glove over in his hands with a bemused expression.

"And I do believe I'll oblige the bastard."

Even at dawn the high heat of August pulsated over the fine blades of grass on Schwab's Green. In a closed black coach sprung with stout leather straps, Horace Rathford mopped his brow distractedly.

"Don't do this, Hance," he said.

"I have to, Horace. I called the man out."

Horace laughed dryly. "That happens every day in the capital; we're all such a feisty bunch. But no one will look askance at you if you withdraw the challenge. I'll see that Artis Judd is ridden out of town, tarred and feathered if you like."

Hance gripped the door handle. "Damn it, Horace, I'm sick of you always doing for me, smoothing things over, tidying up after my mistakes. It's about time I did something for myself."

"But this? Think about it, Hance. You're a young man. Your promise will never be fulfilled if you duel with Judd today. If he doesn't kill you outright, you'll live your life as an outlaw. You'll never be able to show your face in Richmond—in Virginia—again."

"Virginia won't feel the lack," Hance said darkly. He picked up an inlaid iron-maple box, feeling the weight of the loaded pistols inside.

Horace put a hand on his arm. "For God's sake, Hance, doesn't our friendship mean anything to you?"

Hance eyed him keenly, wondering what aspect of that friendship Horace was referring to. The endless hours they'd spent together, reading the laws of the land, creating new ones? Or was it the other, the almost suffocating power Horace had held over him for the past three years? Hance had never made a move that Horace didn't know about; he couldn't even enjoy his mistresses anymore . . .

For the past few months, Hance had been growing restless, another fact of which his benefactor was keenly aware.

He peeled Horace's fingers from his arm, one by one. It was time to stop denying what he'd become. It was time to leave.

"You choose death blithely, my friend," Horace said.

Hance sent him a brash grin. He opened the door and stepped down into the sunlight.

"Goodbye, Horace."

He strode out to the green, taking deep gulps of the sultry air. A mockingbird trilled in the trees that fringed the meadow, and a light breeze rustled the leaves. The idea that Artis Judd might put a ball through him today didn't disconcert Hance. One day was as likely as the next when it came to dying.

He looked down at the pistol case in his hands. He wasn't going to die. He'd been shooting since the day he'd turned seven years old, when his father had knelt behind him, supporting a long rifle while Hance squeezed the trigger. The turkey's head had been blown clean off. Hance had missed very few of his targets since then.

Artis Judd arrived on horseback. Three of his cronies were with him, joking raucously as they approached Hance.

"What do you say, pup?" Judd demanded. "It's not too late to beg off."

Hance threw him a scathing look but said nothing. He stooped and placed his pistol case on the grass, extracting one slowly, assuring himself that it was loaded and primed.

The seconds receded to the edge of the green. Hance paced off the distance, and Judd did likewise. Slowly. Neither was in a hurry to reach the end of the green.

Hance stopped walking and swung about. He'd half decided to vindicate Horace's honor by spending his bullets harmlessly in the air. But by the time he faced his opponent, Judd was a blur, his face drawn into a snarl as he brought his pistol up and fired with deadly aim. Hance felt a ball furrow its way into the flesh of his upper left arm, tearing muscle and shattering bone.

Even more blinding than the pain was the rage that roared through him. Ever the cheat, Judd had taken aim well before Hance had turned around. As blood warmed his sleeve, Hance gritted his teeth and fired, forgetting his idea of shooting skyward. A dot of red appeared on Judd's forehead, square in the center. He fell backward, dead before his body hit the grass.

Hance's ears roared, and he felt suddenly cold. He steeled himself against the trembling that threatened to shake him to his knees. Moving slowly, holding himself steady with a monumental effort, he replaced his pistol in its case and walked away, leaving the elegant weapons behind in the grass.

Hance didn't want them. He'd taken a man's life.

Judd's friends rushed to his body, stunned. One of the men looked up and shook his fist at Hance. "You'll hang for murder, Adair!" he shouted.

Horace's coach pulled up. The older man leaped out, his face ashen and damp with perspiration.

"Hance—"

"I'm leaving, Horace." He began untying his horse from the back of the coach.

"But your arm—good God, Hance, you'll bleed to death."

"I'll make it." Hance felt no joy at the prospect.

Horace gave him a wistful smile. "I dare say you will. That is, until the law catches up with you." His brow furrowed in distress as he watched Hance mount unsteadily. "You'll have to leave Virginia, Hance. Go away, lose yourself on the frontier. You won't be the first man to start clean in Kentucky."

Hance touched the horse's flanks with his heels. He rode westward until the woodlands swallowed him up. When he was a safe distance from Richmond, he stopped by a creek and dismounted. Taking out his knife, he sat at the base of an oak tree. Gingerly, he unbound the crude bandage he'd made from several handkerchiefs and took a bracing swig of whiskey from a flask, pouring some of the liquid on the bullet wound.

Then, with more fortitude than he'd know he possessed, Hance used his knife to remove the bullet. The operation took a long time, the bullet sliding deeper into damaged flesh each time Hance tried to grasp it.

Gritting his teeth, he forced himself to think of other things, anything but the deathly agony of steel probing for lead in his shattered arm. Horace Rathford's advice swirled like an eddying stream through his pounding head: the frontier . . . Kentucky . . .

The corners of Hance's mouth turned upward. He couldn't quite seem to focus his eyes, which were flooded by cold sweat from his brow.

"You know, Horace," he rasped, "I just might do that." He keeled forward. The last thing he felt before blacking out was the ticklish brush of grass against his face.

19

Roarke's back *was* turned, taut and hunched-looking as he worked on a new grain bin for the livestock. He wielded his hammer with inborn expertise, his arm rising and falling in a natural motion.

Genevieve watched him sadly. A different Roarke worked the land now; there was none of the quiet joy that used to color his every task, no pauses to laugh and joke with the children. Roarke's heart hadn't been in the work of the farm since he'd returned, empty-handed and dispirited, from his two-year odyssey into Shawnee territory.

The fruitless journey had cost Roarke more than his high spirits; Will Coomes had been captured by a band of renegade Miami braves, and by the time Roarke caught up with them, the only evidence of his friend was a bloody scalp. Genevieve shook her head. Although Roarke hadn't elaborated on that tale, she was sure he'd exacted a harsh payment from the renegades.

The hammering stopped, and Roarke wiped a sleeve across his brow. As he so often did these days, he paused to gaze westward at the Blue Ridge in heartaching contemplation of what lay beyond.

Genevieve went to him and wrapped her arms around his middle, laying her cheek against his sweat-dampened back.

His big, freckled hand tightened around the hammer he was holding.

"Hello, Gennie love," he said softly.

"What are you thinking about?"

"Ah, Gennie, what am I always thinking about?"

She felt a familiar ache in her throat. "We all miss her, Roarke."

He shook his head and turned to face her with troubled eyes. "'t's not so much the missing," he said. "It's the wondering and not knowing that's so hard to bear. Becky might have died months, years, ago, or she might still be with Black Bear, being treated like, like—" He clenched his jaw and looked away.

"Roarke, don't," Genevieve said quickly, tightening her grip on him. "We've tortured ourselves over this for four years. You did everything a man could possibly do. More than that."

Pain tore across his face. "Did I, Gennie? 'Tis a question I keep asking myself. Perhaps I should have gone ten more miles, twenty . . ."

She placed a finger on his lips, silencing him. "There are just too many places for Black Bear to go. If you'd searched ten years, you'd not have found him."

The tortured look hadn't left his face. "That's just what Will Coomes said. One of the last things he said."

Tears prickled in Genevieve's eyes. Roarke was too good a man to be so laden with guilt. His shoulders, though strong and broad, were hard put to support Will's loss and Rebecca's capture as well.

"We just have to go on, Roarke," she told him firmly.

He rested his chin on her head. Sarah toddled toward them, grinning, arms outstretched. "Papa," she said, clinging to his leg.

Sarah's touch seemed to jar Roarke out of his desolate mood. The child, born during his absence, was a spark of brightness in his life, with hair the color of sunshine and cheeks blooming with health and good humor. Though only three, Sarah had learned that her father was a fathomless source of indulgence, and she exploited that knowledge shamelessly. Roarke scooped her up and balanced her on his hip, tickling her under the chin until she chortled with glee.

"Thank God for this one," Roarke chuckled. "She's the prettiest Adair yet, aside from her mother, of course."

"What's that you got there?" said a voice from behind them. "Another towhead?"

Roarke and Genevieve turned quickly, faces lighting up. "Hance!" Genevieve cried, and flung herself against him. "Hance, oh, Lord, but we've missed you!" Seeing him wince, she pulled back, staring in consternation at the bandages that bound his upper arm.

Noticing her concern, Hance said quickly, "A scratch, Mama. I'm fine."

"Welcome home, son," Roarke said quietly. He extended his hand, and Hance clasped it. Roarke looked at him, suddenly struck by the absurd formality of their greeting. He gave Hance's hand a jerk, bringing the young man into his arms in a huge bear hug with the baby between, giggling.

"Say hello to your sister, son," Roarke said. "This is Sarah Ann Adair."

The baby clung shyly to Roarke, but her wide blue eyes remained fastened on the handsome, slightly haggard-looking man who was grinning at her with genuine pleasure.

"Come inside," Genevieve invited, linking her arm through his. She felt him stiffen at her touch. "Hance?"

He was quick to soothe the hurt that sprang to her eyes. "Sorry, Mama. I guess the arm's still healing."

"What happened?"

His smile faded, and he looked over at Roarke. "I was shot in a duel."

"A duel? You were dueling? Good God, Hance, whatever possessed you to . . ."

He looked suddenly weary, his eyes haunted by self-loathing. "I don't know, Pa," he said with painful honesty. "I never seem to know. It's so easy for me to see the wrong in what I've done. But only after it's done."

Hance raised his eyes to Roarke. "I've done a lot of things I'm not proud of, Pa."

Supper was a quiet affair, attended by more Adairs than had shared a table in a long time. Israel badgered Hance for tales of his exploits in the capital, but Hance had little to say, responding distractedly. He'd closed that chapter of his life just as the wound on his upper arm had closed. All that remained was a long, livid scar and the persistent dull ache of a bone that had no hope of healing properly.

Hance barely touched the roasted meat and steaming bowls of fresh vegetables. He walked out onto the porch, still reeling from the news of what had befallen Rebecca. His hellfire-and-damnation psalm-singing little sister. He tried to picture her in the hands of her Shawnee captors. It was too obscene to imagine.

The baby was put to bed, and Luke and Israel went to settle the horses in for the night. Watching Luke, Hance had the sensation of watching a stranger. He handled the horses expertly, joking with Israel as he worked. Hance sighed. He'd never really known his brother; he'd never really tried.

Only now did Hance feel that loss. Israel looked up to Luke in a way Luke had never regarded Hance. But, of course, Luke didn't need an older brother. He'd already surpassed Hance in height and exuded a confidence rare in men twice his age.

"I'll be leaving soon," Hance said to Roarke and Genevieve, who had joined him on the porch.

She looked at him curiously. "But why, Hance? You've just come back to us."

"I can't stay here."

"Of course you can, son. This is your home."

He brought his fist down on the porch rail so hard that the wood creaked.

"Listen to me, damn it! I have to leave."

"Hance—"

"You didn't ask me about the duel, but I expect you'll find out soon enough." His voice was brittle as he tried to mask his inner turmoil. Behind them the mantel clock ticked loudly in the keeping room.

"I killed the man who shot me."

Genevieve was reminded of the day Roarke had set off into the wilderness. With a leaden heart she made similar preparations for Hance. A single change of clothing, the barest implements of hygiene, which included only a comb, a razor, and a cake of soap. A few cooking utensils, sewing things, and a tool or two were stashed in his saddlebag.

Mimi Lightfoot, putting on a stolid front, although she was shocked by the fate of the boy she'd once nursed at her breast, prepared the food—plenty of hardtack and jerked meat, coffee and dried beans and a supply of sugar. Luke and Roarke saw to the most important provisions—a long rifle, polished to a dull gleam, a bag of shot, flints, a ramrod, a plain brass patch box, and a supply of powder wrapped in oilcloth to protect it from wet weather. Hance was also equipped with a finely honed hunting knife and the tomahawk Roarke had carried during the war.

The family stood in the yard, silent and tense. Hance looked at them, and the corners of his mouth lifted in a self-deprecating grin. He spread his arms, showing off the fringed hunting shirt and buckskin leggings Mimi had made him.

Roarke chuckled. "Where's our young dandy now?"

Hance sent him a sideways glance. "I expect he'll turn up somewhere over the Blue Ridge if what I've heard of Kentucky's to be credited." He scooped up little Sarah, who'd spent the past two weeks toddling worshipfully after him. Brushing his chin across her fair hair, he sighed. "I wish I had time to know you, sweetheart, like I knew Mattie. I once promised her I'd take her to the other side of the world, but it looks like I'll be going alone." Sarah gave him a moist kiss and squirmed away to devil a barn cat that had strayed into the yard.

Israel approached shyly. He was a little in awe of his eldest brother, whose wild ways had been spoken of with scandalized whispers in church ever since the sudden rift between Hance and Janie Carstairs. He gave Hance a Bible.

"What's this?" Hance chuckled. "Am I to find redemption in the wilderness and mend my ways at last?"

Israel swallowed at the sarcasm he heard in Hance's voice. "You used to read it," he said sullenly.

"So I did, lad. What could be more exciting a yarn than the tale of Gideon overthrowing the altar at Baal?" He caught Israel's look and stopped joking. Placing the small tome in his shirt pocket, he said, "I'll read it, Israel. I promise."

Luke sent a sharp look over his shoulder. Although Hance would probably read the book, it was doubtful he'd heed its lessons. Frowning, Luke turned his attention back to the pack saddle he was fashioning for Hance. No one had asked him to do it, but the notion had appealed to him. The result was gratifying—a sturdy fork of white oak with boards fastened to the prongs, boasting a good number of iron rings to carry straps and girths. Unsmiling, he placed it atop the horse and secured it.

"You did a good job, little brother," Hance said.

Luke chafed at the name Hance had taken to calling him, even though Hance said it jokingly, to point out the fact that Luke was the taller youth now.

"My pleasure," he said, drawing a strap through the pack saddle.

"You always were a great one for making things," Hance observed. "The only thing I'm good at making is trouble."

Luke shuffled his feet, trying not to show the resentment that welled within him. He didn't want to feel this way about his brother, but he couldn't stop himself. For years he'd been a dutiful son, smoothing over problems that Hance carelessly left in his wake.

Yet it was Hance the family rallied around, confused but all-forgiving. Sending him off with more money than Luke had ever seen in his life.

His mother had tried to explain. "He needs us, Luke," she'd said in that soft, compelling way of hers. "He needs more from us than you ever did. Ah, you're a good lad; you'll be all right . . ."

It was true, Luke conceded without a trace of smugness. He had a decided gift for keeping unto himself. He turned to Hance and stuck out his hand.

"Good luck," he said simply.

"I'll need it, Luke."

"Stay clear of redskins."

Hance shook his head. "I intend to be in their company constantly."

Luke frowned. "Hance—"

"That is, until I find Becky."

Luke's head snapped up. "What the hell—"

Hance grinned. "If I'm to take to the hills, I'd best do what I can for Becky."

Suddenly, Luke understood why Hance commanded his parents' loyalty as he did. Rakish charm and insouciance masked a true intensity of purpose that was hard to resist.

Fishing in his pocket, Luke extracted a small folded knife, its horn handle worn smooth by use. "Take it," Luke said. "I noticed your own was rusted."

Hance nodded. Now that they were parting, probably forever, there was no point in sustaining the prickle of mutual dislike. He gave Luke a mock salute, then turned to his parents.

Roarke embraced him wordlessly. They'd said all there was to say earlier, late at night over cups of fruit brandy.

"Take care of yourself," Roarke said.

"I mean to, Pa."

"Leave word at the Sheaf of Wheat in Lexington. We don't want to lose track of you."

Tears poured down Genevieve's face as she hugged Hance against her.

"I love you," she told him brokenly.

Hance swallowed against the ache in his throat. "Goodbye, Mama."

The sun burst from behind a cloud as he rode away. A single golden shaft streamed down over Hance as he stopped on the rise above the river road and turned to lift his arm in farewell. He looked glorious—young, strong, and golden, full of promises yet to be fulfilled. Genevieve refused to think of him as an outlaw, fleeing justice to lose himself beyond the Blue Ridge.

Luke and Israel ran down to the end of the drive, and Mimi scooped Sarah up and took her to the house, muttering and wiping at a stray tear.

Genevieve followed Roarke into the keeping room. The hooded clock's halfpenny moon was arcing into view within the dial, signaling the start of a new day. Absently, Roarke gave the clock a wind and then went to the window, leaning his knuckles hard on the sill.

Genevieve stood back, watching her husband closely. His jaw was set, his eyes trained unerringly westward. Lord, how many times had she seen that look lately? That intensity, that yearning.

Something Roarke had said to her, long ago when he'd returned from the frontier campaign, drifted into her mind. "'Tis a beautiful country, Gennie. A paradise on earth. A man could walk a hundred miles and see nothing but nature's bounty. Why, if it weren't for this farm . . ."

And later, when he'd returned from his search for Rebecca: "I knew it was hopeless after the first six months. But I stayed, Gennie. I stayed because I love the feel of Kentucky soil in my hands and because, somehow, it made me seem closer to Becky."

Genevieve knew the restless yearning would never leave Roarke. At night sometimes he would hold her close and wonder aloud if he'd already satisfied life's demands here in Dancer's Meadow. Everything ran so smoothly on the farm. Too smoothly. Roarke, who had once been so busy and full of plans, had become an observer. He had only to watch his lands flourish and then reap the monetary rewards.

With a wistful smile, Genevieve realized that this existence simply wasn't enough for a man like Roarke Adair. He needed a challenge, something new to revive his spirits.

Her smile broadened suddenly to a grin. All she'd just thought of Roarke applied to her as well. And the children.

The family simply wasn't made to sit in idleness and watch their lives go by.

The Adairs were suited to a more challenging existence. In the early years their lives had been unpredictable, sometimes cruel, filled with upsets, surprises, and unexpected pleasures. They were a family who gained strength from adversity, who found joy in building things together.

Building things . . . There was nothing left to build here, at this farm. The work had all been done.

Genevieve drew in a shaky breath. "Roarke."

He looked at her, frowning at the odd note in her voice.

"Roarke, let's go to Kentucky. All of us."

The clock's ticking disturbed Roarke's thunderstruck silence. He stared at his wife and saw eagerness in her eyes, an excitement he hadn't noticed in a long time. The look enhanced her usual soft beauty with youthful fire, which made his blood grow warm.

"Gennie, what are you saying?"

"Only that it's time to move on, Roarke. All we do is grow soft and fret about Becky and wonder . . . We don't belong here anymore. It can never be Hance's home again. What have we to hold us here but the land?" She brightened at a sudden inspiration. "We could give it to the Greenleafs. Lord knows, they need the space for all those grandchildren."

He stood in front of her, looking almost boyish in his wonder. "Gennie . . . ?"

She leaned against his chest. "I'm not ready to grow old yet, Roarke. Neither are you. Let's go to Kentucky, claim the tract of land that was awarded you for serving in the war. Let's build something new together."

"Gennie love, could you really leave all this?" He encompassed the farm with a sweeping gesture.

"Willingly," she replied softly.

He opened his arms to her, and she walked into his embrace. Together they went to the window while the clock chimed quietly behind them. They were turned toward the solid, brooding wall of the Blue Ridge, but their eyes looked beyond.

PART
II

The moonlight is the softest, in Kentucky,
Summer days come oftest, in Kentucky,
Friendship is the strongest,
Love's fires glow the longest,
Yet a wrong is always wrongest,
  In Kentucky.

JAMES HILARY MULLIGAN

PART
II

20

Licking River Valley, 1805

Whispering Rain brought her hand over Small Thunder's mouth to still his whimpering. It had been hours since the white hunters had attacked, but she was still gripped by the fear that some of them lurked at the riverbank below, poking through the burned-out remains of the small encampment. She gathered the little boy closer and brushed her hand over his brow, murmuring words of comfort that she could not give.

There was no comfort for either of them. Whispering Rain squeezed her eyes shut and gritted her teeth against the impulse to keen forth her grief with a high-pitched wail, as her people had done since ancient times. It was imperative that she hold her emotions in tight rein.

Even more pervasive than grief was the anger Whispering Rain felt. The supreme irony was that the hunters had descended upon them just when the small family had been heading peaceably into their midst, to the town called Lexington.

They were going there at the insistence of Whispering Rain's mother, a white woman, Amy Parker had lost her youngest child to the smallpox, had watched the boy slip away in an ooze of pus and fever. Terrified for the rest of her family, she'd begged her husband to take them to Lexington. A trader had told them of a new shield against the scourge. An inoculation, the trader had called it. Something added to the blood to make it immune to the dreadful disease.

Whispering Rain shook her head. There was no shield a Shawnee could erect against this other scourge, this frenzied hatred of whites against Indians.

She wondered if the hunters had been aware that they'd killed one of their own. A woman whose skin was as white as theirs, who'd kept her Christian name. Amy, who had prayed and sung hymns and called her daughter Mariah Parker, doggedly teaching the girl to speak the tongue of the white man.

Whispering Rain despised her knowledge of English now, just as she despised her appearance. Her eyes, a legacy of her mother, were the same scintillating blue of the sky, although her hair, mercifully, was as black as a raven's feather and grew straight and thick. Unfortunately, her other features bespoke her mixed heritage. Rather than the proud nose and fleshy lips of the Kispokotha Shawnee, Mariah's features were so delicate that she considered them weak. If she hadn't been a war chief's daughter, she would have been viciously ridiculed by the tribe.

The war chief's daughter. Once so proud, always striving to overcome the taint of her white ancestry by running faster, weaving more finely, singing more sweetly than all the others. But what was she now? Her efforts to carve out her own identity mattered not at all here in this wilderness, where all her family but a small frightened boy had died.

Coonahaw, her father, lay somewhere below in the charred rubble of the camp, his body chilled by the blast of winter cold that swept over the steaming salt licks.

Whispering Rain would have been among those massacred—by the gods, she almost wished she were—if it hadn't been for Small Thunder, the stocky boy of three winters who had climbed up to the caves on the bluff, then screamed when he couldn't get back down.

His mother, Mariah's half sister, had snorted and declared that he should be made to climb down on his own. But Whispering Rain had been fearful. Small Thunder was teetering precariously at the top of the bluff a hundred spans above and in his panicked state might have fallen to his death.

Whispering Rain had gone to fetch him, not knowing what her indulgence would spare her. No sooner had she reached him than a crash could be heard below. Whispering Rain had thrown herself to the rough edge of the bluff, covering Small Thunder with her body.

From that vantage point, frozen with horror, she'd watched her family die. All of them. Faces smashed by tomahawks, bellies laid open by long knives, bodies shattered by the white man's fire-spitting *metequa*.

The massacre had lasted only minutes. Whispering Rain wondered how it could have happened. The settlers in Chillicothe had assured them that no hostilities were nurtured in the area.

With a leaden heart, Whispering Rain came to her feet. Arrows of pain shot up her left leg, and she glanced down at it, frowning. She hadn't realized she'd injured herself. A sharp jut of rock had torn into the flesh above her moccasin, laying it open. Blood oozed from the wound. She used her belt to wrap it, wincing with pain.

Dusk was settling over the licks, creating a throbbing atmosphere of purple twilight. Whispering Rain glanced down at the boy. He had begun to shiver, and there was a bluish ring about his lips. He wouldn't last this winter night on the exposed bluff.

"Gimewane." His teeth chattered as he spoke her name.

She put her shawl around him and brought the ends of it about her shoulders, fashioning a sling. She was clumsy and off-balance, being so slight of stature, but her limbs were strong and wiry from years of running and hefting great bundles on the tribe's frequent migrations.

Whispering Rain paused to listen to the winter stillness of the woods as her eyes surveyed the steaming licks below her. Her relief came in a little frozen breath; there was no sign of the attackers. Fitting her hands and feet into gaps in the sandy rock, she began a slow, arduous climb downward. It was full dark of night by the time she dropped to the packed-earth surface of the river bank. The impact caused her wound to begin bleeding again. Whispering Rain ignored it and turned slowly, dreading the sight that was about to greet her.

Wisps of smoke trickled skyward, emanating from the pitiful remains of the scattered makeshift dwellings. The camp looked like a battlefield, littered by the dark, still shapes of her parents, her half sister, Melassa, and Melassa's husband, Scotach. Sickness bounded to her throat, and she fought it down with an effort.

Whispering Rain swore softly to Matchemenetoo, the Devil Spirit, when she recognized her father's body. His head was a mass of gore, black in the deepening night. The hunters had claimed his scalp. Many white men sported Indian pelts. Still cursing, she crossed to her mother's body. Amy Parker, it seemed, had died as peacefully as she had lived. A single ribbon of darkening blood circled her throat like a necklace. Her hands were folded on her breast; her face was smooth, its lines softened by the release of her spirit.

Whispering Rain set Small Thunder down beside the caved-in remains of a hut some yards away from the bodies, where the partial walls offered a bit of shelter from the driving blast of wind.

Activity kept her emotions at bay. She had little trouble making a fire. Sifting through a smoldering pile of ashes, she scooped a few live coals into a shard of clay pottery and laid them in front of the shelter. She coaxed a blaze from bits of charred cloth and dried bark chips and then wrapped Small Thunder snugly in a torn blanket.

"Stay here," she told him, her breath coming in visible puffs. "I'll get you something to eat."

But when she returned with a small quantity of jerked venison that had survived the pillaging, she found that Small Thunder had fallen asleep. Tears were drying on his face, streaking through the dusting of dirt on his cheeks. Whispering Rain's breath caught in her throat. Small Thunder understood. He was too little to comprehend everything, but he obviously knew all was lost.

Tscha-yah-ki. Everything.

Whispering Rain put a hand to her cheek. It came away dry. She couldn't remember ever shedding a tear and now, when at last there was cause to indulge her grief, she found she couldn't cry. Years of battling imagined weaknesses had driven the tears from her.

Sighing, she returned to the main part of the encampment, forcing her mind to empty itself of all thought as she prepared to mourn her dead. If she allowed herself to think too much, she'd never be able to cope with the ravaged faces, the slack limbs, the staring eyes.

She worked until the winter cold was replaced by the sweat of exertion, bringing the bodies to a flat where the springs warmed the earth to a sticky mud. Lacking tools, she couldn't provide proper narrow graves and had decided instead to let the earth take them slowly, swallowing their remains.

Using her shawl she cleansed their faces, beloved faces that had once laughed around the council fires. She paused to loosen her hair of its braids, wishing she had paint of yellow and vermilion to draw whorls of mourning upon her face. She covered the bodies with burned and bloodied shreds of fabric and laid a single smooth stone at the feet of each one. The tobacco she sprinkled over them was not the sacred *nilu famu,* but it would have to suffice as the final sacrament.

Then Whispering Rain stepped back and watched the firelight flicker off the makeshift bier. She stared as deep, silent, heartfelt grief gripped her in stillness, until the wind chilled the sweat on her body.

At last she began the breathy, undulating notes of the death chant. Her voice rose to the barren night sky, quavering with melancholy, embodying all the tenderness, sorrow, and despair that she felt.

When her song was done, she trudged to the river's edge to scrub her body with sand until her limbs stung and her flesh glowed pink in the firelight. There should be no anger in mourning, yet Whispering Rain couldn't help herself.

Rage intruded upon the hollow grief in her heart. Surprisingly, she realized that some of her fury belonged to her parents. They had to ride down among the white man, ignoring the elders' decision that the course of wisdom lay west, into the sun. *You should have heeded the elders,* she raged in silence. *Didn't you know what would happen?*

Whispering Rain set her jaw. Of course they knew. The reprisals, the furious vengeance. The struggle went on until fighting meant only death. The hallowed hunting ground, which the ancients had decreed could belong to no tribe, had been measured and surveyed and parceled out by land-hungry settlers who named it Kentucky and called themselves Americans.

They'd never stop coming.

Whispering Rain retreated to the shelter where she'd left the boy. When she tried to settle down, a hard object dug into her back. Frowning, she groped among the blankets and debris until she extracted a rifle. Somehow the weapon, along with all its firing implements, had escaped plunder. Whispering Rain gathered the things close with the cold certainty that she would be needing the *metequa*—the white man's weapon.

What didn't occur to her, as she lay back and stared up at the cold, white points of light in the dawning sky, was how soon she would use the rifle to spit vengeance on one of her family's murderers.

A twig snapped. She would never have remarked on it had it not been for the utter, unmoving stillness of the dawn. She sat up, listening intently now. There was a crunch of frozen mud being trodden upon—by a foot heavier than that of a deer or wildcat.

Whispering Rain took up the rifle, biting her lip as she tried to remember the steps in loading it. Her father, proud of her quickness of mind, had shown her. Twice. She prayed it had been enough.

Her fingers trembled as she inserted a small swab of flax into the barrel and tamped it down with the ramrod. Finding no measuring device, she placed an unknown quantity of powder into the muzzle. The footsteps grew louder, and Small Thunder whimpered and shifted in his sleep.

"Nen-nemki," she murmured, "be still."

Swallowing the panic that rose in her throat, she continued loading. The bullet, wrapped in a bit of greased patching, went down into the muzzle, aided by the ramrod, which, mercifully, slid silently. Quaking with apprehension, she added powder to the firing pan to prime it.

Closing the pan, she rose slowly to her feet, her injured leg thudding with pain. She had no idea whether or not the rifle would fire; she could well have left out a step in the loading. The flint might not work. But there was no time to worry about the weapon's shortcomings.

She stepped away from the shelter to divert the intruder's attention from Small Thunder's presence. And found herself facing a tall man who swayed drunkenly in the dawn light. A man with eyes so yellow and cold that his very stare sent terror twisting down her spine. Behind him, a scruffy young boy of perhaps nine hung in the purple shadows, holding the reins of a horse.

Her breath caught with a hiss as recognition dawned. She brought the barrel of the rifle up, level with his belly. Then she spoke his name disparagingly.

"Elkanah Harper." His clothes stank of the scalps he'd taken; one bitten-off ear marked him as a horse thief.

He swayed a little and laughed harshly. "Aye!" he shouted, not at all concerned by the cold round eye of the gun pointed at his midsection, "'tis Elk, and glad I am that I came back to see that me and my boys did the job up right."

He hooked a thumb into his belt loop, fingers playing on the handle of his long knife. "'Pears we overlooked a couple of redskins, Caleb," he said over his shoulder. "Where's your father and his brother?"

The boy shrugged.

"Goddamned boys o' mine," Harper swore. "Must've stopped below the bluffs to water the horses." He turned his yellow-eyed gaze back to the girl, exuding malevolence.

"Guess me an' my grandson'll have to deal with you ourselves." The boy quailed and shrank back.

Whispering Rain felt sickness well up in her. This was the eldest of the Harpers, the man who had assured her father in Chillicothe that it was safe to make salt at the licks for trading in Lexington. Who had given Coonahaw detailed directions, fed him firewater, won his trust.

She met his eyes. They were bleary with drink and full of gleeful cruelty.

"You knew," she said accusingly. "You sent us here."

He laughed again. "My boys did a good job killin', eh?"

"Not good enough," Whispering Rain told him. "They left me, Coonahaw's daughter, behind. To avenge my father."

Harper was not as drunk as Whispering Rain had hoped. As he spoke, he edged closer. She saw his fingers twitch a little in anticipation of seizing her rifle.

"Don't," she cautioned him. "I do not relish killing as you do, but I will take your life. Go away, Harper."

He shook his head slowly from side to side. "You'll come with me, squaw."

"Never!"

He laughed in her face. But the laughter was meant to disarm her, to cover his sudden lunge.

Whispering Rain squeezed the trigger. The flint struck a spark against the frizzen, and the *metequa* barked its thunder at Harper. The ball struck him, not in the belly where she'd aimed, but higher, piercing his heart.

The boy dropped the horse's reins and scampered away in terror.

"Bitch!" Elk spat raggedly, clawing at the sooty, gaping hole in his chest.

Elkanah Harper's boys appeared over the rise in time to see a young squaw with a little boy clutched to her breast, fleeing southward on their father's horse.

Luke Adair threw himself to the ground at the sharp crack of a rifle report. He grimaced in silent pain as his knee struck a frozen clod of mud, and then he rose slowly, cautiously, to look around. His sigh of relief froze in the air before his mouth. The shot hadn't been meant for him; it was too far away. But now he moved with more caution. Deep in the wilderness, both Indian and white were likely to shoot first and wonder about the target afterward.

Such dangers never dissuaded Luke from his frequent forays into the thick, river-creased woodlands of Kentucky. It was worth the danger to come here, to hear the wind moaning through pines on high ridges, to see the relic stands of ancient hemlocks, to feel his horse's footsteps springing on a cushion of humus. Beyond the hastily tamed regions of central Kentucky were places where a man could still touch the land.

Luke set out hunting whenever he could, especially in winter when work on the farm slowed down and the family settled into their snug house near Lexington to huddle against the chill.

Too much closeness, Luke decided. Too much of his parents' tacit trust in his dependability, of Israel's incomprehensible orations on theology, of pretty Sarah's incessant prattle over her dolls and bright bits of calico. And especially too much of Hance's careless, half-formed dreams of glory, which were constantly thwarted by his own recklessness.

Luke ventured out for the solitude as much as he did for the hunting. Always alone, always on his favorite dun mare, a fleet Chippewa-bred horse. Luke enjoyed the independence of traveling alone, not having to think about planting schedules or sick cows or getting Hance out of his latest scrape. Here Luke answered only to his own needs, and it was a welcome relief after a long season of responsibility.

At the moment his own need was to find the source of the rifle shot, to ascertain that he wasn't the one being hunted. The rifle was Indian; of that much he was sure. Redskins used low-grade powder, which gave the report a slightly different quality.

Hoofbeats sent him and his horse backing into a dense stand of hackberry. An eagle mare burst into view, its eyes rolled back fearfully, showing white. Luke saw a flash of moccasin-clad feet and a well-greased fringe of doeskin. An Indian woman, clutching a child in front of her. She rode past him, ducking low over the horse's shoulder, and disappeared from view.

Luke was about to emerge from his cover when two more riders appeared, well mounted, urging their beasts on with curses. The men reminded Luke of a pair of scraggly wolves.

Stay out of it, Luke admonished himself. But even as the thought squirmed through his mind, he was mounting and spurring his horse in the direction the hunters—and the hunted squaw—had taken.

He couldn't imagine the sort of men who would ride down a lone Indian woman . . .

Yes, he could. Hance was capable of that. And maybe Roarke, too. The two of them had had enough brushes with redskins to develop a deep, abiding hatred of all their kind. Luke despised Indians, too, but his hatred was more focused, more controlled. An entire race of people wasn't responsible for nearly killing him twelve years ago and carrying off his sister. Luke reserved every shred of his loathing for the one brave called Black Bear.

He rode on, bending low beneath a leafless hickory branch. The fires of rage had subsided over the years. Black Bear was probably dead, and Rebecca undoubtedly so. Luke had done his grieving.

The hunters never saw him. They veered northward, toward the river, having lost their quarry. Luke felt a breath of relief escape him and slowed his horse to a meandering walk. He hadn't given the squaw enough credit. She'd managed to elude the hunters with her inborn sense of woodcraft.

Wandering southward, Luke began to seek out a place to make camp for the night. Lost in thought, he didn't realize what he'd stumbled upon until he was in the midst of a burnt-out Indian camp.

Sickness constricted his throat. Four bodies had been laid out on a mud flat in deathly repose. Swallowing bile, he saw that the women had been butchered every bit as ruthlessly as the braves. The sympathy that suddenly burst within his heart felt strange to Luke. Why feel compassion for red-skins?

He supposed it was the waste, the utter senselessness of the massacre. Yet he knew redskins to be equally indiscriminate in their killing. One of them had recently made short work of a white man, Luke saw. Some distance from the rest of the bodies lay a filthy, grizzled carcass, the face twisted into an eternal snarl.

Shaking his head, Luke walked away from the camp, putting a cold hand to his roiling innards. The freezing temperature had preserved the scarlet hue of the blood that crept out across the frozen ground.

A sudden wave of longing for his family welled up in Luke. He'd been gone a month, time enough to forget the tension of all his responsibilities. The cold bodies made him long to embrace someone warm and alive, like Sarah, who was fond of crawling into his lap and begging for stories.

The trail to Lexington took him along the Licking River. He paused to eat, to water his horse, and to savor the last of the day. The bleak winter sun carved deep shadows into the cliffs above the water. A flock of geese appeared soundlessly, hanging still in the air for an instant. Then they wheeled out over the river in perfect *V* formation and were gone.

A small sound drifted through the evening silence. A human sound. Tensing, Luke scanned the cliffs above the river and edged toward a great limestone outcrop.

The sound grew stronger as he neared it. A voice, sweet and clear, issued from a large cave. Tethering his horse to a bush, Luke climbed to the opening in the cliff. What he found made his throat constrict with emotion.

An Indian girl—or was she a grown woman?—sat on a ragged horse blanket cradling a small child in her arms, crooning some sweet melody. Her face was set impassively, and her cheeks were dry, yet the aching mournfulness in her voice indicated grief more poignantly than a flood of tears.

Touched, Luke took a step toward her.

Whispering Rain tensed every nerve when a long, broad shadow closed the mouth of the cave where she hid. Driven by instinct, she clutched Small Thunder closer while her other hand reached for the primed rifle. Her head snapped up, and her eyes clouded with confusion. She was staring at a man far too magnificent to be one of Harper's sons.

He removed his hat and raked his hand through a mane of clay-colored hair. The white winter sun illuminated arresting features that looked as if they'd been hewn from iron maple by a master's skilled hand. A proud, firm jaw and squarish chin, a straight nose and oddly soft lips, lips that made Whispering Rain feel something dreadful and forbidden curl within her.

With an inner tremble she lifted her eyes to his. The color reminded her of a dew-wet leaf in springtime, but he was staring at her with a chilly hardness that made her shiver. She recognized the hardness as hatred.

Whispering Rain swallowed. She was in an awkward position to fend him off, but he hadn't yet taken his knife or tomahawk from his belt.

The speed with which she set Small Thunder down awoke the child, who began to whimper. In one quick movement, Whispering Rain thrust him behind her and seized the rifle.

The man's foot slammed down on the barrel, pinning the weapon on the floor of the cave.

"Don't," he ordered curtly.

With a grunt of fear, she tried to pry it up. The man uttered a curse and took the rifle, twisting it roughly from her hands. He regarded the rusting, dirty muzzle for a moment, his mouth drawn taut in disapproval.

"Now then," he said, half to himself, "what's to become of you two?"

From somewhere in the corner of her mind burst a wealth of English words, words schooled into her by her mother's teaching.

"Do you really wonder?" she snapped. "I should think it is obvious."

His eyes widened in surprise. "So you speak English, do you, little squaw? Damned well, too."

She stared at him, unsmiling.

"You were being chased earlier today," he continued. "How the devil did you lose the hunters?"

"I abandoned the horse and fled on foot. They followed the horse's trail."

He gave a slight nod of approval. "Where will you go?"

His question indicated that he didn't mean to kill her. But Whispering Rain felt no rush of gratitude. She knew she would probably die anyway, alone in the forest with a small child and a leg wound that left a trail of blood to tempt marauding wolves and bears.

In response to the white man's question, she said, "Perhaps I will boil salt to trade for shelter, until I can return to my people." The very thought of her tribe, so distant that they were like a dream, filled her with sadness.

He shook his head. "Salt doesn't bring much these days." His eyes moved over her slowly, igniting a coil of fear within her. "It appears you've gotten yourself wounded."

"What does it matter to you?" she asked hotly.

He pushed back his hat and scratched his head. "I don't guess I know, little squaw."

"Then leave us. You and your marauding brothers have already taken the lives of my family—"

He shook his head slowly. "Nope. I wasn't with them. I've no love for Indians, Shawnee in particular, but I'm not in the habit of riding down peaceful bands."

The silence drew out between them. Small Thunder shifted and trod upon her wounded leg. She ground her teeth against the pain, but a small sound escaped in spite of her.

"Let's go," the man said.

She stared, her heart thumping in her chest. She didn't move.

Impatience tugged at the corners of his mouth. "Come on, little squaw—"

"Do not call me that again!"

He shrugged. "Have you got a name?"

"Gimewane. In your tongue, Whispering Rain."

"Whispering Rain," he repeated. "Hell of a mouthful for a little thing like you."

"My Christian name is Mariah Parker. Given to me by my mother, who was adopted by my people many winters ago."

He nodded. "That explains the blue eyes." He indicated the boy. "Who's he?"

"Nen-nemki. Small Thunder. He is the son of my half-sister."

The man nodded again. "I'm Luke Adair." He hung the rifle about his shoulder, then stopped and picked up Small Thunder, who regarded him with large, solemn brown eyes.

Whispering Rain leaped up and tried to snatch the boy away. "Do not touch him, Luke Adair!"

He turned, ignoring her, and started down toward his horse. "Look, Mariah," he said impatiently over his shoulder, "we're three days from Lexington and you need a doctor. Every minute you stand there arguing with me is a minute lost. Now, you can either sit here and watch the boy freeze to death, or you can try to get some help before it's too late."

She said nothing. But the barely discernible sagging of her narrow shoulders indicated capitulation.

21

Luke felt the coldness of the ground in his left foot where the leather sole of his boot had worn through, but he ignored the discomfort. He was near the end of his trek; in an hour or so he'd have the boot in Mansfield's shop for resoling.

He glanced back at Mariah Parker, who straddled his dun mare, holding the boy in front of her. For three days they'd traveled together, yet he still knew virtually nothing about his reluctant charge. From time to time she would respond to his questions in her curiously precise English; he'd learned that she was seventeen, as nearly as she could tell, the daughter of a Kispokotha Shawnee and a white woman. Her camp had been set upon by frontier bandits, and she'd killed one of them, incurring the wrath of his sons. Beyond that, Mariah Parker told him little; she was hardly a widow's barrel for talk.

Luke found himself watching her frequently, curious and slightly resentful of the fact that he'd made himself responsible for her. She was a small slip of a girl, with fine-boned, regular features and eyes so huge and blue that it hurt to look at them. Luke's deeply ingrained dislike of redskins prevented him from admitting that she was actually quite beautiful.

When they reached the head of the town branch of the Elkhorn, the child called Small Thunder said something in a small, fearful voice.

"Please stop," Mariah said to Luke. At that moment his left foot found a particularly succulent puddle. Gritting his teeth in impatience, he halted the mare.

Mariah drew the child to her breast, and he spoke again, this time with large tears escaping from his eyes. Mariah made a soft, crooning sound of sympathy and hugged him reassuringly. Then she drew one of the leather whangs from her braid and deftly knotted it, instructing Small Thunder to pull upon the end. He pulled, and the knot disappeared as if by magic. Before the tears had dried on his cheeks, he was grinning and begging for more.

Mariah's face was expressionless when she turned to Luke. "He fears the white man's village," she told him simply. "You may go on now."

An unexpected and unwelcome prickle of guilt crept up on Luke as he started toward town. The tenderness Mariah had shown the boy in that brief moment suddenly transformed her in his eyes. She was as human as he. A person who had suffered, a person who now grieved. She'd given him a glimpse of her inner being, and Luke found he could no longer deny how beautiful she was, how fine, how brave.

Still, she came from a race that he hated. Her father had doubtless been among the murderous bands who spread terror throughout the frontier, slaughtering whole families, slashing babies as they lay in their cradles. Luke wondered if he would always have such thoughts when he looked at Mariah.

The trace they were following broadened abruptly into a road. Luke pointed up ahead.

"Lexington," he told her.

Mariah tightened her grip around Small Thunder.

Couched between two undulating hills, the town was a sprawling array of log and clapboard buildings interspersed with a few structures of brick and stone. A main square was alive with the temporary stands of itinerant merchants. Unlike the woodsmen and settlers Mariah had seen, the people here were more grandly dressed, the men in tailored frock coats, the women carrying parasols and wearing sweeping skirts, many of them attended by black slaves.

Luke lashed the horse's reins to a rail in front of a white house bordered by a wooden walkway. Overhead, a painted wooden sign swung in the sharp breeze, bearing a symbol of some sort. He took Small Thunder down and held the boy while Mariah dismounted. She kept her eyes downcast, overwhelmed by the strangeness of the town.

"This is Dr. Elisha Warfield's," Luke said. "He'll see to your leg."

Mariah hesitated outside the office, giving him a dubious look.

"He's a healer, Mariah, like a Shawnee medicine man, I guess," Luke explained. "He's a lot better than those calomel doctors some folks swear by." She drew back distrustfully.

Luke set his jaw. The girl's silent vulnerability stirred something inside him that he couldn't name. He didn't like it, didn't like feeling responsible for the woman and boy. It was easier to hate redskins when they were a mass of faceless, marauding savages in the wilderness, not a beautiful woman who bore the look of a thousand hurts in her eyes.

He stepped into the office and drew Mariah in behind him. Her wrist felt fragile, birdlike. Luke ground his teeth together. Everything about her was fragile, from the soft straight line of her brow to her tiny, moccasin-clad feet.

Luke recognized the two women who waited within. He nodded at Myra Trotter, who ran a dry-goods store with her husband. She was constantly complaining of vapors and ague and paid regular visits to the doctor. Her eyes widened at the sight of Luke's companions. She threw Mariah a look of contempt and drew her well-jowled face into the curved bill of her bonnet.

The other woman in the waiting room was Nell Wingfield. Luke felt, as always, a stab of regret when he saw her, and resentment, too. When his family had arrived in

Lexington in 1796, they'd met Nell again and learned that Black Bear had released her. It seemed the brave had taken a dislike to her; she claimed that her constant complaining served her well.

All those years ago, Nell had ground out the last inkling of hope the Adairs had of finding Rebecca again. When Nell had left Black Bear, Rebecca had been dying of smallpox, her body covered by running pustules, fever burning her life away. Nell had assured the Adairs, not unkindly, that Becky couldn't have survived the illness. A good thing, probably. Even such a painful death was preferable to living with her Indian captor.

Nell had forged a new life for herself in Lexington, much to the dismay of people like Mrs. Trotter. Miss Nellie's Liquor Vault and House of Entertainment, she called her establishment. The neat whitewashed house at the lower end of Water Street was popular among more men than would admit to it.

Nell had the self-possession and overblown looks of a woman who used to be pretty, and still thought she was. The object of a good bit of disapproval herself, she didn't raise an eyebrow at Mariah and the boy. She merely blinked and shifted in her creaky caned chair.

Alvis Mann, the doctor's assistant, entered through a door in the rear. He and Luke exchanged a few words, quietly. Alvis shuffled his feet and made a sound of protest. Luke replied curtly. Mariah heard a clink of coins, and then Luke turned back to her.

"I'll wait outside," he said, and disappeared.

Mariah looked after him, her hands tightening to small fists at her sides. Luke Adair thought nothing of leaving her alone in this strange place, with the fat woman glowering beneath her bonnet, the other staring unabashedly and smoothing the folds of her pink dress. Mariah wanted to leave, to run and hide, but Luke had already paid for the care she would reluctantly receive.

"What's your name, girl?" asked the pink-gowned lady suddenly.

"Gime—Mariah Parker."

"You're a friend of Luke's?"

Mariah shook her head. There was nothing between her and the white man that even resembled friendship.

"What about the boy—what's his name?"

Mariah thought quickly. Nen-nemki was a proud name, one revered by the Shawnee. But they weren't among the Shawnee anymore. Small Thunder would have to go by a Christian name.

"Gideon," she said suddenly, remembering the name of an ancient hero her mother had once told her about. "Gideon Parker," she added, giving him her mother's name as well.

The woman rose and approached her. Mariah caught a waft of heavy perfume and a certain musty odor from the woman's breath.

"I'm Nell Wingfield," she said, imbuing her name with importance. She slid her eyes over Mariah.

"What's ailing you?"

Mariah quickly explained about her injury and also mentioned that she wanted the inoculation against the smallpox for Gideon.

Mrs. Trotter harrumphed sharply. Nell whirled on her. "And what's ailing you?" she snapped.

"You'd best stay away from those Injuns," the other lady cautioned. "They're probably crawling with vermin."

"Why, Mrs. Trotter, I've heard you say the same thing about me and my girls," Nell said with false sweetness. She turned her attention back to Mariah, grinning at Mrs. Trotter's gasp of outrage.

The doctor's assistant appeared and motioned for Mariah to follow him. When she balked in sudden fear, Nell took her by the arm.

"He's a good doctor," she said, elbowing her way into a small, well-lit surgery. She paused to clasp hands with a younger woman in the doorway who had a fresh bandage above her eye. "Wait outside, Doreen," she said, and drew Mariah up beside her.

Elisha Warfield looked more like a backwoodsman than a doctor, in a linsey-woolsey shirt and well-worn buckskin trousers. But his rough-looking hands were gentle, his voice soothing as he removed the strip of cloth that bound Mariah's leg. The wound was healing poorly, the flesh at its edges grayish and growing putrid.

"This'll hurt," Dr. Warfield told her simply, unstopping a green bottle.

Mariah nodded. "I know."

The pain of the clear liquid seared her to the bone. She gripped the edge of the chair she was sitting in, set her teeth together, and allowed no sound to escape her. The doctor eyed her with frank admiration as he finished cleaning and trimming the gash and bound it with white strips of a porous fabric.

Gideon was equally stoic when Dr. Warfield expertly broke the skin of the boy's shoulder and rubbed a thread treated with dried kine pox over the wound. Mariah stood, swaying slightly with sudden weakness and relief. Her mother's wish for protection from the disease had been fulfilled—at a cost so dear that it made Mariah tremble.

Looking slightly ashen, for the operation on Mariah's leg had been an appalling sight, Nell Wingfield propelled Mariah from the surgery. "Do you have a place to stay?" she asked.

Mariah considered for a moment. True, Luke Adair had brought her here, but he'd said nothing about sheltering her and Gideon. She shook her head.

"Well, you do now, I reckon." Nell linked her arm through Mariah's. "I had a darkie, name of Rosalie, who used to work around my place. Cleaning, doing laundry and such. But she ran off a week ago, probably up to Louisville to find her way to New Orleans. Fool girl, she had a good roof over her head and three meals a day. I can give you the same, Mariah, and twelve bits a week if you'll take Rosalie's place."

Much of what Nell said was incomprehensible, but Mariah caught the gist of it. She hesitated, turning the idea over in her mind. Nell Wingfield offered a slave's work. Whispering Rain, who had once run free and played in tumbling rivers and sung to the trees and stars, would be trapped into an existence where her life would be ordered by other people. White people.

Alone, she might have a choice. She might be able to find her way back to her people. But she had Gideon, the son of her half sister, to think about. The risk of such a journey was too great. She lifted her eyes to Nell.

"I will come," she stated at last.

"Good. I'm sure you'll do just fine. Of course, I'll give you time to let that leg mend."

They left the office with Doreen, stepping out into blinding noonday sunlight. Luke, who had been lounging against the rail, swung around.

"I'm taking her in," Nell explained.

His brow darkened, and he raked a hand through his hair. He was seized—not for the first time—by a sudden, fierce protective instinct. The mere thought of this fragile girl being mauled by Nell's unsavory patrons made his insides lurch.

"Look, Nell," he said, "I don't think—"

She waved her hand impatiently. "Now, don't go getting your dander up. She's just going to do the chores around my place in exchange for room and board."

Luke glanced over at Mariah. "Will you be all right?"

She gazed at him, unsmiling. Nothing would ever be all right again. Everything she'd ever known had been taken from her. But there was no point in bringing up a matter that Luke Adair didn't understand and didn't seem to care about. She merely nodded.

He helped her and the others into Nell's cart, pausing a moment to brush his finger over the boy's cheek in a gesture that surprised Mariah. Then he turned back to his horse.

She knew that broad, strong-looking back from days of watching him from between the dun's bobbing ears. Somehow the sight gave her strength.

As Nell took up the reins, Mariah cleared her throat.

"Luke Adair."

He turned back, eyebrows raised at the throbbing softness of her voice.

She forced the barest hint of a smile. "Thank you."

Just for a moment a grin of genuine friendliness lit his face. Then he mounted, and was gone.

A chunk of mud slid down the river bank and plopped into the swirling dark waters of the Ohio.

"Damn," Hance swore, gripping a tree limb to keep himself from slipping.

"Keep it quiet, Adair," whispered Wiley Harper. "We don't want the trappers to know we're here too soon."

A cloud that had obscured the moon scudded away, and a shaft of pale, ghostly light slid over Hance's companions. Wiley and Micajah Harper, acquaintances from his Virginia childhood, were alike in sheer ugliness. They both had the same jutting jaw and protruding brow, beady eyes and thick lips. Spiky hair was given no more attention than their yellowed teeth. Their fingernails had been hardened by wax so that they might be used as weapons in one of their favorite pastimes, gouge fighting. Micajah had a shriveled knot of flesh where his ear had been cut away in retribution for horse stealing. His brother's eyes were scarred by the gouging matches they indulged in. The Harpers represented the lowest-living element of the frontier.

But at this point in Hance's life, they suited him. He was cleaner and better spoken, but was like the Harpers in some ways. He was a man of few scruples, possessing a lust for adventure and a vengeful hatred of Indians. There was as little to admire about Hance as there was about his companions. He stared up at the dripping trees above the Falls of the Ohio and thought about his family.

He'd tried, God, he'd tried to live the life they wanted for him on the farm they'd carved out of the rippling Bluegrass Region, just south of Lexington. But there was nothing about that back-breaking existence that called to Hance.

Lately, he'd begun to suspect that what he wanted would always be out of his reach. He wanted goodness, honor, pride . . . yet those things had never been part of his nature. Instead, he was hot-blooded, self-willed, shrewdly ambitious.

"Get on out there, Adair," Micajah Harper urged, interrupting his contemplation. "You've got to get clear of the bank so you'll be ready when the barge gets here."

Hance crawled out onto a stout limb, watching the dark waters slip by beneath him. It occurred to him that the Harpers were using him, giving him a dangerous role in their scheme to pirate six thousand dollars' worth of prime pelts. But Hance didn't care. He'd been ready for a change when the brothers had taken up with him. He'd followed them up to Louisville, as much for the adventure as for the promise of fabulous sums of money. Money was always a lure for Hance. Not that he was all that fond of the trappings of wealth, but somehow earning it gave him a better sense of his own worth.

Hance pushed aside a sudden, unwelcome image of his parents. He'd managed to stay out of trouble for a good while, consumed by guilt over his part in compelling them to leave Virginia. They'd insisted, of course, that they'd been ready for such a move. But the fact remained that they'd still be living comfortably in Dancer's Meadow if he hadn't killed Artis Judd.

He was smarter now, he told himself. He joined the Harpers with eyes wide open, appreciating—and accepting—the risks of their plan. And the risks weren't that great. The raft they'd spotted earlier in the day was manned by only two Indian trappers, too greedy for firewater to want to split their earnings with guards.

The rain-slick branch he was clutching felt cold beneath his hands. As the moments crept by, Hance began to wonder if the rafters might have put in for the night somewhere up river. Just as he was about to return to shore, a tiny red spot in the distance caught his eye.

"It's them," Wiley whispered. He and his brother were similarly poised in the tree. "Get ready."

Hance tensed and saw the tip of a cheroot in the darkness. It glowed brightly for a moment as the man smoked on it; then it made a red arc and disappeared into the river with a soft hiss. The water stirred as a pole dipped, steering the raft at the precise angle to the tree.

A shoal gave the raft only one option: to pass directly beneath Hance and his companions.

He didn't need the urging of the Harpers to tell him the moment was right. Hance didn't hesitate at the ten-foot drop. He came down squarely onto the raft, feeling it lurch as the Harpers did likewise.

Hance recovered with a lithe movement, spinning. He didn't see much of the raftsmen. The plan was to overpower them, send them into the woods to lick a few well-placed wounds.

But it didn't happen that way. The Harpers fell on the river men with a cold purpose that Hance recognized too late. To the front and rear he discerned dull flashes of steel. Wiley dispatched his victim with practiced neatness, slitting his throat. Micajah struggled with the other. A cry of agony was ripped from the rafter's throat as Harper's long knife slipped between his ribs, was extracted, then buried with a thud in his chest.

Wiley chortled as he wrung a gold ring from his victim's hand, slipping it triumphantly on his own finger. Then, working methodically, the Harpers weighted the bodies with iron pots from the crate and slid them into the river, creating an eddying swirl of bubbles that soon receded.

Hance braced himself against a bale of beaver pelts. Beads of sweat stood out on his brow as a cold feeling writhed through him. He gulped the thick misty air and swallowed bile. Then he shifted his gaze to Wiley.

"There wasn't supposed to be any killing."

"C'mon, Adair, don't say you didn't know what was going to happen tonight. Beside, they were just a couple of no-account Injuns anyway. Probably killed the trappers they stole this load off of, just like Injuns killed my mama in Virginia and my pa up in the licks."

"That doesn't make us any better," Hance said hotly.

"Look, if you want out of this, just say so."

"What's done is done," Micajah added. "Let's sell off this load and do some celebratin'."

They received less than half the actual worth of the pelts, but the warehouseman from Louisville who paid them didn't ask questions. The three men made camp in the woods above the Falls of the Ohio. The Harpers sipped rough corn whiskey and cackled over their success.

"First thing I'm gonna do," Wiley mused, fingering his new ring, "is get me a room and a woman at the Indian Queen in Louisville. Maybe buy a gun for my boy, Caleb. He's had a hankerin' for a man's weapon lately."

"Me, too," Micajah agreed. "And I believe I'll invest some of my share in a good game of draw poker or brag."

Hance joined them in their drinking, but not with the same celebratory air. He still felt sick, cheated, and angry. But rich. Exhaustion and the burn of cheap whiskey eventually dulled his mind to what had happened, and he dragged his bedroll to a cushion of needles protected by a thick, low canopy of pine boughs. He fell asleep with his share of the take tied in a pouch around his neck and a knife in his hand. He knew better than to trust the Harpers.

The sky was still damp and dark when something awakened him. Hance opened his eyes and shifted in time to see three men step into the small camp.

The sudden thumping of blood in his ears was strangely exhilarating. Hance took a perverse pleasure in the tingling sense of imminent danger.

One of the men—tall, tight-lipped, and raven haired—presented himself to the Harpers, hooking his thumbs into his trousers and drumming his fingers casually on his knife sheath.

"I'm Billy Wolf," he said. "Sheriff's deputy." His eyes snapped from Wiley to Micajah. In that instant, Hance realized that the deputy and his men hadn't seen him; the low pines had shielded him from more than the dripping weather.

The Harpers were stupid, but shrewd. Neither of them blinked at the idea that a lawman had walked into their midst.

Wiley grinned crookedly and held out the whiskey flask. "A nip to warm your bones, Billy?" he invited.

Billy Wolf didn't take the flask. With a hand that streaked

like lightning, he grabbed Wiley's wrist in a grip so tight that the flask dropped to the ground.

"Mighty unique bit of jewelry you have there, stranger," Billy growled, eyeing the gold ring on Wiley's finger.

Covering his surprise, Wiley chuckled. "Got it off a no-account Injun," he explained.

Billy gave the arm a twist. Hance gritted his teeth at the sound of snapping bone. As Wiley howled with agony, the other two deputies seized Micajah.

"Stranger," Billy hissed, "that 'no-account Injun' happened to be my brother. And I happen to know he was headed toward Louisville with a load of pelts." The words were gruff with furious condemnation.

Both Harpers reacted in the only way they knew. As Wiley clawed and bit at the deputy's hand, Micajah twisted in the grip of the others. But the Harpers were clumsy fighters and weren't adept at fending off an attack they didn't know about beforehand. They were helpless against Billy Wolf and his tough, silent men.

Hance didn't wait to watch the outcome of the struggle. As he edged away from the campsite, keeping to the shadows, his foot brushed against Wiley's knapsack, which contained the Harpers' share of the money. Hance hesitated for the slimmest fraction of a second. The Harpers would have no need of currency where they were going. Snatching the knapsack, he tucked it under his arm and lunged for freedom.

22

Luke emerged from the public library on the corner of the main square of Lexington, raking a hand through his hair in irritation. Mr. Quick still hadn't been able to acquire the book Luke wanted, a volume by Charles Newbold, which contained ideas on farming so modern that some considered them radical.

Luke wasn't much for reading, but he pored over anything that dealt with farming and livestock. His obsession with improving the farm's yield was the only thing that even faintly resembled passion in his life. There was Hannah Redwine, of course, but what he had with her was too comfortable to be thought of in terms of passion.

At times, Luke wondered at his own discontent. He had so much—a loving family that was working its way to modest prosperity in the finest country west of the mountains, a woman who wanted nothing from him beyond the pleasure he gave her . . . He'd no call to want more from his life.

Preoccupied, he nearly collided with a small, gingham-clad woman who was walking through the square with her arm angled through a large wicker basket. A bonnet fell down her back, hanging by its ribbon.

"Excuse me," Luke said impatiently. "I—" He broke off and stared at her, so amazed at the feeling of utter delight that rippled through him that he forgot to smile. Somewhere he found his voice again. "Hello, Mariah."

She smiled shyly. "Hello, Luke Adair."

Luke knew he was staring, but he couldn't help himself. Mariah had changed a great deal since he'd brought her to Lexington six months earlier. Her pink gingham dress, covered by a serviceable apron, was both practical and demure. She wore her straight ebony hair pulled back and tied with a bit of ribbon. Her only concession to Indian garb was a pair of moccasins peeping out from beneath her dress. The picture she made, standing there with that timid half smile and her eyes as wide and clear as the Kentucky sky, made Luke feel suddenly and strangely alive.

"Well?" she said at last.

"Sorry," he said, flashing her a grin. "I didn't mean to stare. I'm just surprised to see you, Mariah. You look nice, like, like—"

"—Like a white woman?" she asked.

He couldn't decide whether she was teasing or being sarcastic. "You look fine, Mariah. Just fine."

She put her bonnet back in place. "Thank you."

"How's the boy?"

"Gideon? He's well. The girls at Miss Nellie's spoil him terribly."

"So it's Gideon now, eh?"

"I figured he'd best have a Christian name if we're to live among Christians."

Luke laughed. "Among Christians? I'll bet the ladies of Walnut Hill Church would give you an argument on that point."

"Nell Wingfield gave us a home," Mariah stated. "How many of those church ladies would have taken us in?"

Not a one, Luke thought. And neither would I, he admitted, feeling the prickle of prejudice that never failed to sneak up on him when he thought of the Indians who'd intruded upon his life. The sudden guilt that accompanied his prejudice surprised him.

"What about you?" he asked Mariah. "Are they treating you all right?"

She shrugged. "Plenty of laundry and cleaning, running errands and such." She indicated her basket, which overflowed with ribbons and lace from Trotter's store.

He gave her a sideways glance. "So the arrangement agrees with you?"

"Would I have any choice if it didn't?" Suddenly, her good nature seemed to leave her, replaced by resentment. "Maybe you don't understand what my life was like before, Luke Adair. I was free! Free to spend a whole day picking wildflowers if I wanted to. Free to play with the children of the village, to sing songs and listen to the stories of the old ones."

"And free to starve in the winter," he countered, "or die of disease."

She thrust her chin up obstinately. "At least what I did was up to me."

He shook his head. "Sorry to hear you're unhappy."

"How else can I feel, living among the very people who murdered my family? The only thing that makes it tolerable is that my mother was once one of them. She always spoke well of them. And Gideon seems happy . . . He's already forgotten what his life was like before." She stared at Luke, wondering at the expression in his green eyes. And then she realized what she was seeing. She laughed harshly.

"You're angry with me, aren't you?" she said. "Because I'm not grateful for this life you've given me, because I've robbed you of the feeling of having shown great humanity to a lowly Shawnee."

Luke gripped her arm. "Mariah—" She met his eyes again, and he broke off. Some of what she said was true; it did bother him that she was less than content with her new life. He didn't want her gratitude, not in the way she said, but for some reason her happiness was important to him.

"Maybe you're missing out," he suggested, "keeping too much to yourself. This is the first time I've seen you in town."

Her eyes moved over the square and up the length of Main Street. "There's nothing here for me, Luke."

He gestured at the building behind him. "What about that place?"

She gave him a questioning look. "What is it?"

He laughed a little. "The public library, ninny. Folks borrow books to read."

"I'd say you're the ninny, Luke Adair," she returned hotly. "I'm Injun trash, remember? I can't read." She pushed past him and started to walk away.

Luke grabbed her arm and brought her back around to face him. The anger he felt was only for himself, for his own insensitivity.

"Let me go," Mariah said. She spoke softly, but her voice throbbed with outrage.

"Not until you let me apologize. It was a stupid thing for me to say. I should have thought before—"

Her eyes didn't soften the slightest bit. "Let me go," she said again. "Do you want all of Lexington to see you in the company of an Injun?"

"I don't care," he said. "Besides, you're only half—"

"Ah, I see." She gave a bitter laugh. "The fact that my mother was white makes me more acceptable to you. Well, it doesn't matter, Luke. I was raised a Shawnee, and that's what I am, straight through to my heathen soul. These skirts and this bonnet are the only things about me that have changed. Inside I'm a redskin, and always will be."

"I don't hold that against you, Mariah."

"Liar! I know how you feel about Indians."

Her temper was infectious. He let her go so abruptly that she stumbled back, nearly losing her balance.

"I know how I feel about unreasonable women," he snapped. "I can't abide them." With that, he turned and stalked away.

Immediately, he was engulfed by a sense of guilt so overpowering that it was out of proportion with the insult he'd dealt her. Luke had never been given to fits of temper, but something about Mariah rankled, made him want to push her away and gather her protectively against him at the same time.

He walked away with long, angry strides. Damn, but she was a difficult woman. Why did she have to look that way, fragile and hurt, her soft, quiet beauty an unexpected foil for the defiance she showed him? Luke tried to tell himself she was just an Indian squaw, a product of the same savage heritage that had spawned the braves who'd taken Rebecca. But it was no good. Try as he might, he couldn't relegate Mariah to that faceless race that was his enemy. She'd become too human to him.

Mariah leaned against the building called the public library and watched him walk away, pushing his fingers through his hair in an angry gesture. He was so tall and broad, so at ease in his frankly masculine body. Luke had a face the girls at Miss Nellie's would call a real looker— rugged, unyielding features, an easy, self-assured manner about him, and a grin that made one weak in the knees.

God, but he was an Indian-hating bastard. Yet he seemed to want something from her. Mariah's lips curved into a derisive smile. With cold certainty she knew the friendship he offered was conditional. So long as she denied the wild, restless Shawnee blood that pounded through her veins, so long as she dressed, talked, and acted like a white woman, Luke Adair would give her his respect. But she flattered herself if he thought he was worth it.

She turned and looked at the chiseled stone plaque embedded in the side of the building. Placing a finger in one of the grooves, she traced the letters. Her mother had known how to read, had shown Mariah that the strange little symbols formed words. Amy Parker had told her daughter that children not much older than Gideon learned to get meaning from those small symbols.

With sudden purpose, and without pausing to wonder at what compelled her, Mariah entered the library. It was quiet within and smelled faintly musky and sweetish. Forcing away a sudden tingle of nervousness, Mariah approached a table where an elderly man sat reading, holding a thick calf-bound book close to his face.

"Excuse me . . ." she interrupted hesitantly.

He looked up, showing her a wizened face and a soft, almost childlike smile.

"Yes, miss?" His voice whistled slightly through ill-made false teeth.

"How do I go about taking a book home?"

The lines about his face deepened as his smile grew broader. The man was delighted by her interest. Mariah soon learned that Abraham Quick's main calling in life was to share the books he loved with others. Leaning on a well-rubbed hickory cane, he showed her books on every possible subject, from animal husbandry to theology.

Mariah couldn't suppress a smile. Mr. Quick behaved as if he were giving her a tour of the wonders of the world. Finally, he asked her what she was looking for.

She studied the floor. "I—I'm not sure what I'm interested in, Mr. Quick. You see, I don't know how to read." She braced herself for some derisive comment.

But it never came. Abraham Quick hurried to a low shelf of blue-bound volumes, slim, with words embossed on the front. "Never too late to learn," he said happily. "This should get you started. It's *The Royal Alphabet,* a new edition from Boston."

Mariah took the book and flipped through the pages. She liked the feel of it in her hands, the small line drawings and the smell of the print. She gave Mr. Quick a dubious look.

"I hardly know where to begin."

He chuckled merrily. "The beginning's always a good place." Taking her elbow, he drew her over to a table and motioned for her to sit down. "I doubt you'll fancy these dull, preachy tales, but you'll soon go on to more interesting reading."

But Mariah was fascinated from the start by the fact that each symbol on the page stood for a sound, that the sounds blended into words she understood. By the end of the afternoon she was identifying letters and could recite short poems from the book.

" 'C was a cherry tree, pleasing to view,' " she said when Mr. Quick pointed to a letter. " 'D was a drummer, and beat a tattoo. E was an eagle, and soared to the sky, F a fine lady, with head near as high.' "

Mariah giggled at the depiction of the hair style of outrageous proportions.

"Can I take this home?" she asked.

He drew his face into a stern expression. "On one condition, Miss Parker."

Mariah braced herself. Mr. Quick seemed friendly, but like most whites he probably thought of her as a thieving Indian.

But then he smiled again. "I'll only let you take it if you promise to come back for another lesson next week."

Abraham Quick asked nothing in return for his tutelage, nothing but the gratification he reaped in watching her rapid progress through the weeks of the summer and autumn of 1806.

Mariah never allowed herself to wonder why it had suddenly become so important for her to learn to read. As she progressed, the reason ceased to matter. Finally, she'd found something she liked about the white man's world, something that gave her life meaning and purpose.

"Why, Sarah Adair, I never thought you were one to tell whoppers."

Sarah pouted prettily. "It's the truth, as you'll soon see, Lucy. That 'divine gentleman,' as you call him, most certainly is my brother; he just never stays in Lexington for long. His name is Hance."

Ivy Attwater, who had been listening idly to her younger sister's chatter, followed Sarah's gesture. Her gaze slid to the doorway of the Caddicks' ballroom.

Hance Adair looked magnificent in snug butternut trousers and a fashionably cut frock coat, with lace at his throat and wrists. His hair was cropped shorter than fashion dictated, crowning his startlingly handsome face like a golden wreath.

So this was Hance Adair, of whom Lexington's belles talked in fascinated whispers. A man who possessed more than charm or good looks. Through means no one had yet discovered, he'd made a small fortune in a unique shipping enterprise. His ships were deep-draft, oceangoing vessels capable of shooting the Ohio rapids at Louisville and descending to New Orleans, ultimately to make port in England. An amazing concept, Ivy reflected. An ingenious one. One that had made Hance Adair extremely rich in a very short time.

Ivy would have liked to have made his acquaintance, but already he was surrounded by a bouquet of beautiful, tittering women. Hance Adair would never notice Ivy, bookishly plain, and, at twenty-five, with one foot already in the lonely pasture of spinsterhood.

"He never stays around long," Sarah explained to Lucy. "Mama says Hance has always been a restless sort. Come on, Ivy, you must meet him, too. I'd best make introductions before he disappears again."

Hance was used to his sister's simpering friends, with their skillfully batting eyes and fluttering fans, their confidence that the world would fall at their feet should they so command it. Lexington was full of them. But as soon as he took Ivy Attwater's slim hand in his and felt her firm grip, he knew she was different.

He noticed immediately that she wasn't beautiful. Her eyes were too wide set, although the color was lovely, reminding him of a glass of brandy shot through by candlelight. She had a small, impish turned-up nose and thin lips that smiled in a way that was merely friendly rather than fetching. Her nut-brown hair had not been fussed over; it was pulled back to reveal the unadorned honesty of her features.

When he raised her hand to his lips, Hance found himself hoping intently that she wouldn't giggle. If she did so, she'd be no different from all the others.

She didn't giggle. Her smile merely broadened, and she said, "How do you do?" with clear articulation.

"Much better now, thank you," Hance said and swept her onto the dance floor.

Before long the Caddicks' ballroom buzzed with urgent whispers. For Hance Adair, the rakish, golden lady's man, who'd been pursued relentlessly by scores of Lexington's most delectable belles, appeared to be smitten. If he hadn't been dancing attendance on Ivy Attwater before their very eyes, no one would have believed it.

Granted, Ivy was respectable, the daughter of one of Transylvania University's most eminent professors, but the girl was positively *dowdy,* and far too outspoken in matters that should never concern a lady. The bolder gossips also pointed out Miss Attwater's age as yet another defect. At twenty-five, she was well past her courting years.

Hance wasn't impervious to the curious glances, his brother Luke's bemused expression, his parents' fond smiles. Nor did he fail to note the miffed pouts of the Beasley twins, whom he'd been calling on for the past few weeks. But he didn't care. He was fascinated by Ivy Attwater, who somehow managed to move through the steps of each reel and quadrille with careless grace while she spoke knowledgeably on subjects ranging from river shipping to Joseph Buchanan's radical philosophy of human nature.

"I've purchased a tract of land just north of High Street," Hance told her. "I intend to make it the site of the grandest house Lexington has ever seen."

"You said you spend most of your time in Louisville."

"So I do. But I should have a decent house to come back to."

Ivy grinned at him. "How very modern of you, Mr. Adair. So materialistic."

The laughter began in his eyes and then rippled from his smiling mouth. Ivy frowned at him.

"Didn't you think my comment was rather barbed, Mr. Adair?"

"Barbed?" he laughed. "Miss Attwater, it was downright rude!"

"Then why are you laughing?" she demanded.

"Because you delight me. Most young ladies ooze pure rapture when I impress them with my wealth."

She tried to look stern. "Mr. Adair, I am not young, and I never ooze."

"Which is precisely why you're so delightful. Now, if

you're not too disgusted by my materialism, I'd like to take you for a drive tomorrow."

Hance wanted to fill his life with Ivy Attwater. Just being around her gave him a sense of goodness. Never had he met a woman so honest, so utterly devoid of the grasping, smothering qualities he attributed to the fairer sex.

He had two distinct sets of females with which he associated. There were the proper ladies, the ones who simpered and batted their eyes and mentioned pointedly that at thirty-two, Hance should think about settling down. And then there were the others, the bold, lusty, free spirits of the frontier, who didn't hold with repressing their bodies' needs.

Ivy Attwater didn't fit into either category. She was a class unto herself, neither missish coquette nor brash saloon girl. Intelligent and forthright in her opinions, generous of heart, possessed of an honest, captivating charm. She had a direct way of looking at Hance that told him she was more interested in the person he was than in what he had to offer her.

Hance worked hard at courting Ivy. Almost daily he called on her, taking her for drives, for walks, poking through Tilford's bookstore. The Reverend Rankin and his parishioners were astounded to see Hance appear in church with unusual regularity.

But Hance's favorite hours were those he spent alone with Ivy, hours he took great pains to arrange. In May they picnicked on his plot of land, when the delicate flowers of the bluegrass turned the acres to an undulating carpet of lavender.

"Mr. Adair," Ivy said, tucking a mint leaf down into her glass of lemonade.

"I won't answer you until you agree to call me Hance."

She grinned. "Very well. Hance. You've been in Lexington for weeks. Aren't you neglecting your business concerns?"

"A little, perhaps. But my associates, the Tarascon brothers, will take care of things in Shippingport."

"You've never spoken of your business, Hance."

He hesitated, wondering what her reaction would be if he told her the truth. His single exploit into river piracy had convinced him that such a life wasn't for him, but the large amount of money he'd earned had been seductive. The money gave him a sense of worth, a sense that nothing was out of his reach.

He'd happened upon a more agreeable—and more lucrative—way of earning it. Since the port of New Orleans had been acquired by Mr. Jefferson and opened to American shipping, Louisville had undergone an explosion in shipping. The huge rivers of the West provided highways to every part of the world, a resource just waiting to be tapped. Hance had joined the Tarascon brothers in their grand enterprise of building oceangoing vessels below the Falls of the Ohio. They weren't particularly selective in the goods they transported, be it bootleg whiskey, stolen furs, or an honest load of grain.

The profits Hance reaped were astounding.

"Hance . . . ?"

He looked up at Ivy and realized he hadn't responded to her question. Hastily, he said, "I'm into transportation."

"What sort?"

"Anything I sense a demand for."

"You're evading me, Hance."

He smiled the smile that had melted dozens of hearts. Ivy only looked at him steadily.

"It's just that I'm enjoying your company too much to talk of business, love."

She shook her head slowly. "You disappoint me."

Hance chuckled. Other women flattered him, took what he said as gospel, but not Ivy. She demanded more from him, made him present more of himself than he was accustomed to doing. He suspected she'd be fascinated by the intricate workings of shipping, the network of distribution that stretched from Pennsylvania to New Orleans and beyond. But he didn't want her to know about the darker aspects of his enterprise. Her opinion of him had become of supreme importance. He deflected further questions by asking her about herself.

"We're from Boston," she told him. "Father was teaching ancient literature at Harvard College. Unfortunately the faculty there found some of his ideas a bit radical, and they made life rather hard for him. He was ready for a change when he heard about Transylvania University."

"The university is lucky to have him. My brother Israel has spoken highly of his teaching."

"Some of his ideas are quite fascinating."

Hance lifted an eyebrow. "Oh?"

"My parents never discouraged learning, even of things that are supposed to be of no interest to women. Did you know that many of John Locke's ideas stem from his correspondence with Lady Masham?"

He leaned his head back and laughed heartily. "Ivy, I confess I've had cobwebs growing in certain areas of my brain. You're the breath of fresh air that will chase them away."

She flashed him her frank smile. "It appears you've given me a calling, Hance."

She was the only woman Hance had ever met who didn't want either his money or his commitment to marry. Ivy Attwater was a giving person, sharing herself while asking nothing in return. Hance forgot the world as they talked and laughed their way through the summer of 1806, forgot that his life was less than admirable, forgot how he used people and hurt his parents. It was as if some of Ivy's innate goodness had rubbed off on him, minimizing his many flaws.

Lexington society buzzed about the unlikely liaison. The couple appeared everywhere together, much to the dismay of numerous belles and their ambitious mothers. Ivy ignored the talk, but Hance grew weary of it. At the Beasley plantation one autumn evening, he won a horse race and the twins presented him with a coin-silver julep cup. It was customary for the victor to receive a kiss from his hostesses, but Hance merely walked from the racing green, shedding his jacket and loosening his stock.

While the twins glared daggers at his back, he found Ivy sitting beneath a crab-apple tree and gave her the cup.

"You're behaving dreadfully," Ivy admonished.

He took a cup of whiskey from a passing servant, drew long on it, and lay in the grass beside her. "I've never been noted for my manners, love."

She tried not to smile at him, at his lazy grin, at the golden hair ruffled by the evening breeze. "Hance, you cut them dead."

But he only laughed and drank some more and discarded his stock, wresting his shirt front open. His chest glistened damply in the waning light.

Ivy regarded him with frank admiration, unabashedly moving her eyes over him.

"What are all those scars?" she asked.

Hance moved a hand absently to his chest. "Battle scars," he admitted. "But not the soldiering kind. I used to be quite a brawler."

Ivy pressed her mouth into a thin line of disapproval. "I hope those days are over. I despise fighting no matter what the cause."

A lazy grin slid across his face. "I am a man completely at peace," he assured her. He picked up a crab apple that had fallen to the ground and contemplated it. "There's an old saying," he mused, "that if you eat a crab apple without frowning, you'll win the heart of the person you desire."

"Easier said than done," Ivy teased.

He sent her a challenging stare, then bit deeply into the apple. Ivy watched him closely, looking for the first sign of a grimace. Hance chewed slowly, sensually, as if savoring every bit. Calmly, he consumed the apple and tossed the core away.

"Well?" he asked, spreading his arms.

She tried to remain serious. "I've never been more impressed in my entire life."

Laughing, he drew her into his arms. The evening around them was soft and warm, flower-scented and alive with the sound of a fiddler's playing and the murmur of the Beasleys' guests. Hance was a little in awe of the feeling of having Ivy in his arms. He'd held countless women, but none had ever had this effect on him. She was like a soft cushion against the rest of the world, comforting him against all harshness, making him feel as if the two of them belonged to a different world.

But reality came intruding in the person of Farley Caddick. He was a haughty, self-important young man, the son of one of Lexington's leading families. And he despised Hance, despised him for his rakish handsomeness and his ease with the ladies. Only recently, Hance had relieved him of his favorite horse in a card game; Farley was still smarting from the coup.

"Why Hance Adai-ah," he drawled, haughtily dropping his *r*s. "I didn't know you had a charitable bone in your body. But here you are, ignoring all of Lexington's most beautiful songbirds to keep company with a little brown sparrow."

Hance looked quickly at Ivy. The only sign that she'd caught the stab of Farley's insult was a blossom of red smudges on her cheeks.

"Leave us alone, Farley," he said, his voice taut and quiet.

But Caddick made no move to leave. "What are you trying to prove, Adair?" he demanded. "Have you suddenly decided to be a gentleman, or have the belles finally found out what a scoundrel you are?" Farley emitted a harsh laugh. "Imagine, the artful Adair, relegated to entertaining a plain little pigeon. I declare, you're both desperate, aren't you?"

Caddick looked slightly distressed that Hance hadn't risen to his bait. Spoiling for a fight, he went on. "Of course," he drawled, "I could be wrong about the little lady. Could be some of those books she's always reading have finally taught her something. I wonder how long it'll be before she decides to share some of those charms with the rest of us. Tell me, Hance, is it true she's not the dried-up little sparrow we all thought she was?"

No thought preceded Hance's action. Knowing only the heat of blinding rage, he shot to his feet and drove his fist into Farley's smirking face.

Caddick landed with a howl on his backside as blood poured from his nose. Snarling an oath, Hance dove onto him, losing sight of Ivy in the scuffle that followed. The last he saw of her, as Nathaniel Caddick and several others hauled him away from Farley, was her bewildered face, stained with a humiliated flush. A look of bleak disappointment haunted her eyes. Instantly, Hance knew she disapproved of his defense of her.

Roarke appeared like a flame-haired giant, balling up his fists and demanding an explanation.

"He attacked me, the infernal beast," Farley spluttered. "He should be horsewhipped."

"Throw him out," barked Farley's father, Samuel. "Throw him out like the rubbish he is."

Hance wrenched himself from the grips of the two men who flanked him. Glowering, he retreated. "No need for an escort," he growled. "I know my way out."

He paused for just a moment, moving his eyes over the scandalized crowd gathered around the crab-apple tree. He caught sight of Ivy, and their gazes locked.

Her look told him, with dreadful finality, that the image he'd spent weeks building had crumbled. She took a single step away, then turned her back on him.

As he stalked through the dark, dusty streets of Lexington, the only thing Hance remembered with any clarity was that look. The stark, searing disappointment in her brandy-colored eyes, impaling him with disapproval. Hance knew he'd made a fatal error. Ivy would never forgive him for being so rash, for losing control.

Full of self-loathing, he headed for Satterwhite's Tavern and drank enough whiskey to drown a skunk. He did the same at several successive taverns, but the needed effect eluded him. Hance didn't feel as base and worthless as he deserved. Slamming a coin down on the bar, he stormed from the saloon, pointing his feet in the direction of Miss Nellie's. It was fitting, he reflected grimly, for him to turn to Nell Wingfield after being rejected by a decent woman. He'd done it once before, after Janie Carstairs.

But none of the girls, not the lush, brassy-haired Doreen nor the exotic octoroon Cherisse, was to his liking tonight. Even Belle, with her tongue curling into his ear as she whispered an outrageous suggestion, couldn't coax Hance out of his mood of self-loathing.

He was about to leave, disgusted with himself, when a girl he'd never seen before crossed his path, carrying a tray of glasses across the parlor.

The girl was striking—small, with a shining mane of inky hair and wild blue eyes fringed thickly by long, curling lashes. Prominent cheekbones and an arrogant lift to her chin, a well-shaped nose and a smooth brow, added pride to her appearance. Her body was taut and firm, yet at the same time generous in its proportions. She had a delicious-looking mouth and an air of innocence about her that intrigued Hance.

He was seized by a sudden masculine urge. Grinning, he felt more like his old self again. He planted himself in front of her, feet splayed and arms akimbo, smiling lazily as he blocked her path.

"Not so fast, pretty girl," he said. "I wouldn't mind a few hours of your company tonight."

She tried to push past him. "It's not my place."

There was a lilting arrogance in the way she spoke that made Hance pause, considering. Recognition teased his mind, then burst into consciousness.

"By God," he laughed, "why didn't I see it before?" Insolently, he reached out and stroked her smooth, copper-tinted cheek. "You're an Injun, aren't you, girl?" That would be even more satisfactory, spending his anger on such a lovely specimen of the race he hated.

He took the tray from her. "Come on, little squaw," he said. "You and I are gonna have some fun."

"Let me be," she said through her teeth.

Hance's reply was cut off by a meaty hand clapped firmly

over his shoulder. He twisted his head to see Jack, whom
Nell employed to deal with unruly patrons.

"She ain't one of the girls," Jack said.

Hance jerked away from him, reeling a little. "What the
hell difference does it make?" he demanded. "Look, I'll pay
double the usual fee."

Nell edged her way forward, placing her hand on
Hance's arm.

"Mr. Adair," she said with an affected formality that in-
furiated Hance, "I'm afraid I must insist that you leave
Mariah alone. She's not to be had for any price."

Mariah shot Nell a look of gratitude. This wasn't the first
time she'd turned aside a large amount of money for her.
Nell declared that no amount was worth as much as decent
help these days. But Mariah suspected that it was more than
practicality that made Nell so protective of her. Nell's harshness concealed a streak of sentimentality as wide as the Kentucky River. Having ascertained early on that Mariah was a
virgin, Nell had made sure that this quality was guarded as
closely as her cache in the safe.

"Set that tray in the kitchen," Nell said. "You can finish
in the morning."

Awash with relief, Mariah left. After going to the kitchen,
she slipped out the back, crossing the dooryard to the bungalow she shared with Gideon. As she stepped into the cool
night air, gulping it into her lungs, Mariah found she was
shaking. She leaned against the house, hugging herself, rubbing her palms up and down her upper arms.

Mr. Adair, Nell had called him. That name was like a
small needle sticking painfully into her side. She wondered
what relation the handsome, drunken man in the house bore
to Luke. Brothers, probably, although she saw no resemblance in the two. The fair-haired man within was older,
with tiny fans beside his eyes and lines of hardness about his
mouth that made her afraid.

Mariah drew a shaky breath. The predatory look in those
glittering blue eyes, the promise of brutality she heard in his
voice when he discovered she was Indian . . . A man like
that could hate awful hard.

Shuddering, she started across the yard. A chorus of crickets rose up, filling her ears. Mariah had almost reached the bungalow when an arm as strong as a steel band hooked around her from behind, sealing her windpipe.

The reek of whiskey preceded a soft whisper in her ear. "It's me, little squaw."

23

Luke was grateful when Roarke approached him from across the Beasleys' ballroom. Lyla Jessup's desperation to get him to marry her was growing day by day. Tonight she'd boldly extracted him from a comradely discussion of farming techniques and drawn him to the dance floor.

Luke hated dancing. He didn't even like women, not the ones like Lyla. He found their chatter annoying, their laughter forced and artificial. Seeing no use for them, he was never more than distantly polite. Unfortunately, this elusive quality drew women to him like mindless moths to a glowing candle.

Hannah Redwine, who never appeared at these social gatherings, was the one exception to Luke's dispassionate attitude. Two years ago he'd plowed a firebreak around the widow's farm and, with neighborliness rather than passion, had become her lover.

She was ten years his senior, alone in the world, with a no-nonsense way about her that appealed to Luke's practical nature. She'd welcomed him into her life with the ease of a scratch on the back. Temporary, but welcome. That suited

Luke just fine. There were no disappointments because there were no commitments.

Unexpectedly, another image pushed its way into Luke's mind. Eyes of blue, stark against light copper skin, a proud, determined chin . . . He shook his head. Where the hell had that come from?

His father spared him from having to probe his thoughts. His face grim, Roarke took Luke by the arm and steered him out onto the verandah with an apologetic smile at Lyla Jessup.

"Hance has gotten himself into a bit of a scrape," Roarke said.

Luke frowned. "I thought he left hours ago."

"Turns out Farley Caddick's nose is broken. His father vowed to send the sheriff after him."

Luke couldn't fault the Caddicks for that. Although he suspected Hance had been provoked, there was no denying that he'd acted out of turn in smashing Farley's nose. Luke's first impulse was to let the Caddicks have their petty revenge in sending Hance to jail for a day or two to cool his heels.

But he knew better than to say as much to Roarke. His parents had always gone out of their way to smooth things over for Hance. Although Roarke and Genevieve never spoke of it, they were afraid of losing Hance.

"He's probably already left town," Luke ventured.

"We have to be sure," Roarke insisted. "Caddick is mighty tight with Judge Ormsby. Things could go badly." Seeing his son's hesitation, Roarke put out a hand. "Luke. He's your brother."

Luke expelled his breath with a soft hiss. He'd been getting Hance out of scrapes since boyhood, performing the chores he neglected, never revealing to the parson that Hance was the one who tossed bombshell acorns into the schoolroom fire, turning aside one girl's inquiries when Hance was out with another . . . Luke strained against resentment. It was always he who did the covering up, like a harrow over a rutted field.

Of course, there was no one else to do it. Israel was too righteous; he'd see to it that Hance faced up to the error of his ways. Sarah was too young and silly to be any help at all. Only Luke possessed the loyalty, however reluctant, to help Hance.

"I'll go," he said at last, brushing past his father.

Luke's mood darkened more with each successive tavern and gaming hall he visited. Yes, the barkeep remembered Hance; he'd stumbled out, cussing and reeling, a while ago. Finally, at the Sheaf of Wheat, a gambler jerked his head.

"Try Miss Nellie's. The fella wasn't good for much, but I heard him mumble something about that place."

Luke wasn't inclined to pursue the suggestion. Hance was not one to pay for something given freely by any number of girls.

But he'd exhausted all the other possibilities. Feeling weary and irritated, he trudged down Water Street and stopped in front of a two-story white house. Lamplight filtered through a fringe of chintz curtains, and piano music wafted out on the scented breeze, accompanied by low conversation and rippling laughter.

Luke let himself in the picket gate, shaking his head. He didn't much care for Nell Wingfield's girls, with their overblown looks and too-knowing ways. He'd never liked the idea that Mariah Parker worked here.

A scream rent the air, freezing Luke at the bottom of the porch steps. Then he thundered into action, rounding the house to the dooryard in back. In the scant light of a clouded-over moon, Luke discerned two figures locked in an embrace some yards away. The man had his hand buried in the woman's hair. He yanked her head back sharply and leaned forward to kiss her.

Luke started to turn away. It didn't surprise him that some of Nell's patrons treated women roughly; it wasn't any of his business if that's what Nell—

The woman screamed again, a ragged, desperate sound followed by the tearing noise of fabric being rent. Still Luke didn't move toward them. But then the woman began sobbing, and he heard the man curse, his words slurred by drink.

"Injun bitch! I liked you better when you were fighting me."

An icy hand took hold of Luke's heart and squeezed. His brain screamed a denial as he tore across the yard. He grabbed Hance by the shoulders and flung him roughly to the ground.

He dragged his gaze to Mariah, taking in her wide, frightened eyes, lips that were battered and swollen by Hance's mouth. She clutched convulsively at the bodice of her dress but not before Luke caught a glimpse of the flesh exposed by Hance's tearing.

Rage rocketed through Luke. Without pausing to think, he leaped onto Hance, pulling him up by the shirt front.

"Get up, damn you!" Luke ordered, hearing his voice shake with fury.

Hance righted himself and swayed a little, grinning. "What's up, little brother?" he slurred mildly.

"What the hell are you doing?"

Hance shrugged. "Just havin' a li'l fun with the squaw here. Now, why don't you go on back home and leave us be? She was just startin' to enjoy herself."

Luke glanced over at Mariah, wondering if he'd been mistaken. Hance was as handsome as the devil. Maybe she was no different from the others, maybe she . . .

But she was different. Still clutching her dress, she stared at Hance with a mixture of terror and revulsion. Luke placed himself between her and Hance, who laughed.

"Come on now, you're not gonna defend that bit of Injun trash, are you, little brother? It's not like she hasn't had her fun before. I've heard redskins like it a lot—"

"Just get the hell out of here, Hance. Caddick's sent the sheriff after you."

Hance's face grew grim as the unpleasantness of the scene at the party came back at him. But he was too drunk for caution.

"Maybe I ought to get out of here," he agreed. Luke dropped his fists, and Hance seized the opportunity to shove him aside, reaching for Mariah. "Just as soon as I settle things with the little squaw," he added, yanking Mariah's hands away from her bosom.

"You son of a bitch," Luke snapped, and rage built within him again, more intense than before. He took a sort of grim satisfaction in the feel of his fist burying itself in Hance's midsection. He'd never hit his brother before. All the force of years of frustration added impetus to the blow.

Hance stumbled back, his breath snatched away. He gasped for air and then growled, "Quite a punch, little brother. If I didn't know you hated Injuns like sin, I'd think you wanted her for yourself." He swung out in an ill-aimed blow that clipped Luke's jaw, less painful than it was irritating.

Luke hurled Hance against the house. Then he lost track of how many times he struck that handsome, laughing face. He knew only that he was punching his knuckles raw on his brother.

Only Mariah's voice, taut with alarm, finally penetrated his blinding rage.

"Luke. Luke, stop. You'll kill him."

His hands fell to his sides. Hance slithered to the ground with a moan. Luke felt rivulets of sweat crawling down his neck, down his arms, stinging where his knuckles had been laid open. He raised his eyes to Mariah, feeling a new focus for his anger.

"Isn't that what you wanted?" he demanded.

She regarded him steadily. "It's not what you want, Luke."

They stood for a long moment, eyes locked, both breathing heavily. Luke tried to blame Mariah. He wanted to believe she was the reason he'd attacked Hance. But there was more to it than that. Much more.

Nell Wingfield appeared in the yard, taking in the scene with a swift glance. "Should've known he wouldn't leave peaceably," she remarked. Hance began to moan softly. She shook her head. "I doubt he'll mend his ways, though, Luke. What's bred in the bone can't be beaten out of him."

Luke looked at her sharply. "What's that supposed to mean?"

Nell shrugged. "Some other time, Luke. Just get him out of here." She disappeared into the house.

Mariah turned away. "I'll get some things to clean him up."

She walked a few steps, then turned again.

"Luke."

"What is it, Mariah?"

"Thank you, Luke."

Luke didn't knock on the door but lifted the latch quietly and let himself in. The room was swathed in darkness, but Luke knew his way around, skirting the pine trestle table, setting his hat down on the precious, lovingly oiled spinet. The warm, familiar smells of baked goods and lye soap lingered in the air, mingling with wood smoke from the low-glowing potbellied stove in the middle of the room.

Luke slipped through a partition to the bedroom, rounding a highboy and lowering himself to the bedside. Unerringly, his hand found a familiar, softly rounded shoulder.

"Hannah," he whispered. "Hannah, it's me."

She stirred to wakefulness. "Luke." He could hear the smile in her voice.

"I know it's late, Hannah—"

"You know I never mind that, honey." Her hand was warm on his chest.

"I need your help, Hannah. I've got Hance outside." Briefly, he sketched out what had happened at the party.

He brought Hannah her wrapper from a hook by the door and lighted a lamp. They went outside, and Luke brought a groggy and drunken Hance down from his horse. Roused from a besotted half sleep, he swung his fist at Luke with a curse.

"Cut that out," Luke said irritably, dragging him inside. In minutes he was sprawled on the settee, muttering.

Hannah brought a red cedar bucket and some cloths and daubed gingerly at his cheek. The gash was a short split high on the cheekbone, puckered by bruises at the edges. Hannah glanced up at Luke.

"I thought you said he was doing the hitting. Looks like Farley managed to get a few punches in."

Luke winced as Hannah applied bloodroot liniment to the cut. He'd felt its sting plenty of times on various boy-hood wounds.

"It wasn't Farley," he admitted quietly. Self-loathing welled in his throat.

Hannah frowned. "Then who—?"

Hance had come unpleasantly awake at the balm treat-ment. He lifted one corner of his mouth at Hannah.

"My own baby brother's handiwork," he said. His eyes, crystalline despite drink and injuries, glittered at Luke. "Right handy job you did, little brother, defending the vir-tue of an Injun whore." Hance then looked at Hannah, sa-voring her shocked expression. "That's what he did, all right. I was just having a little fun with the squaw—Shaw-nee trash, I guess she was—when Luke took it into his head to rescue her."

Luke tensed. "That's enough, Hance. It's over."

Hance ignored him. "What got you so fired up anyway, little brother? Have you and the squaw got an *amour* going on the side, or—"

"I said that's enough," Luke hissed through gritted teeth.

Hance chuckled and accepted a mug of cider from Han-nah. "Yes, sir," he said softly into the mug, "never thought I'd see the day an Adair got soft over an Injun."

Luke turned sharply away, gripping the edge of the pine table so hard his knuckles whitened. Slowly, the hard edge of rage ebbed away, leaving only the dull ache of anger in its wake.

When Luke turned back to the room, he saw Hannah watching him. Her eyes searched his, and then she gave him a wistful smile of understanding. Her woman's wisdom had already told her what Luke himself didn't know.

*   *   *

The clock's halfpenny moon crept into view as the Adairs sat together on a soft autumn evening. Roarke had designed the room to open out onto the porch, with a view of the verdant acres of their farm.

Soft, metallic chimes, ringing the hour of eight, stirred Luke to his feet. He went to the door and stared out at the land, the sturdy new barn and outbuildings, the granary packed to its walls with corn. He was unconscious of the restless tension in his shoulders and the fist that pressed hard against the door frame.

Genevieve glanced at Roarke and fitted her hand into his. Then she turned her eyes to Luke. "They're saying the Adair men aren't the marrying kind," she mused.

Luke wandered out to the porch and sat on the step, drawing up one knee and resting his elbow on it. The ripe corn stirred in the twilight breeze.

"I reckon I've got enough work to do with the farm," he told his mother. "If I had a wife she'd feel cheated out of my time."

Roarke and Genevieve exchanged a look of amusement. "You don't work any harder than your father did when we were first married. I never felt cheated." She laid her head in the hollow of Roarke's neck in a way that bespoke years of familiarity.

Luke shook his head as he lit a cheroot. "You're different, Mama. You worked right alongside Pa every day. Lexington girls aren't like that. They all want pretty houses and slaves to do their work for them, to raise their children for them, even."

"Those are girls, son. What about the Widow Redwine?"

Luke exhaled a cloud of smoke and gave her a keen look. "What about her?"

Genevieve laughed, that sweet, rippling sound that was so much a part of her. "It's not much of a secret, son, that you've been keeping company with her for over two years. Haven't you ever thought of marrying her?"

Luke had, more than once. But he and Hannah had a comfortable relationship. Too comfortable. If they lived together day in and day out, he knew it would begin to grate on him. Without quite knowing what it was, he wanted more from a marriage.

"Hannah and I have an understanding," he said. And he believed it. She'd never made any demands on him, never asked for a thing.

Genevieve felt a sudden wave of compassion for the widow. Luke truly believed that Hannah wanted nothing from him, and the woman was wise enough to allow him to think as much. But Genevieve knew better. She'd seen Hannah staring at Luke in church, had recognized the stark look of unfulfilled longing, a look she herself had worn during the years of wanting Roarke and denying him. Hannah loved Luke desperately and was not about to make the mistake of driving him away by asking for a commitment.

Roarke glanced at the clock. "Well, we're not getting any younger, son," he said, only half-joking. "We'd love to have some grandchildren to spoil."

Luke shrugged. "Sarah's the prettiest little thing in Lexington right now. In a few years she'll probably be happy to oblige. Or Israel—"

"Israel doesn't take his nose out of his books long enough to tell whether it's night or day," Genevieve explained. "And Sarah may think she's ready, but she's still a child."

"Nathaniel Caddick doesn't seem to think she's a child." Luke studied his parents' reactions closely. The youngest Caddick had been courting Sarah for a few months, as taken by her pink-and-white prettiness as she was by his family's fabulous wealth. The Caddicks were different from the Adairs, acquiring money and slaves at breakneck speed, determined to forget their pennyroyal farming heritage. Luke suspected his parents didn't quite approve of their life style. They had created a tobacco and cotton dynasty, with a stable of house slaves that occupied what amounted to a small village.

"I suppose you're right," Genevieve sighed. "But it's you we've always been able to depend on, Luke. Israel and Sarah are so wrapped up in themselves . . . I once had hopes for Hance and Ivy Attwater, but Hance has been off in Louisville ever since the trouble with Farley Caddick."

Luke's shoulders tensed beneath the unseen burden of his parents' dependence. Trying hard not to feel resentment, he walked down into the yard, to concentrate instead on the coming harvest. Crews would be arriving soon to bring in the corn. And then, Luke thought with relief, he'd be free to lose himself in the wilderness for a time.

He didn't mind thinking about tomorrow. It was the years to come that he avoided considering. The weight of his parents' expectations settled on him, pressing, smothering. All his life he'd worked hard to live up to an ideal of steadfast responsibility.

Luke ground out the cheroot with a savage twist of his boot heel. Just once, he thought, just once he'd like to do something reckless, something totally out of character. Something that went against everything he tried so hard to be.

Mariah walked across the square to the library, her feet moving eagerly beneath her calico skirts. Her visits to the musty-smelling reading room gave her a hunger for learning that filled her mentor, Abraham Quick, with quiet, indulgent joy.

She slipped inside to find Mr. Quick speaking with an aging, rotund man who wore a garish suit of clothes and sported a thick mustache.

"Excuse me," she said, turning back toward the door. "I didn't mean to interrupt—"

"Mariah, wait," Mr. Quick said. "This is someone I'd like you to meet." He made an endearingly formal bow. "Miss Parker, this is Mr. John Bradford, publisher of the Kentucky *Gazette*."

She inclined her head slightly. "Mr. Bradford. I've read your paper."

He puffed his chest out and grinned broadly. "Then you're a friend of mine, Miss Parker. Mr. Quick has been telling me about your achievements."

"It's Mr. Quick's doing," she insisted. "I couldn't even write my name when I wandered in here over a year ago."

"She's quite remarkable, John," Abraham said. "She's been reading a translation of Châteaubriand's 'Atala,' and writes a fine hand, too."

Mr. Bradford cocked an eyebrow at Mariah. "Châteaubriand?"

"Yes, sir."

"And how do you find his work?"

"I—it's quite interesting, sir."

"But you don't care for it."

She flushed. "No, sir. He deviates much too far from the truth. I doubt there's ever been an Indian woman even remotely like Atala. I closed the book when she and Chactas escaped into the 'Allegheny desert.' "

"You sound offended, Miss Parker."

"I am, Mr. Bradford. No wonder the Indian is hated and feared by white settlers. Writers like Châteaubriand lead people to believe we are aliens who live in a fantasy world. But we are human beings, Mr. Bradford, following a way of life we've known for generations. We cannot understand the man who stakes out boundaries and claims the land as if claiming ownership of the very air he breathes."

Bradford stared at her in amazement. His attention had been arrested by the fact that Mariah had used the word *we,* aligning herself with the Indians.

Mariah took a step backward, expecting him to rebuff her. But, still gaping, he grabbed a sheet of paper and a pencil from Mr. Quick's desk and thrust them at her.

"Write it down," he said.

"I don't understand, Mr. Bradford."

"What you just said. Write it down—that, and anything else you'd like people to know about Indians. I'll print it in my newspaper."

Luke held a copy of the Kentucky *Gazette* with a vague feeling of guilt. While the harvest crew labored in the September fields, he'd been reading, fascinated, in the bright light of late morning.

When Luke had first seen the name M. Parker on an

essay in the *Gazette,* he hadn't given it much more than a glance; Parker was a common enough name. But then he'd realized what he was reading. An essay as full of passion and flame as Mariah herself. Where had she learned to write, he wondered, and with such deadly precision?

In the words he heard her voice, saw her blue eyes snapping as she expounded her opinions skillfully, persuasively, demanding to be heard. Luke could sense Mariah's quiet anger as he read. She didn't sensationalize what had happened to her family; her straightforward narrative and subdued description were much more powerful than a graphic tale of the carnage Luke had seen at the Licking River.

He felt a strange ache in his throat as she told of readying her family's bodies for their journey into the world of the spirits. Not once did she beg for sympathy, but Luke felt her pain as if it were his own.

The hooded wall clock enumerated the moments as he continued reading. Cleverly, Mariah had decided to end her lengthy essay by describing other aspects of the Shawnee. Using words like an artist's paintbrush, she depicted her tribe's medicine man, whose gnarled old hands offered cures sent down by the ancients, and a crone named Cocumtha, who spun endless tales at the fireside while the women wove sieves from hackberry bark.

In her fifteenth winter, Mariah had met a woman called Outhoqua—Hair of Red Metal—a mysterious white adoptee who sang the Shawnee songs as well as the hymns remembered from her childhood, who read ceaselessly from her battered red-bound Bible with a curious raised design on its . . .

The words began to swim before Luke's eyes, and the blood drained from his face. His hands clenched convulsively around the paper, rending its edges. Somewhere in the back of his mind he heard a little girl's voice, singing with a militant air. Blinking hard, he reread the words, not daring to believe, yet feeling a terrible hope well up from deep inside him even as he denied it.

The door opened, and he stood quickly, folding the newspaper.

"What's keeping you, Luke?" Roarke asked impatiently. "We've got two wagons full of crew men waiting for . . ." Roarke frowned as he took in Luke's pale, shaken expression, the white lines of shock around his mouth. "What is it, son?" he asked.

"I can't go with you today," Luke said raggedly.

"Are you sick?"

"No, I . . ." Luke swallowed. His parents had accepted Rebecca's death years ago. To resurrect the hope that she lived before he knew for certain was wrong. It would only lay the old wounds open to more hurting.

Luke clutched the paper more tightly. "I've got to go, Pa."

"Son, you're needed here."

The men looked at each other tensely. Pushing his fingers through his hair, Luke said, "You know I wouldn't do this if it weren't important, Pa."

Mariah was humming as she pinned a load of freshly laundered clothing to the line. It was a tune she'd learned from Doreen, who had an uncommonly pretty voice. Mariah's mouth curved in amusement as she shook out a cherry-red petticoat. How the girls loved their gaudy clothes.

But her mind wasn't on the laundry, not completely. John Bradford had been effusive with praise for the first set of essays she'd submitted to him. He'd paid her decently and promised more space in the *Gazette*.

As she worked, Mariah was mulling over a score of ideas that tumbled through her mind. There was something endlessly exhilarating about sharing her ideas with readers, provoking their thoughts.

Luke Adair's sudden appearance startled her into dropping a pair of snow-white breeches onto the dusty yard. She picked them up, frowning at the brown streaks that soiled them.

Luke didn't seem to notice. A look of chilling intensity darkened his eyes as he thrust a crumpled copy of the *Gazette* at her.

"Did you write this?" he demanded. *"Did you?"*

Mariah was a little shaken by his harshness, the hand that bit into the soft flesh of her upper arm.

"I did," she told him quietly. "And it's the truth. Every word of it."

Her quiet dignity seemed to bring Luke to himself. He relaxed his grip on her. "Tell me about the woman you call Outhoqua," he said. "Tell me everything you know about her."

Mariah pulled away and edged toward her basket. "I've got work to do, Luke."

"Mariah, *please.*"

There was a raw edge of desperation in his voice that startled her. This was important to him. She wiped her hands on her apron.

"I never knew her well. There was a strangeness about her, a distance. Outhoqua belonged to a Shawnee renegade warrior. His treatment of her was—dishonorable. Yet he'd made her completely dependent on him. The woman was loyal as a dog. She—"

"What did she look like?"

Mariah hesitated, forming an image from the shreds of her memory. She remembered Outhoqua's head of thick, curling hair, its color always a source of comment among the women. The image came together, and Mariah raised large, disbelieving eyes to Luke. Her hand flew to her mouth.

"Oh, my God," she breathed. "Oh, my God."

Luke impaled her with an intense stare. "Tell me, Mariah. What did she look like?"

She opened her mouth to speak, but no sound came out. Luke's jaw tensed with impatience. Finally, she found her voice.

"Outhoqua looks like you, Luke."

The newspaper dropped unnoticed to the ground. "Not Outhoqua. Rebecca Adair, my sister," he said in a ragged whisper. "Did she never speak of her family?"

"No." A look of pain flickered across Luke's face. "Luke,

she never spoke of anything but her God. You see, she was touched by madness. Black Bear was hard on her."

Black Bear. The name sparked a flame within Luke, contorting his features with rage.

"Where is she now, Mariah?" he demanded.

"I—it's been more than three years . . ."

"But you know them, Mariah. You know where she might be."

She nodded. "There is a set of villages on the far bank of the Wabash . . ."

He inundated her with questions, making her sketch a crude map in the dust. Having exhausted her memory, he started to leave.

"What will you do, Luke?" Mariah asked.

"I'm going after her."

"You can't," she said.

"That's absurd, Mariah. What do you expect me to do when I've just learned there's every possibility that my sister is alive?"

"It's not that simple, Luke. She's a Shawnee now. You can't just ride into the village and take her away. It would be like stealing one of their women."

"Do you think that will stop me?"

"You'd be killed."

"Better to die trying than to live knowing Becky is out there somewhere."

Mariah regarded him solemnly. At last she understood why Luke disliked her, why he'd always begrudged her even the smallest kindness. She was a Shawnee, of the same blood as Black Bear, who had ripped his sister from the bosom of the Adair family.

"I no longer wonder why you hate me so," she said softly.

His head snapped up. "I don't hate you, Mariah, I—"

"You hate all Shawnee," she insisted. "I've always felt it, your disapproval, the way you keep your distance."

She swallowed hard. There wasn't any choice, not really. She couldn't let Luke plunge headlong after his sister, braving the Shawnees' displeasure, the malevolence of Black Bear.

"I'm going with you," she told him quietly, trying not to think about her duties at Nellie's, and Gideon, and the *Gazette*.

"No," Luke objected. "I can't let you do that, Mariah."

"But you will, Luke."

"I don't need the protection of a woman."

"Don't flatter yourself," she said harshly. "And don't overestimate your abilities. I'm a Shawnee, Luke. I speak their language; I know their ways."

"Mariah—"

She held up her hand. "Think of your family, Luke, your parents. If you go alone, they'll lose both you *and* Rebecca."

He stared at her for a long time. "Why are you doing this, Mariah?"

She began hanging the clothes on the line again. Why, indeed? What had he ever shown her but dislike, disapproval? Still, she would have died that winter if it hadn't been for him.

"I owe you my life. And Gideon's. I don't like feeling beholden."

"I never meant for you to feel that way."

The coldness in his eyes sent a chill through her. But she knew he was only trying to drive her away, rejecting her help.

"I'll be ready tomorrow at sunup, Luke," she said evenly. "If you're not here, with a horse for me, I'll follow you."

Anger darkened his face. She braced herself for a lengthy argument.

"Damn, but you're a hardheaded woman, Mariah Parker," he said.

Her head snapped up. She was sure he was insulting her.

But then Luke grinned, that wonderful all-encompassing smile that suddenly made her want to follow him anywhere.

24

    Hance flicked the reins smartly over the twin bobbing rumps of his new matched grays. He'd paid for his four-month absence by having to field Roarke's painful, probing questions and endure Genevieve's long, assessing stares. His parents had always made him feel uncomfortable. They were so damned good, so willing to understand. *Stop me,* he sometimes wanted to scream at them. *The hell with your indulgence, your understanding.*

    But Hance wasn't going to worry about that right now. All the time he'd been gone, traveling down river to New Orleans, keeping company with smugglers and prostitutes, trying to lose himself on the orange-scented levees of the port, one face had haunted him. A face with wide-set brandy-colored eyes and an absurd little turned-up nose.

    He had every reason to believe she'd send him away, or worse, refuse to see him at all. Hance shook his head. Ridiculous, chasing after this churchgoing and far too forward girl, when he could be sure of a welcome at any one of a half dozen houses, with delectable young ladies dancing attendance upon him. Still, no one but Ivy would bring him the contentment he craved.

He rolled his carriage to a stop in front of the Attwater house. It was on High Street, near the university. The brick facing, twined with ivy, gave it a staid, settled look of security.

As he stood on the front steps waiting for his knock to be answered, Hance wondered what he was doing here. Ivy Attwater couldn't possibly need him, not with her indulgent parents and her books and her self-satisfied opinions.

She answered the door herself. Hance tried not to stare, but the intense longing that suddenly pounded in his heart took him by surprise. He placed his foot on the threshold. She looked different—thinner, perhaps, and a little paler than she'd been last summer. But the smile that lighted her face was exactly what Hance had been hoping for.

Ivy laughed, a musical, rippling sound that delighted him. "Don't worry, Mr. Adair," she said, glancing pointedly at his booted foot. "I won't slam the door in your face."

He joined in her laughter, knowing now how very tense he'd been. "I wasn't sure. I guess you weren't too impressed with me after the Caddicks' ball."

"Oh, but I was," she insisted, drawing him into the elegant house. "I was extremely impressed."

"Not in the way I'd hoped." He swept off his hat. "I've come to apologize, Miss Attwater."

She tapped a finger on her chin. "What about the flowers? The bended knee?"

He shook his head slowly, grinning at her playful tone. "Not for you, Miss Attwater. I think I know you better than that." He reached into the pocket of his superfine frock coat and drew out a slim calf-bound volume.

Ivy took it, the smile in her eyes so bright that Hance basked. "Shakespeare's sonnets—the Eld edition! Oh, Hance, you don't know what this means to me. Where did you get it?"

He grinned, shaking his head. What would Ivy say if she knew he'd won it at the gaming table of a New Orleans club?

"No fair asking," he cautioned.

She brought the book to her face, inhaling the smell of

new ink. Hance basked in the warmth of her smile as she flipped through the pages. He watched, delighted, yet feeling as nervous as a schoolboy.

A slip of paper fell from between the pages and wafted to the floor.

"What's this?" Ivy asked, picking it up.

Hance composed his face. "Read it."

She sent him a curious glance but unfolded the note. He heard her breath catch when she saw the words he'd penned once he'd realized that nothing in the world meant more to him than her.

Marry me, love.

Ivy stared at the words for a long time. Then, slowly, she raised her eyes to Hance.

"What does this mean?" she asked finally.

He grinned. His smile had drawn countless women to him, but now he wanted to summon only one. "Exactly that. I want to marry you, Miss Attwater."

"Why?"

Hance hadn't anticipated that question. He himself had spent weeks wondering the same thing. It had something to do with Ivy's wholesomeness, her straightforward ways. She was good, so damned good. Hance knew it wasn't logical, but somewhere deep down inside him he realized he was hoping, by the mere fact of association, that some of Ivy's goodness would rub off on him, reform his flawed character.

"I like you, Ivy," he said at last. Then, with utter sincerity, he added, "Before long I'm sure I will love you."

She laughed, but she wasn't mocking him. "And you decided all this on the basis of our short friendship."

He nodded. "Don't you love me, Ivy?"

She looked at him levelly with those wide, clear eyes. "I don't know. Why did you leave, Hance? Why did you stay away so long?"

He took her hand and kissed it. "I was ashamed of what I did at the Caddicks' ball . . . and after. I didn't think I was good enough for you, Ivy."

"And you do now?"

"No. But I've decided you'll have to accept me with all my flaws."

"Will I?"

He gave her hand a squeeze. "I insist, love."

She looked away. "Hance—"

"What can I do, Ivy? Shall I court you with flowers and pretty speeches, buy you presents—"

She shook her head quickly. "Not that, Hance. Never that." She glanced down again at the slip of paper, crushed now between their hands. "You shouldn't have put it to me like this, Hance. We need time. Time to be together, to get to know one anoth—"

He silenced her with a swift kiss, grasping her by the upper arms and drawing her against him. Hance knew as soon as their lips met that Ivy had never been kissed before.

He also knew, from the barely discernible sigh of longing that escaped her, that she was his.

The world loomed before Luke through the frame of his dun mare's ears. For a month he'd ridden across the stream-webbed wilderness of northwestern Kentucky, through hollows and hills and across great open patches of land, pausing only to eat, sleep, and rest the horses.

He glanced back at his companion and was rewarded by a cheery smile. Mariah's stamina astounded him. She matched his every waking moment, uncomplaining, working as hard as Luke when one of the horses became mired or when it was time to chase away the nighttime chill with a fire.

She knew the wilderness with impeccable woodcraft. She could name scores of plants and knew that one could chew a clean-tasting shrub like spice wood but cautioned Luke against the bitterness of buckeye and the bright poison oak berry. She hunted without blind searching, finding sweet berries growing hidden in the gorse. She could get a fire going in seconds by striking flint against steel and igniting a bit of charred cloth and dried sage.

Luke was hard pressed to best her in anything, until one

day she begged him to show her a more efficient way to load his rifle. Her delight when she bagged a turkey filled his heart with a burgeoning warmth he didn't dare think about too much.

A hundred times a day he caught himself studying her, watching the clean lines of her profile as she shaded her eyes to study the terrain, the glint of sunlight in her inky hair, the way her slim thighs, encased in a pair of buckskins, hugged the flanks of her horse. At night he lay awake listening to her breathing and thinking about her in ways he'd never thought about any woman before.

Fording the rushing yellow waters of the Wabash had exhausted them both. Luke made a small, intimate fire and, too weary to cook, they supped on hardtack and apples. He stared across the fire at her face. The play of light and shadow carved hollows in her cheeks and lent her eyes a depth that made him wonder what she was thinking.

Tree toads piped loudly in the darkness, their shrill voices accentuating the silence of the two people who faced each other across the fire. Luke saw Mariah shift restlessly.

He tossed a stick into the fire with a mumbled curse. She said so little, yet he knew her mind was far from idle. It was ironic; for years he'd avoided chattering women, but now that he was in the company of one who gave him hours of silence, he found he longed to hear her speak. When she rose and slipped soundlessly into the wooded darkness, he cursed again.

At first, Luke thought nothing of her leaving; she never explained her desire for privacy, and Luke never questioned it.

But tension tingled within him as he selected another apple and ate it distractedly. He tried not to notice the deepening twilight, the spectacular glowing cover of the night sky.

Luke's worries took flight. They were in inhospitable country, where the rocks tumbled down to the river from sheer cliffs. Bears and wolves abounded, aggressive animals that didn't fear humans. This was Indian country, too, and—

Swearing, Luke came to his feet. His heart pounded as he

unsheathed his knife and loaded his rifle. With sudden certainty, he knew that if anything happened to Mariah, the rest of his life would be a waking nightmare.

She'd gone toward the river. Luke hacked his way through brambles and wild raspberry bushes, emerging high on a bank of earth and stone. The moon, newly risen, cast a silver glow over the foamy tumble of water that cascaded over the rocks.

Looking down, Luke saw a dark shape at the water's edge. Panic shook him to his soul. Cursing, he tumbled toward the shape at breakneck speed, thinking she'd fallen down the cliff. The form on the bank was as still as death.

"Mariah!" Her name was ripped from his throat.

It wasn't Mariah but her clothes, spread in a damp heap over smooth stones.

"Fool woman," he said through gritted teeth. "Damned fool woman." The water was deep here, the current strong enough to sweep an entire oak tree downstream. Luke shuddered to think what the swirling water could do to a swimmer, especially one so slight as Mariah.

He set his gun against a rock and threw down his hat. He knew that it was absurd, that there was no hope of finding Mariah in the churning, moon-silvered waters, but he couldn't just stand helplessly by and call her name. Stripping down to his breeches, he waded in and then plunged, surging strongly toward the middle of the river. He dove to the sand and rocks of the river bottom.

After exploring until his lungs ached, Luke resurfaced with a strong kick, gripped by helpless panic. "Oh, God, Mariah," he choked.

She was calling his name. At first her voice didn't register in his panic-fogged mind, but then he snapped his head around, scattering droplets of water over the surface. Relief surged through him when he saw her standing on the shore, looking almost childlike in her overlarge hunting shirt.

Luke emerged from the river with great slogging steps. Chasing on the heels of his overwhelming relief came a terrible rage, overtaking the tenderness he'd felt, obliterating reason.

He stopped in front of her, inches from her. His eyes raked her slender form from her slick, inky hair to her bare legs, slim and shapely beneath the formless hunting shirt.

His fingers bit into the soft flesh of her upper arms. "What the hell do you think you're doing?" he snarled.

Mariah caught her lower lip with her teeth. "I was bathing, Luke. What's the matter?"

"What's the matter!" He emitted a sharp laugh. "You disappear for hours, you don't answer my calls—"

"It wasn't hours, and I didn't hear you calling. When I saw you on the bank, I hid. Over there, behind the rocks."

"My God, Mariah, did you think this was a game?" He shook her as he spoke.

She refused to flinch under his rough assault. "I wasn't dressed."

He let her go abruptly, causing her to stumble back. "Damn it, Mariah, I was thinking you'd drowned, and you were worried about your modesty!" He flicked his gaze over her again. The damp shirt did precious little to conceal the frankly feminine curves of her body. Despite his rage, Luke felt a primitive stirring at the sight of her, the smells of water and wind that clung to her.

He turned away sharply. "You'd best finish dressing," he growled. "I wouldn't want to offend your modesty any more than I already have."

She made no move toward her clothes. "Why are you so angry, Luke?"

Her soft query made him pause. Features hard, he replied, "I thought I'd lost you."

Mariah sighed. So that was it. For one spiraling moment she'd imagined another reason for Luke's rage. In the preceding weeks she'd imagined a softening in his attitude toward her, an easing of tension as they rode side by side.

Making a sound of impatience, Luke scooped up their clothes. He clamped his hand around her wrist and pulled her through the brambles, moving so swiftly that Mariah felt as if she were being dragged. When they reached the camp, he hung their garments from trees to dry.

As she studied the grim look on his face, Mariah wondered how she could have ever believed he liked her. She was nothing to him, nothing but his means of dealing with the Shawnee. All he wanted from her was her cooperation in finding his sister. It was clear that he could barely tolerate her.

When he'd finished with the clothes, Luke turned to glare at her.

Pride kept her from lowering her eyes. She was through being ashamed of who she was, through trying to convince him that her Indian blood hadn't tainted her character. She met his murderous gaze with a level stare.

"Do you really hate me so much, Luke?" she asked softly.

A curse burst from his lips as Luke closed the distance between them. "Hate you?" he questioned in a whisper that throbbed with disbelief. "Good God, Mariah, would I have cared so much what happened to you if I hated you? I died a thousand times looking for you tonight."

"But I thought—"

"You thought wrong, Mariah."

And then he was kissing her with all the fervor of suppressed frustration. There was no gentleness in his embrace, no sweetness, only the raw passion of long-denied emotion. Despite the ferocity of Luke's embrace, he radiated a deep tenderness that quelled all Mariah's fears.

When he finally released her, she stared up at him, a hundred questions written on her face.

His smile was soft. "Now do you understand, Mariah?"

"No."

"Neither did I, not until tonight. I was so damned stubborn, resisting what I knew to be true because of, of—"

"Because of what I am. Because my father was a Shawnee."

"I swore to hate the Shawnee because of what Black Bear did to my family." He laid his hand alongside her cheek and smiled again, rubbing his thumb over her temple "But I can't hate you, Mariah."

"You made an awfully good attempt at it." She turned away in confusion.

He caught her arm and drew her around to face him. "I'm not finished, Mariah."

She wondered if he was going to kiss her again. And she wanted his touch.

But he made no move. Instead, his smile disappeared, and he looked at her so intently that she felt he'd touched some part of her beyond mere flesh.

"Mariah."

She studied the darkness of the woods behind him.

"Mariah, look at me. No, don't talk. Just listen." He took her by the shoulders. His touch was gentle now.

"I love you, Mariah."

The world seemed to splinter, to shatter into a thousand pieces. Mariah searched within herself and found that she was afraid.

Because she loved him, too.

"I'd anticipated that question, sir," Hance said, giving Dr. George Attwater his smoothest smile. "I'm well prepared to support your daughter quite comfortably."

George Attwater puffed on a fat cigar and looked across his desk at Hance. Ash from the cigar crumbled down onto his vest. He brushed it away distractedly. Hance Adair's appearance was almost too perfect. Every golden-blond hair was in place, and a white smile glittered in his tanned face. He sported a crisp new suit of charcoal broadcloth. His hands were meticulously clean, the fingernails manicured.

Adair's face was a mask of civility and control. It was impossible to see what was going on behind the smiling blue eyes. Because Dr. Attwater found himself wondering about the man's sincerity, he found himself doubting it.

"Your family's in farming, isn't it, Hance?"

He nodded. "But I've always been one to strike off on my own. I'm into shipbuilding and trade."

Attwater raised a thick, graying eyebrow. "Is that so? What is it you've been trading?"

"Furs, grain, supplies, salt from the licks. Whiskey. With

all the new settlers coming in, there's a demand for just about everything."

Cigar smoke spread in a blue haze across the room. George Attwater looked around, at the long walls of books and stacks of manuscripts and documents. "What a man chooses as his life's work," he said, "tells much about the man."

Hance heard veiled disapproval in Attwater's voice. But he was careful to keep his congenial smile in place. "I agree with you, Dr. Attwater. I've chosen a career that suits me perfectly. Never will I be in a position where laws or other men can tell me exactly what to do."

This provoked a sudden coughing fit, but when Attwater looked up, there was a certain grudging admiration in his face.

"You must be away a lot," he suggested, "since Lexington has no navigable river."

"I intend to keep residences here and in Louisville."

Attwater puffed furiously on his cigar. "You've satisfied me, Mr. Adair, inasmuch as a man can be satisfied with his daughter's choice of a husband."

"I ask nothing more, sir."

Attwater held up a hand to indicate he wasn't finished yet. Setting down his cigar, he grew serious. "We're an old family, Mr. Adair. A proud one. Our ancestors were among the first to brave New England's shores. We've been doctors, ministers, men of learning, and women of great culture and breeding. Never, in either of our families, has there been a scoundrel, a man of questionable character."

Hance's smile disappeared. "What are you saying, Dr. Attwater?"

"That Ivy is a product of generations of untainted breeding. That, in a husband, she deserves likewise. I demand it for her."

Hance's handsome face grew rigid, like cool marble chiseled into a statue of uncommon handsomeness. "Dr. Attwater, I'm a first-generation American. But my parents are decent, hard-working people who take as much pride in who they are as you do in who your cobwebbed ancestors were."

Dr. Attwater's scowl broke into a smile. "By God," he said jovially, "I do believe you're right, Hance Adair. I like a show of pride in a man, almost as much as I like honesty."

"I'm curious, Dr. Attwater. You've barely spoken of Ivy herself."

"I think the world of my daughter, Hance. But it's easy to misread Ivy. Most people think of her as a bluestocking, a sophisticate in many ways. The girl's always been so damned smart it scares me. She mastered Greek by the time she was ten, astronomy by age twelve . . . When she was sixteen, she wrote an interpretation of Helvetius that I actually used in one of my best lectures."

"I'm not at all surprised, Dr. Attwater. Ivy is the most accomplished woman I know."

"But she's innocent, Hance. In every way that matters."

"I know that, sir."

"She tells me she loves you."

Hance's smile returned. "I reckon she does, sir."

Dr. Attwater's hand came down on the desk, hard. "How can she know that?"

"You're not giving your daughter much credit, sir. She's not a little girl anymore."

"Why Ivy, damn it? You're rich, handsome as the devil, and Lexington has more lovely young belles than any town in Kentucky. Why Ivy?"

It was a question Hance had asked himself again and again. He loved what Ivy was, what she represented. Goodness, decency. All that he was not. He met Attwater's gaze.

"Your daughter's perfect for me."

"I'm sure she is. But are you perfect for her?"

"I'll make her happy, sir. When it comes down to it, that's all you want for her, isn't it?"

The lines of age around Attwater's mouth deepened. He stared past Hance at a Jouett portrait of Ivy on the library wall, done when she was about twelve years old. The artist had captured the intent look in her eyes, the intelligence there. Yet the effect had been softened by the presence of a small, wistful smile.

"You're right, Hance," he said at last. "That's all I want."

25

Intriguing patterns of moonlight and shadow danced over Mariah's nude body. She gave Luke a shy half smile that filled him with tenderness so fierce it made him tremble. When she lifted her arms, he came to her swiftly, without hesitation, burying himself in the soul-shattering warmth of her, surrounding himself with her essence, the glow of her love.

It had been this way for a week, ever since Mariah's disappearance had driven Luke to an admission of his feelings for her. Neither Luke's prejudice nor Mariah's distrust had been proof against the emotions that bloomed between them.

They clung together, one moment in desperation, the next in tenderness, until nothing existed beyond the power of their love. The brutality of the wilderness ceased to be real for them; all was cushioned softness and ease as they held each other.

Mariah threaded her fingers through Luke's hair, loving the feel and smell and taste of him. Never had she imagined feeling this way. She wanted to give . . . until her whole being belonged to him and him alone.

She'd learned ways to please a man at Cocumtha's knee, then later at Miss Nellie's. But no one had told her about this ecstasy; no one had even hinted at it.

Mariah knew she had something rare and special. Something precious that would last her a lifetime. The girls at Nellie's spoke of physical love with harsh, world-weary derision. But for Mariah and Luke it was a celebration of all they felt for one another. Every kiss, every touch, was a reverence.

At first she'd doubted herself. How could she, in her inexperience, possibly please a man whose very magnificence overwhelmed her?

With tender patience, Luke had shown her how. And it was easy. Easy, because the love that swelled within her breast dictated exactly what her hands and mouth should do. Instinct—ancient, long buried—burst to the surface and Mariah gained confidence. She knew that Luke loved her touch, the feel of her long hair, loosed from its braid, trailing over his stomach and thighs.

Mariah shuddered beneath him and wished the moment would never end. But when it did, Luke stayed by her side, stroking her and whispering love words, promises that there would be other times, a lifetime of them . . .

"I love you, Luke," she told him. "I love you."

He silenced her with a soft, lingering kiss. "I know, honey. I love you. I didn't know I could ever love a woman like this." He moved his hand over her shoulder and gazed down at her face. "You're so beautiful, so fine."

"Luke," she whispered, winding her arms around his neck, "it'll always be like this, won't it?"

"Always, honey," he promised. "If we weren't out in the middle of nowhere, I'd prove it by marrying you."

She gasped softly. "Would you, Luke?"

Laughter rippled from him. "As a matter of fact, I intend to, as soon as it can be arranged."

She sat up quickly, pulling on her shirt. "Is right this minute soon enough?"

"Sure, honey. But how?" He watched her curiously as she rifled through the saddle packs. She returned with an ear of parched corn and a rabbit's foot that Luke carried to bring him luck in hunting.

She handed him the small bit of fur and bone. "This is supposed to be a deer's foot, but we'll make do." Glancing up, she laughed at the confusion on his face.

"I hope you meant what you said about marrying me, Luke Adair. Because you're about to do it, in the way of the Shawnee."

There was a time when Luke disdained anything remotely Indian, but Mariah had taught him that there was much he could learn from the ways of her people. He stood and drew on his breeches.

"Just tell me what to do, honey."

"We exchange the corn and the rabbit's foot. They are the emblems of our duties to one another."

"That's all?"

She thought for a moment, then reached out to him. "Take my hand, Luke. The handclasp denotes my willingness."

He raised her fingers to his lips and kissed them. She laughed, pulling away. "The Shawnee never kiss, Luke."

He drew one of her fingers into his mouth. "Oh, no? I happen to know one Shawnee who adores kissing. Now, are you going to show me how to marry you or not?"

She nodded, smiling shyly. They exchanged the corn and rabbit's foot with solemnity as the night sounds rose all around them. The simplicity of the ceremony, the privacy, the sharing, lent it a very special meaning. Mariah clutched the rabbit's foot to her breast, her hand trembling a little.

"Niwy sheana," she said softly. "You are my husband."

Luke let out a whoop of pure, unabashed joy, taking her in his arms and swinging her about.

"Mariah—" He broke off abruptly, and she felt his muscles tense, rigid beneath her hands.

The quiet snap of a twig intruded on their embrace. Releasing Mariah, Luke dove for his rifle, priming it as he spun about.

Three metallic clicks sounded in response. Three rifle barrels appeared like cold, round eyes peering from a low stand of hackberry bushes not ten feet away.

Luke conceded his disadvantage. Slowly, motioning for Mariah to stay back, he lowered his rifle.

A satisfied grunt ensued, and a tall, thin brave emerged from the woods. To his right and left two others appeared. Mariah was relieved to see that their faces were not streaked with war paint. They were a hunting party.

She greeted them in the tongue she'd barely spoken in three years and watched surprise replace the suspicion on their faces.

"They're Shawnee," she told Luke quickly. "From the Kispokotha tribe."

She exchanged a few more words with them, flattering them, assuring them of Luke's good will. Of this they were skeptical; many a white man had flattered them and made promises and then knifed them in the back.

Mariah quelled their suspicions with great diplomacy and ascertained that Black Bear was in their village, that the white squaw called Outhoqua still served him.

She turned and looked at Luke. "They know your sister. She is in a village a half day's ride from here."

"Will they take us there?" His voice was taut.

"I'm sure we have no choice, Luke."

Black Bear himself received them. Luke felt the cold stab of recognition when he looked upon that fierce visage, the one eye scarred and the other as dark and chilling as black onyx. Black Bear was adorned with bones and shells and quill work, looking almost princely as he sat in front of the council house. He had the face of a dangerous and vindictive man, a man who would kill without mercy, without feeling.

His cold-eyed gaze swept contemptuously over Luke. "The cub is man grown," he sneered, eyeing Luke's shock of red hair and his tall, broad figure. "He makes bold to come here, into his enemy's embrace."

"We come in peace," Mariah said quickly. "We bring gifts."

"The white man is not a gift giver," Black Bear snarled. "There are always conditions attached."

Mariah nodded. Black Bear was astute enough to understand that. Denying the truth would be an insult to his shrewdness. "Call it trading, then," she said, "a thing of honor that occurs between men. We will exchange our gifts for Luke Adair's sister, whom you call Outhoqua."

Black Bear laughed harshly. "Outhoqua is my woman. She has been so for many summers. Does this Luke Adair think I will give her up so easily?"

Mariah quickly explained Black Bear's position to Luke. She saw him grow rigid with anger and felt cold dread creeping up her spine.

"I want to see my sister."

It took considerable persuasion. But at last, Puckinswah, the old chief, interceded, and Black Bear barked an order at two squaws who were standing nearby. A few moments passed, and then the women returned, a third walking between them.

Disbelief slowly welled up in Luke as he stared at the woman who had been his sister. He didn't know this woman. The color of her hair, which had once been as bright as his own, could not be discerned beneath bear grease and soiled leather whangs. Her figure, clad in skins rubbed with gray ash, was slight and insubstantial, looking as though a whisper could blow her away. Her face—soiled, like the rest of her—had a hollowed-out look and bore the scars of the smallpox that the family had assumed had killed her.

Most unrecognizable of all were the eyes. Slowly, listlessly, Rebecca raised them to Luke. They were as vacant as a pair of empty wells.

Luke swallowed hard, groping for his voice.

"Becky?" He held his hands out to her. "Becky, it's me, Luke. I've come to take you home."

The words failed to penetrate the dreadful emptiness of her eyes. She merely looked away and took a step back.

Black Bear laughed and said something derisive. Then he leaned over to one of the braves nearby. "She may have been his sister once," he sneered, "but now she is what I've made her."

"He still wants to take her back to her people," Mariah said angrily. She'd always hated Black Bear, the way he thought of himself, godlike, answerable to no man. She felt Luke's presence nearby, felt quiet rage emanating from him.

"I will kill him," he told her softly.

She hid her reaction. "You can't, Luke. You mustn't. Even if you manage to kill him, you won't be allowed to live."

"Tell him I'll fight him, Mariah. *Tell him.*"

She wet her lips, feeling helpless and weak. But she told Black Bear, because if she didn't, Luke would merely attack.

Black Bear laughed when Mariah proposed the fight. He accepted without hesitation, eager at the chance to destroy another of the hated Roarke Adair's offspring.

It was out of Mariah's hands now, a man's fight over a grudge that had been sustained and nurtured for thirty years by the darkest of hatreds. In the back of her mind, Mariah had always known it would come to this. Given Black Bear's hatred and Luke's determination, this clash was inevitable.

She didn't speak to Luke. Instinctively, she knew he needed to be alone with his thoughts, to empty his mind of all civility and gentleness. She stood back, leaning against the council house, and watched him.

He removed his hunting shirt and opened the flap of his knife sheath. Sweat glistened on his bare chest, outlining his muscled contours. His face was expressionless yet still so handsome that Mariah caught her breath.

With a surge of dread, she saw that Luke had succeeded in his mental preparation. The hatred in his eyes was as clean and sharp and cold as a finely honed knife blade.

Black Bear treated the challenge as a great jest, although clearly he hadn't underestimated his enemy. He kept a cautious distance at first, dancing lithely in a semicircle in front of Luke, armed with both knife and tomahawk.

Luke was several inches taller than Black Bear, pounds heavier and years younger. But this provided scant encouragement for Mariah. Black Bear had been born and bred a warrior, while Luke was a farmer, unschooled in the dark arts of stalking and killing a foe.

Artlessly, almost clumsily, he lunged. Black Bear's hideous grin widened as he realized his adversary's utter lack of skill.

It was torture for Mariah to watch, to hear the jeers and catcalls of the throng of onlookers. Black Bear toyed with his prey like a bobcat with a rabbit, dancing forward to torment Luke with a quick knife stab, then dancing back, away from Luke's uncontrolled lunges.

Every cut of the knife and blow of the tomahawk was a celebration of his hatred. His glee at the sight of Luke's shoulders and arms, slick and streaming with blood, was hideous.

Black Bear could have finished Luke with a single well-aimed stab, but he wasn't a merciful killer. He wanted Luke to suffer.

Luke bore the attack tirelessly, as if he didn't even feel the stabs and cuts that streaked his arms and shoulders.

Then Mariah realized what he was doing. He was waiting. Waiting for Black Bear to tire himself out. The brave was no longer a youth; his dancing and artful feints were wearing on him. His breathing was slightly labored, and droplets of sweat sprayed from his brow as he jerked his head to and fro.

But Mariah wouldn't allow herself to hope that Luke was gaining an advantage. Black Bear was still a practiced killer. Even when Luke managed, with a powerful kick to the chest, to send Black Bear sprawling, the triumph lasted only seconds.

Luke's small success enraged Black Bear. The brave's attitude of cruel playfulness flared to fierce anger. He righted himself as Luke came at him. His knife sliced into Luke's shoulder, laying open a gash that stained him with blood, from his chest to the waistband of his breeches.

A dullness crept into Luke's eyes, and Mariah could sense the strength draining out of him. Then, high above the noise of the crowd, a thin scream sounded. Mariah whirled to see Luke's sister, standing between the squaws who had brought her from the council house. Eyes wide, arms stretched out in supplication, she strained toward her brother.

Some long-buried spirit had risen to the surface, and there was a light in her eyes: the cold sparkle of terror.

With her stare fastened on the streaming wound in Luke's shoulder, the woman extended her grimy hands toward her brother. "Luke!" she screamed. "Luke!"

Mariah's gaze snapped back to him. He had seen the light of recognition in Rebecca's eyes. He had heard his name on her lips.

With new force, he lunged at Black Bear. His anger was magnificent, terrifying, out of control. He moved so fast that Black Bear's swing with the tomahawk arced wide and missed; then the weapon flew to the ground. The men came together in a deadly handclasp, knives raised and trembling above their heads.

Their faces were close, their eyes pouring hatred. Then, as if by mutual agreement, they ended the deadlock. Both knives dropped. In seconds, the enemies wrestled in a tangle of limbs and curses in the dust.

Black Bear fought with all the feline cunning he possessed, but Luke's power kept his scratching and biting at bay. Luke rolled the brave onto his back and straddled him, grinding his knees into Black Bear's wrists to hold the brave still.

Eyes wide, Black Bear seemed to realize he had been bested. Several braves moved in to defend him. An order barked from Puckinswah stopped them. "Halt! It's Black Bear's fight."

Muttering angrily, the braves fell back.

Luke's anger exploded as he rained blows on Black Bear's face. Even after the brave went limp, Luke continued his assault, cursing incoherently. Mariah saw tears mingling with the sweat that poured down his face.

Finally, the blows subsided, along with Luke's rage. Filthy, bloody, with no trace of the victor's strut, Luke surged unsteadily to his feet. He staggered toward Rebecca, whose screams had subsided to sobs.

Like an awakening wild beast, Black Bear rose. His face was battered almost beyond recognition. His power was nourished by dark hatred. He stumbled at Luke, raising the knife he had retrieved from the dust.

Mariah heard a scream and realized only later that it was her own. Luke wheeled around. Black Bear stabbed out with the knife.

Luke caught his wrist. Black Bear's fingers held the weapon in a death grip. The blade glittered, caressing Luke's pale, stubbled throat and then was pushed away, closer to the brave's smooth, brown neck. Nose to nose, chest to chest, their panting breaths mingling, they faced each other for the reckoning.

Black Bear's hand trembled as he tried to aim the blade at Luke. "You are a killer, Luke Adair," he said in thick, rough English.

"No!" Luke burst out. "You're not worth killing."

"A killer, like all the white man!" Black Bear's mouth twisted in a hideous smile, and he slackened his grip. The pressure of Luke's defending hand pushed the sharp blade into the brave's throat. Dark blood spouted from the wound. Still grinning, as if to savor the triumph of his hatred, Black Bear toppled to the ground. His lifeblood seeped into the dust.

Luke fell still, watching. Mariah hurried to his side. He would need her now. He would need her to help him combat the dreadful self-loathing that shone in his eyes.

"It's over, Luke," she said gently.

"I killed him," he said, as if he had not heard her. "I killed him."

"It's what he wanted, in the end. To die in combat like a true warrior. To make a murderer of you. You can't let him win, Luke. He deserved to die. Look at your sister. See what he made of her."

It was Rebecca's sobs, not Mariah's words, that penetrated his self-contempt. The red-haired woman had crumpled at Black Bear's side and was whimpering over him, like a dog mourning the master who had abused it.

Luke went to her, murmuring softly, having forgotten all

but the fact that at long last, he would be taking his sister home. Only Mariah had an inkling that something was wrong.

Around her, Shawnee voices rang with outrage. Tomahawk in hand, a brave moved toward Luke. Mariah stepped into his path.

"It was a just fight," she said. "Black Bear agreed to the terms."

"The nenothu has killed one of our braves. He must die."

Puckinswah, the old chief, came forward. "The nenothu fought honorably. He will not die. Still, the life that was taken from us must be paid for."

"We've brought gifts," Mariah said desperately. "A fine pacing horse, silver—"

"You know what we want," said Puckinswah, giving Mariah a hard look. "It is you, Whispering Rain."

She stumbled back, incredulous. "I live among the white man now," she said. "It is where I belong."

Puckinswah laughed. "No doubt you like their fine houses and soft beds."

"I work hard in the white man's city; it is no easy life. But I have a place there."

"You will be much happier among us, among your father's people." Murmurs of assent rippled through the crowd.

Mariah argued, but the men would not be moved. With a leaden heart, she realized what she had to do. Luke wouldn't allow her to be kept here against her will; he'd die for her first. She must make him believe that she was staying here by choice. His life depended on it.

She helped him clean and bind his wounds, helped him dress. Not once did she allow herself to think that this was the last she'd see of him. Silently, she vowed to come back to him.

When Luke was ready, she took his beloved face between her hands, memorizing every feature, every line and angle.

"I'm staying, Luke," she told him with quiet firmness.

He looked as if she'd struck him. His face drained to white. "Mariah—"

"These are my people," she said hurriedly. "I've missed them. I've missed the freedom, the songs and ceremonies, the feeling of belonging—"

"But you belong to me!"

Yes, yes, her heart cried out. She blinked to chase away tears that, for the first time in her memory, stung her eyes. "Please, Luke. It's my decision."

"What about us, Mariah?" He gripped her shoulders and shook her. "That was no playacting I was doing last night, when I married you in the way of your people. You're my wife, damn it!"

She looked down. "It was easy for us to dream, Luke, when it was just the two of us in the wilderness. If I returned to Lexington, nothing would be the same. Your family, the people in town, they'd never accept me."

"But—"

"It is my choice. Please accept it." She leaned up and kissed his cheek, nearly shuddering with sadness. "Go, Luke. Take your sister home."

He studied her for a long moment, pushing his fingers through his hair in a gesture of frustration now familiar to Mariah. And then his face grew hard.

"I guess I was wrong about you, Mariah. I was a fool to believe all the things you said to me."

He turned away and helped Rebecca onto a horse, then mounted his own. Mariah forced herself to remain still as he rode away down the wind-swept traces toward Kentucky.

Only when he was out of sight did she sink to her knees. Every tear she'd spent a lifetime holding back flowed freely now, darkening the dust that she pounded helplessly with her fists.

They were two days' ride from Lexington, and Rebecca was still as much a stranger to Luke as she had been in the Indian village. At first it hadn't mattered. His wounds plagued him; the deep gash in his shoulder was healing badly, and his head pounded ceaselessly.

Worse still was the blow of Mariah's rejection and Luke's

inability to tear his mind from her. At night he tortured himself with images of their honeyed lovemaking, remembering Mariah's softness, the shyness that had given way to a passion so sweet it defied description.

Grinding his fist into his hand, Luke asked himself how she could turn her back on that. The one time in his life Luke had dared to entrust his heart to someone, she'd broken it. He felt like an empty shell, as hollow and wooden as a rotted tree.

It was better that way, Luke told himself. Empty shells didn't bleed.

He tried to push Mariah from his mind as he made camp that night. As always, Rebecca was no help. She sat listlessly by, chewing on a bit of hardtack, watching him as he made a fire and rubbed down the horses.

The woods were quiet; it was between the time of the noisy birds of daylight and the nighttime sounds of wolves and owls.

As he sat drinking the coffee he'd brewed over the fire, Luke studied his sister. She was reading her worn red Bible and twisting a grimy braid about her finger. She'd barely spoken a word to him since they'd left Indian country. A snatch of conversation he'd once had with Nell Wingfield crept into Luke's mind.

"Before the first month was out she was touched, Luke. Mad. I suppose it was her way of escaping. She created a world of her own because the one she lived in was unbearable. She took to talking to herself, to the plants and the sky."

Luke squeezed his eyes shut, imagining all his sister had been through, her pitiful retreat into madness.

The next day he knew he had to do something about her. It would be shock enough for his parents to see her again; the least he could do was clean her up a little.

By the banks of the Kentucky River, just short of the road to Lexington, he stopped his horse and lifted Rebecca down from the other. For once he appreciated the unquestioning obedience Black Bear had beaten into her.

"You're to have a bath," he said. He suspected she hadn't

had one since she'd left Dancer's Meadow. He brought a cake of lye soap from his saddle pack and took Rebecca's hand.

As soon as she realized his intent, she began to fight, scratching at him and bucking so hard that she nearly re-opened his wounds. Gritting his teeth, Luke dragged her into the river, both of them fully clothed. He washed her from head to foot, scrubbing her skin and the doeskin dress that had been stained by grease and ash. Rebecca wailed piteously, but Luke was relentless, cleaning her dirt-smudged face, unbinding the grease-slathered braids, washing away the stench that rose from her body.

It was worth it, he decided some time later. Rebecca's face had been scrubbed until it shone, and her hair, drying in the afternoon sun, was now like his, richly red and gleaming. At last he saw his sister, in body if not in spirit. He only hoped she would be healed by her family's love.

The clock chimed gently in the darkened room. Roarke's candle shed light on a small figure at the door, leaning against its frame in a pensive attitude.

"Come to bed, Gennie love," Roarke said.

She looked over at him with a smile but turned back to the door to gaze out into the early-winter night.

"I'm too excited to sleep," she said. "It's not every day one's son announces he's getting married. And to such a girl, Roarke. Ivy Attwater is everything I could have wanted for Hance."

"Aye. Not what I expected, but better. Ivy's got a good head on her shoulders, not all fluffy and frilly like most girls."

Genevieve passed a hand over her hair. There were strands of gray threaded through it now; her hands were lined and careworn, yet as strong as they had ever been.

"I hope her family likes us, Roarke. I always thought the Attwaters so grand, with their house on the hill and all their fine friends from the university."

Roarke came and stood behind her. She leaned back savoring the warmth of him, the loving feel of his hands as they came up to grip her shoulders.

"Gennie love," he whispered huskily into her ear, "you'll have the Attwaters on their knees before you, make no mistake."

She smiled. Roarke always made her feel so fine, so beloved. She was comfortable with his touch but not so comfortable she didn't feel a familiar thrill of excitement when his lips grazed her neck. She sighed and looked up at the stars, thanking the heavens for the miracle of her husband's love.

She pulled away just before the deep eddying pleasure of his touch overtook her.

"Gennie?"

She pointed out the window at the distant dark shape coming over the rise to the north of the farm.

"It's Luke," she said excitedly, recognizing his hat and his stance in the saddle. "He's come home."

They hurried out onto the porch. Luke had been gone for four months, with even less explanation than he usually gave. Another rider appeared around a curve in the drive—a woman.

"Roarke," Genevieve said, clutching at the folds of her wrapper, "who could it be? I'm hardly fit for company."

He lit a lantern and fitted a chimney over the flame. Luke dismounted and helped the woman down, then guided her up the stairs. Roarke held the lantern high, illuminating her face.

The light wavered uncertainly as Roarke's hand trembled. "Holy mother of God," he whispered. "It's Becky." He set the lantern down and leaped from the porch, followed by Genevieve, who was already sobbing incoherently.

Luke stood back, feeling the ache of tears behind his eyes as he watched. Roarke gathered Rebecca against him, running his hands over her hair and murmuring her name, over and over again. Genevieve joined them in the embrace, crying and thanking the stars for her daughter's return.

Rebecca stood immobile, neither responding to her parents' outpouring of joy and affection nor rebuffing it. Only after several moments had passed did Genevieve and Roarke notice.

"She's not the same," Luke explained hurriedly. "Let's go inside."

Genevieve led the unprotesting young woman into the house. Before following them, Roarke stopped and rested his hand on Luke's shoulder.

"How did you do it, son? How did you find Becky?"

Luke glanced away. He could never tell his father how dear the cost of finding Rebecca had been. His quest had brought him together with Mariah; his success had torn them apart.

"It doesn't matter, Pa. Becky's home, and that's all that counts."

"Black Bear . . . ?"

"He's dead."

Roarke studied his son keenly. He didn't miss the sadness in Luke's eyes, the world-weary thin note in his voice. Roarke knew that look; he'd worn it himself, long ago. It was the look of a man who had killed, and who thought less of himself for having done so. But now was not the time to probe the shadows that haunted his son. He picked up the lantern and led the way into the house.

"Stop primping so, Sarah," Genevieve said, guiding the girl away from the bureau mirror. "One would think this was your engagement party instead of Hance's."

"Maybe it is," Israel teased, pulling one of his sister's golden ringlets out and watching it bounce back into place. "She's got her sights set on Nathaniel Caddick."

"That's not so," Sarah declared petulantly. "I just want to look nice for Hance's party."

"Well, you do," Israel said, patting her hand placatingly. "You look as pretty as a spring flower. Caddick would be some kind of fool if he didn't notice."

Genevieve went upstairs, a small smile on her face. Her two youngest children were happy, possessing neither Hance's wild streak nor Luke's quiet intensity. Israel had recently expressed a desire to enter the Presbyterian ministry, and pretty, acquisitive Sarah had never made a secret of her social ambitions. Genevieve didn't understand that, but it seemed important to Sarah, so she allowed it.

Only one of Genevieve's children worried her now. The middle one. The daughter who had tugged on her apron and begged for stories, who had picked wildflowers at the fringes of the garden while Genevieve worked.

And now she was in the room she shared with Sarah, where she had been for a month, hiding from the world.

Taking a deep breath, Genevieve knocked and let herself into the room. Rebecca sat in the recess of a dormer window, the late-afternoon sun slanting down over the yellowing pages of her Bible. She was dressed in a buttercup dimity frock, one of Sarah's that had needed only a few tucks to make it fit Rebecca's thin frame, a flounce at the bottom to lengthen it.

"Becky?" Genevieve crossed the room to her. "You look very pretty."

"Do I?" Rebecca shrugged listlessly.

Genevieve took a small hand mirror from the dressing table and held it up in front of her face. "Look at yourself, Becky. You're lovely. Your father used to say your hair reminded him of wild ginger blossoms."

The girl stared dispassionately at her image—clear gray eyes, clean, regular features, a well-shaped mouth held in a straight line. Her skin was marked by pocks, but not badly.

"Am I pretty?" she asked, truly uncomprehending. She continued to stare, as if looking at a stranger.

"Don't you remember how you used to stand on the bridge over Dancer's Creek and watch your reflection in the water? You must have been just five or six at the time. You used to drop pebbles into the creek and laugh as the image rippled. You were—"

Rebecca raised her eyes to Genevieve. "I don't remember anything about that time."

Genevieve looked away, feeling her heart constrict. For weeks they'd tried to stir their daughter's memory, showing her the sampler she'd once made for Roarke's birthday, bringing up images from her childhood.

"Nothing, Becky?" Genevieve asked. "Nothing about the family we used to be?"

"I . . . When Luke was fighting Muga and I saw him bleed, something stirred inside me and I said his name. But it wasn't really a memory. It was just—"

"Well now, here's my girl," Roarke said jovially, striding into the room. He looked marvelous in his black trousers and meeting coat, his silver-streaked hair combed mercilessly into place. He kissed Rebecca on the head and hunkered down beside her. He grinned, reaching into his pocket.

"I found something for you, Becky. Something I made for your tenth birthday." He handed her a small carved dancing bear.

Rebecca's hands trembled as she took it from him. Something glimmered in her eyes, a bright flicker that hadn't been there before. Roarke and Genevieve watched, hardly daring to breathe, as she pulled the thin hemp string. The bear spun and bobbed on its stick, whirling with a wooden clack.

Rebecca clutched it to her chest. She raised her eyes to Roarke, looking at him as if seeing him for the first time. The sheen of tears in her eyes didn't veil the sparkle of recognition there.

"Papa," she whispered brokenly. "Papa, it's you."

She tumbled into his arms, reaching out to Genevieve at the same time and calling her Mama and suddenly speaking disjointedly of people she'd known, places around Dancer's Meadow that had been hidden away in the recesses of her mind for years.

Hance strode into the room, looking splendid for the Attwaters' reception. He'd been about to give his parents an impatient prod, but his irritation disappeared when he saw them all laughing and talking and crying at once.

"What's this?" he asked, leaning easily against the door frame.

Rebecca extracted herself from Roarke's embrace and

brushed the tears from her cheeks. Slowly, she walked to her brother.

"I'm back, Hance," she said softly. "I'm really back. I remember everything now." Hugging him, she gave a little laugh. "More's the pity for you, big brother. I remember what a wild boy you were, disappearing from church and deviling me with your horrible language."

He chuckled. "You always used to say I'd bring the wrath of the Almighty down about my ears, making me feel like a sheep-killing dog. And here I am, a respectable man, about to marry the most decent girl in Lexington. So if you don't mind, I'd like you to mop your face and comb your hair so my future in-laws won't think my family is completely besotted."

The drive to town was a merry one, the family squeezed together in Hance's gleaming new carriage, wrapped warmly against the chilly air of January. Roarke wondered aloud how Hance had the means to afford such a grand conveyance.

"A respectable man like me deserves a respectable vehicle," he said.

Luke looked at him sharply, at the bright yellow-gold band on Hance's finger as it curled about the reins. He knew exactly where Hance had found the means to buy the carriage and adorn himself with gold. Although his parents were ignorant of their eldest son's connection to smugglers in New Orleans, Luke was well aware of it. In helping Hance move into his new house on High Street, Luke had stumbled across numerous bills of lading for goods that had been traded in defiance of the law.

But he said nothing. Now was not the time to question Hance's lack of scruples, not with Rebecca finally remembering who she was and his parents so happy.

They flanked their eldest daughter, sitting proudly on the high seat of the carriage, smiling and nodding at the people they passed, who paused to stare curiously at Rebecca, whose return had been a source of gossip for a month now.

Only one small incident marred the trip. Rebecca glimpsed Johnny Eagle, an aging Shawnee who frequented the grog shops on Main Street. Although the Indian wore trousers and a linsey-woolsey shirt, he kept his long hair braided and sported a necklace of bear claws, long and curving into his chest.

Johnny Eagle waved unsteadily at the Adairs, giving them a gap-toothed grin. Rebecca made a small squeak of horror and buried her face against Roarke's sleeve.

"There now," Roarke soothed. "He's harmless as a June bug."

"I know," Rebecca said tremulously. "But I just can't stand any reminder of, of—"

"Of course you can't, Becky love. And I'll see to it you don't ever have to be reminded of the bloody savages again. Ever."

26

"*Mr. Coomes,*" *Mariah* said softly, "no words exist to tell you how grateful I am."

Will Coomes grinned and pushed his hat back on his head. There was a dull-white scarred area on his scalp where, thirteen years earlier, he'd lost a good bit of hair and flesh to a Miami brave's scalping knife.

"Well, now, I don't need any thanks, Mariah." He slung his rifle over his shoulder and gazed longingly at the Sheaf of Wheat Tavern. "Beelzebub and me were glad of your company on the way back to Lexington from Indian country."

"You risked a great deal for me," Mariah insisted.

He shrugged. "Not really. It was just a case of good timing and bad weather. I showed up just when the winter decided to get good and nasty. The Shawnee couldn't very well have worried about keeping prisoners during a blizzard like that." He shook his head. "Yes, sir, that was some little storm."

Mariah smiled at his understatement. They'd both nearly died more than once on their journey back to Lexington. But never, not even while wading through shoulder-high drifts or groping, snow-blind, across howling meadows, had she regretted leaving the Shawnee village. Her love for Luke drove her, made her forget fear and discomfort as she focused her mind on him during the six-week trek to Lexington.

Her only thought was to see him, to explain, to erase the shock and pain she'd seen in his eyes at their last parting.

Will Coomes looked again at the inviting tavern, a warm haven in the January chill. Sounds of laughter and clinking glasses issued alluringly from its doors.

"Guess I'll be going, Mariah," Will said. He paused once more to study her. "Damn, but you're a brave little woman," he added.

She turned away with a smile, just in time to see a small figure running toward her.

"Mariah! Mariah!" Gideon Parker hurled himself into his aunt's arms. "You're back! Miz Nellie said you'd never come back!"

Mariah hugged the little boy close, smiling slightly as his nose wrinkled at the smell of her well-greased and ash-rubbed buckskin dress.

Gideon held her hand and skipped happily at her side, "Where've you been, Mariah? Why are you wearing those clothes?"

"I was in Indian country, with my father's people."

Gideon's eyes widened. "Really?" He was worried at first, but after Mariah assured him that she was back to stay, he badgered her for details of her journey. A bit sadly, she reflected that Gideon had been too young to remember his first three years. He might have been born a Shawnee, but he'd be raised an American.

Mariah spoke patiently, ignoring her weariness. "What are you doing in town, Gideon?" she asked. "It's freezing outside and nearly dark."

"Miz Nellie sent me to M'Calla's apothecary in Short Street for some tonic. Come with me, Mariah."

Andrew M'Calla grumbled at having to concoct a draft of calomel and jalap just at closing time, and he eyed Mariah's fringed and soiled Indian garments with distaste.

"Thought you'd stopped being an Injun now that you're

among decent folk," he said uncharitably. "And Mr. Bradford singin' your praises to the sky because of those essays you done for his paper . . ."

Mariah was too tired to take offense at M'Calla's attitude. She took the parcel and thrust it into Gideon's hands, then stalked out of the shop. It was fully dark now; stars had appeared overhead, and the air smelled sharp and clean. Gideon scampered down the street, and she followed more slowly, shaking her head. People like the apothecary would always be part of this life she'd chosen to live. She would have to learn to face their prejudice, to—

A bright orange spark made an arc several feet in front of her, leaving a thin wisp of tobacco smoke. Mariah stopped and looked up at the stone steps of the house to her right, one of the fine ivied residences near the college. Its windows glowed with yellow light and music wafted out on the chilly breeze.

The man who had been smoking the cheroot rose and raked a hand through his hair in a gesture so familiar to Mariah that she gasped.

Gideon turned, frowning. "Go on home," she whispered. "I'll be there later." He shrugged and skipped down toward Water Street.

Mariah clutched the wrought-iron gate at the end of the walk and took a deep breath.

"Luke. Luke, it's me, Mariah."

His body, outlined by the glow from the windows, stiffened. Mariah yanked the gate open and ran to him, pressing against his chest. It wasn't the reunion she'd envisioned; she still wore fringed buckskins and braids and was filthy from weeks of travel, but she didn't care.

"I'm back, Luke," she murmured softly.

He didn't return her embrace. He set her away from him, and she saw anger in his eyes.

"What do you want from me, Mariah?"

"Luke, please listen. I had to stay in the village. I had to pretend it was my choice. Puckinswah, the old chief, would have kept me by force if I'd refused."

"You sent me away," he grated, taking her roughly by

the shoulders. "Damn it, Mariah, I gave you my soul, and you sent me away."

"I didn't know what else to do, Luke. I had to lie—"

"Seems like you lied about a lot of things."

She shook her head vigorously. "Only about wanting to stay with the Shawnee. Nothing else. Luke, why can't you believe me?"

He let out his breath with a soft hiss. "You should have told me."

"I couldn't, Luke. You were hurt; you couldn't have withstood another fight." She winced at the fury on his face, but her gaze never wavered. "I stayed because I was afraid for you, Luke. I came back because I love you."

Tense silence lingered in the cold air between them. Then Luke gave a small gasp of longing and need. He caught her against him, and she was engulfed by his familiar male scent, the feel of his crisp starched shirt front beneath her cheek, and his arms around her.

"You sweet, foolish woman," he murmured. "Do you know what it did to me when you said you wanted to stay?"

She nodded. Her throat began to ache. "Yes. Yes, I do know. Because I was feeling the same thing."

"You could have died getting back here, Mariah."

"I know. But I didn't want to live without you."

The kiss he gave her drew out until her knees felt weak. Then, with a whoop of gladness, he whirled her about. Taking her hand, he led her toward the house.

"Luke, what are you doing?"

He grinned. "There's an engagement party going on inside. We might as well give my family even more reason to celebrate."

"Your family? Luke, no! I'm not dressed for—"

He pulled the door open and brought her into a small but grand vestibule that smelled of polish and lamp oil and rich food. Still she resisted, feeling unwashed and out of place in the house. But Luke pulled her into the drawing room, grinning jubilantly.

The music, provided by a small ensemble of university students, continued. But the people in the room stopped to stare at Luke and the uninvited guest. Roarke and Genevieve approached hurriedly, looking apprehensive and not a little troubled.

"Luke, what's going on?"

"This is Mariah. My wife." Mariah's heart swelled at the pride she heard in his voice. But, seeing shock etched on the faces of his family, she felt a chill grip her.

"Luke," she began, "this isn't a good time—"

"A *redskin?*" Roarke said in a low voice, a voice taut with outrage. Mariah winced at the hatred she heard.

"Now look Pa—"

"No, *you* look." Roarke jabbed a finger at him. "You can't just come waltzing in here with some unwashed squaw and say that."

Luke tensed, holding his anger in check—just barely. "Mariah's been through a lot. I won't have you insulting her."

"Insulting her! By God, listen to yourself. What about what the Shawnee did to your family, torturing Becky for years, nearly driving her insane—"

"Well, well," Hance drawled, approaching slowly, julep in hand. "It's the little squaw from Nellie's." His eyes flicked indolently over Mariah.

"Nellie's?" Genevieve whispered.

Hance grinned. "Don't suppose my little brother told you that, did he? She works for Nell Wingfield. Were it not for the ladies present, I'd elaborate . . ."

Roarke's voice grew thunderous. "You would bring an Injun whore into this family?"

Luke's fist was a blur as it sped through the air, connecting with his father's jaw. Roarke stumbled back less stunned by the blow than by the fact that his son had just struck him. Genevieve's hand flew to her mouth.

At the same moment, Ivy entered the room, her arm linked with Rebecca's. Ivy stopped, sensing immediately that something was amiss. Rebecca's gaze moved about the room, to the music ensemble that had finally fallen silent, then to her father and brother, both of whom were red-faced and breathing fast and sharp.

And then she saw Mariah. Her eyes fastened on the sun-
burst pattern on the buckskin dress, on the greased braids,
the worn moccasins.

Her screams tore through the air, making even the
staunchest of guests shiver with the piercing terror of it.
Rebecca screamed ceaselessly, in hysterical panic, clutching
her arms around her waist and backing away from Mariah
until her back was against the hand-painted wallpaper.

Although Rebecca's screams were incoherent, it was clear
her lapse into hysteria sprang from the sight of Mariah—her
hair braided, her features so frankly Indian, the bold beaded
designs on her dress. Every feature was a reminder of the
savagery Black Bear had dealt Rebecca.

While Genevieve rushed over to calm her daughter,
Roarke leveled a murderous gaze at Luke.

"Get her out of here," he growled.

But by the time Luke turned to Mariah, she was gone.

Sunlight streamed into the brown and yellow bedroom of
the neat clapboard farmhouse, laying golden illumination
over the profusion of wicker baskets that Hannah Redwine
kept for gathering. Luke moved restlessly about the room,
cursing softly when his knee cracked against one of the porcelain knobs of the highboy. He raised a whiskey bottle to
his lips, only to find that he'd emptied it hours ago.

Hannah stirred and propped herself up on one elbow,
brushing aside her blond hair. She looked pretty in the
morning Luke thought. The lines of care etched on her features were soft now, giving her face an endearing quality,
especially when she was smiling.

She wasn't smiling now. Her brow was furrowed in concern.

"Something's wrong."

He lifted the corner of his mouth in the ghost of a smile.
"I figured you'd notice."

She drew her knees up and hugged them to her chest. Her
eyes were soft, but he knew she was looking at him keenly,
studying his every move.

"You were gone so long. I'd just about let go of you, Luke, thinking you'd found someone else."

Luke said nothing. He didn't know anymore. He just didn't know.

"We've been together a long time," Hannah continued, her voice strangely tight. "And it's been good." She drew in a long, shuddering breath. "But I've decided it's not enough for me, Luke. After all is said and done, it's not enough. I need more than just a few hours of closeness whenever the mood strikes you. I need you here, Luke, by my side. All the time."

His mouth went dry. This was not what he'd come to hear. Hannah's words weren't spoken as a strident demand, which he would have found easy to reject. Instead, she spoke softly, a compelling plea.

"What do you want from me, Hannah?" he whispered hoarsely, gripping the door frame and edging unconsciously toward it.

Hannah saw the slight withdrawing movement, the weary ambivalence in his face. And she understood. Her eyes filled with tears.

"Never mind, Luke," she said thickly. "I guess I was afraid to find out until now."

She was brave. So brave she wouldn't allow her tears to fall while he was there. Luke swallowed hard.

"Hannah, I—"

She waved her hand. "Don't worry, Luke. And stop looking so damned guilty. I'll be fine."

"Will you, Hannah?"

Her head descended in a slow nod. "Yes, Luke. I knew this day would come; I knew it from the start." She straightened her shoulders and faced him squarely. "I'm going to marry Zach Houseman. We'll be moving back east."

He looked at her in surprise. "Houseman? He's an old man, Hannah."

A smile twitched about her lips. "Anybody's old compared to you, Luke. Zach is a good man, a decent man. I've never been one to care much about money, but I know I'll appreciate his wealth in my old age."

There was something so melancholy about her whole plan that Luke felt guilty.

"Don't look that way, Luke." She rose and crossed the room, taking a leather portfolio from her letter box.

"Here are the titles to this farm," she said, thrusting the packet into Luke's hands. "I want you to have it."

"Hannah, no. I won't take your farm."

"You've never taken a thing from me, Luke," she said sadly. "At least let me give you this. I know you've always admired the land. With your knowledge of farming, you could make it into something special one day. Indulge me, Luke. Please."

"I'll pay you for it—"

She nearly lost control then, bringing her fists hard against his chest. "Damn it, Luke Adair, don't do this to me. I never asked a thing from you. The least you can do is let me give you the farm."

He'd never seen her like this. Why was it so important that he take her farm?

"I simply want you to have it," she said, answering his unspoken question. "I want to know I've given you something real, something you can hold on to."

"But—"

She gave him a weak smile. "I haven't lost you, Luke. I haven't lost you because I never had you in the first place." He started to speak again, but she held up her hand. "The farm will make you happy in a way I never could, Luke. Don't deprive me of the chance to give it to you."

Mariah's hands tightened around her washboard when she glimpsed a familiar figure with a wide-brimmed hat riding up Water Street toward Nellie's. Leaping to her feet, she went in through the back door and ran through the passageway to the front room, where Jack was cleaning ashes from an iron stove.

"I need your help," she said, nervously looking outside. Luke had dismounted and was lashing his horse to the hitching rail. She gestured at him, and the burly man straightened up, adjusting his breeches.

"I can't—I don't want to see him. Please, will you tell him that?"

"Sure thing, Mariah," Jack said with a grin. He went to the door and motioned for her to stay in the parlor. Flexing big hands, he reached for the brass doorknob.

"Don't hurt him, Jack," Mariah said.

He frowned a little and then nodded.

Mariah hung back, tensing against the chintz curtains, listening. The door opened.

"Christ," she heard Luke mutter, and she could imagine his keen look of irritation when he saw Jack.

"We're closed until sundown," Jack said mildly.

"I'm here to see Mariah Parker," Luke informed him.

"Sorry, friend. She doesn't want to see you."

"Why don't you let her tell me that herself?"

"Now look friend—"

Mariah cringed as she heard the sickening thud of a blow, then an agonized grunt. Finally, the sound of a body hitting the pine-plank floor brought her running from the parlor.

"Jack, I told you not to—"

"Not to what, Mariah?" Luke drawled, inspecting his reddened knuckles.

She backed against the far wall of the entrance way, nearly stumbling over Jack, who was groaning and rubbing his jaw. Above the foyer, Belle and Doreen had run to the railing. They were speaking in rapid whispers and pointing admiringly at Luke.

"Please go away, Luke," Mariah said. "We have nothing to say to each other."

"Yes, we have, Mariah. I want to explain about last night."

She lifted her chin. "You needn't. I found out everything I need to know when I saw your family."

"You don't understand them, Mariah."

"I certainly do," she insisted. "They hate me. They hate me because of what the Shawnee did to your sister. And because I live here. Your older brother has them believing I'm a whore. My presence in your life would go against everything they believe, everything they are."

"They'll get used to the idea, Mariah. Give them a chance."

"Do you love your family, Luke?" She saw the look in his eyes and shook her head. "Never mind, of course you do. You've spent your whole life being their son, pleasing them, building a life with them. It's not in you to hurt them, Luke. I know it."

He took a step toward her. "You're right, Mariah," he said quietly. "I do love my family. They're important to me." He gripped her shoulders. She gasped and tried to wrench away, thrown off balance by his sudden touch. Luke continued with the same quiet insistence.

"It's you I want to build a life with, and to hell with what anybody thinks."

She groped for calm. "But you have everything—a good family, the respect of your friends and neighbors—"

"I don't have you. And you're all I want."

"*Why*, Luke?"

"Because I love you, damn it!"

He almost shouted the words, and was answered by applause and giggles from above. Mariah felt a familiar, welcome jolt as Luke crushed her against him, bringing his mouth down on hers with stunning, fierce tenderness. Suddenly, she knew that nothing could keep them apart, come what may. Gladness and love radiated through her as she returned Luke's kiss with a sweet fervor that matched his own.

Jack groaned again and staggered to his feet, working his jaw. Above, the two girls continued to titter.

"Is everything all right?" Jack asked.

Mariah smiled and laid her cheek against Luke's chest. "Everything's fine, Jack," she said softly. "Everything's just fine."

*   *   *

The amber light of evening bathed the Adair farm in its rich glow, gilding the white house and Genevieve's mountain laurel bushes, which adorned the front of the railed porch. A catbird called and rose from the lawn, winging westward. Luke saw to his horse and trudged up the walk. He'd been over and over what he was going to say to his family. He would be as honest with them as he knew how to be; it was up to them to open their hearts and minds and accept his decision.

The family was at supper when Luke stepped into the dining room, having paused only to remove his hat and splash water over his face and hair. They were all there, even Hance, who had already taken up residence in his nearly finished town house. He was the first to speak.

"So the prodigal son has returned," he drawled.

Luke felt a prickle of irritation, but he swallowed it. Pettiness had no place in this discussion. He took his usual seat between Israel and Sarah, across from Rebecca. She was pale but appeared calm and had eaten a good portion of corn pudding and ham.

"Are you all right?" he asked her.

Rebecca swallowed and nodded her head. But Roarke set down his fork and growled, "She hardly slept at all last night, Luke."

"I'm sorry you were upset, Becky." His gaze moved over the faces of his family, and he took a bracing gulp of cider.

"I didn't quite go about this right," he admitted. "Seeing Mariah again made me a little crazy, because I'd been trying so hard to get used to the idea that she was gone. I should have made the announcement at a more appropriate time."

"You shouldn't have made the announcement at all," Roarke said. "I've never known you to do a fool thing in your life, Luke."

"The Attwaters were a bit put out," Genevieve added, not unkindly. "Their party fell apart after you left."

Luke looked across the table at Hance. "I'm sorry for that," he said.

Hance glowered. "I've spent weeks trying to persuade the Attwaters that my family is better than poor dirt farmers.

They were ready to believe it until last night. Now Mrs. Attwater is taking Ivy on an extended trip to Boston. They seem to be having second thoughts about letting Ivy marry a man whose sister is batty and whose brother has taken up with an Injun whore."

"Hance," Genevieve began, covering Rebecca's hand with hers as the girl's eyes filled with tears.

Luke clenched his fists hard, quelling a longing to smash his fist into Hance's angry face. There had been enough of that last night. Instead, he lashed out with words.

"Maybe you shouldn't worry so much about what the Attwaters think of Becky and me," he said with quiet anger. "Maybe it's their opinion of you that you should concern yourself with. If you're so all-fired certain of your own perfection you wouldn't worry about your family."

Luke saw that he'd hit his mark. Fury flamed in Hance's eyes, and he flung his napkin down on the table. His chair scraped savagely on the floor, and he stalked from the room.

"He's very sensitive, Luke," Genevieve said, her eyes troubled. "Please leave him be."

"Oh, yes," Luke drawled angrily. "Let him paint a rosy picture for the Attwaters so they'll never know what he is."

Genevieve's eyes hardened. "What he is," she said determinedly, "is a fine man who wants to forget the mistakes of the past. And he will. He will, if you let him."

Luke let out a sigh of resignation. "I'm sorry, Ma. I didn't come here to stir up trouble with Hance." He looked at her and then at Roarke. "I wanted to tell you about Mariah."

Everything stopped. Rebecca's fork dropped to her plate with a clatter, and she ran from the room, sobbing against the back of her hand.

Roarke clenched his teeth, and his fist closed around the base of his cider cup. "Damn it, Luke—"

"She's going to have to get used to hearing Mariah's name. And her face and her voice and the fact that her father was a Shawnee."

Luke's words threw his family into disbelieving silence. He cleared his throat, fighting anger. "I didn't mean to cause trouble last night, but I meant what I said, every word of it. I'm married to Mariah. I mean to register it officially as soon as it can be arranged."

Roarke cursed and looked away. Sarah emitted a horrified little gasp, and Israel refilled his mug with an unsteady hand. Genevieve sat and slowly moved her head from side to side.

Anger burst from Luke in a resentful tide. "When a man announces he's been married, he expects a better reaction from his family."

Genevieve looked up, her eyes wet, her sadness tearing at his heart. "How can you do this, Luke? How can you say you've married a Shawnee? Her people ripped this family in two, nearly killing you, taking Becky and turning her into a frightened, confused creature. We'll never be able to look at that woman without thinking of all that the Shawnee brought upon us. We'll never forget, Luke."

"Nor will Mariah," he said heatedly. "She'll never forget the fact that white men murdered her family while she watched. Yet she somehow found it in her heart to live with that."

Roarke gazed at his son, eyes smoldering with fury. "We're different, Luke. We can't forgive what the Shawnee did to this family. And we won't forgive you if you insist on living with that woman."

The words hit Luke with a jolt of red-hot pain. Pressing his knuckles against the surface of the table, he stood up, his eyes growing hard and cold as he looked at the people he'd worked all his life to please.

"Is that it, then?" he asked.

Roarke looked suddenly weary. "Aye. I wish it could be otherwise, Luke, but there you have it. We won't have a Shawnee in our family. And we won't have you if you take up with her."

Genevieve began to sob. Luke went to the doorway.

"I'll be getting my things," he growled. "You're making a big mistake, turning Mariah out before you've given her a chance. It's no great loss losing me, but you're fools to deny yourselves the chance to know Mariah."

He turned on his boot heel and stalked from the room with a silent vow that he would never appear at his father's table again unless Mariah were welcome there, too. He slammed the door behind him.

27

Luke felt a tug, a vague longing that occupied the place in his heart where his family had been until two months before. Already he missed his father's masculine friendship, the long talks with Israel, even Sarah's pretty pouting when he teased her too much. But most of all he missed Genevieve, her laughter, her utter delight in the things he did and said.

Yet now Luke knew how shallow it had all been, the encouragement, the approval. His family's acceptance extended only to things he did that pleased them. The one time he'd done something for himself, they'd withdrawn their approval. They could only love that which they understood, which fit into their way of thinking.

All thoughts of his family fled when he looked over at Mariah, who rode in tense silence in the cart beside him. He brushed his fingers over the slight furrows that marred the fineness of her brow.

"What is it, honey?"

She took his hand and clasped it against her cheek. "I wish today could have been different for you. A man's wedding day should be something special."

He rubbed his knuckles over her trembling lips. "Honey, we already had the grandest marriage in all creation on the banks of the Wabash, with the moon and the stars as our only witnesses. Today's little ceremony was just a formality, to get our union on the books."

"Today was perfect," she maintained. "Nell and the girls made me feel like a princess with all their fussing and silliness. But I couldn't help thinking of your family, Luke. They should have been there. All along I never really believed they could stay away."

"But they did," Luke said, dropping his hand.

Mariah's eyes filled with tears, and she looked away. "I'm afraid, Luke," she stated.

Her tremulous admission tore at his heart. "Of what, honey?"

"I'm afraid one day you'll wake up and realize I'm all you have. Your family has turned from you because of me. I'm afraid you'll resent me for that eventually."

He kissed away the sparkle of tears in her eyes. "God, Mariah, don't say that. Don't ever say that." He took her face between his hands. "You're my whole world, Mariah. I love you. I could live fifty years on one of your smiles."

She kissed him with such gratitude that in the bed of the cart, Gideon dissolved into giggles.

Mariah emerged from the embrace laughing, too, all her uncertainty having been chased away by Luke's loving assurance.

But her smile faded when they came to the top of a bluegrass-carpeted rise, and Luke drew the horse to a halt. They were looking down into a valley watered by a deep, sparkling stream and surrounded by a profusion of honey locust and oak trees. Spring flowers rippled in the breeze, and catbirds sang in the reeds beside the stream.

In the middle of the clearing stood a house. It had a snug, sturdy permanence about it that gave Mariah new confidence. A wreath of dried flowers graced the door.

"Luke," Mariah breathed. "How did you ever manage to—?"

He pushed her bonnet aside and stroked her shining hair.

He'd tell her about Hannah one day, after he himself recovered from the shock of her leaving the farm to him.

A lock of hair strayed across Mariah's cheek, and he brushed it aside. "Ah, honey, if I had my way, it'd be a palace with an army of servants to dance attendance on you."

"I don't need any more than I already have," she insisted sincerely.

With a groan of sudden desire, Luke reached for her again, but this time Mariah eluded him, leaping from the cart and raising her dimity skirts above the swaying bluegrass. Laughing, she ran with a tumbling gait down toward the house.

Luke grinned, enchanted by the sight of her small, lithe figure skipping down the hill. Not even the flowers that graced the slope could match her wild beauty.

"Wait here," he said, tossing the reins to Gideon. He set off after her, plunging through the grass with long-legged strides. Just in front of the house he caught her about the waist, swinging her around and silencing her peals of laughter with a kiss.

Then, grinning, he placed one arm behind her knees and swept her up in his arms. Mariah made a token protest as he carried her toward the door, but she wound her arms about his neck and laid her head on his shoulder.

Luke stepped into the house. It smelled of dried lavender and the freshly hewn wood of new furniture. Bending his head, he gave Mariah a lingering kiss. His heart filled with the pride of possessing her as he looked into her eyes, shining with love for him and him alone.

"Welcome home, Mrs. Adair," he said.

Hance burst into the small, overly feminine office of Nell Wingfield, nearly tearing the door off its hinges. She looked up, startled, and drew away from the anger she saw on his face.

"You owe me, Nell," he said hotly, striding to the wooden secretary where she sat.

"Do I now?" she answered uninterestedly. "Do tell, Mr. Adair."

"You've been stealing my whiskey."

She pretended surprise. "So you're the one responsible for that divine whiskey that's been coming in from Louisville. I must say, it's the best quality I've been able to find. I never could get Mr. Leland to divulge the source."

"You won't see your Mr. Leland around Lexington anymore," Hance said darkly. "He was lucky to get away with his life."

"Pity," Nell sighed. "He was such a cooperative man."

"You won't find me so cooperative," Hance snarled. He dropped a packet of bills of lading in front of her. "I'm here to collect on what you stole, Nell. You owe me close to a thousand dollars."

She brushed the bills to the floor. "I owe you nothing, Hance. Of course, if it's company you want . . . well, my girls always suited Mr. Leland just fine. Perhaps—"

"Not interested, Nell. I've outgrown the need for you and your kind."

A look of disgust deepened the lines of her face. "What an arrogant pup you are; you always have been. Fancying yourself too good for other people."

He laughed humorlessly. "You never have forgiven me for walking out on you all those years ago, have you, Nell?"

The words struck home. Nell shot to her feet and cracked her hand across his face. "Get out," she railed.

He ignored the sting of her slap. "Not until you pay me, Nell. Ivy's coming back from Boston any day now, and I've got a lot of work to do on my house. I'll take the full amount right now."

"For bootleg whiskey?" she snorted. "You won't get a penny from me, and there's nothing you can do about it. Of course, if you decide to be difficult about it, I can always notify the authorities. Judge Ormsby would dearly

"Not as much as James Blair would like to know how you get around paying your taxes on this place, Nell," Hance told her in a threatening voice.

She gasped softly. Blair was Kentucky's attorney general,

as righteous as a Puritan. The local authorities had never given her any trouble, but Blair could ruin her.

"I know him well," Hance continued. "He's not a reasonable man. All it would take is a word from me, and—"

"You bastard!" Nell said, and Hance knew he'd scored a coup. There was genuine fear on that painted face.

"You have until Monday to come up with the money," he said. A stream of curses accompanied him to the door, and Hance smiled. The money was as good as his.

When he stepped down the walk to his carriage, he spied the Beasley twins walking by across the street, accompanied by a pair of Negro women overburdened with parcels.

"Can I give you ladies a lift?" he asked jovially.

The twins emitted simultaneous gasps and flounced away, ignoring him. Too late, Hance realized they'd seen him come from Miss Nellie's Liquor Vault. Laughing to himself, he reflected that women like the twins, who gave themselves away for free, were sure to resent those who turned a profit from it.

"This is getting ridiculous," Hance whispered.

Ivy kept her eyes fastened on the Reverend Rankin, pastor of the Walnut Hill Church, but he knew she'd heard him because she squeezed his hand.

"I was only gone three months," she said placatingly. "I had to go to Boston. My mother has four sisters."

"Who absolutely had to shower you with useless gifts."

Ivy stifled a giggle. "How could we even think of starting our life together without a matched set of silver candle snuffers?"

Hance chuckled softly. Although he'd never admit it to Ivy, he had a secret admiration for the many fine things she'd brought from Boston. The idea of surrounding himself with useless items of luxury pleased him.

"Our life together . . ." He trailed his fingers suggestively up her arm. "I like the sound of that. Lord, but I've missed you, love."

"Have you?" she whispered teasingly. "And I thought

you'd flee to the nearest available arms before the dust settled behind my coach."

"You know better than that, love."

"I do, Hance. Still, you had quite a formidable reputation
with the ladies . . ."

"Only one lady," he vowed. "Lately." His fingers found
the curve of her neck.

Ivy pulled away sharply, not because she was offended,
but because she felt her mother's eyes boring disapproval
into them.

"Stop that," she hissed. "Mother will add another six
weeks to the engagement if she thinks you're too eager."

Hance lifted his eyes heavenward. "God, not that."

Ivy bit her lip to hide her mirth, but the preacher noticed.
He directed his most thunderous look at the young couple in
the boxed pews of the privileged and barked, "Some of us
seem to have forgotten that respect for the church is a godly
thing."

Ivy had the decency to blush, but Hance gave the
preacher a brazen grin, as if to say it was lucky he was in
church in the first place.

After church it was customary to gather on the lawn in
front. The social groups were rigidly marked here, the farmers mingling with their own, while the wealthier planters
kept to themselves. The Adairs were in an unusual position
now that Hance was engaged to Ivy, and young Nathaniel
Caddick was showing signs of interest in Sarah. They stood
in a loose arrangement beneath a honey locust tree, the men
smoking, and the women listening raptly to Mrs. Attwater's
description of Boston.

Ivy strolled away from the group to the long table where
some of the women were cutting pies. She hugged herself,
full of the familiar breezy happiness that enveloped her
whenever Hance was near. She wanted to be with him now,
as he stood talking under the honey locust, but felt she
should take a turn at the womanly chore of serving pie.

She approached the table where the Beasley twins were
unveiling a peach pie. The checked napkin was moved aside

to reveal a lovely golden-brown latticed crust with the peaches glistening and juicy beneath.

"That looks delicious," Ivy remarked. "A masterpiece. I'd love to have the recipe."

Lacey Beasley looked up. Her pleased smile gave way to a feigned look of pity when she saw who had given her the compliment.

"It'll take more than peach pie to keep Hance Adair happy," Lacey told her.

Ivy was stunned by the venom in the young woman's voice. "What do you mean by that, Lacey?" she asked.

The twins looked at each other. "She really doesn't know, does she, Laura?" Lacey said to her sister. "Amazing . . ."

Ivy placed her knuckles on the table and leaned forward, eyes darkening with anger. "I've never been party to your gossip," she said to the twins, "but if there is something you have to tell me, I wish you'd simply say it."

The twins exchanged another glance. "Perhaps we shouldn't . . ." Laura mused.

"But don't you think Ivy has a right to know the sort of man she's about to marry?" her sister asked.

"All men have certain . . . urges," Laura said sagely. "I'm sure even little Ivy can appreciate that."

"Damn you," Ivy snapped. "Stop playing games."

Lacey shrugged. "Since you insist," she said, bending forward conspiratorially. She didn't quite manage to conceal her glee as she said, "Ivy, during your absence Hance consoled himself at Miss Nellie's."

Ivy stepped back, cheeks flaming. "That's a lie, Lacey Beasley."

"I'm afraid not," Laura said. "We both saw him, as did our servants." She shook her head. "Why, it was only last week, wasn't it, Lacey? Pity he couldn't have waited just a few more days. But that's Hance Adair for you . . ."

Ivy fled from the twins, hating them. Then she slowed her pace as a dreadful calm settled over her. The twins were vindictive, to be sure. But it was Hance who had lied. Just moments ago, in the church: *only one lady* . . . How many other times had he lied to her? How many times would he lie again? Could she live with a constant cloud of deception hanging over her?

No one noticed the woman coming up the road until Sarah Adair gave a scandalized little gasp. Genevieve looked up to see Nell Wingfield coming toward them. As always, all she felt at the sight of Nell was a surge of pity, for she felt she was looking at a life gone awry. Nell's yellow hair was streaked with gray, and her once full, sensual face had gone slack, the cheeks and lips too heavy to be considered pretty any longer, no matter how thick their coating of carmine. Nell was dressed in a full gown the color of pink mountain laurel trimmed with black ribbons. Her hat was a ridiculous confection of ribbons and paste fruit, and that, coupled with her large bosom, gave her a rather top-heavy look as she teetered along on bright red-heeled shoes.

Genevieve gave Roarke's sleeve a tug. Nell stopped just on the other side of the picket fence that encompassed the churchyard. Her eyes swept over the gathering.

"Well, well," she said loudly. "So this is the Adair family now. I'm a bit miffed you haven't been to see me." Nell threw back her head and cackled raucously, emitting the smell of whiskey with the laugh. "Don't guess my brand of hospitality would be appreciated," she said. "I suppose it's up to me, then, to call on my dear old friends Roarke and Genevieve."

Genevieve felt Sarah stir nervously behind her and noticed that Mrs. Attwater had stopped her monologue on Boston. She swallowed hard and tried to smile.

"You'd be welcome, Nell," she said in a low voice.

Nell's laughter cracked through the air on a triumphal note. She slapped her thigh. "Did you hear that?" she joked to no one in particular in her loud, brassy voice. "I've been invited to call on the Adairs. Aye, they've not forgotten their Nell, have they?"

Hance saw outrage on the Attwaters' faces and was relieved that Ivy was nowhere in sight.

"You don't belong here, Nell," he said, leaning across the fence.

"I don't, do I!" Nell spat. "I've known that for years." Genevieve and Roarke were the only ones who understood the full force of her resentment. Nell had always been on the wrong side of the fence. Aligning herself with a Tory during the war, becoming an object of scorn in Dancer's Meadow, running her house here in Lexington . . .

"I'm sorry," Genevieve found herself saying.

"Oh, no," Nell shouted, and Genevieve was stunned to see tears glistening in her eyes. Tears of hatred and frustration. "Don't you dare feel sorry for me, Genevieve Adair. *You're* the one to be pitied."

Suddenly, Nell was addressing the entire group assembled in the yard. "They've got you all fooled, I tell you. But look at them. Look at them with all their handsome children around them." She laughed maliciously and leaned over the fence, the points of the pickets pressing into her bosom.

"Oh, no, not quite all, I see. Their Luke has gone to live with a redskin; took her right from my employ without even a by-your-leave. And their Becky, ah, I'm the only one who knows what's with her."

Nell began to strut, feeling the attention of the entire congregation on her. "But those aren't secrets; you all know that. But there's one other thing . . . I think the grand Attwaters have a right to know just who it is their little daughter is marrying." She leveled her malicious gaze at Hance, who scowled defiantly back.

Genevieve's heart missed a beat as the full impact of Nell's words hit her. Nell was one of the few people alive who knew the secret of Prudence Moon, the secret so long buried that it was nearly forgotten. Genevieve clutched at Roarke's arm. From the stiff way he held himself she knew that he, too, understood.

"No," she whispered desperately to Nell. "No, please. You don't know what you're saying—"

"Ah, but I do," Nell shot back. "It's about time folks learned the truth."

"Go away, Nell," Roarke ordered curtly. "Causing us pain is no way to alleviate your own misery."

Nell tossed her head, ignoring him. She turned her attention to Dr. and Mrs. Attwater, who watched her in consternation.

"I'm not here to inflict pain on the Adairs but to prevent the Attwaters from being afflicted by it."

Dr. Attwater cleared his throat. "Miss, er, Wingfield, we have absolutely no interest in what you have to say."

She grinned. "Not even if it's to tell you that your precious daughter's suitor is not what he appears to be?"

She raked her listeners with a malevolent gaze. Her hands gripped the fence like talons. "Hance is not the son of Roarke Adair at all. He's an Englishman's bastard!"

Genevieve leaned helplessly against Roarke as all color drained from her face. In a waking nightmare she forced her eyes to Hance.

He had gone completely rigid. His eyes glittered like two hard, bright jewels in the stony façade of his handsome face. His voice cut through the leaden silence that hung in the air.

"Is this true?"

Roarke held Genevieve steady. "Hance, you're my son in every way that counts. Please, this is hardly the place—"

To Hance the plea was like an admission of guilt. With a vile curse, he spun away, his face a furious red.

He found himself face to face with Ivy, who had just appeared on the scene.

"You heard?" he rasped.

Her eyes were bright with tears. "Yes!" she snapped, mistaking his meaning, thinking he was referring to what the Beasley twins had told her. "Damn you for a liar, Hance."

He held out his hands to her. "Ivy, I—"

"I thought about forgiving you," she said softly. "But I'm afraid this is something that will never change."

"Of course I can't change this, Ivy. I can't help what happened—"

"Stay away from me, Hance," she sobbed. "Don't ever come near me again." She stumbled into her father's arms and asked to be taken home.

*   *   *

The clock with its relentless ticking accentuated the tension in the Adair sitting room. Rebecca was reading from her Bible in a tremulous voice. Genevieve and Roarke were nearby, not listening but sitting together on the settee, gazing out through a rain-lashed window at the dreary evening. Noting her parents' inattention, Becky closed her book and left the room.

"Where could he be?" Genevieve asked softly.

Roarke squeezed her hand, but she could tell from the set of his jaw that he was as concerned as she. Hance had been gone two days. The last they'd seen of him, he'd clattered away from the church, stunned and furious at Nell's revelation and Ivy's rejection. No one had seen him in Lexington since.

"It's a nightmare," Roarke said. "God, I thought everything was finally falling into place for Hance; he had a wonderful girl, a beautiful house in town . . ."

"Maybe it was a mistake for us to keep Hance's parentage from him," Genevieve suggested. "We should have known he'd find out one day."

Roarke nodded. "But he was always such a proud lad. He'd have been devastated."

"I was," came an icy voice from the doorway.

Genevieve and Roarke came to their feet. Hance's wet presence filled the room, his ravaged features shadowed by the brim of a dripping hat.

"Hance, where have you been?" Genevieve rushed to his side, taking the hat and his damp, mud-splattered coat from him. He strode across the room, oblivious to the wet clods of earth he left in his wake.

"I'd rather not say," he remarked. "The places I've been are suitable only for the low creatures of the earth. Bastards like me."

Genevieve gasped and caught the reek of the whiskey on his breath. "Hance, please—"

He whirled on her. "Don't beg me," he snapped. "I'm

through with this family. I never belonged here in the first place."

Roarke felt as though a knife had sheathed itself in his gut and twisted. "Son—"

"I'm not your son!" Hance thundered. Outside, lightning cracked as if to punctuate and confirm his statement. "I should have felt it long ago," he continued. "I was never like the others."

"You're our son," Roarke insisted raggedly. "Have we not always treated you so?"

"How very noble, Mr. Adair. But now I understand why you showed such scant concern for me. Good God, every time I got into trouble, I prayed you'd care enough to punish me, to bring me back in line. But you never did. You just sat back and let me ruin myself. The others felt the back of your hand when it was warranted, but not me. Never me."

Genevieve was crying quietly into her hands. Roarke sighed wearily. "You were different, Hance," he said. "So sensitive, so wild. You had a spirit that defied restraint. I knew no amount of beating would purge you of that."

Hance made a curt, mocking bow. "Thank you for that favor. Thank you for letting me bury myself in iniquity."

Genevieve raised her tear-stained face. "Hance, we can explain."

"That's exactly what I want. An explanation is all I want from you."

"Your mother was my dearest friend in London," Genevieve said softly. She turned her eyes to the window, watching droplets collect and run on the glass. "She was my only friend." She'd told Hance that before, and his jaw ticked impatiently. But then she told him the other things, about Prudence Moon and Edmund Brimsby.

Hance sat perfectly still, his face an unmoving mask.

"She loved him, Hance. She never stopped loving him."

"She was a whore," Hance said tonelessly.

Roarke's arm shot out and grasped Hance's collar, twisting it savagely. "Don't you dare," he said. "Don't you ever, *ever* refer to Prudence in that way."

"It's what she was. You were the only reason she didn't die in disgrace. I suppose I should thank you for that, too."

Roarke released Hance and threaded his hands into his hair. The one thing he would never tell Hance was something he didn't even want to ask himself. Would he have married Prudence if he'd known she was carrying another man's child?

"You're part of this family," he said. "I've never thought of you as anything but my own son."

Hance didn't react. Instead, he asked about the man who'd sired him, probing until Genevieve told him the whole story. And then he left.

28

Even hours after they'd tumbled from their sturdy rope-frame bed each morning, the taste of Luke still lingered on Mariah's lips. She knew it was ridiculous, but a perpetual smile tugged at her mouth, and she went about each day's work full of blithe, breathless feelings that made it seem as if her feet never quite reached the ground.

In the three months she'd lived with Luke on the farm, she'd known a happiness so intense it was almost frightening. He was as much a part of her as her own heart, as the tiny throb of life that she was now certain quickened within her.

For a week or two she'd been bothered by queasiness and certain tender aches. Welcome signs, because they confirmed her hope.

Holding Gideon's hand in hers, she made her way up a gentle slope to where Luke was tending corn. Aided by some of the girls at Nellie's, Mariah was learning to bake and cook. The still-warm loaf in the basket was her best yet, and she was eager to share it with Luke.

She paused just below the field to watch him for a moment. Only Luke could look so much a part of the land he worked. He knew just how to plant and where. Never would Luke make the mistake of putting sweet potatoes in the swollen, rich lowlands that would yield corn fourteen spans high. He was a consummate farmer, with an innate knowledge of earth and seasons.

In the burgeoning warmth of the June day he'd stripped off his shirt. Sunlight glinted over his tautly muscled torso in a way that made Mariah's mouth go suddenly dry. His mane of burnished copper hair framed a face Mariah found so endearing that she—a woman who had always disdained weeping—was sometimes moved to tears.

Luke glanced up and gave her the smile she would gladly have laid down her life for. The smile that told her how much she was loved.

Gideon ran ahead and was promptly swung about and wrapped in a bear hug. The two were fast friends now, Luke's hearty indulgence matched by Gideon's idolizing love.

"I'm going rock hunting today, Luke," Gideon told him proudly. "Mariah said she'd help me. Tomorrow you'll be able to eat your hominy out of a geode bowl just like the Injuns!"

"I'd like that, Gid."

"What about your lunch?" Mariah asked the boy.

"Golly, Mariah, I'm still full from breakfast. Can't I go now? Please?" He was dancing impatiently from foot to foot.

"Go on," she said indulgently. "Start in the woods at the edge of the stream. I'll join you in a little while."

She and Luke looked fondly after the boy as he scampered down the hill. Luke put on his shirt and paused for several greedy swallows of water from the can he always kept close at hand. Finally, he bit into the bread. A grin spread across his face.

"So that's what you've been doing all morning," he said. "And I thought you were writing."

"I managed to finish my piece for Mr. Bradford as well," she said smugly.

He brushed a crumb from his lips and kissed the top of

her head. "An accomplished writer who also knows her way around the kitchen. You certainly look proud of yourself."

Mariah took both his hands in hers and stared into his eyes. "I *am* proud, Luke. But not for the reasons you think."

He frowned at her sudden grave look. "Then what—?"

She brought one of his hands to her lips and kissed it. "Luke, I'm going to have our baby."

Even though it was a natural outgrowth of the love that filled their nights with splendor, Luke gasped in surprise. Every smile he'd ever smiled paled in comparison with the one he gave her now, as he pulled her into his arms.

"Mariah . . . honey," he whispered against her hair. Then he covered her face with kisses so ardent that Mariah soon realized the day's work would never be finished if she let him continue. Reluctantly, she moved away.

"We've both got things to do," she told him, drawing a shaky breath. "Gideon's probably half a mile up the creek by now."

Luke helped her to her feet, then stopped to pluck a single perfect daisy from the fringe of the field. He folded her fingers around its stem and pulled her into his arms for a last lingering kiss. Leaning down, he curled his tongue wickedly into her ear.

"Tonight I intend to finish what we've started," he promised.

Color flooded Mariah's cheeks as she backed away. "Luke Adair, if you know what's good for you, you'll—"

"Yes?" He grinned challengingly.

"You'll do just that!" she retorted. His rich laughter followed her as she ran up the hill.

Hance rode until his horse quivered and snorted in protest. Noting the sweat that glistened over every inch of the beast, Hance slowed to a walk. The fact that he'd nearly ruined a good horse on the wild ride from his parents' farm the night before only heightened his anger. He should have known better. He should know that no horse was swift enough to ride down the demons that plagued him. Two quarts of whiskey hadn't purged him of the bile of betrayal.

He rode through a thick wood where the floor was carpeted by ferns and the mountain laurel had burst into bloom. Hance grabbed savagely at a dogweed twig and broke it off, deriving little satisfaction from its destruction. He took a long swig of whiskey from his flask; his throat was so used to the liquor that it had long ceased to burn. Cursing, he tossed the flask away.

That was the problem, Hance decided darkly. There was nothing, no one, to lash out at. His mother was long dead. He couldn't condemn Genevieve and Roarke for their self-lessness. Even Nell Wingfield couldn't be blamed; her only sin was telling the truth that his loving, misguided family had so carefully concealed from him.

Tension twisted in his gut. The murderous rage he'd felt the day he'd killed Artis Judd was nothing compared with this. The bottom had dropped out of his life, and he was falling into a void, powerless to stop his descent.

"Gideon!" A voice, clear and sweet as a bird song, pierced the silence of the forest.

Hance drew his horse up, stiffening with recognition. And then he saw her. Mariah Parker. No, Mariah Adair now. She had a more legitimate claim to the name than Hance had. Framed by a pair of pokeberry bushes, she looked as fresh and sweet as summertime itself.

"Gideon!" she called again. "Gideon, where are you?"

Although her brow was furrowed slightly in annoyance, it was clear to Hance that she was a supremely happy woman. Even as she called and scolded, she held a daisy in her hand and from time to time would run it across her beautiful cheek, a soft smile tugging at her mouth.

The tension inside Hance burst. He dropped from his horse and lashed its reins to a shrub, feeling almost relieved. At last he'd found an outlet for his rage.

He didn't stop to examine his reasoning. Mariah and Luke had no right to be happy, to mock him with the perfection of their own lives. Hance wouldn't rest until he'd ruined that happiness with his brand of revenge. Luke was the eldest son now. He had it all—the premier position in the family, the mate of his heart, a farm that promised to be successful.

And Hance had nothing. Not even a name of his own. And not Ivy. Oh, God, he thought, a red haze of rage swimming before his eyes. This time he'd really lost Ivy.

He wanted to even the score, to take from Luke the one thing he cherished above all others, just as Ivy had been taken from him. Clenching his fists, he stepped into Mariah's path.

The fury in his face was obvious. Instantly, she recoiled, dropping the daisy to the forest floor.

Hance laughed maliciously. "You're right to back away, little squaw. My feelings for you haven't changed since that first night we met. I mean to finish what we started."

Just a short time ago, Luke had said those very words to her, and she'd been filled with warm anticipation. Coming from Hance, the words filled her with terror. She clutched unconsciously at her midsection.

"Hance, please."

It was exactly what he wanted to hear. Luke's wife, begging for mercy. He seized her, winding his fingers savagely through her hair and jerking her head back, forcing her to look into his eyes. Mariah could see nothing but his rage, the cruelly twisted smile he gave her.

Neither one of them noticed the small boy who appeared on the scene briefly and fled.

Ivy toyed with the food on her plate, managing to avoid eating even the smallest bite. Her mother held her tongue for as long as she could. But finally it became too much.

"Dear, you must eat your lunch. And you're far too pale. You should start thinking about getting out."

Ivy stared out the window. She didn't see the twining yellow jessamine there but Hance with that irresistible smile on his beautiful face. *Why did you have to lie?* she asked him. By now the ache in her heart had become familiar, almost comforting despite the pain. It was the only thing that told her she was still alive.

At that moment the houseboy approached the table. "Someone to see you, Miss Ivy," he murmured.

Grateful for an excuse to leave her parents' sympathetic looks and shaking heads, she went to the foyer.

"She's waiting at the kitchen entrance," the houseboy explained. Frowning, Ivy went to the back of the house.

An elaborately garbed woman stood on the doorstep, her face concealed by a huge ornamented hat.

Ivy stopped and stared in surprise. "Miss Wingfield."

Nell's hands moved nervously over the ribbons that adorned her dress. She attempted to smile.

"Hello, Miss Attwater. May we talk?" She hesitated, as if fully expecting to be ejected from the house. But she didn't know Ivy, who possessed none of the false propriety of her peers.

"Come in," she said immediately, guiding Nell by the elbow.

"No, I—" Nell looked pointedly at the cook and a maid, who had stopped working to listen. "Could we go outside, Miss Attwater?"

"Of course," Ivy said, leading the way to the rear garden.

"I have something to say to you," Nell announced hesitantly. "I should've spoken up three days ago. But it was only today that I learned to regret the things I've done." Absently, she plucked a jessamine blossom and toyed with it. "I've just seen Reverend Rankin," she continued. "Lord, that man had every right to condemn me for upsetting his parishioners last Sunday, but he didn't. He invited me into his fold."

Ivy wasn't surprised. Adam Rankin was the epitome of Christian tolerance. "I'm glad for you, Miss Wingfield," she said.

"Miss Attwater," Nell said, "I've come to ask your forgiveness. I feel responsible for driving you and Hance Adair apart practically on the eve of your wedding."

Ivy looked away, feeling a familiar stab of pain. "You had nothing to do with that," she said brokenly. "It was all

Hance's doing that he went to your—your house. His disloyalty had nothing to do with you."

"My house . . . ?" Nell looked confused. She thought for a moment, then shook her head. "Ah, yes, I remember now. Hance *did* come by." She caught the look on Ivy's face. "It wasn't like that," she added hastily. "He had quite another reason for coming. I owed him money, you see, and—"

Ivy's shoulders began to shake with sobs.

"Honest, Miss Attwater," Nell continued, "that's all that happened. God forgive me, I did offer him some, ah, company, but he refused. Quite adamantly."

Ivy swiveled around, eyes wide. "Really? That's all there was to it?"

"Of course."

"But when I asked Hance about it he—he made no attempt to deny it!"

"The way I remember it, you didn't give him much of a chance, Miss Attwater."

"Oh, my God," Ivy murmured. "I didn't, did I? I'd been talking to the Beasley twins and I—" Suddenly she flung her arms around Nell. "Thank you, Miss Wingfield!"

Nell looked nonplussed for a moment, then her face broke into a grin. "I hope the two of you can patch things up. Hance and I have had our differences but I've always admired the man. Reverend Rankin says it's never too late." Nell laughed. "If he thinks *my* soul is salvageable, then anything is possible!" She stood up, looking as if she'd relieved herself of a great burden. "I've got to go, Miss Attwater," she declared. "I mean to spend all this month training my girls to cook and make beds and draw baths. The Liquor Vault is about to be converted to a proper boarding house!" She went away humming to herself, leaving Ivy staring after her.

It was as if the sun had reappeared after days of darkness. Ivy sprang up, running into the house. "Sanford," she called to the houseboy, "have the chaise brought around. I'm going out immediately."

She went to her parents, who were still in the dining

room. "I've made a terrible mistake," she said hurriedly. "Hance was wrongly accused of—Oh, I was so damned stupid to listen to the Beasley twins! He didn't lie to me after all!"

"Ivy, what are you saying?" Dr. Attwater asked. "You're not making any sense."

"Of course it makes sense," she said jubilantly. "I still love Hance. Oh, God, I never even gave him a chance to explain—"

Dr. Attwater landed his fist on the walnut table with a clatter, silencing Ivy. "Now listen to me. You can't just go running back to Hance Adair, or whatever his name is. Nothing can change what he is."

Ivy's eyes widened. "Whatever are you talking about?"

Mrs. Attwater's face crumpled. "Oh, Lord, George, *she doesn't know* . . ." She stared at Ivy with pity in her eyes. "Darling, we found out that Hance was born illegitimate. *That* is why you can't marry him."

Ivy drew a deep breath, stunned. So that was what Nell Wingfield had been trying to tell her. "Can't I? Can't I?" she asked. "Sweet, merciful God, Mother, do you think I'd let a thing like that stand in my way? I rejected Hance because I thought he'd lied to me about something that *mattered*."

She grabbed an apple from the bowl on the table as she ran from the room. Her appetite had suddenly returned.

The sound of Mariah's screams made Luke run even faster, leaving Gideon far behind. He had no doubt it was Hance; Gideon had described a yellow-haired man with a black horse.

Luke knew why Hance had chosen to vent his rage on Mariah. The gossip was all around town, repeated with relish by those who'd witnessed the scene at the church last Sunday. Luke had reacted with shock to the idea that Hance wasn't Roarke's son. He'd even felt a measure of compassion that Ivy Attwater had broken their betrothal.

But all Luke felt as he pounded through the forest was

rage. And cold, abject terror. Mariah was in the early stages of pregnancy and in no condition to fend off Hance.

Luke rushed headlong onto the scene. The daisy he'd given her earlier lay trampled beneath scuffling feet. Hance had torn Mariah's bodice and was groping savagely at the shift beneath.

The towering fury that roiled within Luke gave him more strength than he'd ever possessed. He grabbed Hance by the collar and ripped him away from Mariah. With one swift movement, Luke spun him around and drove his fist into his face, laying open the flesh above his cheekbone.

Hance tried to elude Luke's rain of blows, putting up his arms. Uttering disjointed curses of loathing, Luke penetrated the defense and slammed his fists at Hance again and again. A thunderous kick to the midsection sent Hance sprawling to the forest floor, and Luke immediately dropped to his knees, preventing Hance from rolling away. Again and again he beat that face, hearing the sickening crunch of his own blows with dark satisfaction. Somewhere in the back of his mind he remembered another fight. A fight that had ended in the death of Black Bear, his enemy. Luke found himself craving that result once more.

Finally, Mariah's voice penetrated the red fog of rage that engulfed Luke.

"Stop, oh, God, Luke, please stop! He's not fighting back!" Luke felt her hands on his shoulder. "You'll kill him!"

"Exactly," Luke snarled, not letting up.

"You'll never forgive yourself, Luke."

At last he stopped and straightened slowly, feeling drained and somehow unclean, as if soiled by his own dark desire to kill. Shuddering, he pulled Mariah to him.

"Are you all right?"

She nodded. "He—he's been drinking. He was half out of his mind, I think."

Together they stared down at Hance's inert form. His face ran with blood, cut raw by Luke's fists. His nose was shattered, and one eye had swollen shut.

Wordlessly, Mariah plucked Luke's handkerchief from

his pocket and daubed at the wounds. Hance moaned and stirred, then opened his good eye. He put his tongue out tentatively, touching a deep split in his lip.

"Get up," Luke ordered roughly.

Hance gave a slight nod and complied, staggering a little. Gideon appeared, wide-eyed, the black horse in tow.

"When you ride out of here," Luke gritted, "I want it to be for the last time. If you ever come near me or my family again, you're a dead man."

Again Hance nodded, giving Luke a hard look. "I should have appreciated you more when we were growing up, little brother. Seems you were the only one who knew better than to put up with me." He lurched toward his horse. "I've taken a lot of thrashings in my life, Luke. But no one's ever dealt it out like you." He struggled onto his mount, and Mariah gave him his hat. Their gazes locked for a moment.

"Sorry is too weak a word to apologize for what I just did to you," Hance said.

She nodded and then, unexpectedly, took his hand. "I've always been good at forgiving, Hance. But I'll need time to understand how you could be hurting so badly to want to attack me like that."

Hance set the hat on his head and touched the brim in an unsteady salute.

"So long, little brother."

"He may need doctoring," Mariah whispered as they watched him ride away.

"He'll find one in the next county if he knows what's good for him."

29

Hance saw his reflection in the oval glass of the front door of number 36 Bedford Row. With a satisfied nod, he adjusted his stock and smoothed the front of his superfine morning coat. His tall boots gleamed as richly as the polished beaver hat on his head. His face still bore the scars of Luke's attack and various other scuffles, but time had faded them. There was a small crescent-shaped depression above his left cheekbone and another on his chin; his nose bore only the slightest irregular bump.

Hance didn't mind the scars. At one time his vanity would have been mortified, but now he looked upon them as badges of lessons learned hard. And learned too late.

As he stood waiting for his knock to be answered, Hance reviewed the events that had brought him here, to the house of the man who had fathered him. He had never gone back to Lexington after that day with Luke. For three years he'd wandered the length of the Mississippi and the Natchez Trace, sliding effortlessly into the life he'd led before. Before Ivy. The dreadful wrenching that twisted his gut when he thought of her faded to a dull ache, which he battled in vain with whiskey and women.

With some vague notion of restoring his sense of self-worth Hance had finally become a passenger on one of his ocean-going vessels from Shippingport. He gave in to the curiosity that niggled at him incessantly.

He sailed to London to see the man who was his father.

A stern-faced butler led him into a grand, overheated salon. Hance waited in front of a marble fireplace, taking in the dainty blue Grisson harpsichord, the gilt-edged books that lined the walls, a collection of Sèvres vases in colored porcelain. He could imagine Ivy in such a room, surrounded by luxury and learning and breeding. *Breeding.* A word Hance had come to hate, for the accident of his birth had driven Ivy away from him.

"Hance Adair?"

He swung around to see the source of the voice. Edmund Brimsby arrived in a rolling wicker chair pushed by a footman. The man's feet, too swollen by gout to be fitted with shoes, were wrapped in bandages. He had a ruddy, florid face that might have been distinctive at one time; now its features were slack and timeworn.

"You are Hance Adair?" Brimsby asked again.

Hance gave him his most charming smile. "That's the name I was given."

At that moment a woman swept into the room. Stiffly gowned and grandly coiffed, she had hard, glittering eyes and a look that hinted disapproval of the world in general—and of Hance in particular.

"You must be my cousin Roarke's son," she said, touching her coiffure with a disdainful but trembling hand.

With sudden clarity, Hance realized why he'd come. He wanted to show these overly comfortable, self-satisfied Londoners that he would not be forgotten as his mother had been.

"Roarke Adair raised me," he conceded. "I was born November 14, 1774, in Dancer's Meadow, Virginia, to a woman named Prudence Moon."

The mention of that name caused different reactions in his hosts. Angela Brimsby's eyes hardened to twin gemstones of loathing. In contrast, Edmund grew pensive, looking like a man who had lost some part of himself and had no idea where it had gone.

"She died bearing me," Hance added coldly.

Edmund's shoulders sagged, and the sadness that came over him was as genuine as any emotion Hance had ever seen.

"Why have you come here?" he asked raggedly.

"I think you know," Hance replied.

"We owe you nothing!" Angela declared.

"Relax, Mrs. Brimsby. I want nothing from you. Only to see the man who used my mother and abdicated his responsibilities to her." Coldly, he eyed Edmund Brimsby and strolled around the wheelchair. "You're not such an old man, are you, Mr. Brimsby? Yet you've a dissipated air about you. Perhaps your life of ease and privilege hasn't brought you the contentment you crave."

He was neither surprised nor disappointed by Brimsby. Hance refused to admit a certain underlying admiration of this grand, comfortable, eminently proper life. A life that, had the circumstances of his birth been different, might have been his.

He expected to be asked to leave. Instead, Edmund Brimsby, shaken and pale, begged Hance to stay for tea.

Hance was taken aback. His curiosity piqued, he handed his hat to the butler.

As tea was served in an overdecorated, stuffy room, Angela impaled him with her hard stare and was clearly trying her best to find fault with his manners.

But his deportment was excellent. Horace Rathford had taught him well in his youth, in Richmond, where English ways had hung on well after the war. He wielded his utensils and teacup with an expert hand.

His host asked him questions, not hard, probing ones intended to make Hance squirm but questions of genuine interest. He wanted to know about America, the people who had fought so desperately to free themselves from England, the seemingly limitless possibilities the land in the New World offered.

"The Americans are a singular lot," Hance explained,

"so diverse as to resemble patchwork, yet somehow united, all of the same fabric. The things they value are different from what I've observed in London. Faith, individual liberty. A child is raised to rely on no one beyond himself for his own destiny."

Brimsby was smiling at him. "You talk like an American. I can't think why you'd leave that life."

"There are some things even Americans can't forgive," Hance said. The hard edge to his voice left no doubt as to what he meant.

Brimsby looked wistful again. And curiously eager. "May I call you Hance?"

"Of course."

"I'm an old man, Hance, despite what you said earlier. I've done nothing in my life but improve my family's fortune in a modest way. Aside from Angela, I have no one to share that fortune with. My only son, Andrew, was killed fighting against Bonaparte. My daughter died giving birth to a still-born boy, and her husband succumbed to consumption soon after."

Angela took a gulp of tea. Her cup quivered as she set it down on its saucer.

"Edmund, really, don't you think we should keep such matters private?"

Hance sent her a charming smile. "I've already told you, ma'am, I make no claim to anything you have."

"But that's the point," Edmund persisted. "That is exactly what I want you to do."

Angela gasped, and Hance felt his hand tighten around the cup he was holding. A keen feeling of resentment gripped him. Edmund Brimsby had ignored his existence for years. Now, old, broken, and lonely, he wanted to absolve himself of the wrong he'd done by tossing Hance this double-edged opportunity.

To agree to this would be to deny everything Roarke Adair had been to him. Roarke Adair, the man he'd called father. The man who had loved him, had forgiven him everything.

"No," Hance said quietly. "No, it's not what I want."

"Perhaps this is too abrupt. But give me a chance. I have a distinct feeling about this. Stay with us, Hance, as a guest in our home. I'd welcome the opportunity to know you better. Not as your father, of course. Roarke Adair is the only man deserving of that title. But as a friend. Please."

Hance took a snifter of brandy from a silver tray proffered by a footman and swirled the amber liquid thoughtfully. He looked around the room with its gilded cornices and painted doors, at the chandelier sparkling over the table, the rich Gobelins tapestry that graced the mantel. Hance found that he was comfortable in these surroundings. Very comfortable indeed.

He didn't bother looking at Angela; he knew what her completely justifiable reaction would be. She was reluctant to open her home to her husband's bastard. But Angela's opinion meant nothing.

Only this gouty earnest old man with his wistful watery eyes and nervous hands mattered. It had been a long time since anyone had wanted to know Hance, to be his friend.

"I'd be obliged," Hance said, flashing a grin. Then he raised his glass to Brimsby.

A filthy finger with a wax-hardened nail curled around the brass trigger of a new rifle. The clearing just south of Lexington buzzed with the music of summer crickets and bird song.

"Now listen to your Uncle Micajah, boys," the man said. "Guns ain't worth the wood they're made of unless you learn to shoot properly. And you can't learn to shoot unless you aim at something."

"Aw, I know that," Caleb Harper said.

"Me, too," added his younger brother, Spruce, wiping a sleeve across his nose.

"We'll see about that, boys," Micajah said. He hunkered down and shouldered the rifle. "Takes practice, y'hear? I ain't held a gun in seven years, ever since Billy Wolf hauled me and Wylie in . . ." Micajah's protruding brow darkened. "Damn, I'd like to put this bullet through Hance

Adair; pay him back good for running out with our share and leaving us to take the blame."

"We won't find Adair in Lexington," Wylie Harper reported, ambling toward Micajah and the boys. "I done some checking around; 'pears he lit out five years ago."

"Ah, well, let's give these youngsters a shootin' lesson anyway," Micajah said. "Now." He laughed wickedly as, in the distance, a child appeared. "Say we want to plug that little half-breed yonder. Here's what you do . . ." Micajah made a great show of sighting down the barrel at the dark-haired boy in the clearing.

"No!" screamed a female voice. A flurry of gingham and shiny black hair descended on Micajah, knocking him to his backside.

"Aw, see here, lady," Micajah laughed, "we was just makin' a little joke." His eyes roved appreciatively over her. "Didn't mean no harm, did we, boys? The Harpers don't go around pluggin' kids, even 'breeds. Say . . . you're one yourself, ain't you, lady?"

Mariah stumbled back. She'd gone completely cold at the mention of the Harper name. There was no doubt in her mind that these were Elk's sons and grandsons, cruel and crude in the tradition of the man she'd killed at the Licking River seven years earlier.

"Gideon," she said quickly over her shoulder. "Take Hattie up to Trotter's store and wait for me there. I'll go fetch Benjamin." Sensing Mariah's alarm, Gideon snatched hold of Hattie's hand, and they ran up Main Street into town. Mariah was about to run across the clearing to her son when one of the younger Harpers stepped in her way.

She brushed past him toward Benjamin, but not before recognition had dawned in the youth's small, cruel eyes.

She'd seen the same look on the same face at the Licking River. This boy had watched her kill Elk Harper.

Mariah forced the encounter with the Harpers from her mind as she and Benjamin went to find the others. The outlaws couldn't harm her, she told herself, not here in Lexington. But when she heard from Myra Trotter that the Harpers had staked a claim a few miles down the Kentucky River, she vowed to stay well out of their way. She scolded her four-year-old son for wandering off, then squeezed his hand with a bright, reassuring smile.

Trotter's mercantile was jammed with women. Lexington suffered both from war shortages and the lack of a good river port, so a delivery the size of this one was a rare thing indeed. Mariah seldom ventured into town, relying instead on Luke's foreman, a man called Jake Hopkins, to do the shopping. But Gideon, Benjamin, and his sister, the three-year-old Hattie, were badly in need of new clothing. The children were growing faster and taller than tulip poplars.

Gideon stopped before an array of hunting knives in a glass case. Mariah left Benjamin and Hattie lingering over a tantalizing display of licorice and horehound candies while she examined several huge bolts of material, trying not to be crushed by the press of women groping aggressively for the prettiest bits.

Mariah smiled, fingering the material. Five years ago she never would have believed that this life of domesticity could bring her such happiness. Her hand strayed to her midsection. The new presence there delighted her and quickened even more actively than the previous two had. Her arm ached for a day three months hence, when she would be able to hold the new life close.

She made her purchases, feeling a thrill of pride in Mr. Trotter's eager extension of Luke's credit. Her husband's farming methods had been a source of skepticism among other farmers in the area. Men had laughed at Luke's use of manure to fertilize his crops, at his rigid program of rotation and irrigation.

But now that Luke's crop yields had become legend, amused indulgence had given way first to disgruntled envy and then to unabashed imitation.

Mariah sighed a little as Mrs. Trotter reckoned her purchases. Lately, Luke hadn't been as enthusiastic about his farm. Everything had become easy—too easy. She'd noticed some of Luke's old restlessness. At times she'd seen him sitting on their new wraparound porch, staring west-ward, dreaming things he wasn't ready to speak of yet. Mariah knew better than to badger or push Luke. He'd tell her what was in his heart when the time came.

She added some cinnamon sticks and licorice to her purchases and handed one to Benjamin.

"Time to go," she said. "Where is your sister?"

Genevieve tried not to smile as Bridie Farrell, the maid she'd grudgingly engaged at Sarah's insistence, grunted under a load of parcels from Trotter's store.

"Sure it's enough to clothe a church choir," Bridie scolded. "Or maybe Miss Sarah has some aversion to wearing the same frock more than once. So spoiled even salt and vinegar wouldn't save her."

"You're a saucy thing, Bridie," Sarah snapped, but she was smiling. She and the fifteen-year-old Irish immigrant were fast friends. "As Mrs. Nathaniel Caddick, I'll need gowns for all occasions."

Smiling at the prospect of her daughter's impending wedding, Genevieve handed the last of the parcels to Bridie, who managed to load everything into the chaise. She was about to climb to the seat when the sound of childish crying caught her ear.

The pedestrians jostling each other on the wooden walk-way in front of the store took no notice. But Genevieve's ears were sharp, perhaps as nature's compensation for her ever-weakening vision.

She edged her way through the crowd to find a small girl crouched fearfully on the walkway. A maternal feeling en-gulfed her as she bent and touched the child on the shoulder.

The little girl looked up, blinking huge blue eyes mourn-fully and twisting a lock of hair with a small, nervous hand.

Genevieve gave a gentle smile.

"I'll bet you've lost your mama," she said.

The child nodded gravely. A man carrying a new plow blade came out of the store, narrowly missing the girl with its metal edges. Genevieve lifted her up and set her on a pickle barrel out of harm's way.

The child was remarkably pretty, with wide, clear eyes, a trembling rosebud mouth, and hair of glossy black. Genevieve's smile widened as she reached into her pocket.

"I've a lemon drop, just for you. Bet I'll find your mama before you can make it disappear."

The worried face blossomed into a smile. Genevieve was amazed by the intensity of feeling that swept over her. For some reason she felt a deep-seated longing that almost hurt.

Thank God Sarah was about to marry; Genevieve could hardly wait for the blessing of grandchildren.

When the little girl was sucking contentedly on the candy, Genevieve cautioned her to stay put and started into the store.

"There you are, Hattie!" a voice exclaimed. "Child, you gave us a fright."

Genevieve turned to assure the woman that Hattie was fine. She found herself staring into a face she'd seen only once before—at the Attwaters' disastrous reception five years earlier.

Gasping, she stumbled against the pickle barrel. The idea that she was in the company of Luke's wife and children struck her with stunning force. Instantly, she recognized Hattie's habit of twisting her hair in her fingers. Luke had soothed himself to sleep in the same manner when he was a child.

The little boy at Mariah's side was dark and exotic looking, like his mother, but the handsome form of his face and the sturdiness of his body were unmistakably Luke's. Oh, God, and Roarke's.

"Good day, Mrs. Adair," Mariah said stiffly. She handed the boy her packages and lifted Hattie from the barrel. "Come along, Benjamin," she added, taking Hattie by the hand. "We'd best find Gideon now."

"Wait," Genevieve pleaded. She'd known of Luke's children, of course; people loved to talk. But until this moment they'd been nameless, faceless. Not really people at all. Now that she'd seen them, she ached for them. Even more than she'd ached for the past five years for Luke's smile.

Mariah hesitated, clutching Hattie and moving slightly in front of Benjamin, unconsciously protective. She waited for Genevieve to speak again, her face unreadable.

Sarah interrupted. Luke's pretty sister moved in on the scene, her brow puckering as she recognized Mariah. Unlike Genevieve, she was utterly unmoved.

"Mother, let's go," she said impatiently, tugging at Genevieve's arm. She lowered her voice and hissed, "This is the worst possible time to get involved with—well, you know. The Caddicks, they'd never understand . . ."

Genevieve looked torn as Sarah pulled her away. But she didn't protest. Five years of silence were not to be breached by a chance meeting.

"Who was that, Mama?" Benjamin asked as Mariah walked away. "She seemed nice."

"Perhaps she is," Mariah said. "But not to the likes of us."

A howling wind sculpted the snow into great drifts against the fences, obscuring the landscape in a cloak of white. At high noon it was impossible to see beyond the well house, which was located just a few feet from the kitchen window.

Luke squinted out at the blizzard. He was weary to the bone, having spent the better part of the night battening the livestock into the barn and stables. Ordinarily, Jake Hopkins would have been there to help, but the foreman had taken his family to spend Christmas with relatives.

Just as he'd finished with the animals, Luke had crept into bed to find Mariah shifting restlessly with the early twinges of labor. She'd assured him that all was well. But now he wasn't so certain.

Turning back from the window, he studied her, lying on her side on the cot in a recessed alcove of the kitchen. She was so brave, not uttering a sound as the ebb and flow of pains held her in a deathly grip.

Luke's heart swelled with love and pride as he sat beside

her and smoothed a sweat-dampened lock of hair from her brow. She managed to smile through her pain.

"The children?" she whispered.

"They're all sleeping in Gideon's room." Luke sent her a sheepish grin. "I gave them rum toddies after breakfast."

Her hand tightened around his as another pain gripped her. Luke ached for her, wishing there were some way he could shoulder the pain himself. When her hand finally relaxed, he bent and brushed his lips across her cheek.

"I love you," he said.

She tried to smile. "I know, Luke. I wish this were over. It was easy with the first two, but . . ."

He leaned forward. "But what? Oh, God, Mariah, what is it?"

"I'm afraid there's something wrong," she admitted finally. "It's been so long, and the baby is still high—" She broke off and braved another squeezing pain.

"I'll get the doctor from town," Luke said.

"But you can't, Luke. The snow . . ."

He sat with her, mopping her brow and feeling helpless. The other two times Essie Hopkins had been present, assisting Mariah with quiet, womanly competence. But now Luke was alone except for the children. And he could see Mariah weakening by the minute. She drifted in and out of sleep, awakening with each squeezing pain and then slipping away again. Luke raked a hand through his hair and stood up.

"I'm going for the doctor," he said again. He kept his voice quiet, trying not to betray the stark terror that gripped him. He roused Gideon and instructed him to stay with Mariah.

Nearly shaking with fear, he dropped a kiss on her forehead. "I won't be long, honey," he told her.

She nodded, too weak to protest now. "I'll be waiting, Luke."

He dressed in layers of wool and buckskin and fought his way out to the barn to harness the sleigh.

*   *   *

Lexington had drawn in on itself for the blizzard. Doors were locked and windows shuttered against the howling wind. Luke stood at the door of Dr. Warfield's surgery, suddenly remembering the last time he'd come here. Bringing Mariah and Gideon, his unwelcome burdens from the wilderness.

Recalling the brave, silent, proud Indian girl, he felt his heart constrict. Never could he gave guessed that she would be the one to break down the barrier of his prejudice and penetrate the cynicism of his heart. That their destinies had become entwined was a strange and splendid thing. That he was in danger of losing her was an intolerable and unthinkable horror.

Knowing his knock wouldn't be heard, Luke pushed open the door to the surgery and stepped inside, stamping the snow from his boots.

A ragged scream of pain greeted him. The scream rose and crested and then dissolved into a disjointed plea for mercy. Luke cursed inwardly. Of all the days for Dr. Warfield to be occupied with some emergency . . . Stamping his feet again, he removed his hat and unwound his muffler.

A soft gasp issued from a corner of the room. Turning, Luke saw his mother. Her face, absent from his life for years but never completely out of his thoughts, was drawn with deep concern. He cleared his throat.

"Hello, Ma."

"Luke! How could you have heard?"

He frowned. Genevieve looked old, old and haggard. And terrified. "I didn't hear anything. How could I have?"

Her eyes were dry, but he could see she'd been crying. "It's Israel," she said. "He was helping stable the horses during the blizzard, wading in snow up to his waist. His leg struck a scythe one of the hands had left out. The cut nearly severed—"

Genevieve swallowed hard. Her small, strong hands twisted in her lap. She raised pain-filled eyes to Luke. "The doctor has to take his leg."

The shudder that rippled through him had nothing to do with the cold. "Oh, God, Ma, are you sure?"

Another scream rent the air. "The doctor said there's no other way, Luke." She looked confused. "If you didn't know about Israel, then why are you here?"

Luke's first impulse was to keep his dread to himself. He'd neither seen nor spoken to his mother in years; she had nothing to do with his life anymore. He didn't want to share his terror with her.

But then she touched him. She crossed the room and laid a paper-dry hand on his cheek. It was a small gesture, hesitant, but it opened a place in Luke's heart that hadn't been touched in years.

"It's Mariah," he rasped. Tears poured from his eyes. "She's having a baby, and there's something wrong. Look, Ma, I can't take Dr. Warfield away from Israel now." He turned away helplessly.

"Wait." She placed her hand on his arm.

"She's alone, Ma," Luke said impatiently. "My foreman is in Danville. I've got to go back."

"One minute, Luke," she begged. "That's all I ask."

At his curt nod she fled into the next room, where Israel's cries had dissipated into incoherent mumblings. Luke heard Roarke's voice rise high in anger and fear, answered by Genevieve's pleading tone. Then his mother reappeared, wrapping her head in a shawl and drawing a cloak around her.

"Let's go," she said to Luke.

Gideon greeted them at the kitchen door, his eyes wide and frightened.

"She's bad," he said fearfully, trying not to cry.

Peeling off her wraps, Genevieve hurried to the bedside. She soothed Mariah with a few soft words and worked gently, a look of intense caring on her face. A few moments later she turned back to Luke.

"How long has she been like this?"

"She—It started yesterday at sundown."

"That's nearly twenty-four hours."

"Too long," Luke said brokenly.

Genevieve rubbed her hand comfortingly over the small

of Mariah's back. "She's a strong woman, son. But she's going to need you while I take the baby."

"Oh, Lord God—"

Tears rimmed her eyes. "I must, Luke. Mariah's getting weaker, and I doubt the baby can take much more. It was the same way with Sarah, remember? Mimsy Greenleaf finally had to give nature a bit of help."

A small cry of pain slipped from Mariah. Luke's eyes grew moist as he looked at her.

"Do what you have to do," he told his mother.

Genevieve was full of confidence. Despite the pain she'd suffered, she remembered every detail of Sarah's birth, as if the agony and terror had heightened her awareness. She refused to think of how weak Sarah had been, half-dead at birth.

While Luke cradled Mariah against him and held her shoulders, Genevieve set to work. For the first time since the labor had begun, Mariah screamed. The savage, elemental sound of agony caused Luke's heart to shatter. It went on and on as Genevieve worked feverishly, using her hands to do the work that nature should have done.

Mariah fainted from the pain as the baby was born, tiny buttocks first. It was a boy, perfectly formed and with a mat of dark red hair. His limbs were slack and bluish.

He wasn't breathing.

"No . . ." Luke rasped. "Oh, God, no . . ." He gathered Mariah to him and started to tremble as a terrible storm of grief welled up in him.

Genevieve didn't pause to look at her son or Mariah. She cleared the baby's air passages and, covering his mouth and nose with hers, blew air into him. She repeated the process in a desperate rhythm, drenching the baby's face with her tears but never wavering in her determination.

Vaguely, Genevieve realized that there was more to this than saving the tiny life. She needed this baby to live, as much for herself as for Luke and Mariah. The child was the link that never should have been severed. If he died, Genevieve knew she'd lose Luke for good.

"Ma." Luke's voice penetrated her desperation. "Ma, it's no good."

Genevieve ignored him and continued breathing into the baby's mouth and nose.

"Ma, stop!" Luke said more loudly. "I can't stand to see you—"

Genevieve hesitated, but not because Luke had begged her to. She'd sensed a difference in the baby and paused, studying him, silently summoning every prayer she knew. She didn't dare believe the minute rise of the baby's chest. Then the child gasped and coughed.

And, blessedly, began to cry.

It was the sweetest, most miraculous sound Genevieve had ever heard.

30

Hance liked London. He liked living in a city that never slept, where amusements abounded on every street corner: dancing dogs, small mice spinning in gilt cages, a fiddler playing for the price of a tot of gin, markets that offered everything from jasper chessmen to Turkish sabers.

And he liked the gentlemen's clubs, Crockford's and White's, Boodle's in St. James's Street, where fortunes were lost at the turn of a card or a spin of the rouge-et-noir.

Night after endless night he frequented the pleasure gardens of Vauxhall and Ranelagh, where he was as likely to meet the Duke of Cumberland as a child from the Foundling Hospital.

Hance found the Londoners an excitable, learned group. Everyone, even the ladies, discussed politics, be it the Whiggish Prince Regent and the Tory government or the boundless vulgarity of Princess Caroline. Hance's friends enjoyed being in a constant state of alarm over the king's health or whether they'd been invited to a fête at Carlton House.

London liked Hance, too. The fashionable acquaintances of the Brimsbys took an immediate liking to Angela's distant "cousin," charmed by his rakish good looks and smooth Virginia accent. It was quite a distinction, being considered "an original" at a time when the unique was pursued with an abject horror of boredom and a distaste for the mundane.

Since Hance had arrived in London, he and Angela had settled into an attitude of mutual tolerance, while he took an unexpected liking to Edmund Brimsby. The elder man often declared he was in his dotage, but it was only in body. Edmund conversed aptly, having well-formed opinions on a variety of topics from universal suffrage to the abolition of slavery. His chess game was impeccable, although he failed miserably at the games of faro and *jeu d'enfer* that went on at Crockford's.

Never did Hance think of this intelligent, gouty, weak-willed man as his father. He declined to think about the circumstances of his birth at all.

That was the beauty of London. He didn't have to think; he had only to indulge himself. When he was in the mood for lighthearted pleasantries, he called on Melinda Speed, a daring woman with a too-bright smile and a sense of humor that was both bawdy and rich.

When Hance craved a darker pleasure, a dangerous one, he sought the lovely Agatha, Countess Carey. A sultry beauty two decades younger than her husband, she had a carnal appetite that challenged and enticed. She was too wealthy to expect presents from Hance and too wise to demand his love. Agatha knew better than to risk asking for things Hance wasn't willing to give.

Amid the social flurry of the high season of 1813, Hance noticed through a haze of brandy that his father was dying. Edmund had become positively slight in the past several months. No amount of the doctor's tonics and diets could revive him.

Hance wasn't surprised when, as an autumn chill gripped London, he was summoned to Edmund's bedside.

The older man eyed Hance admiringly, taking in his elegant figure. "Lord, but you've got character," Edmund wheezed. "You're hot-blooded and willful, to be sure, but as shrewd and wise as any man I've known, Hance. I can't help but wonder how you came by those traits."

"Doesn't matter," Hance said with a shrug. "I'm my own person."

Edmund nodded. "Aye. You're a lot of things, Hance. But you lack the one asset that truly counts."

"Oh? And what might that be?"

"Happiness."

Hance chuckled. "Since when does a good Londoner consider that important?"

"It occurred to me too late, my friend." Edmund gestured weakly at Hance. "But you—you're young still. Don't give yourself up to cynicism at this stage of your life. Tell me, Hance, what you've been longing for. Ever since I've known you, you've been hiding something deep inside, covering it up with rakish bravado."

Hance looked sharply at Edmund. He hadn't realized until now how well the man knew him. He began talking then, telling Edmund about Ivy. Hours later, having consumed half a bottle of brandy between them, he finished his story. He was amazed to see tears in Edmund's eyes.

"Shall I get the doctor?" Hance asked.

"No. Not yet." Edmund brushed at a tear. "I haven't started feeling sorry for myself, Hance. But I just heard you say you let go of the one woman who could truly make you happy." He sent Hance a knowing look. "I believe I was guilty of that myself. With your mother."

Hance's hand shook as he added more brandy to his glass.

"That won't help," Edmund pointed out.

"I know."

"There's only one thing that will, Hance. You've got to go to her."

"Damn it, Edmund, haven't you heard a word I've said? I just told you she turned her back on me when she found out I was illegitimate. That'll never change."

"Maybe not, Hance. But people change. You didn't even give the girl a chance for the shock to wear off."

Hance wavered. He recalled Ivy's white-lipped fury, but there had been regret in her eyes, too. Longing. Maybe . . .

"Do it, Hance—don't spend your life wondering," Edmund prodded.

Hance clasped the older man's hand. "You've always given me good advice, Edmund. I won't ever forget that."

Edmund brought Hance's hand to his heart and looked at him steadily. "Thank you, son," he whispered, claiming Hance with that word for the first time. "And now I believe I'd like you to send for the doctor. And my wife."

Angela protested the terms of the will, of course, because it divided the estate between her and Hance.

Two days after the funeral she was waiting in the drawing room. Hance had been out all night with Agatha, reluctant to be alone with the idea that his only link to humanity was gone.

"I expect you to be out of here by evening," Angela said. "The house is mine, you know."

Hance sighed wearily. "Yes, Angela." He had no desire to stay anyway. Edmund's advice lingered in his mind, impossible to ignore even when he was with Agatha. As a footman was helping him fill his trunk and clothespress, Edmund's valet appeared with an old wooden letter box.

"Mr. Adair, I found this while going through the master's effects. I believe the contents might be of interest to you."

Hance set the letter box on the bed and extracted an assortment of papers and small certificates, a small supply of dried ink and a well-whittled quill.

At the bottom of the box was a calf-bound book, its cover embossed in flaking gold leaf with the initials PM. Hance dismissed the footman and valet, poured himself a generous glass of brandy, and took the volume to a chair beside the fire.

The journal was written in a tight, precise hand. Hance was surprised to see that the handwriting had an uncanny resemblance to his own. He flipped through the descriptions of the Brimsby children, pausing to grin at Prudence's assessment of young Andrew: "A fat, sneaky individual who resists learning as if it were a deadly scourge . . ." Even Edmund had admitted that his son had been no scholar.

Impatiently, Hance skimmed through disjointed, meticulously penned entries. There was a short bit on Prudence's opinion of Rousseau's philosophy, a recipe jotted here and there, a note to herself to share some thought with her friend, Genevieve Elliot . . . And then the handwriting changed slightly. It became more careless, spilled over the pages by a hand that seemed to be trembling or overly tired.

"He is more than the man I love," Hance read. "He has become the reason I take nourishment each day and draw each breath that keeps me alive. God forgive me." With a jolt, Hance realized that he was reading of his mother's relationship with Edmund Brimsby.

He felt her longing as she mentioned a chance meeting in some part of the house, the electricity of a casual touch. She'd resisted him for months, burying her feelings, secreting her private longings in the diary.

At last she stopped denying what was in her heart and gave herself to him. As Hance sat reading, his image of his mother was transformed. For so long he'd carried around an impression of the wily governess using her charm to entice the master of the household, to win favors from him.

It wasn't like that at all. Prudence Moon had felt a deep, abiding love for Edmund Brimsby. Hance understood. He'd loved Ivy with the same pureness of heart, the same disregard for convention. The words on the page swam before his eyes.

He still loved Ivy.

His dead mother's words, shimmering ghosts from the past, brought back all the intensity of that love.

Closing the book and putting it in one of his bags, he finished packing.

Hance looked at Dancer's Meadow from beneath the brim of his beaver hat. The town had matured since his boyhood. Its main street had been paved by brick, and a number of storefronts had sprung up where only dust and tree stumps had once existed. The horse he'd purchased in Yorktown bore him down the river road to the farm where he'd been born.

The house looked the same. A little more careworn, the trees taller, but the white clapboard with its breezy porch was still familiar. Hance dismounted and secured his horse, calling out a greeting.

"The Lord be praised . . ." called a voice from the door.

Hance snatched off his hat. Mimsy Greenleaf looked grand, with a puffy white cloud of hair, erect posture, and the plumpness of a life well lived. Her embrace was firm.

"It's good to have you home," she announced, filling her eyes with him. Then she hurried off to ring the kitchen bell, summoning her family and sending one of Eustis's sons down to Genevieve's old place to fetch the others.

Hance said little as he shared their meal. Instead, he marveled at what the Greenleaf family had become. Joshua, the proud patriarch, presided over a table long enough to encompass the whole of his brood, which now included his sons' wives and five grandchildren.

Two of the Greenleafs were absent, though obviously in their family's fond thoughts. Calvin, restless as ever, was involved in the dangerous business of abolition; his parents didn't elaborate but hinted that Cal had been responsible for the escape of a number of slaves. Rose was teaching now at a Quaker school in Philadelphia, Joshua informed Hance with pride.

After the meal the men retired to the front porch. Evening was settling over the distant blue haze where the mountains melted into the western sky. Phillip cleaned his gun, while Curtis hummed softly, playing checkers with Eustis. Inside the house the children were giggling and being scolded by their mothers.

Hance inhaled appreciatively on his cheroot. "Best smoke in Albemarle County," he declared with a grin.

"You should know," Joshua said. "You sure stole enough tobacco from the curing sheds when you were a boy."

"How did you know about that?"

Joshua's eyes danced. "That's the trouble with twelve-year-old boys. They tend to think they're invisible. And invincible."

Hance gazed out at the farm. Years ago it had been his whole world. Somehow he wished that had never changed.

"Well, I don't believe it anymore," he said humorlessly.

Hearing the world-weary note in his voice, Joshua frowned. "Where've you been?" he asked.

Hance shrugged. "Everywhere. And I still don't know where I belong. I've learned a lot about myself, Joshua. Things I don't much like."

"You've got to like yourself, my friend. You're all you've got."

"I don't even know what I'll do with the rest of my life, Joshua."

"Well, whatever you decide, make sure you like it. Because you're gonna be dead a long time."

Hance looked up, startled. Then, seeing the twinkle in the old man's eyes, he burst out laughing.

There was one thing left to do before leaving Dancer's Meadow. While the morning dew still glistened on the fields, he rode up the hill beyond the house to the tree-shaded knoll where the family buried their dead. Only two small markers jutted up from the ground. Dismounting, Hance approached the first. As he dropped to his knees before it, his chest tightened, and he was flooded by memories that had been hidden away in the back of his mind for years.

Matilda Jane Adair, 1787–1790. Hance read the verse on the headstone aloud: " 'I will both lay me down in peace and sleep; for thou, Lord, only makest me dwell in safety'."

Hance traced his sister's name with a finger, remembering. Little Mattie. A golden child, a child of sunlight and springtime. Hance recalled her bubbling, babyish laughter as he used to tickle her chubby chin with a twig of pussy willow. And her smell, the sweet, milky scent that clung to her. The soft moistness of her laughing mouth as she kissed him and gurgled his name.

Mattie's death had been the beginning of his withdrawal from the family, he realized. After that nothing seemed to matter. Perhaps nothing ever would. Brushing a tear from his cheek, he plucked a single white flower from the dogweed tree above and laid it at the base of the grave. Then he moved on.

The date of Prudence Moon Adair's death was Hance's birthday, a grim reminder of the cost of his life.

His mother had been twenty at her death. Barely emerged from the chrysalis of girlhood.

"Would she have liked the man you've become?" asked a thin, reedy voice.

Hance turned and jumped to his feet. "Mimi!" he cried, embracing her. She felt frail and insubstantial in his arms. "I was going to come and see you, but Mimsy wouldn't let me call on you at this hour. She said you've been ailing."

Mimi shook her head. "Not unless you call getting old an ailment. Mimsy's good to me, though. They built me a cottage down by the springhouse. They spend too much time fussing and worrying that I eat too little and sleep too much."

He squeezed her bony shoulders. "It's good to see you."

She nodded. "And you. You're a handsome devil, and well off from the looks of you. But you haven't answered my question. Would your mother have liked you?"

"No," he answered without hesitation.

Mimi sighed and spread her homespun skirts, lowering herself gingerly to the grass. "Why not?"

"Because I'm no good. I've lied and cheated people. I've used women and stolen from men. In almost everything I've done in my life, I've hurt people. The whole family left Virginia because of me."

"What do you intend to do about it?" Mimi demanded, fixing an unrelenting stare on him.

Hance shrugged. "The answer's obvious. I'll stay the hell out of their lives."

"Do you think you could hurt them any more than that?"

"It's to spare them, Mimi. To spare them."

She shook her head. "What a fool you are, Hance. Your parents—"

"They're not my parents."

Her dark eyes snapped with anger. "You're wrong, Hance. Genevieve and Roarke Adair are your parents in every way that matters. If you deny that, you're denying every decent thing they've ever done for you."

"But—"

Mimi waved her thin hand at Prudence's grave. "I never knew her." She watched his fist clench. "But Roarke understood his wife, Hance. And he forgave her. So should you."

"What does it matter whether or not I forgive a woman who's been dead almost forty years?" he demanded.

She held his hand. "Because it's the beginning of forgiving yourself."

The kitchen door banged behind Genevieve as she entered Luke's house, arms laden with groceries. Mariah hurried to relieve her of her burden, putting the jars of wild honey and preserved fruit on the kitchen sideboard.

"You didn't have to do this," Mariah scolded.

But Genevieve wasn't listening. She'd dropped to her knees beside the cradle near the hearth and was already cooing at Dylan, fat and cherubic at the age of nine months.

The baby blinked his wide, clear eyes, and his face blossomed into a wet, one-toothed smile of recognition.

"So you know your old grandmother," Genevieve said with satisfaction.

"I should think so," Mariah laughed. "You spoil him shamelessly."

"That's exactly what I mean to do," Genevieve said happily. Reaching into her apron pocket, she extracted a wooden rattle, honed smooth and carved just right to fit a small grasping hand. She closed Dylan's chubby fingers around it. "Israel made this for him."

"How is he, Genevieve?"

"The leg's still mending after all these months, but soon the stump will be ready for a wooden peg. Israel swears he'll be back teaching at the university next term. I think I've shed more tears over that leg than he has."

"Grandma!" Hattie and Benjamin burst into the kitchen

from the garden, hands and lips stained with berry juice. Genevieve gathered the children into her arms and allowed them to search her pockets for the ever-present barley sugar.

"Anything in there for me?" Luke asked, walking into the kitchen.

"You emptied my apron pockets years ago," Genevieve told him with mock severity. "But I have something for you, Mariah."

"Really, Genevieve, I don't need—"

Genevieve placed a small black object in Mariah's hand. "This belonged to your mother," she said softly.

Mariah turned the lacquered box over and over in her hands, running her fingers over the design etched in gold, opening it to find a small supply of rusting needles.

"Mother's etui," she breathed. "She told me about this."

"You'd have had it long ago it I hadn't been such a thick-head about it. Took me all this time to realize Amy Parker was your mother. Roarke found this at the farm in Dancer's Meadow, after the Indian raid."

Mariah gave Genevieve a quick hug and murmured her thanks. She placed the etui on the mantel and went back to putting up the honey her mother-in-law had brought.

Luke had crouched down by the cradle, and was soon joined by Genevieve. The two of them discussed the infant's various accomplishments with absurd gravity.

Mariah smiled. Dylan's birth had been the impetus that propelled Genevieve back to her son. The Shawnee would have said Moneto, the Supreme Being, had taken a hand in the reunion. Whatever it was, Mariah was thankful. Luke and Genevieve shared a bond that should never have been broken.

There was still a rift in the family, Mariah reflected sadly. Roarke Adair remained steadfast in his hatred for her people; Rebecca still couldn't look upon or think about Indians without going into hysterics. Although Genevieve had never admitted it, she doubtless had to do battle with Roarke each time she came to visit her grandchildren.

But it was a start. Perhaps one day . . .

Gideon arrived, breathless and sweating. "Sadie's gone,"

he announced, referring to the family's favorite dog. "Must've gone to the woods to whelp her pups." He looked regretfully at Benjamin. "Sorry," he said. "I know you spent a long time making a nest in the barn for her. I'll go see if I can fetch her back."

"I'm coming with you!" Benjamin piped, already diving for his hat. With his eyes, he begged Luke and Mariah not to deter him.

Luke gave him an indulgent grin, fondly ruffling the boy's hair. "Go on, son. Round her up."

Ben let out a whoop of joy. He threw his arms around Luke and then hugged Mariah. She felt an unexpected jolt of emotion as she held her son. Her firstborn was a sweet boy, full of life and good spirits. He had a boundless love for animals, singling out Sadie and a family of barn cats for his special brand of affection.

He was off and running after Gideon in the blink of an eye, winding down the hollow and into the western woods.

"You leave Sadie alone!" yelled a childish voice. Hance drew up his horse and peered into the woods near the road leading into Lexington from the east. A few yards away four boys struggled, each trying to capture a rope that had been slung around the neck of a cinnamon-colored hound dog.

Hance dismounted and walked over to the arguing group. The dog seemed to be straining toward the younger boys, at the same time snarling at a pair of youths. An instant wave of dislike came over Hance. The elder youth was pock-faced and ugly; the younger was handsome, yet no less cruel looking.

"Give her over, Caleb," the youngest boy said to the pocked youth.

"See here," Hance said loudly. "What are you doing to this poor beast?" The dog did indeed look poorly, its belly sagging with pregnancy.

"Spruce and Caleb are trying to steal my dog," the little boy said.

"We ain't stealing," Caleb retorted. "Done found her on my daddy's property."

Hance gripped Caleb's wrist and squeezed until the boy dropped the rope. "You boys are to be commended," he said sarcastically, "for bringing the little lad's dog to him."

Caleb and Spruce exchanged a glance, then looked back at the well-dressed gentleman. All it took was a stare from Hance, and they were thoroughly intimidated. They hung back sullenly.

Hance gave the rope to the small boy. "You'd best keep your dog at home, son," he advised, turning back to his horse. A well-shaped brown hand touched his sleeve, and he hesitated, looking down into a pair of steady brown eyes.

A boy of eleven or twelve was staring at him. "You're Hance Adair," he said quietly.

Hance stiffened. He barely noticed that the two youths had lit out on hearing the name. "Sweet Christ," he murmured. "You're Mariah's boy, aren't you."

"Gideon Parker. Her nephew." The boy's gaze turned to one of loathing. "Luke told you never to come back here."

Hance expelled a sigh. "That he did, son. But it's been six years. I mean to make peace with my brother—"

The boys left before he could finish, pulling the dog back through the woods. Hance sighed again, shaking his head. If Gideon's reaction was any indication, he might be making the mistake of his life in coming back to Lexington.

But only Ivy Attwater could prove or disprove that. He mounted and urged his horse into town.

Ivy looked without interest at the array of hand-tatted lace in the milliner's shop as her mother exclaimed over it.

"Really, Ivy," she scolded, "you could show a little enthusiasm for the Caddicks' ball. Mr. Clay of Ashland is sure to be there. I dare say Sarah is a bit young to hostess such a to-do. Imagine, a farmer's daughter . . ."

Ivy turned away, closing out her mother's denunciation of Sarah Caddick. Mrs. Attwater made no secret of her dislike for the Adairs, and Ivy was tired of hearing about it. She was tired of being pitied for her love affair gone awry, tired of being pushed at Farley Caddick, who had sneeringly offered for her, openly declaring that surely George Attwater would have to settle a generous dowry on his thirty-two-year-old daughter.

No one seemed to understand that Hance Adair, gone so long his memory was like a gilded dream, had ruined all other men for her. No one had his vibrance, his brash nerve. Right from the start, Ivy had been aware of the passionate side of Hance's nature. But now, it seemed, she'd cheated herself out of the chance to sample that passion. Hance had already left Lexington by the time Nell Wingfield had told Ivy the truth about him.

While her mother was making purchases, Ivy looked wistfully out the shop window. Her breath left her as she made out the form of a well-dressed man riding up the street, his beaver hat set at a rakish angle over a shock of thick blond hair.

Nothing existed at that moment but Hance. Nothing mattered but having him in her life again. Oblivious of the scandalized gasps of the ladies in the shop, Ivy picked up her skirts and ran.

Outside, into the sunlight, into Hance's welcoming arms.

31

"*Everything's changed*," *Hance* commented as the chaise rolled along a well-traveled road just south of Lexington. The forest, once so dense that sunlight never touched its floor, had given way to productive fields, small homesteads, and large, townlike plantations.

"I'm not sure I care for all this," Hance added, scowling at a shoddy claim in a hollow off to the left. The farm was an unkempt jumble of buildings, log mixed ungraciously with clapboard. The cornfields around the compound were scruffy and crow infested; steam rose from an ill-concealed still. An unkempt youth who had been idling in the dooryard took note of their passing and disappeared around the back.

"The Harper place," Ivy said, moving closer to him on the seat. "They moved into the area about—"

Hance gripped her arm. "*Who?*"

She frowned at him. "The Harpers, darling. A rather strange family. Two brothers. I've heard one of them has two wives . . ." Ivy frowned slightly. "There are two grown boys as well."

Hance had a sudden unwelcome image of the youths he'd

stopped from stealing the dog from Luke's boys the year before. Now he knew why they'd fled on hearing Gideon speak his name. He should have recognized then the brand of gleeful cruelty unique to the Harpers.

"Listen, Ivy," Hance said urgently. "I don't ever want you to go near those people. Don't speak to them, don't tell them your name. They must never know you're my wife."

His intensity worried her. "Hance, why?"

Flicking the reins, he urged the pair of pacers faster. At last he spoke of his first and only experience in river piracy. Once he'd feared telling Ivy about his past. But no longer. There was nothing he couldn't say to the woman he loved more than his own life.

"Hance, that was years ago. Surely, they've forgotten."

He shook his head. "Wiley and Micajah Harper are vindictive men. They've killed for smaller things than what I did to them."

"They can't harm us, Hance. You're a very important man in Lexington now."

He leaned over and kissed her temple softly, still a little in awe of the miracle that she'd waited for him, that she still loved him. "What would I do without your faith in me, love?"

She gazed at him seriously with her brandy-colored eyes. "You'd be fine, Hance."

"No, I wouldn't."

She watched him fondly, thinking back over the year of their marriage. Ivy still felt she hadn't awakened from the dream of happiness cloaking every moment of every day. Her parents had resisted the marriage at first . . . until Genevieve had spoken to them. Genevieve, who knew the pain of alienation in a family.

And so the Attwaters had proven amenable. Over the months, Hance had given them no cause to regret the marriage. In fact, he seemed intent on proving to Ivy's parents that the circumstances of his birth had nothing to do with the person he was.

One hurdle was left to surmount—the rift with Luke. The road they traveled now led to Luke's farm and to, Ivy hoped fervently, a truce between the brothers. Hance drove in thoughtful silence.

"You're nervous," Ivy said in surprise, noting an unaccustomed tightness in his jaw.

Hance nodded. "If ever a man had cause to hate me, it's Luke."

"I think he's ready to forgive you, Hance. Mariah has; she's the one who asked us to come today."

His hand closed over Ivy's, but doubt crept through him as they descended the drive to Luke's farm.

Rows of corn hugged the hills flanking the farmhouse. Behind the house, a newly whitewashed silo and barn jutted proudly beside a winding stream. Luke's home looked snug and charming, pristine in its setting of wildflowers and blooming morning glories.

Mariah greeted them on the porch, stepping over the cinnamon-colored hound dog. Hance sensed her nervousness, although she was smiling and more beautiful than he had ever seen her. Luke's children were beautiful, too: six-year-old Benjamin, the lad Hance had seen defending Sadie against the Harper boys, appeared with a large barn cat in his arms to greet them with polite affection. Hattie, an adorable childish version of her mother, had baby Dylan in tow. The stocky little boy, his hair the color of rain-wet clay, looked so like Luke that Hance caught himself staring. Gideon Parker, a slim and handsome boy with frankly Indian features, seemed possessed of a boundless assurance as he greeted Hance and Ivy. Yet he seemed wary of Hance, not quite so forgiving as his aunt.

Luke was nowhere in sight. Mariah explained that he was out hewing logs for a new harrow and would be back in time for supper. Ivy followed her into the kitchen while Hance stayed on the porch, talking to the children, delighting them with a description of a street show he'd seen in London.

Ivy inhaled the warm, fresh smell of bread and watched Mariah as she moved quickly about the room, preparing the evening meal.

"Luke doesn't know we've come," Ivy stated with sudden insight.

Mariah almost dropped the knife she was using to slice the bread. "I—No, he doesn't. In fact, when he heard Hance had returned to Lexington, he wanted to run him out of town."

"You shouldn't have done this, Mariah."

"I had to. It's bad enough Luke and his father haven't seen each other in seven years; this family doesn't need another rift. Besides, it's up to me to forgive Hance." Her eyes were bright with determination. "And I have, Ivy. We both know he's not like that creature who attacked me. He's changed. We all have."

"They'll fight. They've always fought."

"I don't think so. Not this time. Too much has happened."

They worked in silence for a while, listening to the sounds of the children's laughter on the porch and the occasional trill of a mockingbird in the dooryard. Ivy poured cream from an urn into a small pitcher while Mariah checked the roast. The routine chores of preparing the meal seemed to calm the women, although both were still tense about what would happen when the two brothers met.

Two shots rang out. Ivy's urn fell to the floor and shattered. Mariah gasped. Even in her darkest imaginings, she hadn't believed Luke would react like this.

Together she and Ivy raced to the porch. Hance had pushed the children into the house.

"Where's a gun?" he demanded tautly.

Mariah stiffened. "No, Hance. I'm not going to let you settle things this way."

He grasped her by the shoulders. "It's not Luke, damn it. The Harpers are outside. They must have seen Ivy and me, and followed us here."

Mariah's blood chilled as she looked out the window. She saw riders in the trees at the sides of the slopes. Buckskin-garbed riders. The Harpers with their stringy hair and gap-toothed grins and hard-drinking ways. There were four of them—Wiley and Micajah, and Wiley's two sons, Caleb and Spruce. Without another word, Mariah went to a cabinet and took out a rifle, handing it to Hance.

She took the children to the root cellar, a tiny underground cave behind the kitchen. Ivy hesitated, placing her hand on Hance's arm as he loaded the gun.

"Hance—"

He paused and gave her a grim look. "I know. I'll be careful. Now, see to the children."

Gulping air, Ivy went back through the kitchen. Mariah was holding the slanted wooden door open as she spoke calmly to Hattie, instructing her to keep Dylan quiet. Benjamin hung back, loath to enter the cellar.

"What about Papa?" he asked.

Mariah swallowed. She'd never told Luke about killing Elk Harper, nor about the more recent encounter with Wiley and Micajah in town. Those were things she didn't want to share with her husband, to heap on him like an unwelcome burden. "He's all right, Ben," she forced herself to say.

"But he doesn't know about the Harpers, Mama. He could walk right into this. And what about the animals? I saw one of the men going down toward the barn." Suddenly, Ben began to shift from foot to foot.

"Get in the cellar, Ben," Mariah ordered.

"Just a minute, Mama. I—I gotta—" He pointed at the privy across the yard.

Mariah felt frustration grip her as another shot sizzled through the air. "Be quick about it."

Ben scampered off. Too late, Mariah realized his ruse. He bypassed the outhouse and ran down a path toward the woods, disappearing into a stand of elm trees. Mariah called his name and nearly went after him when her attention was diverted. To her right, Gideon was thundering away on his Chickasaw pony.

Inwardly cursing the two willful, foolish boys, Mariah settled Ivy, Hattie, and Dylan into the cellar.

"Stay quiet," she cautioned them again, placing her hand on the door.

"Where are you going?" Ivy asked.

"Back inside. Hance won't be able to handle the four of them alone."

"Then I'm coming, too."

Mariah shook her head. "You don't know how to shoot, Ivy. And the little ones need you." She closed the door firmly and ran back to the house.

One blast had shattered a window. Hance was crouched beneath it, trying to draw a bead on the elusive targets that hung slyly back, in range but out of sight. Hearing Mariah loading another gun, he swiveled around. He was about to object when he noticed how smoothly she fitted the ramrod into the barrel and checked the firing pan.

"I'm sorry about this, Mariah," Hance said gruffly. "I'm sorry about everything."

She squeezed his hand and set the rifle butt against her shoulder.

Israel's uneven gait added its rhythm to the ticking of the hooded wall clock. The sound brought Genevieve to her feet. "Welcome home," she said, hurrying out on the porch to take his arm. "I thought the university had swallowed you up."

Israel grinned and allowed her to help him into the sitting room. She insisted on fussing over him, even though he could now walk and even sit a horse with his peg leg. All Lexington had buzzed in admiration when Israel had danced with Bridie Farrell's flamboyant sister Margaret at a recent cornshucking.

"Roarke," Genevieve called, "Rebecca, come see who's here for Sunday dinner."

They sat together in the quiet of a soft summer afternoon, talking and smiling, wrapped in the comfortable peace of familiar closeness. They spoke of the farm, of Israel's career teaching theology, and Sarah's recent social triumph of hostessing her first formal party as Mrs. Nathaniel Caddick.

Talk meandered around to Hance. Hance, whom they'd thought lost to them forever. It was a different man who'd ridden home to them, with new lines of maturity and understanding etched on his face. A man who had done a lot of soul-searching and had come up wanting. And had finally decided to do something about it.

He was content now, with Ivy at his side in their handsome house in High Street. The old restlessness was gone. Hance was happy.

As were all the Adairs . . . almost. Genevieve could accept Israel's disability and Rebecca's reticence. The young woman had become almost a recluse, folding in on herself, poring over her Bible and her copies of the *Home Missionary*. Sarah, too, had her flaws, which included her utter delight in the fact that she was now mistress of several slaves. Yet she remained a loving girl, still close to the parents who were no longer her social equals.

The only thing Genevieve couldn't accept was the estrangement between Luke and Roarke. It simply wasn't meant to be, yet the rift hung over them and tinged her life with melancholy. So many times she'd argued, begged, and browbeaten Roarke, only to encounter the cold wall of his hatred and prejudice. She tried to play on his softer emotions, regaling him with anecdotes about the grandchildren he refused to know.

Somehow he managed not to hear. He didn't care that Ben had shot his first wild turkey, that Hattie was reading by the age of five, or that Dylan was miserable with the croup . . . Still Genevieve tried. She would never stop trying to pull her family together.

The sound of hooves pounding up the drive startled them. Sundays were generally quiet, the hands in town for some time off and the family together for their supper.

Rebecca parted the drapes and gasped. "An Injun, Pa," she breathed. Her eyes were wide and the edge of hysteria was there in her voice—the hysteria that always surfaced when she saw an Indian.

Roarke grabbed his rifle with a curse. But Genevieve recognized the visitor.

"Put that down, Roarke," she ordered sharply. "It's Gideon Parker."

"He's not welcome here."

Genevieve brushed past him and opened the door. "He wouldn't have come without good reason."

Roarke allowed her to go out on the porch, but he kept his rifle trained on the boy. Gideon was handsome and self-assured as he dropped from his horse, his face a placid, unreadable mask.

Rebecca began to whimper. Disgusted, Israel silenced her with a sharp order and joined his mother on the porch.

Gideon noticed Roarke's rifle, but he showed no fear. He nodded at Genevieve and then at Roarke.

"Luke needs you," he said simply.

Anger flared in Roarke's eyes. "Luke hasn't needed me since he disgraced this family by marrying a Shawnee."

"The Harpers are attacking the farm, Mr. Adair."

Roarke hesitated. Genevieve heard his sharp intake of breath. The Harpers' reputation was known—and feared—throughout Lexington; even back in Dancer's Meadow, they'd been a wild and unprincipled family.

Still . . . Roarke looked at Genevieve. She threw back her head and sent him a challenging stare. Israel limped down the steps, already armed and heading for his horse. Roarke's expression wavered in indecision.

It was Rebecca who made up his mind for him. Hesitantly at first, then boldly, she went to Gideon and touched his sleeve, giving him a smile that trembled but was full of conviction. It was the first time she'd touched another human being outside her family since her return from Indian country.

Then she turned to Roarke with tears in her eyes.

"Go to them, Papa. Please. I've been selfish long enough."

The words propelled her father to the stables, to fetch his horse.

Just before Roarke mounted, Genevieve kissed him, smiling with pride.

"Ah, God, Gennie," he said, rubbing his cheek on her hair. "I've been more a fool than a man has any call to be."

She nodded her head, eyes shining.

"But I love you, Roarke Adair," she said.

*   *   *

Luke scowled, thinking the shots he'd heard were from Ben and Gideon. He hadn't given them permission to go out hunting. Angrily, he put up his whipsaw and brass rule and mounted his horse. The boys knew better than to be shooting so close to the house.

His anger dissipated when he spied Ben running toward him. The boy gulped air, chest heaving with exertion.

"The Harpers, Pa! They're attacking the place!"

Luke reached down and swung Ben into the saddle in front of him. A fearsome tightness gripped his chest. "What's happening?" he demanded.

"Uncle Hance says there's four of them—"

"Hance?"

Ben bobbed his head. "He and Aunt Ivy came for supper."

Luke felt a prickle of displeasure but a more pressing emergency was at hand. He hadn't trusted the Harpers since Caleb and Spruce had tried to take Ben's dog; he'd forbidden the boys to go near the dilapidated farm after that. Naomi Harper had come by selling eggs one day, trying to conceal livid bruises on her face beneath the brim of a battered poke bonnet, confirming the rumor that the brothers treated their women with indiscriminate brutality. The Harpers were stupid, unpredictable, and dangerous.

Luke drew the horse up on the crest of the big slope in front of the house. On either side he could see movement, but the Harpers seemed to be lying low. Cautious devils.

And then he saw the reason for their caution. The two front windows of the house had been shot out, the curtains wafting outward on the breeze. A rifle barrel protruded from each of the windows. Just for a fraction of a second, he saw the blue-black sheen of Mariah's hair.

Terror thundered through Luke's vitals, robbing him of breath. This was no casual game of aggression but an all-out battle.

Almost unconsciously, Luke wrapped his arms about Ben, inhaling the scent of the boy's hair. He smelled of the summer breeze and boyish sweat and innocence. Leaning down, Luke kissed Ben's cheek.

"You've got to go, son," he said quietly. "There'll be no getting back to the house now, so I want you to take the path down behind the barn. If things get out of hand, you take to the river, you hear me?"

"But I want to stay with you, Pa."

Luke shook his head grimly. "All I've got is this pistol and enough shot for a few rounds. I can't trust myself to defend the both of us."

"But—" Another shot cracked through the air. One of Mariah's flower boxes dropped to the ground below the window.

"Go, Ben," Luke said urgently. He kissed the boy again and plucked him from the horse, sending him on his way with a firm pat on the shoulder.

Ben hesitated. "Pa?"

"What, son?"

Ben blinked his eyes and swallowed. "You're a brave man, Pa, and I love you."

Luke lifted the corners of his mouth in an attempt to smile. And then Ben was gone down the path.

Luke tethered his horse and primed his pistol. Then he crept through the woods, crouching low to keep out of sight. The breeze brought on it an ominous crackling sound and the scent of burning. Pulling himself up into a tulip poplar, he looked down into the hollow. A savage curse exploded from him.

One of the Harpers had set fire to the stock barn, the first place accessible from the slope. Already a plume of smoke rose from the rear section, and flames were licking up its back wall. A horse squealed, panicked by the scent of smoke.

Luke cursed again. All that livestock. The shoats he'd borrowed money to buy. Mariah's gentle milch cow. Ben's pony, and his cats. The boy's most prized possessions.

The cats . . . Suddenly, Luke dropped from the tree and hit the ground running. If Ben knew the barn was burning, he'd head straight for it, to free the animals. Luke ran so hard he could barely see. Vaguely, he was aware that he'd been spotted; a ball tore a large splintered bite in the trunk of a tree as he passed. But he didn't care. He was sure Ben would try to get to the barn, and—

He arrived to see the rear part of the roof and wall in flames. Even from a distance he could feel the heat and hear the dreadful roar. Thankfully, Ben was nowhere in sight. Luke stopped and looked around. There was no noise but the squealing and bellowing of panicked animals and the roar of the inferno.

Then the barn door swung open. A huge cloud of smoke issued from the barn, and the fire inside, fueled by the rush of fresh air, grew redder and hotter. Animals burst from the building: one of the cats with a kit clamped firmly between her jaws, the shoats, running with uncharacteristic speed to safety, the milch cow. Then, finally, Ben's Indian pony and the dun mare, both squealing and pawing the air before thundering down to the blessed coolness of the creek.

Luke's relief was only momentary. He knew the animals' escape could only mean one thing: that someone was inside. Forgetting caution again, he ran toward the door of the barn.

Heat issued from the building. The inside was an unholy inferno fed by dry hay and timber. In the back several roof beams had collapsed and the ones in the front didn't have long to stand.

A gust of wind blew the smoke aside for a moment, and almost choking with terror, Luke made out a small form running toward him.

Ben.

Beneath splotches of soot his face was dark red and contorted. His arms were full of kittens; he was determined to save the whole litter.

A crossbeam flared and crackled and then collapsed just behind the boy. The one in front of that was about to do likewise.

Luke heard himself screaming at Ben to run, and then he was running, too, toward the raging heat. The falling beams seemed to be chasing Ben. The boy eluded every one, managing to hold the kittens as he ran for his life.

Before Luke reached the barn, Ben emerged. Spying his father, he let go of the kittens, which scattered in all directions. Luke dropped to his knees and stretched out his arms toward the boy, thanking God and all the stars of heaven that his gentle, brave, foolish son was safe.

In dropping to his knees, Luke eluded the bullet that had been aimed at the middle of his back.

It hit Ben instead.

The boy was just a yard from his father's arms. His feet left the ground as the explosion rent the air. The impact threw him back. He died instantly, even before the blood started to blossom from his shattered chest.

Luke couldn't stop to grieve over his son's body. That would come later, after he reacted to the maniacal rage that possessed him. Somehow he found his pistol.

His body was not his own. It belonged to the cold, demonic hatred that possessed him, not allowing him to think or feel anything but rage and determination.

Micajah Harper had fired the shot. He was looking with dreadful amazement at Luke.

Micajah ran. Then Luke cocked his gun, and he froze.

"Turn around, Harper," Luke ordered coldly. "I want to see your face when I kill you." Slowly, sobbing, Micajah turned.

Luke felt no cathartic rush as his bullet bored into Micajah's head, blowing off the back of his skull. Justice had been done, but that didn't change the fact that Ben was dead. Luke felt nothing but a cold wind blowing through his heart.

When Wylie Harper appeared, assessing the situation with a quick glance, he shouldered a gleaming rifle and aimed at Luke.

"You're goin' to die," he informed Luke.

"I know." Luke supposed Wiley wanted him to be terrified, but he wasn't. His impending death would merely spare him the pain of living without Ben. He found himself almost eager for the release.

Until he remembered Mariah and the others. They needed him, more than ever now that Ben was gone. But it was too late. Wylie was aiming his rifle, and Luke refused to beg for his life. He planted his feet and waited for the impact of the bullet as Wylie squeezed the trigger.

The shot that rang out didn't issue from Wylie's weapon. Luke watched, dumbfounded, as Wylie crumpled, shot through the gut from the back. Blood bubbled from his mouth and midsection as he slithered, cursing, to the ground.

Hance emerged from a cover of bushes near the path from the house. The blood drained from his face when he saw Ben's body.

"Oh, God, Luke, they shot your boy."

Luke looked at Hance for the first time in seven years. Hance's agony was so genuine that Luke found himself not caring about all the old enmity. Hance had saved his life and was convulsed with grief over Ben.

Hance held out his arms. "Luke," he choked, his face streaming with tears. "Little brother, come here."

Their hands clasped desperately, hopelessly, frozen with grief and agony and a sudden understanding that had eluded them all their lives until this moment.

Until the twin clicks of rifles shattered the agonized silence of their reunion.

"We've got the two of you now," raged Wiley Harper's son Caleb. "You owe us for what you done to our daddy," he said furiously. "Both of you." Caleb looked over at his brother.

"What say, Spruce," he inquired casually. "Do we finish 'em here and now?"

Spruce shook his head. "Not now, Caleb. First they're gonna watch what we do to their womenfolk."

Luke heard Hance's hiss of indrawn breath and felt him tense. He gripped Hance's arm.

"Not yet," he whispered.

"Right," Caleb agreed. "We got some things to do before we put you to rest."

"Damned right you do," growled a voice from behind.

Slowly, the four men looked up. Upon a winded horse sat Roarke Adair, magnificent in his rage, like a great flame- and silver-haired avenging angel. He was flanked by Israel and Gideon, also armed and angry.

Keeping his gun ready, Roarke dismounted. Never had he looked so fiercely protective.

"Drop your guns," he told the Harpers. "If you can manage to get out of my sight in five seconds, I won't kill you. I'll give you until sundown to leave the county."

The Harpers didn't hesitate. Hurling their weapons to the ground, they scampered into the woods.

Roarke drew an unsteady breath. Without looking right or left, he went straight to Benjamin. Gathering the limp form into his arms, he leaned down and kissed the boy's cheek. Then he approached Luke.

"Son," he said brokenly, "son, what can I say? What can I do?"

Luke took the boy from him, feeling his insides splinter into shards of sorrow. Tears streamed from his eyes as he started toward the house. He paused a few yards from Roarke and turned back, just as the last supporting beams of the barn collapsed and were engulfed by the fire.

"You can help me bury my boy, Pa," he said.

32

Tick, tock.

The clock above the mantel sent a quiet rhythm through the house. Genevieve glanced at it, reflecting. The timepiece had witnessed all the events of her life in America, from her struggles to wrest a living from Virginia's soil to the present moment. The little halfpenny moon in the dial was privy to all the family's blessed triumphs and bitter disappointments, its joys and its tragedies.

Tick, tock.

Genevieve stepped out on the porch and inhaled the sharp, cold air of the fall morning. Hoarfrost, a creature of the low, moist clouds, clung to grass and trees and hung in the valleys of the distant hills. Pulling her shawl more tightly around her, Genevieve shivered, feeling her age.

Tick, tock.

Not that fifty-eight was such a bad age to be. She was comfortable in a body that had served her well, from the backbreaking toil of her first tobacco farm, through the birth of five children—four of whom survived, praise God—and into the settling twilight of her life.

Tick, tock.

Feeling a familiar presence behind her, Genevieve leaned back against Roarke's broad frame. Always he was there, sensing when she needed him. They stood in comfortable silence, breathing the cold air and listening to the clock, fingers laced together.

A creaking sound intruded upon the moment. As one, they turned and watched an ox-drawn wagon lumbering toward them, its canvas hood arching above the passengers like a halo.

A lump rose in Genevieve's throat. Roarke slid his arm around her waist and drew her to him.

"I never thought it'd be Luke leaving us," she said.

"I think I did, Gennie. Ben's death only made it happen sooner." Roarke sighed warmly into her hair. "This land's not big enough for a man like Luke. It's gotten damned crowded these past few years. Luke needs a place with room to grow, a place where he can make his mark. His farm's just a piece of land now."

Genevieve nodded. Even after an estrangement that had lasted seven years, Roarke understood his son.

"Do you think he'll find what he's looking for in Missouri country?" she asked.

"I don't think it's so much a question of looking as it is of creating something." Roarke moved his hands slowly upon her shoulders. "At least I've made my peace with him. I couldn't have stood it if he'd left before I came to my senses."

Genevieve turned to lean up and kiss him. "You were magnificent with him about Benjamin."

But Roarke shook his head. "There's no comforting a man who's lost his son, especially like that."

"Still, you managed to reach him when no one else could." She smiled sadly. "We were all a little shocked when you took him fishing right after the funeral, but it worked."

"We had a lot to catch up on. In his grief, Luke forgot he had a damned fine wife and two other children who needed him."

The covered wagon was joined on the road by Hance's elegant chaise. He sat flanked by Ivy and Sarah, both of whom were flushed and plump with early pregnancy. The two vehicles rolled to a stop in front of the house.

"Hance left us so many times," Genevieve said. "It never surprised me. But Luke . . ." She blinked fast. "Luke was the steadfast one. The one we could depend on."

"We leaned too hard on him," Roarke admitted, his voice rough with regret. "'Tis a miracle he's forgiven us." Arm in arm, they started down the porch steps.

Rebecca and Israel joined the family in the yard. For a while, the men stood smoking, talking about conditions on the western trails. The women spoke of more homey things: Did Mariah have enough flour and lard, bacon and coffee? What about tonics for dosing the children? Cotton scraps for stitching extra quilts?

Gideon Parker hung back from the group, flushing to his ears when Mariah announced proudly that he had won a place at Joshua Fry's renowned school in Danville. He would be preparing to study the medical arts. The farm, worked by Luke's foreman, would be Gideon's when the boy came of age.

The rising sun touched the frosted grass, turning it to a field of glistening green. Luke glanced up at the sun, and then at Mariah. An unspoken message passed between them, which everyone felt. The family drew together.

Luke gave a final tug on one of Sarah's ringlets, and for once, she didn't scold him. Rebecca embraced Mariah, murmuring how wrong she had been to let her old fears rule her.

"I cheated myself out of the chance to know you," she said.

"Look after Gideon for me," Mariah said. "Do that, and we'll always be friends."

Hance bowed to Mariah. He and Luke shook hands. Then, both of them laughing, they abandoned formality and yanked each other into a bear hug. Sitting on the steps, Israel held Hattie and Dylan on his lap, allowing the children to explore his wooden leg one last time before relinquishing them to their grandparents.

Genevieve stroked Hattie's silky hair, then, with shaking hands, tied her poke bonnet in a crooked bow beneath her chin. She gathered both children to her breast. Her aching senses devoured them, absorbing their smell, the texture of their skin, their sweet voices. They were children of an American family, as much a product of the land as they were of her and Roarke. She knew Luke would teach them to love the land, to make their mark in a way that would do homage to the nation Roarke had fought for, bled for and nearly died for.

She straightened up and kissed Mariah, whose face was stiff in a losing battle against tears. Nearby, Roarke and Luke shook hands, and the love and forgiveness that flowed between father and son was written on their rugged, unsmiling faces.

Genevieve broke away from Mariah and went into the house. She returned a moment later with the beautiful old clock and placed it in the back of the wagon.

"Mama, no," Luke protested. "The clock belongs to you."

She shook her head and struggled to speak through the thickness of tears. "It belongs to all of us, Luke. Having the clock will remind you that you'll always be a part of us."

"Thank you, Mama." Luke closed his eyes and pinched the bridge of his nose. "Lord, this is hard."

Suddenly Genevieve was in her son's arms. There was nothing left to be said; they had talked of this move for many weeks. So she whispered, "I love you. I'll think of you every day." And then she let him go.

As Luke and his family climbed into the wagon, Genevieve took Roarke's arm. They walked back into the house, to the quiet of their sitting room, never again to hear the click of the halfpenny moon. But their heartbeats matched the steady echo of the clock, marking another milestone in their lives, another parting. There had been so many of them.

Genevieve gazed out the open door at the wagon lumbering westward along the road. The rising sun swept the landscape in a blanket of gold, and her heart swelled as she lifted her hand in a last farewell.

Roarke's arm slid around her shoulders. She leaned her

head against his broad chest. "We'll never see them again, will we, Roarke?" she asked.

He smiled down at her. "That depends, Gennie love, on how you feel about traveling."

COMING NEXT MONTH

SONG OF THE NIGHTINGALE by Constance O'Banyon
A mesmerizing historical romance from bestselling author Constance O'Banyon. This enchanting love story sweeps from the drawing rooms of London to the battlefields of Waterloo as a beautiful woman fights for her family's honor and finds her one true love.

LOVE WITH A WARM COWBOY by Lenore Carroll
When her boyfriend returns from a trip abroad with a Croatian bride, Barbara Door is crushed. She heads for a friend's dude ranch in Wyoming to find confidence, adventure, and love with a warm cowboy. A sassy, moving story for all modern women.

SWEET IVY'S GOLD by Paula Paul
Award-winning author Paula Paul brings the Old West back to life in this winsome turn-of-the-century romance about a feisty young woman who sets up a gambling parlor in a small gold-mining town in Colorado. Adventure and true love abound when she meets Langdon Runnels.

THIEF OF HEARTS by Penelope Thomas
From the author of *Master of Blackwood* and *Passion's Child* comes a story of love and intrigue in 17th century England. Forced to flee her village home after accidentally killing a local squire in self-defense, Damorna Milfield seeks refuge in London. She is rescued by mysterious "Lord Quent," a charming but duplicitous man-about-town, who teaches Damorna the art of deception and love.

SUNBURST by Suzanne Ellison
A sweeping tale of love and adventure in the Mohave Desert and the Sierra Nevada. Bostonian beauty Mandy Henderson goes out west in search of her fiancé, Rodney Potter, who has disappeared while doing survey work for the railroad. Drew Robelard, a handsome army captain, is assigned to help Mandy find Rodney, but he actually has his own secret agenda.

PRIVATE LIES by Carol Cail
The lighthearted adventures of a young woman reporter who sets out to investigate her boss's death and ends up solving a different crime, discovering unexpected romance along the way.

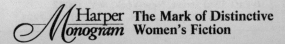 Harper Monogram The Mark of Distinctive Women's Fiction